The
Sweet Life

Also by Lynn York

THE PIANO TEACHER

The
Sweet Life

LYNN YORK

A PLUME BOOK

PLUME
Published by Penguin Group
Penguin Group (USA) Inc., 375 Hudson Street, New York, New York 10014, U.S.A. •
Penguin Group (Canada), 90 Eglinton Avenue East, Suite 700, Toronto, Ontario,
Canada M4P 2Y3 (a division of Pearson Penguin Canada Inc.) • Penguin Books Ltd.,
80 Strand, London WC2R 0RL, England • Penguin Ireland, 25 St. Stephen's Green,
Dublin 2, Ireland (a division of Penguin Books Ltd.) • Penguin Group (Australia),
250 Camberwell Road, Camberwell, Victoria 3124, Australia (a division of Pearson
Australia Group Pty. Ltd.) • Penguin Books India Pvt. Ltd., 11 Community Centre,
Panchsheel Park, New Delhi – 110 017, India • Penguin Books (NZ), cnr Airborne
and Rosedale Roads, Albany, Auckland 1310, New Zealand (a division of Pearson New
Zealand Ltd.) • Penguin Books (South Africa) (Pty.) Ltd., 24 Sturdee Avenue,
Rosebank, Johannesburg 2196, South Africa

Penguin Books Ltd., Registered Offices: 80 Strand, London WC2R 0RL, England

First published by Plume, a member of Penguin Group (USA) Inc.

First Printing, March 2007
10 9 8 7 6 5 4 3

"Apologia for Your Death" from the collection *Let Me Explain,* by Gaylord Brewer
(Oak Ridge, TN: Iris Press, 2006).

Ⓟ REGISTERED TRADEMARK—MARCA REGISTRADA

LIBRARY OF CONGRESS CATALOGING-IN-PUBLICATION DATA

York, Lynn.
    The sweet life / Lynn York.
      p. cm.
    ISBN 978-0-452-28822-5
    1. North Carolina—Fiction. 2. Church musicians—Fiction. 3. Grandmothers—
Fiction. 4. Granddaughters—Fiction. I. Title.
    PS3625.O75S94 2007
    813'.6—dc22   2006021324

Printed in the United States of America
Set in Simonici Garamond
Designed by Eve L. Kirch

PUBLISHER'S NOTE
This is a work of fiction. Names, characters, places, and incidents are either the product
of the author's imagination or are used fictitiously, and any resemblance to actual per-
sons, living or dead, business establishments, events, or locales is entirely coincidental.

For Anna Lee and Will

Nobody has it easy, and too often these days
that choice bit of fat is a hard swallow
even holy rivers of wine can't clear, even
celebration dissolve. You fine generous man.
You man apart.

—"Apologia for Your Death"
Gaylord Brewer

The
Sweet Life

Chapter One

Roy

*O*ne time—it had to be thirty-something years ago now, during his army days—Roy had been walking down a tiny backstreet in Seoul, Korea. It was a hot afternoon. He was sweating through his uniform. He stopped to take off his hat and wipe down his forehead with his handkerchief. Sometime during this operation, he looked up through the watery shimmer of the heat. The street was narrow and lined with four- and five-story apartment buildings, old, with crumbling cement. He stopped there amid the clamor of a street market, the drone of foreign music from cheap radios. And he looked up—by chance, just a small tilt of his head—a quick survey of the open shutters, laundry, power lines, antennas. A tilt of his head, nothing more.

He saw a woman leaning out of a second-story window.

Her elbows were propped on the sill, her small hands folded in front of her. He had seen many beautiful Korean girls during his tour of duty, lovely girls with very smooth faces, shallow features, and hooded, mysterious eyes. However, he had never seen any girl as lovely as this one. She was a perfect sculpture: completely still, her graceful neck wrapped in a filmy yellow scarf, black hair piled on her head. She did not look at him, for even from that distance, he could see she was wholly taken up in her thoughts. From her expression, he'd bet they were very sad thoughts—a wrong done to her long ago and never repaired, maybe, or something profoundly lost.

Roy was taken, literally taken, by this sight—removed from anything else he had ever wished for. His immediate and inescapable need *was to find the right door, to climb the necessary stairs, to tear into her room, if need be, to get to her. Roy knew, here these years later, that he had measured every moment with every other woman against that one. Nothing matched the quickening of those few minutes. She beguiled him, awake and asleep, through three decades, that girl way off in Korea, way up on the second floor, suspended, unreached and unreachable.*

Of course, he had not looked for her door. He had, in fact, put the handkerchief in his pocket, adjusted his hat, and walked on. There was a war to fight, after all, and his own parents had died just the year before, these things leaving him little courage to spare—on other foundlings or on what his mother might call an ill-advised detour. Oh, he had regretted it all right. He had come back to the street on every leave; he had looked for her in the little GI cafés and bars that he and his buddies frequented. He had looked over the girls. There were a lot of girls. Many of the guys ended up romancing them for a night and some for a lifetime, brought them home, married them, the works. Maybe he had seen her among them. He'd often spot one across a bar and think, maybe, maybe that's her, *and then he'd walk closer, and a flaw would appear—a thick nose, a slightly flattened forehead, thin arms, or else a face faintly marked by worldly harshness. In the end, not one of them was her, not one was quite right.*

But no matter, he came back to the States, and there were more girls to look over. Someone was always wanting to set him up with this young lady and that. He had seen quite a string of girls, one precious pearl after another. If someone asked him, as they often did, why he didn't pick one and settle down, he would always say that he hadn't found the right girl, never found one that could completely measure up. Secretly he wondered if he wasn't just walking around with the wrong damn yardstick.

He had given up and, truth be told, almost stopped dating altogether by the time he had noticed Wilma right there in Swan's Knob, in his own church, both of them riding out their late fifties on their own. He'd love to know if there was a psychiatrist or someone who could explain it. For the life of him, he couldn't figure out how she'd done it, how she'd gotten him to throw out every notion he had about love and just start doing it. Wilma looked nothing like the other girl, of course, not in any way he could name. Her beauty was borne of motion, of hands and curves and a comely step—though on occasion, in a rare light, he'd caught her in a moment of fragile stillness. But that wasn't it. There was some other trick to it, whatever it was that changed his mind, and he thought maybe it had to do with him being right there with her—in her room, in her bed, in her corner altogether—and not standing out on the street.

Wilma

Nineteen eighty-eight had been, Wilma saw with no small measure of despair, a good year for tomatoes. Two bushel baskets, the fruit of only the last five days, sat on her kitchen counter this morning, left there by Roy, who had lovingly cleaned them, and layered them in those baskets according to approximate diameter and degree of ripeness. What would look enticing at any farmers' market Wilma could only weigh at this moment in terms of the jars and the hours it would take to put them up.

Sad, because this was a job that she normally enjoyed. It was a pleasure somehow, a break with life in the last part of the century, to take out your nice paring knife, the one that your husband kept perfectly sharp, to wash over the tomatoes, dunk them down in boiling water, and whisk the peels off. This was something she had always loved, her hands busy for the morning in the pulp and the seeds, hands without a care in the world, not obliged to strike the right key, to stretch for the chord. She had loved this kind of task especially since she and Roy had been married, and they had set up house in his beautiful old childhood home.

It mattered that these were Roy's tomatoes, the ones that he grew himself, the ones that he picked on just the right day and brought to her. So the peeling and cutting and putting them up in shiny jars for the basement had always seemed to her to be an act of love, though that was not ever what she would say to a soul. It was not the kind of thing she would say even to Roy, but of course he understood. She saw it just in the way he would stand in the kitchen at the end of days such as this one. When she had all the mason jars lined up across the counter, he would step back and look at them and let out a low whistle and say, "Well, woman, you would have made someone a fine little farm wife back in those days. I can see it on the tombstone, *goodly wife of farmer Roy Swan, all the fruits of the earth*." Roy was all the time quoting the things that he found on tombstones. It didn't seem to him even one bit ironic that these were dead people he was talking about, and that by association he was making Wilma dead too. "Oh, dolly, it's all just part of life," he would say if she objected. "We're all dying someday, doll. Might as well have a colorful tombstone."

Wilma picked up a few of the topmost tomatoes, checking to see if they could wait a day or two before she did something with them. But, no, they were ripe and it was late in the season. There would only be more tomorrow. She took a little breath and pulled out her pots—one for the parboiling, the other for the jars. It came to her that the dread she was feeling had little to do with the tomatoes and everything to do with the rest of it—the way things were going with her and Roy right now, the things that she didn't want to think about for three hours standing in front of her kitchen sink. She dried off her hands and went into the den to cut on Roy's fancy stereo. A little music might distract her.

From the den, she could see that Roy was hacking around in the front bed again, kneeling on a burlap sack. He had come home from the nursery with a bucket of bulbs yesterday—probably the pick of the bargain bin. Come spring there would be one of every single type of tulip, hyacinth, and daffodil known to man, flower confetti across the front yard. Roy had a wonderful green thumb and the aesthetic sense of a plumber. Everything he planted lived, flourished in a wild display of inappropriate color. He was bending down across the bed now, trying to make a hole in the far corner of the plot, still fairly agile despite his potbelly, though the back of his shirt was soaked from the late August heat. He stood then with a little bit of effort and stomped his plantings with the kelly green clogs that he had ordered from a gardening catalogue when Wilma was not looking.

Wilma headed back to her boiling water, tied on an apron, and set up her little assembly line for canning. As she rewashed the first batch of tomatoes, she looked over at her new phone, half willing it to ring and interrupt her. Roy had gotten her one of the new kind with a receiver end that was completely detached, so she could walk all over the house while she talked on the phone. Wilma was not one to live on her telephone—though she enjoyed talking to her daughter Sarah out in New Mexico at least once a week. And the new phone made it so that she could fix herself a cup of tea and then sit by the window and she and Sarah could chat almost as if she was in the room. So she could see how some women in town could spend their days talking first to one and then another of the circle.

Most of the time, Wilma counted this kind of thing as a waste of time—why, everyone in town saw each other at least once a week at church, twice, if they went to prayer meeting. Then there were football games, chance meetings at the drugstore, the beauty parlor, and on and on. Still, at choir practice, she would often hear Grace Snow or Mamie Brown say, "Well, just like I was telling you on the phone, *I am at the end of my rope over the prizes for the Halloween raffle . . . and you-know-who is not helping the situation . . .*" Wilma did not care a flip about the Halloween raffle, but she imagined that between such trivial details, women often shared those things that troubled them most—that a woman could slip in, between talk of the centerpieces and the new sweater, the fact that her formerly amorous husband had not approached her in any way for over six weeks and had not offered the first word of explanation.

Wilma tried to imagine a discussion about this very topic, the one that now occupied her every waking thought. She was sure that Grace and Mamie had learned how to discuss these delicate subjects. Maybe it took hours of going over the program for the garden club, years of idle comments about the foibles of your children and of the husband in question—how sweet he was, how attentive, how he always dropped his socks, inside out of course, right in the middle of the bathroom floor as if he were leaving a gift for you, how the two of you had such lovely Sunday afternoon "naps" (this said maybe with a little laugh or a wink). Maybe that was what it took, this kind of talk that Wilma had always had little patience for. Instead, she had elected to go it alone. She had not been completely alone—there had been Sarah, and they had grown a bit closer over the years—but this current problem was not something she could talk to her daughter about. And Roy, well, they had always been able to talk. But this, this was a sticky subject. She was not sure what to ask, and even if she could get up her courage, asking him might make things all the worse.

The phone did ring then, of course, the second she dropped the first batch into the water. She dashed to answer it. The tomatoes would need no more than sixty seconds to swell enough to split their skins.

"Hello?" She made an effort not to sound reluctant or harried—it might be Reverend Berry trying to finalize the bulletin—and cradled the phone between her shoulder and ear.

"Hello. Am I calling at a bad time?" said Sarah, her voice a half-octave higher than usual—Wilma heard this after two words—the curse of a mother's ear. Probably some kind of bad news.

"No, no, just putting up a batch of tomatoes." How long had they been boiling now? She stirred the pot, then went to the drawer to find her slotted spoon.

"Oh, God, that's a load of work. I can't imagine why Roy makes you go to all that trouble. Can't he just grow one little bush on the patio and be done with it?" Sarah had never been short on opinions, especially when it came to her stepfather—though she never called him that, never called him anything but Roy, and said even this with a little hint of—what?—not quite disdain. Maybe this was to be expected, but Sarah's father had been dead for over twenty years now, and Sarah was thirty-five—old enough to have a little charity.

"Dear, Roy does not make me do anything. I enjoy putting up tomatoes," Wilma said as she used her slotted spoon to transfer the cursed things into ice water.

"You do not. You just think that you should," said Sarah, laughing. This was typical of Sarah—a little gentle argument to forestall the real conversation.

"How are you all?" Wilma said. "Jonah? The girls?" Sarah's oldest, Starling, was about to start her senior year in high school, while the little one, Verity, would be a first grader. Organization was not Sarah's strong suit.

"Jonah is great," said Sarah. "His latest show opened in Albuquerque last week and sold out in three days. There has been a lot of interest in it, really. We've even heard from *National Geographic*. He's very excited, going to buy a new lens he's had his eye on." Jonah was a photographer and Verity's father, presumably, though he and Sarah had never bothered to get married. Wilma tried to step around this mishmash these days.

"You must be so proud," she said. "What about the girls?"

Sarah told her about Verity's lost front tooth then, and about the latest song that Starling had written and played for hours on end. The exchange went on for a few minutes—Sarah's summer school class, the novel by an East Indian author her book group was reading, the new music store Wilma had discovered in Greensboro—the workaday knickknacks that mattered little in the scheme of things, though sending them back and forth across the phone gave the two of them something to say, a way to live their lives together. It had taken them years to learn this simple thing between them—Wilma was not sure now why it had been so hard—but as they went on—Roy's obsession with his grapes, a new kind of herbal tea—she set aside her tomatoes, cooling in the water, sat down in her favorite rattan chair out in the Florida room, and nearly forgot about that earlier worried half-octave of Sarah's voice.

"Listen," Sarah said finally. "I need to ask a favor. A big one." Wilma had time to draw a breath and pray that Sarah was not going to ask for money. "It's about the *National Geographic* people. You know, I said before they were interested in Jonah's show . . . Well, they saw his photographs of the potters—his latest ones—and just a few days ago came to him with a big opportunity. They want him to sign with them and go to South Asia and the Pacific—Nepal, Korea, Indonesia, Sri Lanka—to photograph craft artisans in the remote areas of the world. You know—rug makers, weavers, the people who make those metal bells . . ." Her voice trailed off. This was going to be a big favor.

"Here's the thing: I want to send you Starling. Verity and I are going with Jonah. He wants us with him. I want to go and Verity can wait a year to start school, but Starling, Starling needs to stay, and I can't leave her here in Santa Fe on her own."

"Well, no, you can't," said Wilma.

"Just until Christmas," Sarah said quickly. "We'd finish up in Sri Lanka in mid-December." Sri Lanka. It figured. Not Paris, the Sorbonne, like Mimi Salter's daughter. No, Nepal, Korea, Indonesia, with a six-year-old.

"We'd come straight back," Sarah said after a few seconds of silence. "Straight back," as if she were trying to get permission to go to the beach with the wild crowd from high school.

"What does Starling think of this?" Poor Starling, her senior year. From her chair, Wilma could see out beyond her hanging ferns to the yard, where Roy was watering his newly planted bulbs in complete tranquility.

"This just came up and we haven't talked to her about it yet. I wanted to run it by you first. To see what you thought. And Roy, Roy too."

"Roy," said Wilma. She couldn't imagine what he would think. She wasn't sure that she could even begin to explain what it would be like having a teenager in the house.

"I know you'd have to talk to him. And we'd have to talk to Starling. It is her senior year, but she'll be back for the end of it, and well, you know she's always loved our visits with you, always wants to know when we'll be going to Swan's Knob again . . . This is such an opportunity for Jonah, and for me." This tone was meant to be persuasive, but the tentative, please-please-can-I-please nature of the argument only reminded Wilma what Sarah herself had been like when she was seventeen.

"I'll have to talk to Roy," was all that she could manage, but somehow Sarah found this an encouraging response and then poured out what meager details she had gathered about the plan for her trip. Planning was not Sarah's strong suit either—she planted sunflowers in mid-June, her car often ran out of gas, and she hadn't been married to either of her girls' fathers at the time of their conceptions. So

now, of course, the most that she knew was that her little family—
minus Starling—would depart from Los Angeles in ten days. Thankfully, Starling had never quite been her mother's daughter. She was a
wonderful student, straight As, always neat, and according to her
mother's crude calculations, she had already accumulated most of
what she needed to graduate with honors from Santa Fe Academy.
Her college applications were done.

"You can let her go to East Surry High," said her mother vaguely.
"It will give her some social interaction. She could probably teach
them a thing or two anyway." Wilma wanted to mention that the
school had sent a Morehead Scholar to Carolina this fall, but she
didn't bother. Sarah would never be convinced that Swan's Knob was
anything but a backwater town, which it surely was—population of
2,500 on a busy Saturday, four stoplights, one brand-new Hardee's
hamburger place—but that didn't mean some wonderful things
didn't happen right there in those ten square blocks at the foot of
their little mountain.

Sarah went on then about the bell makers of Nepal, their fires,
their little huts—these people living, in fact, in real backwaters, but
somehow more noble, in Sarah's mind. Wilma listened, made sounds
of interest, but then she got a picture, not of the crude metallurgy, but
of her granddaughter sitting on the chintz sofa across from her,
telling her about the boys at East Surry, about the fascinating Latin
teacher. She thought of the great scarf Starling would wear to the
homecoming football game, the royal-blue-and-white stripes of the
East Surry Rebels. She pictured Starling playing her piano again,
studying at the kitchen table, hot chocolate at midnight. She thought
of four precious months with a granddaughter whose presence she
had always craved. She had never quite gotten enough of Starling in
those brief summer visits over the years, and here, here was her
chance. Suddenly she was in a terrible rush to get Sarah off the phone
so that she could think for a minute, think clearly about how she
might talk Roy into this venture and how they could have Starling
with them and not ruin their marriage and their health before
Christmas.

Josh

Josh's calculus teacher, a pretty woman except that she had no tits to speak of, had decided to give his class an extra unit on statistics this year. Josh saw no good reason for this. Maybe she was on a mission to find out why she had been dealt a lousy hand, tit-wise. Maybe the answer was found in the numbers—the probability of X given Y, like the chance that he, Joshua Diamond, would get laid in this decade, given his height (5'9") and the condition of his chin (pimples). Or the joint probability that he would be at home—as he was at this moment, lying on his bed, listening to U2, surveying his chin with his fingertip—and that there would be no one around for the first time in who knows when.

Josh hated statistics. He hated math, though let's face it, he was better at it than most people. What was the point? What could you solve, really, that hadn't been solved already and listed in the back of the textbook? However. Last Tuesday in class he'd run into a word that finally satisfied him. *Outlier.* There it was, the entirety of his existence. An outlier was not a person who spent his spare time lying on his bed. No. It was a dot of data. Lonely. Hanging out there on the blank white quarter of the graph paper. It represented some schmoe, some disaffected thing—a piece of information so different from the rest that, according to Miss Grimsley, you could almost ignore it. An outlier. He loved this word. Loved it for what it meant and also because it sounded like "outlaw." When he became a recording artist on the Vista label, he would go by that name: the Outlier. The album cover would picture him hanging out in the desert in cowboy clothes. Two chicks in peasant blouses would be in the background. Admiring him. He'd have a badass look on his face. The whole thing would look like the ZZ Top poster he had pasted on his ceiling between the rafters.

"With or Without You" finished and the cassette deck clicked off over on his bureau. He got up to turn the tape over, but before he could get there, he thought he heard the front door slam. Too early for his folks to be back. Maybe it was Tommy, home to do laundry again. He looked out the dusty dormer that faced the front. Reprieve: Tommy's truck wasn't there. He lay back down and listened to the static at the beginning of the tape. Instead of starting his homework—he had a ton of math—he checked out the chicks that ZZ Top had on their poster. A blonde and a redhead were sitting on the hood of an old Cadillac, wearing short jean skirts and cowboy boots. It looked good.

Josh was an outlier by birth, the last of six children. Tommy, two years older, in junior college now, was the next youngest. Josh was an afterthought. His parents would say that to other adults when they thought he wasn't paying attention. When you looked at him beside his siblings, he had nothing they had. Not a single athletic ability, unless by magic next spring he showed up to baseball practice with a pitching arm. Not going to happen, though maybe if he listened to his dad for once and prayed for it . . . Presto. The immaculate pitching arm. In lieu of an arm, he had been granted brains—this was clear to him by now. He wasn't sure anyone else had noticed.

Side 2, "I Still Haven't Found What I'm Looking For." No kidding. It was a waste for him to be holed up in his room when he had the whole house to himself. Maybe he'd go down to his parents' room—the sanctuary, Tommy called it—and read on their bed. He was halfway through a racy book that he found in his mother's bedside table. It was called *Fear of Flying*. He wasn't too sure what his mother was doing with that book. Probably never read it, just crammed it in her drawer. It was for sure that his dad had not taken a good look at it. The contents would cause a riot if he bothered to read two sentences. He wouldn't. Josh could walk around with the thing hanging from his neck, and the guy wouldn't say a word. Just like everything except Tommy's game stats, it would go unnoticed. This was fine with the Outlier.

That was the thing about being the last of six. Everyone was worn down. Not past caring, just past any sustained concern. His room was Exhibit A. His parents had run out of house by the time he and Tommy came along, so the two of them got the attic and a pull-down stairway. Josh could have moved down to another room by now, but he'd stayed. He liked his privacy and he was used to it—he could fly up the narrow steps and fold them behind him in ten seconds flat. Travis and Celeste didn't care. They weren't even embarrassed if someone asked about it. *Six kids,* they'd say, *how else would you manage?* They said this matter-of-factly, like the choice was reasonable, thought-out in advance—loading two boys up into an attic with a single bare lightbulb every night. *Josh likes it now. He won't even move downstairs,* they'd say. *There's a heat vent and a little fan.*

Josh was not buying Travis and Celeste's game these days. He knew human biology. Six children. That wasn't something that was all that reasonable, not all that thought-out. No, you didn't get six children by praying fervently, as his dad would've had him believe early on. Communing with the Almighty was not what was required.

But this was not what he wanted to think about.

He shook it off and trotted down to the kitchen, where he fished around in the pantry. He found a bag of chips and chomped through five or six, then realized they'd been sitting open on the shelf for a while. More foraging uncovered a full bag of Oreos. He grabbed it and got the milk carton from the refrigerator. He'd chow and then he'd find out who little Ms. Erica Jong was going to do today.

Chapter Two

Wilma

She was late, though no one seemed to mind. This had become her habit, this ten minutes behind everything, so that the choir members didn't bother to even take the pews when they arrived, just mingled in the little space of carpet in front of the altar, scarcely noticing her as she pulled her electric keyboard out of its hiding place and set it up in front of the choir loft.

"Celeste saw them right after they checked Rufus in over at Baptist Hospital," Travis Diamond was saying to those gathered. He was always the first with the news of the injured and infirm since his wife Celeste worked as a nursing assistant in Winston three afternoons a week. "His goiter was the size of a grapefruit, isn't that right, honey?"

"Well, an orange," said Celeste, taking her place on the soprano row, "or maybe a tangerine . . ." Celeste's voice tended to trail off at the end of her sentences, so Wilma didn't think the group even heard this last part, which was said with the barest tinge of sarcasm. This surprised Wilma, because she had always seen Celeste as the kind of woman Wilma's mother always wanted her to be: modest, pleasing, pink lipstick, few opinions. But tonight she had made a little joke. She looked around to see who might have caught it, and spying Wilma, she smiled broadly. Her husband, his back to his wife, continued to enthrall the group with Rufus Ingram's goiter surgery.

Wilma unrolled her extension cord and plugged it into the keyboard. She was not fond of the instrument—the sound quality left much to be desired, and unlike the church organ or her baby grand at home, it was not big enough to hide behind. Roy had bought her the keyboard once it became clear last winter that Dan Mayhan's case of the flu was something far more serious and that he wouldn't be back to direct the choir. The job had fallen to Wilma—that in addition to being the organist. She didn't mind really; she liked the job most of the time. She didn't teach many piano students these days, so this extra work suited her.

Roy had come along with her one night and noticed that she was wearing herself out during practice, always coming down from the organ loft to give the choir some direction, then running back up to accompany them. Next chance he got, he'd taken her to Strain's Music in Winston, bought the electric organ for her as another man would buy his wife a toaster—that's just the way he was. Early on in their marriage, she had objected to this kind of extravagance, but then she saw that Roy took pleasure in giving her things, so she let him. He bought the organ. And she had made good use of it.

She turned on the keyboard and began to pass out the music for the Sunday anthem. It was a beautiful Fauré piece, "Ave Verum Corpus," with a wonderful part for the sopranos—they were her strongest section. As she sent the sheets down the pew to her tenor and bass sections, she braced herself. There were those in the choir who did not like this sort of music—who thought the standard hymns and your basic eighteenth-century anthems were enough. Charles Wesley made everyone happy. Some people just wanted to come to church and hear "Amazing Grace" for the umpteenth time and be done with it. But then she had run into sheet music for Fauré's *Requiem* and his other choral pieces in her catalogue. They were so lovely. She was going to try to do several of them over the fall. There were a few choir members who would actually appreciate this, like Cynthia Trolley, who smiled at her now from the middle row. Cynthia taught voice at the high school and even had some private students. She was always trying to get people in this town to reach a little further.

The choir was quieting down now as everyone took their places. Travis Diamond flipped through his pages briefly, then held them down by his side like a poker hand. He drew his lips together in a thin line and wrinkled his forehead, this display aimed at his wife Celeste sitting in the opposite pews of the soprano section. Celeste, usually the soul of serenity despite her crop of children, looked back at him and mouthed, "Please," which meant, Wilma would find out in a second, "Please don't make a fuss." Travis, who was not known for listening to much of anything from anybody, cleared his throat. This was one of those times when Wilma wished to goodness that Roy Swan had even a passable singing voice.

"For who?" said Travis. "Fauré? French, right? Next you'll have us singing in Latin." He said this in a light tone, though you couldn't miss the sarcasm. Everybody in the choir made themselves busy looking over the music, stealing a look or two at Wilma. She tried to retain a neutral expression, which involved clenching her teeth and trying not to stretch her skin tight around them.

Cynthia Trolley spoke up—though Wilma was not sure this would be to anyone's benefit. "Well, Travis, this piece is in Latin, but it's beautiful, if you'd just listen a minute." Beside her, Celeste looked down at her lap and pressed her thumbs against the creases of her slacks.

"I'm sure it is. Perfectly nice. But this is not just music we're producing here. We are not here on this earth to glorify ourselves with this fancy French music. We have a mission." He said this last word like a TV preacher and hit his rhythm. "We're a choir. We are part of worship, WOR-ship."

A few of the tenors began to nod in agreement. Wilma wished that Travis had not taken this up as a cause. He was vaguely convincing and he would not go gently. She had to quell his little rebellion before it spread out of the choir loft. The choir ran the church. It was a known fact. The organist, the choir director, even the minister were just hired hands. If the choir didn't like something, well, it would go the way of the unity wedding candle. This part of the ceremony— where the bride and groom each used a candle to light a single large one at the end of a wedding—had become popular in other churches. After it was incorporated into a ceremony last spring by an unsuspecting bride (whose mother was originally from Pennsylvania), Mimi Salter remarked that she had never seen such a thing in a

Protestant church, that she thought all that candle play was for the Catholics. That was all it took. Now there was a rule that limited candles to the modest matching set that sat on the altar at all services. Of course, exuberant floral displays—those that overwhelmed the altar, perched on the ends of the pews, real or fake, hot pink, bloodred, Wilma had even seen Day-Glo orange—all allowed.

Wilma's impulse was to muscle through the situation, treating Travis like one of her students who balked at her piano assignments and begged for Pink Floyd sheet music. "Take it or leave it," that's what she felt like saying, but she was afraid that Travis would leave it and take Celeste with him. Wilma needed their voices. She looked at Cynthia Trolley then, who was about to let loose on Travis. It would not be the first time. This would not do. "Why, Travis," Wilma said in a conciliatory tone that made her hate herself. "We all appreciate your spiritual leadership, we do, and in fact I was about to ask you to lead us in a prayer before we got down to work on this piece."

"Well, now . . ." he began, as if he needed to consider the situation.

"Wait until you hear the last section. It fairly well sparkles," said Cynthia in a perky tone that made Wilma hate her as well, but then Travis assumed the position: arms folded carefully to the front, fingers interlocked, eyes commanding their attention just before he lowered the lids.

He prayed over them then, prayed longer than was seemly, and more elaborately. As much as Wilma disliked the idea of getting his blessing on the proceedings, maybe it was the price for fancy French music. When he was finished, she warmed them up with the offertory hymn for Sunday, a standard, blessedly composed by Charles Wesley, and then she got down to business. And she had been right: the Fauré was beautiful, and toward the end, when she asked that they sing the entire piece through, she noticed in the coda section how Travis Diamond's voice was perfectly suited to the high tenor range. She smiled at him then, and he could probably guess why she was doing it, but he did not smile back.

She ignored the small snub and said, "Good job, everyone. Just lovely, tenors!" She tried to say it in an enthusiastic way—this was one thing that Roy had gotten on her about over the years. He said she was slow to praise anyone. He would say, "I cannot live on *humph, you'll do*. I want to hear about how I am the greatest man on earth." He was right. Even though he was the greatest man on earth, good grief she hated to say that to him. It caused untoward behavior. Same with the choir. Rather than dole out praise, she would have liked to work through the piece for another fifteen minutes. However, everyone had taken her last remark as their dismissal and people were now filing out of their places, like children released from school. Chatter filled the loft where ten seconds before there had been music.

The quick transition bothered Wilma every time—though she wasn't sure why. She thought everyone should take a moment, somehow. It gave her the same feeling that she had after a graveside funeral service, when everyone walked away from the casket, turned their backs, and began talking and hugging one another, no one looking at all when the cemetery people lowered the casket. She would say things like this to Roy every once in a while, that choir practice seemed over too fast or that people ought to stand by a grave a few minutes—the kind of remark that was out of your mouth before you thought—and he would always laugh a little and then ask her what was for dinner. As people began to drift down the aisle, Wilma thanked Cynthia Trolley for her support, and Cynthia left with the other sopranos, looking pleased. Feeling rather pleased herself, Wilma took her pile of sheet music back up to the sanctuary organ, the real one, and then went back down to unplug the toy. Celeste had gathered the music folders the choir had left behind, as she usually did, and brought them to Wilma.

"It was a beautiful piece," she said. "I never heard another thing like it and I been singing in one choir or another since I was little. Those harmonies, I mean, so different from what I'm used to. You don't listen to them, Miss Wilma. You go on with Mr. Fauré. I thought we sounded like the angels."

"Well, angel, hang up your wings there, and let's get on home," called her husband from out in the darkened sanctuary. Celeste stiffened, as if someone had pulled on all her strings. She shoved the remainder of the music sheets into Wilma's hands.

"I'll be right there," she said to him, and then to Wilma in the lowest voice possible, "Walk me out." Wilma did. She noticed that even when they reached the vestibule and walked across the terrazzo floor, Celeste Diamond's footsteps didn't make a sound.

Roy

When he saw Wilma come down the steps of the church, happily chatting with one of the women from the choir, Roy felt a rush of pride, the kind of thing that a parent must feel when his kid comes home with a new buddy. Sure, his lovely bride, the sweet reward of later age, she had friends. Everyone in town knew her, respected her, but usually she was the last one out of the church, a lone straggler, which was why he drove over to pick her up most Wednesdays. He didn't want her walking around in the parking lot after everyone had gone, fumbling with her car keys. She didn't much like it. "How do you think I've managed all these years?" she said. "Stay home. I'll take my car." She said this every week.

Roy had learned over time that when it came to Wilma, it wasn't a good idea to take everything she said as gospel. Not that she lied, really, that wasn't it. In fact, mostly she told him to do something (or not to do something) and she darn well meant it. He'd learned that the first time he left a towel on the floor in that Hawaiian hotel on their honeymoon. He'd been hanging up those babies ever since. Other times, though, she said something plain out, and Roy knew, he just knew instantly, that she didn't mean it at all, and he could go right ahead and do the opposite and she would love him for it.

For the life of him, he did not know where he got this second sense about her, how he could see right into her so much of the time, see a thunderstorm from miles away, see that she was tickled pink even though she was wearing that scary piano teacher scowl. Lord knows, before he married Wilma, he had never had much of a clue about what women were up to, not in the least. He'd had several pretty ugly surprises along the way. One had had a complete hissy fit right in the middle of Skipper's Seafood over a chance remark about somebody else's sunburned ankles. He'd received several Dear John letters out of the blue. He'd even been slapped, though that one had been a little crazy. His courtship with Wilma had contained not a single such miscue. He was right as rain about her from their first date at the Coach House Restaurant downtown until the day they said, "I do." As far as he was concerned, from there, things had only gotten better.

Their wedding was a case in point. "Let's not make a big fuss," she'd said. "It's unseemly." At first he'd been inclined to go along. That's what everyone told him to do, anyway. "Just sit back, Roy, and enjoy the ride, if you can," is the way Clyde Erath had put it. "Grin and bear it," is what Chief Henry said. Of course, everyone down at Squirrely's pool hall had had some little thing to say the minute word got out. Wilma had let news of their engagement slip at the end of choir practice on a Wednesday, and by Thursday night, when Roy walked into Squirrely's, there had been quite a stir. Clyde, who, being the mayor, had to make a ceremony out of everything, stood at attention and hollered, "Boys, raise your glasses. After six decades in the forest, a mighty oak has fallen," and some such like that on and on. Roy had expected this kind of thing, but he had been surprised that he'd also received detailed wedding advice from some of the biggest good old boys in the county. It was Charlie White, who owned Squirrely's and tended bar most nights, who got Roy thinking. He'd said Roy ought to go on and do it up, this being his first wedding.

Roy had realized right then what Wilma had meant by "unseemly." She thought they were too old to be in love like they were, that she in particular didn't deserve this thing that had come to them, that she ought to hide it from the view of the world. Heck with that, is what Roy had decided. Even though he'd had about four beers and a few sips of Charlie's brandy, he had marched right over to Wilma's house and told her so in no uncertain terms. He had made a big lecture out of it and then he had done some major smooching on her.

She relented, sort of. She agreed to a church wedding and a reception in his backyard. She agreed to let him invite the whole choir

and his buddies and about a dozen other people, though it had taken
him some talking. He insisted on hiring a string quartet and of course
she could not resist that kind of thing. Neither could she object when
he offered to fly her daughter and granddaughter and even old
what's-his-name, Jonah, out for the proceedings. She assumed he was
done after that, that he would leave her alone to make the arrangements, and he did, or at least that was what she thought.

In truth, he had called around and checked on every order she
made. He told Dewey's Bakery that they had changed their minds
about that two-layer pound cake. He told the lady they wanted one
of those tower things, triple-decker with all kind of curlycues and she
knew just what he meant. For the other food, he called Grace Snow,
who had recently started up a catering business. He let the punch and
cheese straw orders stand but added a big old roast beef and an entire array of international fruits and cheeses.

When he found out that Wilma had picked out only one little
bitty vase of white roses for the church, he had gone down there to
Gladys Teague's shop himself to fix things up. He ordered every
white flower he and Gladys could think of, except carnations. Wilma
hated carnations for some reason. He'd told Gladys that he wanted
that church to look like a dadburn garden. And it had. He'd had
flowers everywhere, even little sprigs of things on the pews. The smell
alone had been something. That was one of his best memories of his
wedding, the look of complete surprise and delight on Wilma's face
when she came into the back of the church. She had looked so beautiful that day in her suit that was the color of candlelight. He would
never forget her looking at him soft and sweet when she got up to the
altar. She had the most beautiful eyes. They were dark blue, the color
of the Knob at daybreak. It was right then he had seen it, seen it there
in her eyes while they were standing in front of God and everybody:
that he knew all about what was best for Wilma Mabry Swan, he sure
did.

Just like now, he knew that his Wilma could use a friend. He
couldn't figure it out, but she didn't really seem to have any. Sure, she
and Roy were close, but there were some things that a man and a
woman just couldn't talk about. He wasn't really sure what these

might be, especially the topics that might interest what they were now calling postmenopausal women. And Lord knows, he did not want to know, any more than Wilma wanted to know about hunting licenses and jock itch. So it gave him a spark of hope to see her standing on the steps there with some woman from the choir. He couldn't see who it was, but they were laughing now, like one of them had told a good joke on her husband. "And I'm sure he never saw it coming," he heard Wilma say as she got close to the car.

"Oh, no, of course not," said the other woman. Celeste Diamond, that's who it was. He knew the voice, and by now she was right up on the car, so Roy could see her long face in profile and her black hair that was braided in a rope down the middle of her back. Too bad. Celeste would not be his first choice. He had known her all her life, grown up on the farm next to where she'd lived with that awful mother and daddy. She'd had some kind of crush on him at one time, though that'd been a long time ago, before he had gone to serve in Korea. She wouldn't even remember it, she'd been married to Travis for years, but still, he didn't want her running around with Wilma, somehow, telling tales. He couldn't see himself sitting in the Coach House, he and Wilma, Celeste and, of course, Travis, who was a real piece of work all on his own. No sir.

Celeste

Celeste could tell—just by the way that her husband's shoulder blades jerked up and down underneath the thin Western shirt she'd been trying to get him to throw away for two years—that Travis was mad as a hornet and would be letting her have it just as soon as they got into the truck. Oh, he had heard what she said to Miss Wilma all right; he'd heard it real good. It was the very thing that he could not tolerate—her contradicting him. And now he fairly well stomped through the church parking lot, ignoring everyone else around them—the plain folks, as she thought of them, those that just went about their lives: Roy Swan sitting in his car waiting for Wilma, leaning over to open the passenger door for her; Mimi Salter, a longtime widow, riding tonight in Joyce Freeman's blue Taurus, a car picked out and paid for by Steve Freeman for Joyce's fifty-fifth birthday. Marriage, whole lives, she'd bet, running along most of the time without incident, without need to tiptoe across eggshells or hot coals, or whatever else. Travis unlocked her side of the cab and stood holding the door with the kind of boiled patience that scared the living daylights out of her every time.

He wasn't going to hurt her—she knew that much. He had never touched her in anger during all the time of their marriage, nearly twenty-five years. He had pointed this out many times, pointed out that it was her family, her mama and daddy, who did that kind of thing. He was right. If anything, these days, she was the one who felt prone to violence. She climbed up into the cab carefully, keeping her head raised, trying to maintain that quiet dignity that they were always talking about when they described the widows of fallen heroes.

Not that she wanted to kill Travis. No, that would be a sin, and say what you would, she was still scared of eternal damnation. No, she did not even fantasize about putting a knife in his chest or shooting him between the shoulder blades right where that Western shirt yoke came down to a point. This was not what she thought about when she was hanging out the laundry or cutting up onions. In those idle moments, she thought about pearls, a lovely string of pearls, real ones, like those they had on sale at Belks over Labor Day. Pearls lying on a simple black wool dress. That was the style now: she'd seen it on that *L.A. Law* show. Three-quarter sleeve, boatneck. Travis cranked up the truck and pulled out onto Main Street. For the moment, he kept whatever he was fixing to say contained in his cocked jaw. He didn't look at her, but held the steering wheel tight and drove with robotic precision.

As those few streetlights passed over them before they ran out of town and rode out into the countryside, Celeste thought of herself, alone, bereaved, sitting in the back of a limousine, the streetlights falling across her beautiful troubled face as she mourned the untimely death of her beloved Travis. It had happened when he was working on that roof leak the boys were always complaining about, maybe. He'd been putting down the roof shingles in the heat when all the pork chops and the butter biscuits and those awful pork rinds that he ate the minute he was out of her sight—they would all catch up with him and clog his arteries and he would be struck with a single pain and fall off the roof. He would be dead before he hit the ground. And she would have been inside at the time and would hear only a muffled thump.

"For the life of me, I cannot believe that you would do me like that," said Travis in a quiet voice. "It is not a great thing to ask, I don't think, for a wife to stand behind her husband." So he was not going to explode at her, but they would be going home via the guilty, guilty route. She pressed her hand against her throat, fingered the imaginary pearls. The widow Diamond. Our Celeste, who lost her husband last year. It made her sweat a bit, she could feel it on her neck, to think such thoughts. She cracked her window and let the fall breeze come through.

"Roll that up," said Travis. "I do not understand you for a minute. We have discussed this. You know how I feel about the choir. This is God's work, not yours or mine. I am trying to build up and you tear down. Do you think I like creating a fuss at choir practice? Do you think I like being the squeaky wheel?"

"Well," she said, meaning it only as a placeholder.

"Well?" he said. "Well? Are you going to do it again? Don't tell me you're going to contradict me again!" He pitched forward in his seat and the truck swerved, though it didn't matter much. No one else was on the road this time of night.

She gripped the handle on the door to keep steady. "No. Maybe I better not say anything else. I might get it wrong." And, she thought, you always liked me better that way anyway. Quiet. Modest. The quiet and modest widow Diamond.

"Maybe not," he said and then was quiet himself until they hit the gravel of the road onto their land.

"Looks like one young man has learned his lesson," he said, and this too was a reprimand. "I said don't light up the house like a Christmas tree, one lamp at a time, and look up there. Why, I can't see that there's a light on in the house. That's my boy!"

When they pulled up in front of the house, she could see that he was right. There was literally not a single light on, not even a little glow out of the end of the house from the attic. Celeste was not the hysterical mother type—raising a bunch of children stamped that impulse right out of you—but something about the totally dark house made her nervous. Was Josh there at all? It was nine thirty—too early for him to be in bed.

In his satisfaction, Travis seemed to have completely forgotten he was mad at her. He was like that, tear her all to pieces over something, and then by bedtime, Mr. Lovey-Dovey. He jumped out of the truck, ran around to her side. Then he grabbed her hand and helped her feel her way up the walk in the dark. "Careful, honey. Don't you fall now," he said in that voice that told her bedtime wasn't too far off. He leaned up against her in that way he had, and she picked up the scant scent of his body, sweaty, but more of a little boy sweat, and a bit of sawdust from the work he had done in his shop in the afternoon. A nice smell in all. She had always liked it.

The house inside was quiet. She started to call out, but Travis stopped her. He flipped on the dim hall light. They walked into the hall where the stairway to the attic was all folded up, just like Josh always left it when he turned in for the night. "Let him sleep," whispered Travis and led her down the hall and around the corner to their room. Celeste still had her doubts. There was something in her that wouldn't rest unless she put her hands on those kids at the end of the day. Josh was the only one still home and close enough to check on. She'd go up once Travis was asleep and snoring to oblivion.

Travis was in their room now, hadn't bothered to switch on the light. He found the bed and went to sit down and take off his shoes just like every other night of their marriage. She didn't even need a light to know that he would hitch one foot up on his knee to undo the double-knotted lace on those brown work shoes. Next he would loosen the other the very same way.

"Good God Almighty!" Travis yelled and jumped up from the bed.

Celeste's first thought was that a snake had gotten into the room and Travis had been bitten. It had happened to a distant cousin in her girlhood. The man had been dead before morning. She fumbled and found the light switch by the door.

"What? What?" came the confused voice of her seventeen-year-old, her baby Josh, on the bed.

"Good God Almighty!" said Travis again. "Son, you liked to scare me to death. I didn't know what that was on my bed."

"What? What!" Josh yelled now, sitting up suddenly and grasping the book that was open facedown on his chest. Celeste saw then what he had. It was that smutty *Fear of Flying* book that Cynthia Trolley had loaned her. Oh God, she should never have accepted it. Look what had happened. Josh fumbled around on the bed now, closing the book, holding it behind him, horribly embarrassed. And how had Josh got hold of that? She saw that he had been in her drawer, the one that held those things that she didn't want anyone in this world to see. It was pulled out from her bedside table, open two inches, just enough so that you could see the packages of Modess and OB that she kept on the top. This made her furious, but she kept still and tried not to look at Josh or the drawer.

"Son, what in the world were you doing in here?" Travis said.

Josh looked at Celeste then and blushed deep. She thought for a moment that he might give her up—hand her the book or say something awful to Travis—but mercifully he just collected his tall but incredibly skinny frame up off the bed, and with an impressive nonchalance, he said, "Man, sorry, Dad. I know I shouldn't have been in here, but I laid down for a minute to read and I pure-t fell asleep. Sorry that I scared you, really." He ambled past his dad, who still looked a little spooked, and almost made it past the door frame.

"Wait a minute," said Travis. "Since when have you been afraid of flying? I thought you wanted to be an air force man."

"Ah, I'm real tired, Dad," said Josh.

"No, really, it surprises me. You've hardly been up . . ." Travis was pulling his shirttail out of his pants, the next step in getting ready for bed. Celeste was watching their whole marriage flash before her eyes.

"It's about that, really. It's about this flier," said Josh, a much better liar than Celeste would have figured. "See, this military guy, who started out being afraid, see? And he, he . . . well, I didn't get too far in it yet . . . Anyway, good night."

He left them then, closed the door behind him. In a few moments, Celeste heard the creak of the attic stairway spring—the whole thing pulled down, the weight of that skinny boy, her youngest, her co-conspirator, on the stairs, another squeak as the contraption came up into the ceiling. By the time Josh's footsteps fell overhead, her husband's clothes lay in a puddle on the floor, and Travis, the man of her dreams, was an expectant lump in the bed.

Chapter Three

Roy

*H*arper Chilton was late. Roy had rushed his morning routine in town and driven out to his farm in a cloud of dust to be there to meet him, and now he'd been waiting on the front porch of the old home place for half an hour. The coffee in the bottom of his cup was cold. Of course, he should've known. It was real unusual for Harper to make an appointment at all. He'd come by almost a dozen times in the last year—always showing up in the shank of the afternoon, just at the earliest possible time that a man could legitimately break out a bottle. Roy didn't mind: he was happy to have someone to share some wine or even a drop or two of bourbon. This time, though, Harper'd called two days in advance and asked Roy to meet him out here, so Roy had to wonder what he was after. Something more about that fiddlers' concert, most likely. He'd already talked Roy into letting him use the farm. Now maybe he needed something else.

Roy hoped he wasn't going to ask for money. It was always awkward to be the richest man in the county and to have everybody know it. And Harper, Harper in a roundabout way was kin to Roy, not by blood, but by the uncertain chain of marriage. That was not the kind of thing that Roy could say in front of Wilma. No, his little woman was not about to claim Harper; she didn't want to have a thing to do with him, even though he had been her son-in-law at one time, even though he lived in King, just a county over from them. Roy had never really understood this. He'd always liked the guy okay. He was a little shiftless was all, but with him being the artistic type, a musician, well, that was pretty much par for the course.

The sun was starting to get a little hot on him, even though it was getting into September. If he was going to sweat, he might as well get some work done. What he ought to be doing was figuring exactly what he needed in a production winepress, but that was too complicated to get into right this minute. Instead, he went around to the back of the house and got his clippers and his basket, and went out to his little vegetable garden. He stopped first at his grape arbor, the original one that he and his father built when they planted the first scuppernong grapevine. The thing was huge now, the main vine thicker than his leg and gnarly. The grapes were just at the point of ripeness.

On days like this, with a sweet breeze coming down from the Knob into the valley of his land, with the sun beaming down on his little crop of grapes, on his tomato vines and his face, Roy Swan imagined that he had been such a man for centuries, overseeing his land on a hillside, that he was reincarnated somehow—though that was in no way a Protestant teaching—that he had stood in such a field on a hillside in Umbria in 1730 maybe, holding warm grapes in his hand, more pleased with life than anyone on earth.

Though he loved his house in town, and he loved Wilma Mabry Swan, his bride of seven years, he could not abandon this land at the foot of Swan's Knob. In fact, over the years, he had made small improvements to the clapboard house his great-grandfather had built. He had kept up the little vegetable garden, the grape arbor. He'd experimented with several varieties of grapes until he'd found some that would do well on his land. Three years ago, he had let the tobacco leases go and planted grapevines across every acre. Travis Diamond, who'd had the leases so long that he thought he owned them, had been mad as hell when Roy told him. Wilma had said he'd lost his mind—importing little sticks of vines all the way from California. "Your hobby, sweetie, has gotten out of hand," was what she had said, and she was right.

He had almost fifty acres now, mostly chardonnay and cabernet franc, plus a couple of acres of riesling. He was pretty sure they'd all do well with this Swan's Knob soil and climate. One more year and his very first production crop of grapes would be on the vines—a few acres of cabernet franc in the back field would even yield decently this year. They'd be ready to harvest in just a few weeks. They were looking mighty fine, was what he thought, and with a little luck, some dry weather, and a few more visits from those vineyard consultant people from California, he might just have some decent wine on his hands. Hell, he'd even had a label made up from a woodcutting with the outline of Swan's Knob on it. It looked real nice.

And Wilma, well, she was less critical these days. If nothing else, he'd gotten all of those big plastic bottles out of her piano room. The juicer, all the bottles, the whole operation had come out here. Many days, he could leave her to her lessons, her practices, and whatever else it was that kept her running around from dawn to dusk—and come out here to work on his little wine operation without getting underfoot. They'd both lived alone so long before they married, it was only natural for them to each need their own stomping grounds. And this land was his. His own mother hadn't cared much for coming out either, so, growing up, the place had been his and his daddy's. Just inside the back door, there was still a wall full of fish rods, hats, all kinds of tackle. Everything hung up there on hooks, ready for Roy should he get the urge here one day to go fishing.

His basket was full now with the grapes he was going to press the minute he was done with Harper. He'd still use the little press for the scuppernongs and the cab franc just like always, and next year he'd have the big press. He didn't mind using the old way for now. He was getting to be a pretty good winemaker. He fancied that in his red blend he would taste a hint of the minerals in the clay and the sweetness of the mountain sun. Before he got totally carried away, he looked around the house out toward the road to see if he could see Harper coming, but there wasn't a thing, not even a dust cloud from the road turnoff two miles north. He was sweating pretty good now, and as he hauled the basket onto the back porch, he got that swimmy-headed feeling he'd had a couple of times last week. It was the heat. He was going to have to break down and start wearing the silly hat Wilma was always trying to put on his head: this was one thing that didn't agree with him about being married. There was always another precaution about some damn thing or other that he was expected to take note of. Dang, Wilma was nearly as bad as his mother some days. It could be hard to take.

He went in for some water. The plumbing was a little rusty, but once the water had run through it a minute, you finally got the stuff that came up straight from the well. It was cold and clear and tasted so much better than the city water. He was going for his second glass when he heard Harper's van on the gravel outside. It crunched to a stop in front of the house, and Roy heard ten seconds of Doc Watson singing "Tennessee Stud" before Harper cut the engine.

Harper was a man always in motion but never in a hurry. He rustled around in the van for a few moments and finally came up onto the porch, whistling the tune as he knocked on Roy's screen door. "Come on in," yelled Roy.

Harper let the screen door slam behind him and stood in the middle of Roy's front room, his hands on his hips. "Roy, old boy, how you doing?" he said, his standard greeting.

"Fine, just fine." He was a little uncertain as to how to proceed, since it was a little early for drinking. "Coffee? Or water, or something?" he said, but Harper shook his head. It was too hot still to sit inside, so he took Harper back out to the porch. Harper made himself at home, not saying much yet, took a seat on one end of the swing and put his feet up. Roy couldn't ever remember seeing Harper wearing anything other than what he wore today—jeans and some musician's T-shirt. He noticed he had on some kind of sandals, big leather things Roy had seen before, some German brand. Harper had big feet for being such a small man otherwise. You could see two or three toes on each foot, not a pretty sight. Still, Roy liked the way he seemed to feel at home here, wiggling those ugly toes and folding his arms back over his head, no need to rush a conversation. Roy liked how they had come to know each other over the last couple of years. He had known Harper's daddy too, not well, but enough to speak off and on. Wally Chilton had served on the rescue squad for King, and Roy the same for Swan's Knob, so they'd seen each other at the county meetings, at the big wrecks, fires, parades. And Harper had really seemed to appreciate it when Roy had come to Wally's funeral a few years back. That was, come to think of it, when Harper had started dropping by.

"So how's that old Wilma woman getting along?" said Harper, also a standard question. He always said that with a smile and a little conspiratorial laugh—as if he had a good idea of what kind of trouble Wilma really was, and what kind of fun. Maybe he did. He'd been her son-in-law long enough to find out that there was more to her than that strict schoolmarm act. Of course, Harper must also have had some idea that his name was mud as far as Wilma was concerned. He knew better than to show up at their house in town. He had cheated pretty bad on Sarah, cheated up one side and down the other, as far as Roy knew, though that was over ten years ago. Sarah was out in Santa Fe raising their daughter Starling, happily coupled with someone. None of that mattered to Wilma. Harper would not be forgiven. No sir. That was the way she was.

"Wilma's doing fine, spent last week rushing around the house getting ready for . . . a bunch of company." Roy caught himself. He wasn't quite sure what Harper knew about Starling's visit, if he knew at all. Best not to go into it.

Harper didn't ask who might be visiting, and they went on for a few minutes about not much of anything—the weather, the tobacco crop, Roy's grapes. There was a little silence then, and Harper put a foot down on the porch and used it to push himself in the swing. He stared out at the fields for a minute, gathering his thoughts maybe, winding up the pitch.

"So, tell me how it's going with the festival," Roy said, hoping to get things rolling. "Are we all set?" About six months ago, Harper had come to him and asked if he could have a bluegrass concert out in Roy's far pasture. Hadn't seemed like a bad idea at the time—just a matter of a flatbed truck for a stage, some old-time bands, a couple hundred people, and a pair of Port-o-lets. Now he wondered what shortfall or complication had turned up.

"Oh yeah, it's going to be *great*," said Harper, overselling the last word. "That's why I'm here. It's going to be *even better* than we planned. I thought we could walk the land today and figure out where to put everything." He sat up then and hopped off the porch seat just as it swung up. He waved his hand for Roy to get up. Roy obliged, worrying the whole time about what *even better* might mean.

"Let's go out there to that little rise where you've got the oak grove," said Harper. "That way we can see the whole layout." Roy had to smile as they walked down the driveway. The whole layout, huh? Just like Harper to say it like that. He always had a grand way of thinking about things that amounted to nothing in the end. As they walked, Harper started naming off the musicians he had lined up for his concert, though Roy didn't know enough about these local bands to recognize them. At least Harper was trying to do some advance planning. This was an improvement.

Harper walked ahead of him as they took the path up to the oaks. He moved around like he was a big guy, throwing his shoulders back and forth, like he was unaware that he was no more than 5'5" or 5'6". He was a wiry sort, as his daddy had been, more muscled than you'd think for a man who didn't ever seem to do an honest day's work, unless you counted teaching chorus at the community college or substituting for the East Surry band director.

At the top of the hill, Harper stood with his hands on his hips again and looked back, fit as a fiddle. Roy, still huffing up the path, reminded himself that once upon a time he'd run all the way without getting out of breath. "You okay?" said Harper, which pissed Roy off. *You'll be sixty-eight one of these days,* he wanted to say, *if you're lucky.*

Roy loved being up in this grove. All of his kin from four generations were buried just on the other side of the trees, facing up to the mountain. From this side of the hill, where he and Harper stood side by side now, you could look out over the rest of the land. The first few seasons after he had let the leases go, Roy had missed the lush green and yellow of the tobacco plants, but the farm was truly a vineyard now and there was a certain geometry to the fields. It was ten kinds of satisfying to see all the acres of vines tacked up on a run of wire, row after row. The plants had wrist-thick trunks, and leafy arms had grown out down the holding wire. This time next year, they'd be heavy with grapes, skinny men showing off their harvest. Just down the slope were the few unused fields that captured Harper's attention.

"Well," he said, "it's a little smaller than I thought, now that I'm up here to see it. How many acres down there before you get to the grapes?"

Roy started to figure it, but Harper went on, "We are going to need more room. Here's why—I've saved the best for last. We're going to have a big headliner. I know, I know, you're thinking that we already have a good list. The Dixie Ramblers and Ralph Stanley, those acts alone can draw a good crowd, not to mention all those old fiddlers. But here's the kicker, and you're not going to believe it. I've got—are you ready?—Delrina Kay and Little Charlie. Can you believe it?"

Now, Roy had heard of these people. In fact, he thought he'd seen them on TV sometime. Delrina Kay had been a well-known country singer for a while, he thought, but then she'd added her son to the act when he was little bitty, seven or eight, and then things just took off. They had been really big, as Roy recalled, a few years back, and not just as a bluegrass family, big in country music too. But he hadn't heard about them for a while. "Are they still around?" he said. Something had happened; he couldn't remember what.

Harper looked at him, his eyes all lit up, his mustache twitching a little. "Yeah. Yeah, man, you're right. They haven't been around. That's the great part. Remember, they retired a few years back, when Little Charlie was in his early teens. He got a real bad case of mono, then got on drugs. Delrina just pulled him out of everything almost five years ago. They're coming out of retirement, and get this: their debut performance will be right here, at my little festival."

"Well, good. Real nice," said Roy, though Harper had a certain brand of smile on his face that worried him.

"There's more," said Harper. "I've gotten the word this morning that there's to be an article about this in *Rolling Stone* magazine pretty soon, all about Delrina and Charles, that's what he wants to be called now, Charles. Their manager called me on Monday, saying they'll talk the festival up big in this article and to get prepared."

"*Rolling Stone?*" That had a pretty big circulation.

"So I've come on over here to start getting us ready for more people than we thought," said Harper. "We wouldn't want to have all that trouble they had at Woodstock."

"Woodstock?"

Harper kept the silly smile on his face and gave a nervous laugh without moving his lips. "Oh, well, no, now, not Woodstock, Roy. Lord, five hundred thousand people showed up at Woodstock."

"Five hundred thousand?"

"Well, that was the wrong thing to say, truly." Harper tried to rub out the thought by waving his hands in the air.

Roy looked out at his pretty fields of vines. "What was the date, again?" he said.

"November twelfth," said Harper. Ten weeks away.

"And how many?" he said. "Truly, Harper. How many?"

"I don't know," said Harper, his voice flat and quiet for the first time. "Ten thousand maybe, with good weather. I don't know, maybe more."

"Lord. God."

"I know," said Harper. "I don't know what to say, Roy, except for this: I can call it off. I can call it all off as of this minute. I'll tell folks we just can't do it and that'll be the end of it."

"Damn straight," said Roy.

"Or," said Harper.

"Or what?"

"Or," said Harper, "we find a way, Roy, we just find a way to do this. Listen to me a minute. This is big, Roy, really big."

"Yeah, it's big, all right." Oh God, this was way worse than lending money. Roy wished now that he could take out his checkbook. Here it came. Harper was winding up now, taking a deep breath.

"Now, Roy, listen, this is a big thing for me. Finally, a big thing that is my doing. You've known me, on and off, for a while now, and let's just face it, I've been sort of a fuck-up. Yeah, yeah, I made all that noise about the Smithsonian Institution study—music of the Plains Indians, on and on, but let's face it, that was not any great gig, and since then, what? I play a little bluegrass, teach a couple of courses over at Surry Community. I'm lucky they'll take me. So, here it is, Roy, here's my chance. Let's do this thing. You can help me pull it off. Come on."

Harper finished with his voice in a near whisper. Roy had to hand it to him, Harper was persuasive. It was no wonder that he had sweet-talked about half the women in the county out of their underwear. And, of course, all that confessing about his messed-up life, well, Harper knew it would work on Roy, who was the damn king of pulling his sad bachelor's life out of the toilet at the last minute.

"I don't know," he said.

"Well, how about this?" said Harper. "How about we spend a few days trying to think about how we might handle a bigger crowd? That's all, a few days. We'll decide after that. What do you say?"

"I'd say, we're shit-fire going to need more than two Port-o-lets, that's what I'd say."

They talked for a few minutes more, tried to calculate how many people could really stand in that front pasture, how many cars could be parked along his road, but Roy knew that he would agree in the end, and he knew, of course, that he would have a heck of a hard time explaining to Wilma just exactly why.

Harper left eventually, but Roy stayed up on his little hill. He hadn't bothered to climb up here for a time—the laziness of age. He watched Harper drive his van down the long driveway and out to the road, and then he went back around the grove to the family graves. He loved graveyards. Even though he was in no way a mortician and had never thought to be one, he loved to walk among the dead and had ever since he had first discovered this little family plot at age nine.

He and his Walkertown cousins had been playing army on a fine spring morning. In some corner of him, Roy was still that sweaty little boy: buzz haircut, the soft hand-me-down clothes of the Depression, his skinny chigger-bitten legs taking him up the hillside path quick as you please. He had ducked behind one of those big oak trees and sat down. There they were in the shaded clearing—a line of headstones, more than a dozen, each one a bit more crumbled, more weathered than the last. Roy had forgotten about the fierce battle in progress, forgotten his new cap pistol, and the scent of the wild strawberries that called him from the field on the other side of the hill. He got up and walked down the line of the stones, knowing exactly what they were, feeling older and important up here in the place of Death, but knowing it only partially, having seen it for the first time on the last Thanksgiving Day, when his uncles hauled a load of stiff deer carcasses home in a pickup truck.

The stones themselves were familiar—they were made from the gray quartzite of Swan's Knob, the mountain that sat just over his shoulder, presiding over strawberry picking and fishing in the creek, over chores and war games and even sleep. It was nothing more than a foothill, a small mountain hunched up a hundred miles shy of the rest of the Blue Ridge. It began properly just beyond the farthest field of their farm, a gentle slope at first, then a steep incline covered with pines. At the top was a long ridge, then a dip—and from that rose the knob itself, like a huge scoop of ice cream taken out of the mountain. Roy spent many of his days rooting around that knob. They said at one time Indians used it as a lookout, and Roy had found arrowheads up there, all made of the same stone. Roy bent down and touched the names and dates on the grave markers. Lichens—clinging to the letters and the numbers—fell to the ground as he traced the grooves with his fingers. Most of the headstones bore Roy's last name— Swan—just like the mountain, just like the town three miles down the road. This all seemed normal, a bunch of facts without any particular meaning to a boy of eight, as normal as the still faces of the deer in the truck, as normal as the rectangles of settled dirt in the oldest graves, where coffins and bones below had collapsed into nothing.

Leaves from last fall bunched up against the markers; the spring grass was long and gangly. Roy wondered why his daddy and mother had not bothered to show him this graveyard, why it looked like no one had tended to it in a while. A chilled breeze seemed to pass by him. Roy was a boy who loved the movies, who tried to go to the show every time they went down to Winston. He'd seen horror films and how decrepit skeletal beings could rise up out of the graves and stalk the living. He looked down and saw that he was standing on a grave, standing right on top of one Cantrell Thomas Swan, who according to his daddy had died driving an ambulance in early World War I. He jumped back to a safe distance. "Sorry," he said out loud. Out in the strawberry field, he could hear the Walkertown cousins,

his father's sisters' boys, who, his mother said, had pinworm, ringworm, and God knows what else. They were calling to one another
across the field, each convinced he had found the best cache of
berries. Before Roy went down to join them, he ran down the row of
headstones, petting them, saying, "See ya, see ya, see ya . . ." They had
been his kin, he decided, and there wasn't a thing to be afraid of.
They were dust now, nothing more than dust, and they would appreciate his coming to call.

Swan's Knob, as far as Roy could tell, had not changed one iota in
those years in which he had been transformed in the way of flesh
from a chigger-bitten boy to an aging man in need of a sun hat. The
graveyard, though better tended now, had not changed much either.
There weren't even any new occupants. His parents, for reasons he
could never understand, had opted to be buried down in God's Acre
in Old Salem with his mother's Moravian kin. Of course, he would be
here on this little hill someday—he had made that clear to Wilma,
though she was less keen on the idea herself. That was okay, of
course, maybe she'd change her mind—or not, it hardly mattered,
really. Still, the thought of an eternal resting place, even one as perfect as this one, had lost its romantic appeal over the years. The idea
had been more comforting when he was eight and as far as he would
ever get from the day.

Chapter Four

Harper

Harper tried to lower the windows of the van a bit, but couldn't take them down too far because of all the dust kicked up by the dirt road leading out of Roy's farm. It was unusual for him to sweat so profusely in the face of such little physical exertion. Just a short climb up a hill, that was nothing for him, especially since he was running like a banshee these days. It hadn't been the climb that had made him sweat. He had started to get warm just as he was letting Roy in on his festival news. It had been the usual until that moment—the usual, meaning it was just another thing he had to pull off. This was a standard condition in his life, the need to pull something off, the need to explain the not quite kosher situation, the pretty pickle. He thought a lot of Roy, though—he was the kind of guy his father had always been—do anything for anybody. Easy to con, in a way, if that's what you wanted. But that was just it. Standing up there on that hill, Harper had suddenly wanted to tell the plain dang truth, as his daddy would call it. He hadn't wanted to con Roy as much as convince him that he, Harper, could make the whole thing right. And that's what he would do, starting now.

The breeze from the cracked windows in his van was only helping cool him so much, so when he hit the asphalt and turned the van toward town, he leaned over and rolled them down all the way. This caused him to swerve a bit, nearly taking out the old mailbox from the farm next to Roy. *Diamond*, it said. God, another rescue squad guy, if Harper remembered right. Harper slowed and pulled the van onto the shoulder. If he was going to have a big crowd at the festival, he might need to use this land for parking. No doubt, Roy was on good terms with this guy, with all his neighbors. Harper made himself a note right there, the first in a long list of things he needed to do now that it looked like Roy was going to go along with the plan.

Harper smiled as he headed into town, the wind from the window cooling him down, the dampness on his shirt almost making him cold. He couldn't remember really having a plan before, not one that he could talk about at least. He pictured himself up on the festival stage, with an outrageous sound system humming around him. There was a sea of young faces filling Roy's pasture, beautiful girls waving their bare arms and chanting as he introduced Delrina Kay and Charles.

He made town now and whizzed through the stoplight on Key Street just as it turned red, but slowed down as he approached the police station. He was a solid citizen these days, hardly ever did anything very illegal, but all the same, visiting the cops—even these guys, whom he'd dealt with before—still gave him the impulse to check his ashtray. However, Roy had mentioned permits. This was the kind of thing he better get right on or he'd have a big gotcha on his hands.

The police station was a low brick building with tiny front windows. It couldn't be less imposing, and for God's sake, he wasn't some stoned teenager anymore. He walked into the place like the adult he had become, trying not to think about when he'd been in there last, but of course no one in a small town lets you forget much of anything.

"Mr. Ponytail," said Earl Leech, the deputy on duty at the desk, with a kind of ridiculous enthusiasm. "How the hell are you?"

"Fine, Earl," he said. Earl had been in PE with him in high school, the kind of guy who did the watusi in the shower, strutted around in his full glory, just to show the little guys how it was done.

"Brought any interesting hitchhikers into the county lately, hey, hey, hey?" said Earl. Right before his breakup with Sarah seven years ago, Harper had given Jonah, her lover, a ride across the Blue Ridge Mountains and right onto the doorstep of Swan's Knob. Of course, that was before he had known the guy was her lover and before he had known he was a murder suspect.

40 *Lynn York*

"No, Earl. I don't think I'm wanted for questioning right now." He tried to adopt a good-natured tone. On that prior occasion, they had ended up questioning Harper in the back room here. Ironically, Harper had cleared Jonah's name. He was sure these boys down here thought that was cute, yep, cleared the guy just in time for him to take Harper's wife.

"Course not," said Earl. "What can I do for you?"

"I need to talk to someone about getting permits for a concert . . ." he began, but Earl was distracted by the rattle of the door. He turned to see Chief Henry Lynch blow into the room. Chief Henry, never a slim man, had only gotten wider over the years, thick in the neck and louder.

"Well, look who's come to call," boomed Chief Henry. "Earl, you should've got me on the radio if someone had something to confess . . . We're all ears, son. Earl, take this man's statement."

Harper never enjoyed this brand of teasing, though he had been a ready target all his life, beginning with his dad and brother. He had no clue what it was about him that invited it.

Chief Henry laughed at his own joke, laughed longer than it merited, making his face and neck go all red. It was Earl who stopped him finally. "He's come about a permit, Chief, but you're going to have to help him because I haven't ever come up on something like this. It's for a concert, right?"

"Yes," said Harper. "We're going to have it out at Roy Swan's farm. Roy and me were going over the layout this morning, and it occurred to me to come down here and let you know what we're thinking. I don't know that there's anything official we need, it's more of a courtesy."

"Rock and roll?" said Chief Henry, like Harper was a larceny suspect. This seemed to embarrass Earl, who gave Harper a look. Good. Harper was going to need some help.

"Not really," said Harper. "Not what you're thinking, at least. More traditional music than anything else. "

"Traditional? Traditional what?"

"Well, you know, bluegrass, mountain music, fiddlers, mandolin, that kind of thing."

"So like a fiddler's convention, like Galax, then?" Chief Henry worked his way behind Earl's desk, chased Earl over to the Coke machine, and took his seat.

"Something like that. We've got a good lineup, should be a nice crowd, and I've got a nice headliner act, as of yesterday—Delrina Kay and Charles."

"You're kidding!" said Earl. "Delrina and Little Charlie, coming out of retirement. That's big, Harper, real big. Wow, in Swan's Knob, man, you're going to draw a crowd from the whole state." Now this was not the kind of help he needed.

"Wait a minute, wait a minute, here," said the chief. "When are you planning to do such a thing? In the spring, I take it?"

"Well, no. We're set for November, Chief, November twelfth."

"I don't see how," said the chief, in the tone of a man who got his way a lot. "How many people are we talking about, a thousand? Three thousand? And is that a Friday? Because you know, we would have a football game on that same night and then we'd really have a mess."

"Saturday," said Harper.

"Three thousand, hell." Earl pulled up chairs for himself and Harper. "I'm thinking five, ten thousand, what'd you think?"

"And Sunday," said Harper, "so it won't interfere with the football game, if there is one."

"No," said Chief Henry.

"And Earl's gotten a little excited here. I think that ten thousand number is way high," said Harper quickly.

"No, no, no way in hell." The chief stood up with a bunch of file folders in his hands, turned his back, and starting banging file cabinet drawers back and forth, as if he had dismissed both him and Earl.

"Now, Chief," said Earl. "We've handled a crowd before. This is a great opportunity for our town."

"Great opportunity, hell, a great chance to get a bunch of hippie kids and punk rockers together to bring in illegal substances, throw beer cans out on the highway, and roll in the muck." Chief Henry was unable to find an official location for his file folders and brought them back to his desk.

"What about that tractor pull in Dobson last year?" said Harper. "How many did you have there?"

"Four thousand, but it was County that handled that," said Earl, shaking his head vigorously at Harper from behind the chief.

The file folders sailed across the room and landed on the floor, spilling the photographs of wanted men in front of the Coke machine.

"County, hell, we don't need Garson and his boys in our business," the chief said. "Those numskulls can't direct four pickup trucks on a farm road. I can't believe you'd bring that up, Earl."

Earl began to respond, but Chief Henry put his hand up like a stop sign in his face and addressed Harper. "Lord God, I guess you could go on over to the county sheriff's office. They'd be happy to help you out—get you some official permit, put their deputies with those new baby blue uniforms on the road. When the day came, they'd let everything turn into a brawl, and then, when the thing got finished, they'd direct the traffic right down the middle of our Main Street and call it a parade."

"Not if we take on the job," said Earl. "Isn't Roy's farm in our territory?" This Earl was a good fellow, Harper decided. He caught on fast.

"Jurisdiction," said Chief Henry. "Yes, Earl, it surely is, we could make that argument. It's our jurisdiction, which is why I think we need to ask you, Harper, to call this thing off. We just can't handle it on this short notice."

"I don't think that is even practical," said Harper. "It's already been announced and it's been in newspapers and things."

"Well, unannounce it. How about that?"

Harper began to get that panicky sweaty feeling he'd had earlier talking to Roy. He smiled at the man, trying to look like the kind of guy who had an inside straight, instead of a pair of fours. Maybe he'd have more luck at the Surry County Sheriff's Office, jurisdiction or not.

Just then Earl, whom Harper had completely underestimated going all the way back to high school, stood up and walked over to the Coke machine, all casual, and said, "Awhh, you're probably right, Chief, this could be a rough thing to handle. We could stop it right

here, but I'll tell you—I'm not sure the town council will go along
with you. You know how Clyde has been ever since he got back from
that mayors' weekend in Southern Pines—economic development
this and economic development that." He went on then, and though
he had a time explaining to Chief Henry just how a bunch of degen-
erate concertgoers would spend money and help put Swan's Knob on
the map, Harper had to admit he put out a pretty good argument,
and in the end Chief Henry turned back to him.

"You say, now, that Roy Swan is all in this with you, right?"

"Oh yeah," said Harper, "from the beginning. It's his farm."

"And you say how many people do you think?"

Harper took a breath, calculating the average of the truth, what
was believable, and what was acceptable. "Five thousand, tops," he
said. "Less if it's bad weather."

"Lord God, let's not even think about mud," said Chief Henry,
putting both hands in the stop sign position again. He let a long moment pass, no doubt the kind of thing he'd seen a judge do.

"I'll tell you what," he said. "You have Roy Swan come down here
and see me. If he'll come and stand by this thing, then I'll go along
with it."

"You'll give us the permit?" said Harper.

"Son, in this town, my word is the only permit you'll need."

Star

The soda fountain lady placed a grilled cheese sandwich with a
mound of chips and extra pickles in front of Star just two seconds before her dad walked into the drugstore. Grandma Wilma had her
back to the door, so she didn't see, but Star saw him appear in the
flash of white light from the sidewalk outside. He saw her too and she
knew right then that she was busted, big-time busted.

Okay, so she had meant to call her dad, really she had. Her mother
had reminded her in the car to the airport in Albuquerque, as in,
"Oh, God, Star, don't forget to call your father the minute you get to
your grandmother's. I've forgotten in all the rush."

"Real nice, Mom, thanks," was what she'd said, as in, *Thanks for leaving me to tell my dad where you've parked me while you wander off around the world,* as in, *Thanks for leaving me,* period. End of sentence.

And, of course, she'd planned to call him. He was part of the reason she'd agreed to be sent to Swan's Knob in the first place. He'd moved back out here three years ago, and she'd hardly seen him since. She missed him. Excuse her if she liked him—he was her father, though once she'd overheard something . . .

"Dad!" she said, hoping that he would see that she was really, honestly, really really happy to see him. On the other side of the booth, her grandmother looked like someone had run an electrical charge through the seat.

She couldn't tell what her dad was thinking as he made his way through the comic book racks and candy displays to the soda fountain. His face was all still, stuck in the place it had been when he saw her, but he didn't look mad exactly. By the time she stood to hug him, there was nothing but happiness on his face. He did say, "What are you doing here?" but he said it without a trace of accusation.

It had been—what?—at least six months. Someone she had seen most every day of her life and now . . . He had a ponytail, which was cool, but it made her freak out to think of all the things that had happened to him and to her, things they couldn't cover in ten minutes on the phone now and then. He could have told her, all right? As in, *Hey, my little Star, I have a ponytail now.* All right? He could have said that, just to keep her in the loop.

"You have a ponytail," she said about the time he finished the hug, but it came out wrong, like he had committed a crime. This made her feel bad again. Still, he knew what she meant.

He grabbed the end of it and waved it, said, "Yeah, babe, it's getting long, isn't it?" This caused Grandma Wilma to shut her eyes and hold her crinkly lids down, as in, *Good Lord, deliver me from these heathens.*

Her dad noticed this too. He was that way, didn't miss much. "Well," he said. "Well. Well.

"A visit?" he said to her grandmother.

"Yes. Like I told you." Grandma Wilma blushed now and kept up the slow blinking. "I left you several messages on your machine."

"And I was supposed to call," Star said. "Only I didn't get a chance yet, with school starting—"

"School?" said her dad. "Wow, I just spent an hour with Roy and he didn't say . . . You here for a while?"

Star nodded. "Mom and everybody went to Asia."

She expected him to lose it then—the way he would do in Santa Fe when he and her mom were arguing over which weekend Star would come or whether she could ride with him on a motorcycle—but he didn't. He stuffed both hands in his jeans, like he was putting all that away for later, and smiled at her broad and plain, like she had seen him do in his gigs up in front of a crowd. "Then," he said, "we'll be getting some time together. Right, Wilma-woman?"

Grandma Wilma said, "Why, of course. Of course."

"Of course!" he said and leaned over and kissed her grandma on the cheek, kissed her loud before she could even move away.

Then he left, but first he looked at Star again and put his arms around her as if she had been lost for a long, long time.

Harper

Harper was out on the sidewalk and walking fast to nowhere before it hit him that he had gone into Surry Drug for limeade and had come out without even ordering the damn thing. No way was he going back in. *Goddamn, Sarah.* He kept walking. It'd have been even better if he could just start jogging, but he would wait for that, wait until he could get back to the house and change. Then he'd haul it out for a long run. He crossed the street and headed to the new Hardee's. *Goddamn, Sarah, goddamn all over again.* Had Sarah bothered to tell him? Had she thought to send Star to his house? Apparently not.

He walked to the drive-up window and placed his order, noting the puzzled expression on the attendant's face. "My car is down the street," he said, but she had closed her window already. He pictured the look on his ex-mother-in-law's face back in the drugstore, a slightly pained expression is what he would call it, the kind of thing she'd have for a vagrant who wandered up to the lunch counter. The attendant opened her window and handed him a large Dr. Pepper. It tasted watery, like someone had forgotten to change the syrup bottle this morning, but it was wet, so he drank it down and carried the cup of ice back to his van. He'd left the windows down, but it was a steam bath inside. He munched his ice, put his keys in the ignition, intending to go on home, but couldn't resist waiting for one more minute to see if she'd come out.

Of course, his little Starling had been embarrassed to run into him like that, standing there beside her grandmother in her Madonna getup, little ripped T-shirt with the black lace thing underneath, stammering, blushing when she saw him, him—her own father—all apologizing and all. It killed him, those charcoaled baby eyes, heavy black boots on her little feet. She probably thought she was all grown-up, but she was the child in this situation. Didn't anyone see this but him? Sarah was unbelievably casual about a lot of things in life—and good God, that woman was always running off, leaving everybody else to clean up her mess. She had run off on him more times than he could count. He'd even followed her a few times, until she left for good. Poor Star, her mother'd done the same to her—all the way to Asia. Of course, Star was more like him, steady, taking everything on herself.

There was still no sign of her or her guardian grandmother. Harper started the van. He was just pulling out onto the street when the two of them walked out of the drugstore. The light at Key Street was red, so he got a good minute or two to watch them in his rearview as they headed toward him. Starling seemed to be telling Wilma a story. She was waving her hands around, all those silver bangles flashing in the sun, and rocking her head back and forth as she talked. And he had to hand it to Wilma, she was enjoying herself—completely unaware of the sight they made: shirtwaist cotton dress beside flouncy mini, serviceable pumps beside boots. The Material Girl and the frumpster. It made him smile for a few seconds before the light changed.

On the drive back to the house, he tried to think about his last phone call with Starling. Star, she wanted to be called Star now. He had to remember that. They talked at least once a week, maybe more—one would call the other whenever the mood struck. But he'd been so busy with the festival. Was it possible he'd missed Wilma's messages? Maybe Sarah had left a message for him earlier in the week. He couldn't remember. He wasn't always real prompt about calling her back. And Star, they'd talked, right? The last time had been ten days ago, before the Delrina Kay stuff hit the fan. Or two weeks, maybe. That was a little longer than he liked. He'd been busy, but that wasn't much of an excuse.

He pulled into the driveway of his parents' house. It was his house now, had been for two years since his mother had gone down east to live with her sister, but he wasn't quite used to thinking of it that way. He needed to mow the yard before one of the neighbors got on him again, but other than that, it was perfectly respectable. He'd added a bunch of those hand-forged bells to the front porch since Star had been here last Christmas and moved out some rocking chairs for the times his friends came over to pick with him. The inside still looked the same, though thankfully, his mother had taken the lace and the glass figurines with her. He'd filled in the gaps with the pots he'd collected from New Mexico. Star liked it fine. There were magazines and newspapers stacked up on the furniture, and yeah, there were a few days' dishes in the sink, nothing horribly stinky, nothing he couldn't clean up before she came over. Hey, he was just a guy living alone these days. He was more or less between steady girlfriends. There were a few in-betweeners he saw from time to time, but he mostly showed up at their places.

When he got to the kitchen, he saw that his answering machine was blinking. He pushed the button that would let him hear everything on the tape, new and old messages, half hoping he'd hear Star's voice and half dreading that somewhere, he'd find one that he'd flatout neglected.

The first message started with the static of a pay-phone call, and then Harper heard a little series of coughs, like the person was testing out a microphone.

"Huh? Harper? Harper Chilton? Well, I hope that I've got the right machine since there's an old woman's voice on the message. Well, hey! Hey, then. This is Delrina, Delrina Kay? I was just calling to say in person, how much Little . . . Charles and I are looking forward to your festival. Lots of excitement, honey, I tell you what! Well now. I was just calling to find out when we . . . Usually, honey, with these festivals, there are some practice sessions afore things get going, so I wanted to make sure we get plenty of time to be at our best."

There was a pause in the message. Harper heard more static and the sound of several semitrucks running through their lower gears. The machine did not cut off as it usually did at the end of a message, and finally he heard a muffled noise away from the phone and then Delrina again saying quietly, "Can't you see? I am on the phone." Then, loud again, "Sorry, honey. Anyway, we are looking forward to being in Swan's Neck, let me tell you that. And also, while I've got you here, I wanted to know about our accommodations, you know, where we'll be staying and all. I'm sure they've told you about what all we need. You just let me know where and we can be there anytime. Well, got to go. Oh, and honey, Harper, we're on the road right now. It's real hard to reach us, so you just leave a message with the record company. Just call BJ and all them and tell them the plans. You take care now! Bye-bye!"

The machine clicked for the next message then, only it began mid-sentence. Maybe his machine was messed up after all. It took him a moment to place the voice: ". . . so if you would give me a call, son, and I can put you in touch with Del McCoury and his boys, and then, like I said, me and Tony Rice would love to come sit in one night, if that's all right with you. Now that word's out, you might get a few others calling you soon." Jesus, it was Doc Watson. It couldn't be anyone else. Amazing. Harper had called his booking agent months ago and was told that Doc would be off on tour all of November. Now here he was jumping on the bandwagon. Maybe he'd heard about Delrina, maybe he'd canceled his tour, who knew? Harper turned off the machine. He'd listen to the rest later, and hell, he'd worry about the crowds, the accommodations later too. A little celebration was in order. Doc Watson, the man himself, and Tony Rice.

Harper pulled out the bottle he kept in his freezer and had a little swig of Jose Cuervo.

He had one more pop at the bottle before he took off for his run. Not your conventional training drink, he knew, but hell, he was having a lucky day. The big boys were going to play his festival and his Star was back in town.

Chapter Five

Wilma

"Well, hey you two!"

They had nearly made it home without running into a soul, when Cynthia Trolley came out the front door of the library just as they were passing by. Cynthia was wearing her signature color purple from head to toe. She ran right up to them and introduced herself to Starling, and then spent a moment looking her up and down. "Your grandmother mentioned you were on your way, and here you are. Wilma, I know you are just thrilled to have her! And look at you, Star honey, aren't you fun!"

This made Star smile in that open fresh-faced way she'd had since she was a little baby. Wilma just loved Cynthia at that moment. Most anyone else in town would have engaged in small talk just long enough to catalogue the details of Star's getup and then rushed off to start the phone tree. But Cynthia started right in asking Star all about herself and her plans for her visit and somehow had her going on in two seconds about her musician friends in Santa Fe.

Though Wilma would never consider Cynthia a fashion authority, she was exactly right—fun. That's what it was, this sort of trampy, vamp raccoon look of Star's. Wilma got that new MTV station. She had watched it a time or two. This was the thing right now, even if those ripped clothing fashions hadn't quite made it to Swan's Knob yet. Wilma tried to remind herself that Sarah—at exactly Star's age— had worn nothing but blue jeans, Top-Siders, and broadcloth shirts. Those shoes, God, if Wilma could have gotten her hands on them for a minute, she would have put them in the garbage can. She reminded herself that back then she had repeatedly urged Sarah to fix herself up a bit—put on a little lipstick to go out on a date. No one could accuse Star of laziness in that department. No. Of course, she did hope that once Star got to school and saw that none of the other girls used quite that much makeup . . .

Of course, Wilma wasn't going to say a word. That was the absolute fun of being a grandmother. She had seen it all before. This behavior was nothing more than a little bit of the rebellion of adolescence. Every daughter had to design her wardrobe to attract her friends and mortify her mother—or grandmother, as the case may be. Well, mission accomplished. And Star was just having fun with her 1988 version of wardrobe rebellion. Cynthia's purple outfit probably caused her mother the same kind of pain.

"Fun, fun, fun," said Wilma, hoping she sounded sincere. "That's what we're having all right."

"I'm sure you are," said Cynthia, as she climbed into her little Honda Prelude. She cranked open her sunroof and waved her hand out of it before she zipped down the road. "Ta-tah, y'all!" she yelled over the engine.

When she was safely down the road, Star crinkled up one side of her face and grinned at Wilma. "Who, pray tell, was that?" she said. "Pray tell" was her newest catchphrase, borrowed from Wilma.

"Cynthia is our voice teacher," said Wilma. "She also consults with local girls and their mothers on beauty pageants and offers a cotillion class for junior high children."

"And what, pray tell, is a cotillion?" said Star.

A few more cars passed them now, one of them containing a member of the choir, who slowed her car and waved. "'Cotillion.' That's just an old-fashioned word for a dance. A 'formal' is what it was called when your mother was a teenager. Cynthia teaches children basic manners, how a boy asks a girl to dance, everyone gets all dressed up, sips punch, that kind of thing. What would you all call that in Santa Fe?"

"Another planet," said Star. She laughed again and fished her arm through the crook in Wilma's arm. "Nobody worries about that kind of thing anymore, Grandma. You just go to a dance and dance. End of story."

"Well, don't tell Cynthia," said Wilma. "It would be a big disappointment."

"I won't say a word," said Star. "Now, what's for dinner?"

In the four days since Star's arrival, this was the time of day Wilma enjoyed most, the hour she and Star spent making dinner together. Okay, it had taken a little adjustment on her part. She had never really shared her kitchen. Sarah had never been interested and wasn't easily pressed into service. Even during their recent visits, it had been Star, and sometimes Jonah, who helped. Wilma got the feeling that the two of them did the cooking at home in Santa Fe as well.

When they got to the house, they went straight to the kitchen. She began pulling things out and without much discussion, they went to work, Starling chopping onions and Wilma washing chicken. The kitchen was the last room to lose the light, so it was the best part of the house in the late afternoon. It had been built on right behind the back parlor for Roy's mother when she was a young bride. When Wilma had married Roy and, after some negotiation, moved in, the kitchen had every modern convenience available to a woman in 1919: running water, a stove with an oven that had to be lit with a match every time you used it, a single porcelain sink. The only concession to the last half century had been a refrigerator that had been installed in the adjacent mudroom right after World War II, the damn thing still miraculously running.

Roy had not changed another thing since his parents had died in a train wreck in 1952, but only painted and repainted the room every few years in the same yellow his mother had picked out. It was the same all over the house. If most of the upholstered furniture and every one of the caneback dining room chairs had not been completely falling apart by the time they got married, Wilma might have been forced to sell many of her beautiful things to Ronny Snow and his wife when they bought her little bungalow down the street. Fortunately, Roy had become more reasonable after they found mice in his front room divan. Wilma was able to move in with her own nice living room couch, the Henkel Harris buffet, her etched mirrors.

She brought over these things and all her other accessories and mixed them with Erma Swan's better pieces. It looked nice. Even so, it had still been a delicate exercise in marital politics to bring the woman's kitchen up to workable condition. Over time, she'd been able to convince Roy that an undercounter dishwasher and freshly stained cabinets would not banish his mother's spirit from the place. He himself had stripped the umpteen layers of paint from the walls, though in the end she'd had to settle for a color only a few shades off the original.

She found herself telling all of this to Star without thinking first whether it was something she should discuss with someone seventeen and her granddaughter. It had been this way with Star all of her life, easy, somehow much easier to talk to her than Sarah, though she felt guilty admitting this to herself. She never knew how Sarah would take things, when she might seize on an uncalculated word or two and use it against her. How Sarah might easily blow up these very comments into a diatribe on how Wilma ought to conduct herself with Roy, how desperate and sad it was for her to subsume herself to his judgment, on paint colors no less. With Star, it was easy to gently make fun of Roy, to laugh with her about how he had come home bearing paint cans with a "whole new color" for the kitchen. Sunshine instead of lemon. Star was laughing exactly the right kind of laugh, too, the kind that had some understanding and acceptance mixed in.

"I'll bet he was real proud of himself," said Starling. "Though it did turn out nice in here."

"It's grown on me," said Wilma. "Like a lot of things." Of course, what she would not tell anyone was that some days she still felt a little like a stranger in the house, as if she were just keeping house until Roy's mother, the formidable Erma Swan, came back. Starling was finished with the onions and had started snapping the green beans. She was fast, but she tended to take off a little too much of each end, wasting a good part of each bean. It was okay—they had a gracious plenty.

"How about we just steam these a little tonight and make them into a salad?" Star said. She ran the beans under the water and tossed them a bit. In addition to the bangles on her wrists, she had all kinds of silver rings on all kinds of fingers, even her thumbs.

"Sure," said Wilma. Roy would never voice disapproval over such a thing, but he did not take so well to life's little changes. He'd tell the world and himself how much he loved moving a brand-new wife into his house after fifty-eight years of being a bachelor, but just let her bake a pound cake and put it on Erma Swan's sacred cut glass cake stand. Polite silence.

"He looked good, didn't he? Real healthy," said Starling.

"Well, I've always thought Roy was a handsome man," said Wilma.

Starling laughed, the nice laugh again. "No, not Roy—my dad. He seemed good today."

"Well, yes, I guess. He was in and out of Surry Drug before I got a good look at him." This was Harper's habit, of course, in and out of everyone's life, according to his own whim.

"He's been running, you know. Maybe I'll go out and run with him one day." Star didn't look up as she said this, just let the statement hang in the air, a little question in her voice, wondering if Wilma would object. Well, she did, a bit, though this was unfair. He was Star's father. He had a right to see her anytime he wanted, this she knew. But there were other things Star wouldn't know about, things Wilma could not forget. She couldn't forget the Manhattan tenement where Sarah had fought roach wars and nursed Star while Harper played jazz in clubs all night. There were the checks Wilma had written when the power company shut them off, and there was the sullen silence that came over her daughter after Harper had moved her to Santa Fe and continued to bed everything but the lamppost.

"In the drugstore, did he seem mad to you?" said Star. "That I hadn't called him or anything?"

Star shouldn't have to worry for two minutes about hurting that man's feelings. "Why would he be mad at you?" Wilma said, trying not to sound too harsh. "You just got here. You have jet lag, you have school tomorrow."

"I don't have jet lag. He looked surprised, not angry, don't you think? Maybe I'll go to see him after school tomorrow. Do you need the car?"

She did need the car, but she couldn't think at the moment what she needed it for specifically. She was not sure why, but it hadn't occurred to her that Star would be driving.

"I wonder where Roy could be," she said. "He's usually home by now, though I guess he's about to start harvesting his grapes." She busied herself with setting the table, watching Star out of the corner of her eye. Star was not buying it. She stopped work on the salad and stepped back a bit from the counter. She folded her hands up into her armpits as if the entire kitchen was full of things that might cause a nasty infection. There it was, Sarah's old gesture, the folded arms of disgust, practiced a million times in the dinner hour of her adolescence and now passed down to her daughter for all posterity.

For the first time since Star's arrival, Wilma felt a small creep of terror in the back of her neck. To think, she had been excited about having her for a long visit. She had been worried only about how Roy would react. He had not spent a lot of time around children or teenagers and she knew there was no way to completely brief him about just what the visit would involve, and look, already here was something big that she had not even thought of—driving.

"There will be a lot of noise," she'd told him, "loud music and tromping around, kids in and out of the house. There will be shouting." She worried that Star—or any company—might get on Roy's nerves, especially right now when he seemed so faraway. But Roy had been more than enthusiastic.

"Let's redo the guest room," he said, and he would have insisted, had there been time. This worried her further because sometimes Roy couldn't tell how he would feel about something until he was slap dab in the middle of it. This had made for a bit of a rocky honeymoon week a few years back in Hawaii, when he'd kept disappearing every few hours "to get a breath of fresh air." He'd adjusted, though, hadn't he?

On the way to the airport to meet Star's plane, she had given him a few last-minute warnings, about moodiness, eye rolling, the silent treatment, sudden outbursts.

"Oh, dolly," he'd said. "It's all going to be fine. We could use a little shaking up." She'd wondered what he meant by that, if things had gotten too boring for him, too routine. She had worried about this, she had worried about whether he would enjoy the reality of having a teenager in the house as much as he liked the idea, she had worried about what reduced privacy might mean to their other little problem. But she had not worried about how she would feel mothering a seventeen-year-old again.

Star stood with her back to Wilma now, her fists still balled up in her armpits. From this vantage, she could have been her mother twenty years back. She flexed her shoulder blades slightly and sniffed. "Well?" she said. "This isn't going to be a problem, is it?"

God, Wilma was a woman without an answer, and she found herself blinking, blinking back the rush of the past. She reminded herself: here she was in her nice kitchen, wrapped up in her altogether lovely life with Roy Swan. Her old life with Harry Mabry, Sarah's father, was nearly twenty-five years past. And it occurred to her then what it was she had been thinking in some sad and desperate corner of her mind—that she could rewrite history—that she could take Star in and do a good job of it. She was crazily, stupidly bent on making up for the miserable job she had done with Sarah as a teenager. Sarah had been fifteen, in ninth grade when her father killed himself. He had been drunk for at least five years before that. Wilma had spent those last years Sarah was home denying, mourning, hanging on by her fingernails, anything she could just to get through. This accounted for a lot of things in her life and in Sarah's. And though they had both moved away now from her old house, from the rose garden out back where Wilma had found Harry dead, she was still auditioning for the part of the woman who could make all things right.

Star

Roy came in about the time that she was finishing up the salad. It was completely silent in the kitchen. And Star was, what? She was waiting, that's what she was doing, waiting for an answer about borrowing the car. And worried. She was getting sort of worried that she was going to end up being a girl without a car.

"Hey there!" Roy's voice boomed from the mudroom, disagreeably cheerful. "Something smells good, girls. When's supper?" There was the thud of two work boots on the floor and Roy shuffled into the kitchen wearing leather bedroom slippers, something only her grandmother would order. His initials, RS, were embroidered on the top of them, and Star could see his veiny, puffy heels sticking out the backs. Roy noticed her looking at his feet, read her thoughts. He smiled and tilted his head toward Wilma, who was standing at the sink. Star had to smile too, even though she was about to be totally pissed about the car. Roy came up behind Grandma Wilma, put his arms around her waist and kissed her neck in a way that made Star want to leave the room.

"Wash your hands, old man," said her grandma, breaking away from him and carrying serving dishes to the table. "And y'all come on." This meant, "Dinner is served." Her grandma always said that when she got a meal ready. It drove her mother crazy, as did most everything else about a meal in this house: saying grace, passing the dishes around, the salt, the pepper, the waiting until everyone was served. "We eat in hour two," is what her mother said.

Sarah did not know when or how she had gotten the idea that what went on in her grandma's house was the yardstick for normal, but she loved normal. She preferred a nice table over serving herself from the stove, liked a perfectly square pat of butter on her oatmeal, loved a life without dust or spiders or the little whiff you could get of the cats in their Santa Fe house from time to time.

Roy said grace fast, blurring the words together like they were worn down from overuse. Then he helped himself to doubles of everything. He smiled at Star and winked for no particular reason. He was a nice man, nice to everyone, nice enough to help a girl borrow a car, maybe. He dug into his plate while Grandma Wilma got up to rescue the rolls that she had left in the oven.

As she put the basket with the linen napkin on the table, Wilma looked over at Star's plate. "Something wrong, honey? Don't you like the chicken?"

"Sure, I do. I was just getting to it." She liked to eat her food in sequence, veggies first, then starch, and so on, and yes, she liked to take her time, but God, was that anybody's business to remark on? It was funny. At home, she often thought about this kitchen, about eating at this table. She thought especially about it on those nights when she grabbed a bowl of granola and milk since no one else seemed hungry or when Verity was crying because she was up way past the time any little kid ought to be. But tonight she wondered what her mom and Jonah were up to. They would be in Seoul by now, eating dinner out in some exotic place, trying to teach Verity how to use chopsticks. That is, if they used chopsticks in Korea. She didn't know.

Her grandma was chronicling their day's activities to Roy in minute detail: the meeting with the principal, the conditions of the hallways over at East Surry (apparently things were in disrepair since her mother's time there), their walk to town, the new door on the Baptist Church ("Who in their right mind would choose red? Have you ever seen a red door on a church?"). Star finished her green bean salad and went on to her potatoes, half listening to them talk, searching for a place to bring up the car situation.

"Of course, we had to stop by Surry Drug for Star's limeade. That's our little ritual when she gets to town," said her grandma. "We ran into Cynthia Trolley on the way home. You should've heard her complimenting Star."

"Don't forget about Dad," said Star. "We saw my dad at the drugstore. He was real happy to see me. He said he'd really like to spend some time with me, which I think is a good idea. Don't you think that's a good idea, Roy?"

Roy was looking down at his plate, puzzling over the green beans. "Of course. That sounds great," he said.

"I was thinking that I'd like to drive over there, you know, to his house in King to see him," she put in quickly.

"Well." Her grandma pulled her lips over her teeth in a way that made her look old, old, old. "Let's get you settled in school first. Plenty of time to see your dad. He could even come to Swan's Knob. It's just a twenty-minute drive."

"Just twenty minutes, so it'd be easy for me to drive over."

"Which reminds me." Her grandma turned to Roy, who was all business cutting his green beans into little pieces. "Harper said he'd seen you today. Did he meet you at the farm, all the way out there? What was that about?" She narrowed her eyes then, the same way she had this afternoon when Star's dad had come into the drugstore.

Roy pushed his chair back from the dinner table a bit and wiped his mouth with his napkin. "So it's the driving you're thinking about, missy. Don't want to be stuck in town with the old fogies, hey? You know, I do have an old Chevy truck out at the farm. Don't use it much, mostly drive my T-bird. Maybe you could drive that."

"Wait a minute, now, I don't know about that," said her grandma. "Sarah didn't say a word about Star's driving. Do you even have your license, honey?"

"Yes, for months now."

"Sure she does," said Roy. "And I'll bet you can drive a stick too, can't you?"

"Sure," said Star. "Jonah's Datsun is a five-speed and I use that all the time."

"Well, this one's on the steering column, but I can show you how to do that in two minutes. Come on out tomorrow and . . ." Roy stopped talking a moment and looked over at her grandma, who had her eyes wide open, sort of buglike. She jerked her head to one side. It was one of those signals that married people had between them, this one meaning *ixnay on the driving lessons.*

"Roy, you are getting way ahead of yourself. I'm not sure that I like this idea at all," said her grandma, with a finality that made Star see months of doomed existence flash before her eyes. Roy didn't seem to pick up on that and launched into a long list of the things he needed to have done to the truck so that Star could drive it.

"Roy Swan." Her grandma was getting mad, Star could tell, but Roy just kept smiling at Star.

"You know, my daddy taught me to drive out at our farm," he said. "I must have been twelve, thirteen. It was a truck too, two or three models before the one that's out there now. I ran it into a ditch the first day."

"That's what I'm talking about, Roy Swan," said her grandma. "What would Sarah say if we let Star drive into a ditch?"

"Well, as I recall, Sarah is not the greatest driver herself," said Roy. "Besides, there's no harm in trying a few practice runs out there. I'll certify her roadworthy before I let her drive to see her daddy."

Her grandma kept talking to him on and on about licenses and different states and insurance, but Star could see that Roy wasn't listening to a thing she said. Her grandma seemed almost resigned now. "I don't know," she said. "I don't know how we can get in touch with Sarah to make sure it would be okay." She had angled her knife and fork across her plate just so and was watching to see when Roy would finish up.

"Why don't we just ask Dad?" Star said, but then regretted it. This might queer the deal.

"Hmmph," said her grandma, which meant, *I'm not putting what I think about that into words.* Star had seen before that her dad wasn't her grandma's most favorite person, but honestly, why did she have such a big problem with him? Get a clue: he was her dad, all right?

"She's seventeen. She has her license. I don't think we need anyone's permission," said Roy helpfully.

"Hmmph." Again. It was getting annoying.

"Oh," said Roy, drawing the word out so that it sounded like an endearment. "We'll work something out." This was better than she had ever hoped. A pickup truck. Well, that was kind of cool, really.

"We'll see," said Wilma in a way that meant yes. She started collecting the dinner plates. "Roy, you never did say what Harper was doing at the farm. Don't tell me he's working the tomato harvest." She laughed.

Star had seen this music video the other day. Was it Deborah Harry or Rickie Lee Jones? She couldn't remember, but at the end of it, the girl climbed in an old green pickup truck and took off down a straight country road, kicking the dust up behind her. Pair of jeans, plain white T, tousled hair. Oh yeah.

"No," said Roy, "and he's not picking grapes. He came about the festival. I told you about it a while back. Remember?"

"No." Wilma had sat back down now, so Star took the dishes from her and started carrying things to the sink.

"Oh, I know I did. He's having a little concert in my back pasture." Roy shook a cube of ice out of his tea glass and into his mouth and started chomping on it.

"What? This is the first word I've heard." A pause. Star could feel both of them looking at her standing at the sink. "I can tell you that I most certainly would have . . . would have . . . remembered and perhaps commented on that news," her grandma said. God, Star was reminded here of home. Jonah and her mom were constantly having some fight over money or the garbage or something. Jonah didn't believe in holding back just because Star was in the room. Her mom, on the other hand, was all the time doing exactly what her grandma was doing now, saying things like "I would've commented on that," as in, *I am fiercely angry and plan to yell at you in the bedroom later.*

"I thought I told you," Roy said and put another ice cube in his mouth.

"Please don't chew the ice, you'll ruin your teeth. Now, what concert and where are you talking about?" said her grandma. Star started loading the dishwasher. Whatever dishes were left on the table could wait until later.

"It's going to be great," said Roy, like he didn't get what kind of trouble he was in. "Harper is organizing a little showcase of traditional music from this area. You know bluegrass, old-time music. It's getting to be a big thing these days, you know. And he stopped by a few months ago—"

"A few months?"

"Honey, I thought I told you, but I guess I didn't. I'll tell you now, okay?"

Her grandma didn't say anything, but shifted in her chair. Trouble. Roy was in trouble. Star wondered what this would mean for her driving situation.

"It's a concert. It will be in November. Harper is using the pasture by the barn and a little of the frontage for parking. He has gotten some wonderful acts lined up. That's why he stopped in this morning,

to tell me how things are coming. It looks like he's got Delrina Kay
and Little Charlie coming . . ."

"Wow! I've heard of them." Star was excited. Could it be something might actually happen in this town while she was here? First
Roy and the pickup, and now her dad putting on a big concert. She
rushed over to Roy and hugged him. "Delrina and Little Charlie!
They're big! Didn't they have that hit song a few years ago? What was
it, kind of a rockabilly thing? 'Standing Tall, Thinking Big'?"

Roy laughed big-time and hugged Star back. "I think so," he said.
"That's them!"

"My God, Roy Swan, what were you thinking?" said her grandma.

"At the time?" said Roy, still acting like he was having fun, instead
of getting all this grief. "I was thinking that we'd have a few hundred
people, some music, and a big time. What do you think about that?"

"Roy, you know as well as I do that it won't turn out that way.
Consider, consider the big picture, the history. Something's going to
happen. It'll turn into a big mess. It always does when it comes to,
well, you know, this kind of event." Star had gone back over to the
sink, but she could see her grandma look at Roy and then jerk her
head toward her silently—that marital signal—and for a minute, Star
thought she might say, *Little pitchers have big ears.* That was okay.
People were always forgetting that Star was nearly an adult, but come
on, she got it. She wanted to say, *My dad, you're talking about my dad.*
She wanted to say that so bad, but somehow she didn't dare.

She didn't want to hear whatever her grandma might say about
him, just like she didn't want to hear those tiny things her mother said
over the years, bits of stories you couldn't forget, that buried themselves in your skin like burrs—how her mother had to remind him of
Star's birthday the year he gave her that great guitar, how he had
bought it at the pawn shop on Guadalupe and not gotten it from
Willie Nelson's road manager like he said. They were quiet over by
the table then, and Star kept washing the dishes, feeling like she'd
never left home, because this was the same kind of house, a place
where she was the only one who favored her father's version of the
world.

Chapter Six

Harper

The tequila did its work on him in the first part of his run, and he went out a little fast through the neighborhood. The aging houses were not quite as well tended as they had been in his childhood. The original owners—his family's friends and kin—had mostly gone and now the places belonged to other kinds of working people, mechanics, carpenters, beauticians, people who drove down to RJR in Winston, even a Vietnamese family who ran a restaurant in Mount Airy. Most everybody was out of the house working during the day, and there was no one like his mother left, no one to stay home and plant pansies and sweep her porch.

Harper ran right down the middle of the empty street and left at the end of Beekins Road. This road would take him down a slight incline all the way to Danbury Creek, if he was of a mind to run the whole six-mile round-trip. Of course, Jose Cuervo told him, yes, let's go all the way right now—but Jose, Jose would be long gone on the uphill home. He thought he'd set his sights on the Meadow Glen Trailer Park, which was just a bit more than a mile ahead. He would turn around just short of the place. That way, there was no chance of running into his little friend. He found his pace now, an easy rhythm that put him in a place he couldn't get in a whole evening of partying. Of course, this was why he had taken up running five years ago. He was creeping up to forty and needed to cut down on the booze, the pot, etc. And here he was, healthier than he had been in years. He followed his breathing for a moment and tried to think about nothing else. This hardly ever worked for more than a minute or two, but still, he found that out here with his heart going hard, he could take his little problems out of his pocket, look at them in the daylight. This was where he had come up with the idea for the festival. And this was where he would figure out how to pull it off.

From the very minute it had occurred to him, the very second, the idea had been like a fat candle lighting up a dull and familiar room. He imagined for a moment what songs Doc Watson would play at the festival. The strains of six or seven possibilities floated across in his mind—he thought of what Del's band would play and of Little Charlie's bell-clear voice. He pictured the whole group—himself among them—everybody assembled on the stage, their faces gleaming in all the softly colored stage lights.

His breathing became ragged. He had gone out too fast again. He slowed down a bit and ended up having to take it to a brisk walk. Up ahead a quarter mile or so, he could make out the white signboard for Meadow Glen. It was one of those signs where you could change the letters, but ever since Harper had been back in town it had always said Vacancy. The vacancy advertised was nothing more than a rusty, long-ago-abandoned trailer on the far back row. Harper knew way more about Meadow Glen than he wanted to, having crashed there for two weeks with his buddy Steve. This was right after his dad died and just before he figured out that there was something worse than living with your mama.

He turned around and headed back to town, jogging along pretty well, when a familiar car came barreling toward him. His little friend Candace. The car came to a stop twenty feet past him, throwing up a load of gravel from the shoulder. He kept going, back to running now, but within ten seconds, he heard, "Well, hey there!" He turned around and continued to jog a little bit backwards. Candace, a remnant of his Meadow Glen days and, he'd have to admit it, his occasional in-between girl, had her head and half of her torso out of the window of her old Buick Le Sabre and was waving with enthusiasm all the way down to her waist. He waved, a little wave, still jogging backwards, hoping she would accept this short greeting and let him finish his run.

"Come here a minute, you manny man," she said. "I gotta question for you."

This was what he had hoped to avoid, the why-haven't-you-called shakedown. He jogged lightly across the road toward her car, reluctant, but then thinking ever so briefly about Candace's insanely small patch of pubic hair.

"And where were you going in such a hurry?" he said when he got to her window. She had climbed back in and had one lovely arm draped decoratively over the steering wheel.

"Nowhere," she said. "Got done with my shift, so I was headed home." He was really sweaty and hoped he didn't stink too much, though some women liked that. "Listen," she said. "I heard about your festival. That's sounding like a real good time."

"It's going to be great. You won't believe who all I've got booked." He pulled his T-shirt away from his chest. In a pinch, he could shower at her place.

"You booking any local acts?" She looked at him. He did love her eyes. They were real soft and welcoming, as long as you didn't focus on the slight weathering of the rest of her face.

"I guess you heard that I have Delrina Kay and Charles lined up, and I just heard today, Doc Watson heard Delrina was coming and now he's there, Tony Rice's there, who knows who else."

"Well, how about the Rondalays?"

"The who?" he said. "Oh, I didn't mention Del McCoury."

"Us. The Rondalays. My band," she said. "You thought about us?"

Candace had a group of four or five girls she'd been singing with since junior high. They made sort of a parlor trick out of harmonizing late at night at parties when people were so drunk that most any music sounded good. "The Rondalays, huh? I didn't know you had a name now. You girls still singing together?"

"Well, yes." She seemed irritated with him suddenly. "We sang at the Autumn Leaves Festival last year, played a few parties too."

"That is great," he said quickly and with enthusiasm. He bent his knee and raised his foot behind himself until it reached his hand. As he stretched, he tried to think what other noncommittal thing he could say. He was going to start getting a lot of this—all kinds of local yokels hitting him up for a spot on the program.

"Well?" She looked at him with those eyes again, which quickened his pulse and made several steamy little scenarios flash across his mind—none of this helping him with the situation at hand.

"Well, we'll just have to see," he said. "I'm working from a pretty long list right now, and the town is likely to limit how late things go, but I don't see why in the world I can't add the Rondalays to my list of, of, of possibles."

She smiled at this and said, "Really, really? You'll consider us?" She reached up and curled her beautiful arm around the back of Harper's neck. He was starting to think again about that shower at her place, when she released him and said, "You're so sweet." Before he knew it, she had put her car in gear and pulled off down the road.

There was nothing to do but finish the run, but the uphill portion was no fun and was marred in particular by the fact that a woman, a woman whose bed he had shared a dozen or so times off and on, had used the word "sweet" on him. He concentrated on heaving air in and out, expelling Candace and her little patch of pubic hair along with his used-up breath.

As he got into town, he chose a connector street that was slightly flatter than the others. This took him by the school, where it was recess and dozens of kids were out on the athletic field playing soccer. All kids played soccer these days. Star had played goalie. Sarah always nagged him about making it to her games. One day he'd shown up at her elementary school like he was told. It was hot as hell, and there were ten games in progress with hundreds of little children running around. Sheer fucking chaos. And had Sarah told him the colors for Star's team, or even its name? Hell, no. He'd wandered all over the place, trying to find her for a good fifteen minutes, walking up and down the little fields like a piss-poor fool of a father until he heard, "Daddy, Daddy, over here." It was Star who had found him, finally. She probably wouldn't remember the day, or even recall that he was there, but he still had dreams that he was on that field and trying to find her.

Celeste

In room 432 east, someone on the night shift had turned the TV to the all-weather station. Celeste changed it to the channel where the *Dynasty* reruns came on. Her patient, a Mr. Stone, wasn't going to object. He had been comatose ever since they brought him to the ICU a week ago, so it was just wishful thinking to believe he had a single bit of perception left, much less a television preference. She had worked critical care for a long time, almost six years now, and of course, many of the patients who came here were already gone. Long gone really. Just enough brain to keep the heart beating. The worst, though, were the ones like Mr. Stone, who would occasionally open his eyes, roll his head around, and move his mouth like he was about to say something. And maybe he was. That was the terrible part.

She pulled the sheets up from under one side of the man's bed now and folded them up under him. "I'm going to change your sheets, Mr. Stone," she said. "You just lay still and I'll have it done in two shakes." It was always easier to assume, like they told her in training, that some patients could hear what was going on, even if they couldn't let you know about it. This was the lie they told everyone to make the job easier.

Mr. Stone's wife and his daughter had been in the room this afternoon when Celeste was changing out the water pitcher. She had to put fresh ice and water in every room, no matter if it was needed. She'd offered it to the two of them. They'd looked like they needed something; that was for sure. They were pale as daybreak and huddled all around the man like something was going to happen. "You won't believe it," the daughter had said to her. She'd been wearing a beautiful Echo scarf around her neck, probably hoping to get some color on her face. "I called his name before and he squeezed my hand. It was faint, but I felt it, plain as day. 'Daddy,' I said and he squeezed my hand." On the ward, they'd been instructed not to dash out all of a family's hope, so Celeste hadn't told them that this was what most everybody said.

On the TV, that cute couple that was on *Dynasty* and also married in real life were talking about something or other. Celeste couldn't really follow the story. She mostly turned the show on to see what everyone was wearing. That was her interest, the fashions. She tried to tell this to Travis, but he thought the show was put on by Satan. He wouldn't leave her to watch in peace for even two minutes. "Jezebels," he'd yell at the screen if he saw someone in a hot tub. "Lord forgive them." Celeste tried to point out that this was playacting and nothing real, but he would direct her to some scripture or something and carry on until she just turned the show off. Once the scripture started, she knew what was next.

She had new sheets on the bare side of the bed now and pushed them tight against the man's body. The next step was to roll him up on one side and get the old sheets off the rest of the bed and the new sheets on. Any of the other LPNs would call an orderly to turn a patient of this size, but she prided herself on being strong enough and clever enough to get it done by herself. She had a method. It wasn't pretty, nothing you'd want a family member to see. But a shoulder here and a firm hand on the man's posterior did the trick, and in two minutes the whole bed was changed, giving her a few minutes to watch the end of *Dynasty* before her shift was up.

As she sat there, engrossed in these TV people's big problem with a wicked woman's divorce, she could almost forget there was someone else in the room. Finally, she looked over at the poor man, colorless, hopeless, still. She thought about what it would be like to be his wife, a woman who was likely to be in this gray limbo for weeks, maybe months. They would move him soon to another floor and after that, to a long-term care place, where he would linger and not even know that he was using up all of his wife's hope and retirement money. And Mrs. Stone would have all that time to sit there and wonder if maybe, just maybe, he had squeezed her hand. Celeste thought vaguely of what a stupid shame it was and how, if she just stood there and pinched Mr. Stone's nose for a moment, put her hand on his mouth, he would go to peace to his everlasting home. Of course, doing something like that was surely a worse sin than divorce, worse than hot tubs or even adultery, but there was also a kind of good about it, a good of the kind that you saw on those Bible pictures, like the way they showed Peter's face when he was hanging upside down on the cross or Stephen when he was about to get the rock.

She turned off the TV, went over to Mr. Stone, and smoothed his covers as lovingly as she knew to do on a man who was half dead and a stranger. She was not living in those biblical times, and Lord, one martyr in the family was enough. Travis had gotten to where he was quoting scriptures right and left, claiming folks persecuted him for his beliefs. Celeste didn't think it was persecution. People liked Travis well enough; he was a decent man, an honest contractor. He did a good job with cabinetry. They were just tired of hearing him talking so much, telling them how they ought to live their lives. Lately, he'd sensed this; he knew he wasn't getting through anymore, so he'd started having an extra devotional time at home right before bedtime. She endured the devotional. After thirty years of marriage, you learned what might be worth objecting to, and this wasn't it. Besides, sometimes, Travis got all stirred up in these sessions, and they would end with the kind of fervent lovemaking that Celeste still enjoyed—craved, in fact. So, amen and amen on that.

Star

At the stroke of noon on her first day at East Surry High School, the bell rang for lunch and a short girl wearing an old lady's dress had an epileptic fit in the courtyard. Star did not see her fall to the pavement. She was, just three hours into the ordeal of being the new girl in Petticoat Junction, still trying to find the cafeteria entrance, and by accident, found herself in the crush of kids surrounding the fallen victim. Maybe this had happened before, because no one really freaked. They just stood in a little circle staring as the girl vibrated on the ground, her feet twisted around each other, the muscles in her neck red and straining. The cotton dress tangled around her legs. The ample fabric managed to cover her, but it was so thin that you could see the faint flower pattern on the girl's underpants. Star wondered if there wasn't something that someone should be doing.

"Oh, gross," whispered a girl with perfectly puffy bangs standing next to Star. She looked at Star and rolled her eyes. "That's Hannah," she said.

"Get Mrs. Hensley," said a boy near the front of the crowd.

"Stanley's going," yelled someone near the hall door. Everyone else stayed put, still staring at this train wreck of a girl who was making little mewing sounds now. God, Starling could not stand it. She turned around and tried to get out of the crowd, but of course, since she was apparently the first new student that ever showed up in this town, everyone had to stop and stare at her too before letting her pass.

It had been the same all day. No one had been hostile; they would just pause in the hallway and get a confused look, like, *Hello, who is this?* The quicker ones, like some of the people in this crowd, would smile then and give her a drawn-out kind of "heeey." She would have to practice this so that she could do it for her friends when she got back to Santa Fe. "Heeey," she would say and then put on that goofy grin. Oh God, they would fall down laughing.

But that was months away, and she was in Swan's Knob, standing against a courtyard wall, like some sad lost thing. Her little band of friends, les artistes, they called themselves, were carrying on in Santa Fe without her. Kiara, Holly, Joseph, Marianna, and the awesome Cameron. There'd be a fall play, *Our Town*, she'd heard, with Kiara in the lead; Halloween—where they'd smoke a little weed and walk around with tragically white faces, capes, and small flesh wounds. In November was the battle of the bands, though she wouldn't be there to help organize this year, so that cheap folk duo, the Pooles, would take the prize. By the time the luminarias were out on the roofs for Christmas, Cameron would've picked out someone else, and she would return to Santa Fe as much a stranger as she was in this school at this moment. "Heeey," she would say, and les artistes, they wouldn't get the joke.

Two or three adults came out of the school now, and the kids did move to let them through. One of them knelt and picked up the girl's rigid arm and checked her pulse. "Hannah, Hannah," she called out, and the girl began shaking her head back and forth, as if she was saying no, no, she didn't want to wake up. Star was sweating now, though she had been told it would be cool in Swan's Knob. She could feel a large drop rolling down her back. The girl seemed to be coming around but she did not open her eyes. Star couldn't blame her. If that were her, she'd just keep her eyes shut until someone called an ambulance and they took her out on a stretcher. Forget it.

The crowd was losing interest now—lucky for Hannah, who was sitting up and untangling her tragically awful dress. Star looked around to see if she could figure out how to get to the cafeteria without having to ask someone. She saw then the tide of kids streaming to the left.

"Okay, that must be it," she said to herself, but also out loud. And then, "Though who knows what I'll eat." Again, audible. This was a bad trend. This was what happened when you were shipped to Petticoat Junction for your senior year.

She followed the others, attempting not to slouch or commit other pointless felonies. First impressions were important. That was what her grandma had said this morning, and it was true, though the way Wilma had said it in that singsongy lilt—reMEMber, that first imPRESSion, it's imPORTant—that was going to bug her, okay? That melodious thing was going to get on her nerves.

She had to admit that the cafeteria looked just about the same as any others she had been in, except, and this was notable, there was a crude mural on the wall of the school mascot, a blue-and-white Rebel soldier. Tragic. And the food. Odious, of course, though halfway down the line, she found a tray of cornbread that looked nearly edible. As the guy in front of her finished paying, he turned and looked at her. He was pretty cute; his curly blond hair was long in front and hanging down in his eyes. She wondered suddenly if she had been talking to herself out loud again. "Jesus," she muttered. He looked instantly stricken.

"Pardon?" he said, like he was trying to decide if she was a freak.

"Nothing," she said, and fished in her purse for money. She picked up her tray and slowly walked out to find a table. The place was crowded, and she was a girl without a country. Okay, she would figure it out. By the end of the week, she would know the whole hopeless hierarchy—geeks, jocks, freaks, artistes, and maybe, come

to think of it, farmers—but for now what she hated was all this thinking and talking to herself, this hyperawareness. She wished that she
could just sit down and eat her lunch without planning how to get her
food to her mouth, how to chew.

The boy was standing beside her. The food on his tray was the
same as hers—cornbread and two milks. He smiled at her in a decidedly ungeeky way and said, "You know, in this school, we cornbread
eaters sit right over there." He had big ears, and when he talked they
moved a little, but, okay, she was grateful anyway. She followed him
and found herself at a table that included an odd assortment of kids,
including Hannah, who had recovered and was drinking a Coke that
someone must have retrieved from the teachers' lounge. Even though
Star was sure that she was now doomed to the kingdom of the misfit
toys, she sat down at the first seat she saw, and the boy took a chair
at the other end of the table. He smiled at her several times during
the meal in a way that was meant to be reassuring, and she tried to
smile back. She tried to talk to the girls around her, but she could not
shake a creepy, creepy feeling that she had to learn everything all over
again, that she did not know anything about these people and this
place, that she did not know even herself.

Chapter Seven

Star

Wilma and Roy turned in early most nights, which was totally great. After supper, they seemed to have no clue about what to do with her. When Star said she had homework and stuff to do in her room, they smiled little relieved smiles at her.

"Homework," Roy said. "Been a while since I heard that word. I wouldn't mind a little homework myself. What about you, Wilma? How about you be my tutor?" Then he winked at her grandma, and squeezed her shoulder. Her grandma frowned at him, but when they got up to the top of the stairs, Star heard her giggle and say, "You better watch yourself, Roy Swan." She said this in a playful way that Star was not meant to hear. Gross.

Star had a horror of overhearing private conversations and other things. Her mother and Jonah were careless in this way. She had heard disagreements about topics way before she understood them. Once, late at night, she'd heard her mother exclaim, "Jesus, Jonah, does it really matter who the child's father is?"—which left her wondering to this day, which child? Which father? Just as gross was that Jonah and her mother were always leaving the wrong door open. They were immodest about what clothes they had on, or not, and kissed each other in the kitchen, or wherever. Star complained, but her mom had only said that what she and Jonah had was beautiful and nothing to be ashamed of.

"Beautiful to who?" Star had said.

"Whom," said her mother, who was an English teacher when she wasn't sucking face in a beautiful relationship.

Star made her way up the staircase to her room. Roy's house was big and old with long creaky hallways. Her grandma and Roy had closed their door, but she could still hear them shuffling around in the room, whispering. As if she wanted to overhear anything. As if. She tiptoed quickly toward her room.

Her room was at the far end of the hall at the opposite end of the house, so once Star was inside, there was nothing she would hear, and there was nothing they would hear, even if she played her guitar. Pure luxury. Jonah's was a cool enough place, but cramped. He had added a couple of rooms onto his house on the hill when she and her mom had moved in, but then Verity was born a few months later, and they were all on top of each other and they had been ever since. Star had been eleven when this happened and stupid about a lot of things. She had been drawn in by Jonah, drawn into liking him, to it being okay that he was with her mom. For a while it had been fine to live in his house on the hill with the colorful tile floors, the kiva fireplace, and the funky winding pathway lined with rocks that led to the door. She could get worse for a stepfather, or actually, an unofficial stepfather. He was always encouraging her songwriting, sticking his head in her room about this time of night, when she was working on something, and saying, "That's sounding real good, Star. Very cool." He was okay, really, as long as he remembered to close the bathroom door.

Now, of course, there was no one to bother her. Pretty nice. She wandered around her room for a few minutes, enjoying the perfect order of the bed she had remembered to make up this morning, pulling back the lacy eyelet curtains to look out at the yard. She raised the window and a nice breeze came in. She could hear crickets, which she never heard in Santa Fe, and bird calls. Night music, that's the way she thought of it.

She picked up her guitar and tried to come up with a groove that would match what she heard outside, but it was hard to imitate. She noodled around with some old tunes that she'd written last year, and then pulled out a pen and paper. Sometimes the lyrics would come first for a song, and they would suggest their own music, just like the pulse from the crickets. She foraged around in her head for ideas from the last few days. The epileptic girl presented possibilities, all that thrashing around on the ground. Star could identify. *Thrashing and fashion and fastening on/The something and something the season would bring.* Maybe that was a little too gross, though, a song about epilepsy, even if that was a good metaphor for the human condition. She smiled now, wishing that she had a phone in her room here, so that she could call Marianna and they could laugh about the whole epilepsy metaphor thing.

Marianna got her totally, just like the rest of les artistes. Marianna had been totally cool when Star's mom had sprung the news about the trip to Asia and the whole exile to the boondocks thing. "God," she'd said. "I'd love to get away for a few months. What's so great about here? You'll totally blow those kids in North Carolina away. You'll rule. And the guys, they won't be the same guys we've all known since kindergarten. Have a summer romance in the fall and come back and tell me all about it." Marianna was all the time harping on the fact that she and Star were the only virgins left in Santa Fe Academy, which was probably true. Marianna's theory was that it was best to lose your virginity with someone who didn't matter very much. "That way," she said, "when the good stuff comes along, you'll know what to do."

"Two words," she said, Star's last night in Santa Fe. "Practice boyfriend." Now that had song potential: *He was my/Practice boyfriend/My temporary romance/My practice boyfriend/He never had a chance/He was my . . .*

Of course, the cornbread guy, Josh, his name was, was a total possibility. He'd reappeared in her math class the first afternoon, hard to miss since only seven people in the school took calculus. She'd gotten to sit beside him, which was kind of lucky, him being sort of nice and fairly cute, and tall—she liked tall. He wasn't the athletic type bodywise, but that had always been Marianna's preference and not hers. He tried to hide behind his hair in front of most people, so it was cool that he always raked it back when he talked to her. He had these amazing eyes, the kind that really seemed to take the world in. Deepwater blue.

It occurred to Star about halfway through the period that the scrawny math teacher, Miss Grimsley, who seemed oddly obsessed with statistical analysis, knew less about calculus than either she or Josh did. She'd looked over at him and seen that he'd already worked out the proof Miss Grimsley had been droning on about for the past half hour. He was scribbling away in his notebook with a pencil stub that looked ridiculously tiny in his hands. She liked his hands. They were big and tan and looked older than the rest of him. He'd glanced up and rolled his eyes at her and then gone back to drawing what looked like some kind of punk rock album cover on the bottom of his paper, featuring a rudely buxom Joan Jett look-alike. Star had studied his proof, seen a small error in the sign of the second term. As Miss Grimsley labored at the blackboard, she'd leaned over and corrected Josh's mistake using her purple ink pen. She'd also taken the liberty of marking over Joan Jett's ample cleavage.

"Hey," he'd said, loudly enough to get them both in trouble, though she'd stifled her laugh and he'd come up with some dumb question to throw Miss Grimsley off track.

Very cute. He'd sort of shadowed her in a casual but eager way since then. He ended up, if she'd understood correctly, asking her out. At least, she thought so. He shoved his hands in and out of his pockets, then mumbled something about going up to the Knob and climbing around.

"Sounds fun," she'd said, and he'd pulled his hair back out of his face again and smiled. It was a little scary, all these alien mating rituals. In Santa Fe, everything was pretty cut-and-dried—hanging out, a couple of trips to the Taco Cantina for dinner, some making out and other stuff in someone's rec room or in a car. By the end of a month or two, it was sort of understood that Grey Horse Canyon was next. That's where you went to do it. It was nice out there, all kinds of little hidden ledges and rock rooms. It was private and very cool in the full moon, according to Kiara, who had a college boyfriend. It was almost spiritual, she said. That was the kind of thing that Star was looking for, but she didn't want to wait until she got back to New Mexico. No big hurry though. She had a whole semester, so she hoped this boy was not somehow jumping the gun, and expecting this climb up Swan's Knob to be the equivalent of a trip to Grey Horse Canyon.

Wilma

It had started out hopefully enough, Roy taking her by the hand and leading her into their room. He closed the door and pulled her near and looked down on her in that way that could always get her going. Wilma had drawn in a long, silent breath and held it there while Roy touched the small of her back. It was these little things between them that always made her forget that she had thick ankles and a slightly wobbly chin, made her forget her age (somewhere in the mid-sixties, she couldn't be more precise).

"Is it okay?" he whispered, meaning there was someone else in the house. He kissed her lips, then her jaw, then just below her ear.

"Sure," she said. "We'll be quiet." He giggled, something he did rarely, and she ducked into the closet to change into a decent gown. Please, she thought, for his sake as well as mine, please, let it be like it's been before. Easy. Easy and as simple as swimming.

"Hurry up," he said, as she left for the bathroom.

She made short work of her going-to-bed routine, sprayed on a little White Shoulders at the end. When she came out, there was still a light in Star's room, but her door was closed, which was good. Wilma could hear her strumming on her guitar: even better.

It was dark in their bedroom, though at such times Roy usually left on the closet light. As she slipped into bed, he turned over toward the other edge. "Oh, dolly, lost the moment there, I guess," he said, trying not to sound the least bit pitiful.

Another woman, in another generation perhaps, a younger woman might have known what to do, how to rub her hand across just the right spot, unbidden but entirely welcome. Someone freer might be able to say, "Come on over here now, let me find that moment for us again." Surely, there was a whole list of things to try, but she was afraid, as always, of making things worse. She turned toward him, keeping her body on her side of the bed. She laid her hand on his shoulder and tried to sleep.

Josh

The Outlier lay in his bed in the attic, not quite ready to pull the covers over himself. He had officially abandoned his worship of that junior varsity cheerleader and his longtime ritual bedtime fantasy of finding her lost in the woods naked. No, tonight, he thought of that new girl, Star, of her standing there in the cafeteria in those black clothes and boots that the other girls said were weird. He thought of the way she looked at him, like she might possibly, in some century, be interested in the Outlier, in what he might have to offer. The Outlier would arrange it. The two of them would meet up in the dark alley behind Squirrely's pool hall. She would look him up and down, and then she would lean back against a brick wall, unbutton her blouse, and say "Come over here now, take a look that this." He tossed and turned in and out of this scene, it must have been an hour, and though eventually he relieved himself, he could not stop his brain: the wall, her lips, her neck . . . Pretty soon it was back, like some kind of crowbar, and he wondered if there'd ever come a time again when he could sleep on his stomach.

Wilma

Of course, there was no sleeping. It was. this way when Roy got her charged up, embarrassing to admit. She supposed it was just plain biology. Perfectly natural, that was the way she thought about it, though if you went by what you saw on TV, you'd think only the young cared a thing about it. Maybe it was true: love (physical love, at least) was for the young, for the thin-ankled. The best you could do later on was comfort. Maybe by the time you swapped out those high heels for comfortable shoes, you were supposed to be doing the same in your bedroom. She had a hard time believing that Roy thought this way. Maybe he'd just lost interest in her. Possible. There were plenty of women in town who would love to turn his head, always had been. She still had no idea why she'd been put at the front of the line.

What if that Mamie Brown just showed up out at the farm one day? Or Lily Strong, for that matter? She'd been in Daytona Beach ever since Franklin died, but what if she came back wearing one of those sundresses with the plunging necklines? Roy was human, wasn't he? Lord knows she wasn't the most intuitive person in the world. Hadn't her Harry shot himself cold dead before she'd had a good idea things weren't right with him? What if all the time Roy spent out at the home place wasn't just about all those grapevines? She took her hand off his shoulder and flipped over the other way. She had to stop this. It was giving her terrible indigestion, another sign of old age. But God, he had been out there a lot lately, and he didn't always answer when she called. What if it was more than a big crop of tomatoes? What if that ag extension agent, the grape expert, was some cute forty-something redhead? Roy hadn't said.

Okay, she just had to go to sleep. To sleep.

No use. She was going to be up all night.

Fine, she would be up—she just wouldn't spend another minute with her mind in the gutter.

Roy was snoring, a light whistle through his nose. There was nothing to do but roll onto her back and review the music for Sunday (a Bach prelude, easy hymns, the choir anthem mostly ready). Okay. Now she'd think about the Greensboro Symphony concert they'd be going to next month. That was a pleasant topic. Her former student, James Moody, her pride and joy, was the featured piano soloist, coming down from Boston. He was doing so well, better than she would have ever imagined. He'd written her, as he always did when he was booked in the area, and asked if she would come to the concert, to the reception afterwards. Of course they would go. She thought about the last concert, a few years back in Raleigh, how much fun that had been. She and Roy had been married then only a year or so. She tried to think, had he spent quite so much time at the farm then? Wait, none of that. Back to the concert.

Roy had understood what a big deal it was for her—her own piano student, a concert soloist. He'd insisted they go down early, make a weekend of it. He'd booked them a room at the Velvet Cloak Inn downtown, taken her to the Angus Barn before the concert.

James had gotten them seats in the first row, right along with his family. You'd have thought Roy was James Moody's teacher or the mayor of Swan's Knob, the way he shook everyone's hand and smiled. James's relations, a large black family, most of them working a tiny tobacco farm down the road from Roy's home place, seemed just as astounded as she was by all James's high-blown success, and just as proud. Roy chatted them all up, had all of them laughing and beaming. He kept looking at her the whole time, wishing maybe that what all this meant to her would show on her face. He said that to her a lot, that he didn't think much of anyone could tell whether she was happy or sad about anything. Maybe that was the problem. Maybe she should try to be more like that, more expressive or peppy or something. She wasn't sure.

That night, when they sat down and the lights started dimming, he'd been so sweet. She couldn't forget that. He leaned over and said, "Look what you did. You are an amazing woman." That was what she needed to remember: she and Roy sitting there in those nice Raleigh auditorium seats, her knowing right there, in a flash, what they were for each other, how they were one, like the vows they said. James played beautifully, movingly, as always. It had been Rachmaninoff and Wilma had been flooded, with Roy perfectly still beside her, with a rare assurance that no matter what showed on her face, he knew what she felt, the joy of things, the infinite little happinesses that can come at you in life and the sadnesses too. Her presence in the world, her sense of it, was more acute for his witness. It was all wrapped up in his being there beside her, in his feeling it too.

She tried to hold on to that assurance as she fell asleep, tried not to worry that it was leaking slowly out of their life, their marriage. Slipping away, the fate of so many good things.

Roy

Before he was even good and awake, it dawned on him that he'd drifted off last night once again without doing what he'd intended to do. He smelled the coffee, that good coffee that Wilma ground in an old-fashioned grinder though he could have done fine with Maxwell House. She was up and gone, then. Dang. She wouldn't say a word. Maybe she hadn't taken note, though that was unlikely. He thought for a moment about going down to the breakfast table in his Skivvies. He'd done that for the first time early on in their marriage. Wilma had made a big show of not noticing but blushed all the way through breakfast. Of course in the end, she'd noticed all right. Ever since, if he'd showed up like that in the morning, well, she was just waiting for the meal to be over, knowing he'd pull her into his lap.

Maybe it was time to do that again. He'd hit the bathroom, smack on a little Aqua Velva, and he'd be set.

He sat up and was about to bolt out of bed but then remembered to slow up and just sit on the side, take a minute to let the water drain out of his head. Otherwise, he'd feel all cattywompuss, like he was swimming at the bottom of the ocean and didn't know which way was up. This morning, damn it—for some reason, he had a headlight burned out. His left eye didn't exactly work right. Actually, it didn't work at all, but once he rubbed the eyelid for a minute, his vision came right back. It needed to get warmed up, was all. No need to panic. Everything was slowing down, just part of the deal. Aging—a hell of a deal considering the alternative, that's what his daddy always said.

He took a couple of breaths and everything seemed to be in order, so he headed out. He needed to get to the bathroom before he ran into yet another problem. About the time he put his first foot in the hall, the door at the other end opened. Now this woke him up for sure. Star. Good God, he'd forgotten for a second. He'd have to amend his thinking here, no Skivvies in the hallway or anywhere for the moment.

He went back to the room and got dressed in a hurry, but decided to do it up right for a change—a decent button-down, the pressed khakis, not the worn-in comfortable ones, loafers instead of work shoes. If need be, he had more comfortable clothes out at the farm. He could change into those later. For now, he wanted to make some gesture since he wasn't going to be smooching on Wilma and such. Plus, there was one other thing. He'd waited long enough: he needed to tell Wilma all about this festival that Harper had cooked up. He could see a few days back that a storm was brewing and of course, he should've seen it coming. Something not so different had happened between his mother and dad, and before it was over there was enough bad blood to keep his mother away from the home place for the rest of her life—and then some.

One time and only one time, there had been a traveling carnival out at his daddy's farm. Roy had been thirteen or so, old enough, his father said, to earn a little pocket money helping the carnival folks pitch their tents. They had shown up one August morning when he and his father were out back in the garden restaking the tomatoes. A tall man with dark crinkled skin and a dirty gray shirt had come around the house. When he saw them, he took off his cowboy hat and rolled it up in his hands as he talked. He'd stated his business without any fanfare: carnie show, looking for a field for forty-eight hours. He'd pay five dollars a day, ten if they could use the well water. Roy's dad, who in that moment looked like a poor farmer instead of the owner of half the tobacco warehouses in four counties that he surely was, didn't say anything at first. It was his way, Roy knew, to size up a situation, and a man, before speaking. He did this to Roy every day.

He handed Roy the tomato stake, walked out of the garden and around to the front of the house. Roy and the man followed. Across the wavering heat, they could see a caravan of ten or so vehicles, trucks and wagons, painted and maybe even gilded at one time, but now, in the middle of the Depression years, faded and clouded with stinky exhaust trails, several sitting low on their tires. The lead man's car, an old woodie station wagon, sat in front of the house. The remaining vehicles still idled out on the road at a respectful distance. Roy's dad pushed his own hat back on his forehead and said, "What kinds of acts you got?"

And the man told him: acrobats, fortune-teller, world's largest pig, freak show, kiddie rides, and so on.

"Hoochie choochie show?" his dad asked, though Roy was shocked to hear him say it. The lead man looked back at his daddy, trying to size him up.

"Naw," said the man firmly, making a bet. "No sir, none of that. Revival tent, though. Got us a woman preacher."

Roy's dad smiled. "Okay. You can pull into that field there, but here's the thing: come Sunday morning, you all be gone and that field there will look the way it does right now. You hear?"

The man nodded vigorously. Roy's dad had a way of speaking that made people stand up straight and say "yes sir" in just the way the man did now. He turned to leave, but Roy's dad called him back.

"My name is Charles Swan and this here is my son Roy. And yours?"

"Tolley Nance," said the man, finally remembering to offer his hand.

Roy's dad shook and Roy followed him. "Well, Mr. Tolley Nance. I hold you responsible," said his daddy. "And I don't want to hear of any woman preacher prancing around any way she shouldn't be, you hear?"

"Yes, sir. Understood, sir." The men laughed then and Roy laughed with them, though he wasn't quite sure what was funny. Tolley pulled out a glass bottle—looked like a tonic—and offered it to his daddy, but his daddy turned it down. He arranged then for Roy to help with the tents for fifty cents. By the time he and his dad drove home for supper, both of them bone tired, the women from the show had been all over town tacking up handbills on the telephone poles. The carnival was open for business.

Their Friday night supper was usually a pleasant meal followed by a fresh-baked pound cake, but it was dismal that evening. The news of the "godless pack of gypsies" preceded them. Not only had his mother seen the fliers, with "Swan's farm" scrawled across the bottom, but three women from her Circle had stopped by during the afternoon just to let her in on the development. His mother was furious with his father, the pound cake had been dispatched to an ailing neighbor, and Roy found, for the first time in his life, that by brutal association he too was in what his father called "the doghouse."

"Erma," his father said, after she had lectured them both with a red face for several minutes. "I cannot fathom why you and your Methodist Circle group can condemn these poor souls. We all need a little fun these days and these people surely need a little money. What does it hurt?"

"Harumpft," said Roy's mother, followed by another lecture, followed by Roy being sent up to his room, where his model airplanes had never looked so interesting.

The argument lasted for hours in his memory, with the loud parts drifting upstairs to Roy's room: "Charles, you mark my words . . ." and "Just take me out and shoot me, Erma," and "I've said I'm sorry, what more . . ."

By Saturday, though, things were better. Every man in town and a few of the women visited the show. In the end, all but the most strict Circle women let their children see the animals and the acrobats. Roy's mother, of course, was a holdout. She stayed in town. Roy understood, as a pact between him and his father, man-to-man, that he would never mention what he had seen at the freak show: a nightmare of dwarves, a half-he and half-she, and most disturbing, a full-size man with legs and arms the size of a doll. In the light of the tent, he was almost yellow and he coughed like he had swallowed up a bunch of dust. Roy's buddy Bob Geary told him that some of his older brothers had been around late on Saturday night when the woman preacher dropped off all her clothes in a fit of religious ecstasy. Roy could never find a direct eyewitness, though this image, the very thought of her, fueled his imagination for several years to come.

Two weeks later, Roy found the fresh grave up on their hill. He was not smart enough to make the connection and spoiled another Friday night pound cake by asking about it at the dinner table. His mother paled instantly, and when Roy looked at his father's face, he felt for the first time the awful sting of regret that one man feels when he has let down another.

"Yes," his father said finally, "one of the carnival folks passed while the show was in town. There was nothing else to do."

"Which?" said his mother.

Roy knew the answer then. The grave had been small, just big enough for a man with doll limbs. He didn't say a thing.

"Not sure," said his father, looking very carefully at the new little man across the table. "One of the hands, I think. His heart gave out, they said."

"Charles!" his mother said, and nothing more.

Wilma

When Roy came to breakfast, all spiffy in his button-down and khakis, and all smiling and rested from his long night of snoring, Wilma found herself in the kind of foul humor that she had last experienced during the years of menopause. She thought she'd run all out of those nasty hormones, but apparently not. Maybe it was related to having a teenager in the house, though Star was doing nothing more than quietly finishing up her breakfast. Or maybe it was related to living with an old man in his old house, an old man who sat right down and helped himself to more bacon than he should eat in a month, and more pancakes.

"I haven't had any of those yet," she said, making a supreme effort to sound civil, but not succeeding apparently, since Roy replaced several of the pancakes on the serving plate and looked at Star for sympathy.

"It's such a nice day, I thought I'd walk to school," Star said. Wilma wondered exactly how many black T-shirts she owned. This morning's had ripped sleeves, which was the style, of course, but Wilma just couldn't get used to it.

"I don't mind taking you. Won't take but a minute," Roy said.

"Thanks, Roy. I'll walk."

"How about I pick you up, then? I'll bring the truck."

Star brightened immediately and bestowed an amazing smile on Roy. Wilma had lost this battle, that was clear. "Deal," Star said.

"Deal," said Roy, all proud of himself.

Wilma waited until Star was packed up and out the door before sitting down for her own breakfast. The pancakes were cold and she was tired. *Easy, girl,* she thought. "Well, you're all dressed up this morning. Are you going down to Winston to see your broker?" *There. Much better.*

Roy put down his fork. "Well, no, I hadn't intended to. I'll prob-ably end up out at the farm." He looked down at his shirt. "I put this on, well, I don't know. I thought you might be getting sick of seeing an old man slouching around the house in his work clothes."

Wilma had read her share of women's magazines and every now and then there was an article on infidelity. She'd read about the top ten signs that a man was cheating. Wasn't one of the signs a sudden interest in looking nice? This came close behind a man taking show-ers at odd times of day.

"These pancakes are sure good. Nice to have Star around if you're going to make breakfasts like this." Roy smiled at her with those kind eyes of his, light blue with crinkled lids. His eyebrows arched up a lit-tle, made him look mischievous, but not devious. It was hard for her to look at him across their breakfast table like this and actually believe he was up to something. Besides, Mamie Brown was not looking that good these days.

He went out for the paper then and Wilma got herself more cof-fee. When he got back, she watched the routine: a glance at the head-lines, then straight to the sports page. In ten minutes, he'd be looking at the stock quotes. This was the male way, as far as she knew, to start the day hidden behind a large piece of newsprint. Her Harry had done this too, same order, same tilt of the chin. He'd done it every morning of their marriage, even the last one, just an hour before he shot himself. She hadn't thought he was up to anything either.

She was surprised when Roy put the paper down before he even got to the business page. "Dolly," he said. "You okay? You seem, you seem . . . You happy to be in Carolina in the mornin'?"

"Nothing could be finer," she said with what she hoped was a con-vincing lilt.

"Well," he said. "I for one would be a little bit finer this morning if I had not fallen asleep so early last night."

Were they going to talk about it? "Oh," she said. "That. We were both tired."

"Well," he said.

"Well."

What could she say, really? *It's been eight weeks.* No. *What does*

Mamie Brown have that I don't have? Well. *Would it help if I rubbed your back first?*

Roy picked the paper up, but held it so that she could still see his face as he read. Wilma was running out of things to do at the breakfast table. She started collecting the plates but stayed seated. What could she say? She'd just wait a few more weeks. Things might clear up all on their own.

"You know," he said, after a few minutes. "I want to explain about all the goings-on out at the farm, especially since I'll be spending a bit more time there this fall."

"What kind of goings-on?" Did Roy have a shower in the old home place? Wilma could not remember. There was an old claw-foot tub.

"I think we mentioned the other night about Harper and his music festival. I just wanted to explain, that's all."

"Oh, that." Yes, there was an ugly claw-foot tub, no shower, but what was she thinking? The man could barely keep his eyes open after nine o'clock. He was probably out at the farm drinking in the middle of the day with Harper Chilton, planning this hootenanny and then taking a nap. She stood up to get started with the dishes. This was what all that late-night worrying did to her.

He had launched now into a long explanation of what a great thing the festival was going to be. She tried to follow what he was saying, but she just could not shake her peevish mood. Maybe she should be relieved to realize that Roy was in no way cheating on her. But in a way, this whole Mamie Brown notion, it was a brand of wishful thinking—to consider that Roy might have the get-up-and-go for her and another woman on the side. No such luck, apparently.

He was going on now in the animated and energetic manner that had first attracted her to him on their first date at the Coach House Restaurant, but his charm was not working on her this morning. Yes, he could go on . . . and on and on . . . in a conversation, of course, first thing in the morning, of course. By tonight, slap-dab worn out. That or terrible indigestion.

"It'll be a disaster," she said, not bothering to wait for him to pause for breath.

"What?" he said.

"I can't tell you what will go wrong, but let me tell you, if this is something that Harper's come up with, it'll be a disaster. No question in my mind."

He finished his coffee then with his eyes on the paper, his little crinkled eyelids turned down. Disappointed.

"Go on with it, of course," she said. "Knock yourselves out, but I don't want to have a thing to do with it."

He left the house soon after that, kissed her like he always did. She wasn't particularly proud of herself, but she didn't have sense enough to say something to him, even something like *Sorry, sweetie,* which would have been enough.

Chapter Eight

Roy

As Roy pulled his truck into the front circle of the high school, he could pick out Star immediately among all the girls wearing pretty pastels. Travis and Celeste's youngest boy was standing next to her, his skinny frame bent over like a grasshopper caught in a spiderweb. Roy had a pretty good handle on the situation before his wheels stopped rolling. Josh, that was his name. That boy had it bad, falling all over himself now to help Star into the car. His face was flushed and sweaty from overcirculation. Roy hated to think what other problems that might be causing. Roy had not forgotten. Mercy! He feared for the boy for a moment. Star was standing on the sidewalk, looking bored and about four years older than Josh. Maybe she was sizing up the situation and finding him "decidedly uncool." That was what she'd called the school bag that Wilma had offered her at breakfast the other day. She hadn't said it in a mean way, really, just like this was for their information.

Roy braced himself for disaster, but as Josh opened the truck door, Star did a quick pivot and then looked up at him with a fresh smile that looked all happy and white, as opposed to the rest of her. Woo, boy, this caught Roy by surprise. Star hadn't been in school even a week yet, and already these two were in for some full-blown teenaged love.

Roy could never resist this sort of thing. He wasn't that far from it himself. He decided to help out. "Hey, Josh," he said. "We're headed out to the farm. Do you want a ride with us?"

"Well, sure," said Josh in a voice a tad lower than Roy remembered. "Yes, sir! If it's no trouble."

"Slide on in, Star, and we'll have plenty of room for him." He tried to lean forward a bit so he could see Star's face, make sure he'd done the right thing. She looked carefully neutral, but he noticed her swallow real fast once or twice. He was new at the whole thing, but he guessed this was teenager for *I am very excited to be riding in this truck with this cute boy*. He sure hoped so.

They pulled away from the school and set out for Dobson Road. For a few minutes it was quiet, no sound at all except the sound of a black miniskirt and worn dungarees moving across the bench upholstery as the two young people adjusted to sitting right next to one another, for the first time, probably. Roy's T-bird was roomier, of course, but he'd promised Star he'd bring the truck. Now these close quarters were more than they all had bargained for. He noted that the position the pair had settled on had her right leg and his left nested against one another from knee to hip, which was almost necessary within the confines of the cab, but nevertheless . . . Best for Roy to take no further notice of this. Already, he had the impulse to wiggle his shoulders back and forth to get rid of an uncomfortable feeling in the small of his back, and, of course, there was no room for that kind of maneuver at all unless he wanted Star sitting on the kid's lap before the ride was done.

The silence went on until Roy remembered that he had been married for seven years to the queen of small talk. All he had to do was ask what Wilma would: "So, how's it going, Star?" he said. "Are you settling in here with the rest of the East Surry Rebels?"

She laughed. "Yeah. The Rebels. Yeah, it's fine. Not that bad." Very few of the kids said "yes sir" and "yes ma'am" these days.

"Your classes, teachers, okay?"

"Sure, I guess. The English teacher is kind of a dork."

Josh guffawed at this. "You must have Mrs. Parrish. Is she doing *Moby-Dick* in your class?"

" 'Call me Ishmael,' " said Star. Josh laughed again. Now they were getting somewhere.

"That's the one about the whale, right?" said Roy.

"Yeah," said Star. Silence again. Roy tried to adjust his shoulders without knocking into her. He wondered how the boy was getting along sitting over there with all that circulation. "We did have a girl fall down in an epileptic fit on Monday," said Star, like she was wanting to help Roy out with the small talk. "That's something I never saw in Santa Fe."

"Hannah Smothers?" Roy confirmed it with Josh. God, he wished that girl's family would keep her on her medication. Roy had taken care of her himself several times when he was working with the rescue squad at football games. Lord, he hated dealing with a grand mal seizure and it was mostly preventable.

Josh and Star spent the rest of the trip chatting about Hannah and about others at the high school, and once they got going, Roy made sure not to ask any more whale questions. For his part, he began making a list about what he wanted to do to the truck. It needed more than a tune-up, that was for sure. There was a knocking noise he didn't like. He needed to get under the thing and check out the crankshaft. He thought he still had that wooden creeper out in the shed. He could roll right under the truck if he could find that thing.

By the time they drove up to the Diamonds' house, Josh seemed reluctant to get out of the car. He kept looking at Star like he might never get the chance to see her again, and finally leaned over to her and mumbled something just before closing the door. As they drove away, Star turned her head and then her torso all the way around to watch as the boy marched up his front stoop. It was like watching some kind of romantic old movie.

Before he married Wilma, he would watch old movies on a Saturday night, he would notice the nice couple out for an evening stroll holding hands, and it would give him an awful kind of feeling in his stomach that would last late into the night. In these last years, that was all gone. And he felt a keen happiness to see these two kids get a big crush on each other, though Lord God, for Wilma, this kind of thing might be a little like the driving. Maybe it had not occurred to her that she would have to deal with teenaged romance and no telling what all to follow.

Celeste

Celeste came home hoping to find Josh alone in the house. She'd only seen him for a moment at breakfast, and Travis had been at the table with them. Travis's truck was parked in the driveway, but she held out hope that he was back in his shop and that Josh was in the kitchen doing homework. No such luck, though. No sign of Josh. The house was quiet. The kitchen was just like she'd left it at six, breakfast dishes in the sink, butter left out by the toaster. The smell of oatmeal lingered in the air. She hung up her bag and turned on some lights. Once in a while, usually when she was late getting dinner on the table, Travis would complain about how he hated coming home to a dark kitchen, how her housekeeping was getting to be like her mother's. This was a low blow, of course, for him to say this.

Celeste's mother was about the least tidy and most unhappy human being that ever walked the earth. Granted, Celeste had as many children as her mother, but she'd been able to feed hers three meals a day. And unlike her mother, she didn't rank children only a hair above farm animals. She didn't beat them; she didn't call them trash. As Travis was fond of pointing out, Celeste had brought them to the Lord, since she herself had managed to know God in some fashion, though maybe not as thoroughly as Travis would have it. Therefore, she would not burn in everlasting hell like Ramona Clay. So.

So, when Travis had the nerve to bring up her mother like that, as he had sometime around last Easter, it just burned her up. She didn't know what to say for a minute. In the end, she'd just used her mother's favorite expression on him. "It'll have to do," she'd said, drawing out that last word so he could hear the long-departed Ramona Clay in her voice.

She washed her hands and started clearing the sink. Of course, Travis hadn't said a word about the kitchen lately. He knew better. Winter was coming and he darn well liked Celeste's paycheck at the end of the month, especially since he'd had a smaller tobacco production this year.

She heard the truck about the time she finished the breakfast dishes. She looked out her window over the sink. (This view was something Ramona had never had. Travis had put in the window the summer after she died, while Celeste was pregnant with Dora.) Josh was getting out of Roy Swan's truck, smiling and waving like he was a little boy who'd just been taken out for ice cream. Then Celeste saw why: Wilma's granddaughter, Sparrow or some such, was sitting in the truck with Roy. Her face was as pale as someone who lived in a cave; her hair, an unnatural black, was hanging all around it. Her expression was somewhere between dewy and wanton. As they pulled away, the girl fairly leaned out the truck window to focus those big raccoon eyes on Josh. Celeste knew instantly that this one was trouble. As her son trudged toward the house, she spent another thirty seconds of regret for bringing that Erica Jong book into the house. There was no telling what kinds of zipless notions were flying through her baby's head right now. Travis would kill her if he knew, and for once he would be right.

Roy

Roy had to hack through a bunch of honeysuckle to even get in the shed where he stored his tools. He hadn't done much work on the truck in quite some time. Sure, he could take it up to Gregory Chevrolet and let Ellry Mabe do the tune-up, but he took some pleasure in doing this for Star, especially since she was so excited about the entire enterprise. Before he could even find his jack, she was asking about how long it would be before she could start driving. To give himself some time, he handed her some clippers and an old bucket and put her to work cutting some of the coneflowers and Gerber daisies so they'd have a bouquet to take home for Wilma. Wilma needed a little something from him right now. He could see over breakfast that she was tired and off center with Star in the house, and then of course . . . He wished he could borrow some of the good stuff from the teenagers right about ten o'clock tonight.

"Roy, I'm going for water for the flowers. Do you want some too?"

Star looked at him like Wilma did when she thought he was coming down with something.

"Sure," he said, and tossed her the keys to the farmhouse.

Maybe it was the heat getting to him all the way around. Even now, he was sweating straight through his shirt. It had to be at least eighty, and without that old stupid hat Wilma'd gotten him, he was seeing Star make her way up to the house through that shimmer in the edge of his vision that made him feel like he was in the desert. He tried to ignore it and get his tools hauled out to where the truck was parked. It just took a couple of trips, but it was a disgrace to be so tuckered out before he even started the job. Dadburn old man, that was what he was turning into. He was thankful when he found that old creeper so he had a prayer of getting up under the truck.

He got the thing situated and was about to lie down on it and here came his swimmy head again. As he scooted himself underneath, it occurred to Roy that maybe he should've asked Josh over to the farm to help him out. Too late. Roy dug in his heels and inched forward, but he wasn't far enough under the thing to get a look at the crankshaft, and he wasn't sure that he was actually going to fit in the space he needed to be without jacking the whole truck up. He bent his knees so that he could push himself toward the center of the engine, and when he did, he banged his left kneecap on the brake cable.

"Hell!" he yelled. "Goddamn it."

"You okay, Roy? Anything I can do?" Star was back from the house.

"No, no, fine," he said, though he had gone farther underneath the truck than he intended. Right above his head, where a minute ago he could see the crankshaft, it was now dark. More darkness poured under the truck like fog. He lifted the wrench to tap on the engine, but it fell from his grasp unbidden and hit him on the forehead and clanged to the ground. This barely hurt, but it made him mad, and then, of course, his heart started pounding like a demon in his chest.

"Roy? Roy?"

To hell with this. He'd take this baby up to the Chevy place in the morning. He went to pull up his knees again, to push himself out from under that truck and into the sunny afternoon, and it was the funniest thing, nothing moved. Though he told them to, his knees didn't do anything at all. Now there was no light at all. Maybe they were having some kind of storm or eclipse, because it was darker than night, and his heart beat like a six-cylinder and it was not fog, not a storm, not night, but it was him. He could not see; he could not move his arms and legs.

"Roy? Roy?" He could hear this perfectly well, and opened his mouth to tell Star what had happened, but nothing came out, not a sound, and he started for one long moment to panic, to flail himself around, but this he could not do, and after a few more seconds, this was not something that he even wanted to do. He wondered, without any real concern, if he was dying. Maybe this was what it was like.

"Roy? Roy? Please answer! Are you all right?" He could still hear her, hear the girl call to him, but he was too far away to answer. Maybe the truck had fallen on him, its weight pressed on his chest, his heart forced to beat in the tiniest of spaces. Something gave way then and he began sinking into the earth, deeper and deeper, burrowing, becoming a very small thing.

Josh

His mother, still in her nurse's uniform, was popping him some popcorn in the microwave, breaking beans for dinner, and circling around some point she wanted to make with him. "We see so much these days, Josh, on the TV, in books and such, and I think you young people just grow up too fast." She was getting close, and Josh was stuck at the kitchen table, trying to think of a way to exit with his bowl of popcorn before she got to whatever it was.

"Take that book that I saw you with the other night." Too late. The book, that was it. His mom leaned back against the counter and crossed one white nurse's shoe over the other, in a way that she meant to look casual. "Now, I know I'm partially to blame—"

"Hey! What's cooking?" His dad appeared suddenly in the threshold between the sitting room and the kitchen, making them both jump.

"Not much yet," his mother said, recovering. "I just got home a few minutes ago."

His dad cut his eyes between the two of them. "Am I interrupting? You two planning my birthday party or something?" His mother put the bag of popcorn in front of Josh. He made sure to get a big handful in his mouth immediately.

"Not hardly," said his mother. "It's three months off. Where have you been? I couldn't find you when I got home."

"The usual place." The wood shop out back. His dad made cabinets for people when he wasn't busy with the tobacco. "No kidding. Josh here looks like he swallowed a mouse. What's the big secret?"

"Can we have one single moment—" his mother began, just as the siren went off in the distance. The volunteer fire siren. Josh had to smile. That thing had interrupted a thousand other moments of his life, taking his father away from him during Little League games, bedtime stories, trips for ice cream, but never before had it ever sounded at exactly the right time. *Thank you, Jesus.* That was all Josh could think. *Thank you, thank you.*

His dad ran back to his bedroom to grab his boots. The phone rang, and as his mother went to answer it, Josh took his popcorn bag and headed for the stairs. He was halfway across the room when his mother stuck her hand out to stop him. She had an alarmed expression on her face. "Okay, okay, did she say anything else? Is he breathing or what? Okay, we'll get over there. Yes no I'll call you bye." She hung up and headed toward the back door in a single motion. "Travis!" she yelled. "Come on. It's Roy."

Celeste

Up until this very minute, Celeste had always thought of Roy Swan as a man who led a charmed life. She had known Roy Swan since she was a little bitty thing, climbing the apple trees that bordered their two farms. She got up too far in the big Macintosh one day when she was four, and it was Roy who found her, talked her down, and brought her home to her mama just after sunset. She had gotten switched good after he left, had stripes up and down her legs for Sunday school that week, but he was her hero anyway. He had to have been sixteen or so then, and she saw him only once in a while, though she searched for him constantly after that in the orchard and on the little road their farms shared, the road that she was driving down this very minute with Travis and Josh.

In those days, way before Travis had rescued her and the farm, her whole life had been lived literally on these few acres, the little tobacco barn that was hot as a firecracker most of the time, the ramshackle house that held more brothers and sisters and cats than she had numbers for. That was all there was. Those were the only places she knew to look for Roy Swan. She had a hard time taking in what her mother said about him, that his daddy owned that big farm next door with its pretty white house and painted barn and more tobacco rows than anybody ever thought of. Roy didn't really live in this house, her mother said, he lived in another one in town. Celeste never could understand that, never could figure why anyone needed two houses, especially when they had a nice white one with a good spring and an orchard full of apples.

So Celeste had thought of him as the luckiest man she knew, even though he'd lost his parents to a train wreck while he was in the service, even though he'd never married until he was past sixty, even though he never really had much of a job to speak of, and Travis and probably half the town called him the gentleman farmer behind his back. Lucky. And now, according to Grace Snow, whose husband doubled as the ambulance driver and the funeral director in town, he was stuck under a truck, unconscious and no telling what, the nearest hospital thirty minutes away. All the luck he had at the moment was the three of them, and maybe Wilma's granddaughter, who was probably the one run over him in the first place.

"You think he's still alive?" she asked Travis, who just shrugged his shoulders and pointed at the road, to remind her that she was in charge of driving. He didn't like to talk in a crisis. She glanced back at the road, which was unnecessary. She could drive down it blindfolded. She felt a hand on her right shoulder, then a firm squeeze. It was Josh. He was riding in the far side of the cab, but had stretched his long arm out behind his dad, and when she looked over, he gave her a grown-up nod. This would have pleased her seven ways to Sunday if she had not been in the middle of being so nervous. She was going to be the only person there with any medical training to speak of. Travis just thought he knew what to do from a little EMT training. She would do anything in the world she could for Roy, but this was why she was an LPN and not a nurse: no one put her in charge of a split-second crisis. Death, if it came to one of her patients, didn't have much of anything to do with her.

Harper

Harper could not even turn on WPAQ these days without it putting him into a reverie about the festival.

"I'm a-fixing to play you some Del McCoury here in a few minutes, and then Sally over in Level Cross has requested 'Sauratown Mountain Blues.' First, here's Delrina Kay and Little Charlie, 'In My Loving Arms,' " said the announcer, Tippy Bowman. Harper made a mental note to try and call the guy. A little free publicity wouldn't hurt, even at ten kilowatts. However, first things first. It was time he nailed down the permits for the farm and that meant getting Roy to go down to the police station with him. He'd tried to phone him several times already, before his class at Surry Community and during lunch, but there was no answer at the farm. He'd even tried the house in town. When Wilma had answered, he'd asked for Star, just so he didn't have to get into the whole thing with Wilma.

"She's at school," she said, using that flat disapproving piano teacher voice.

"I knew that," he said, but she didn't seem to get the joke.

He'd tried the farm again just a few minutes ago before leaving school. The line was busy, so he'd just gotten in the car, hoping to catch Roy before he headed back home. If he did, he and Roy could scoot into town and get this police thing all taken care of. Harper whistled along with Delrina for a few minutes and then thought back to his little exchange with Wilma. God, that woman, how did Roy stand living with that? He and Sarah had had their problems, but Wilma? Lord God. He felt sorry for Star as well. Maybe he'd go over and get her later on, take her back to his house. They could play some music, maybe even work up a number or two for the festival.

He was close to the turnoff to Roy's road now, and Delrina segued into Del's band singing "Rain and Snow." Harper liked that song. He wouldn't mind trying to work that up himself sometime. Saturday was his turn to host the little group of musician friends. They played together a few times a month. Star might enjoy that. He could ask her. Roy's dirt road came up then on his right, a bit faster than he remembered. He slowed and pulled in. On second thought, though, those pickers were sure enough a partying bunch, and he was in charge of the party. He'd think of something else for him and Star to do, maybe Sunday.

He heard a horn blast behind him. A glance in his rearview and he saw Ronnie Snow's ambulance behind him with the red light rolling around. Jesus. There was nowhere to get his car off the road. There were ditches on both sides and fields beyond that. His first thought, paranoia from the old days, was that Ronnie was trying to pull him over. He slowed down, but Ronnie laid on his horn, which meant, *Get going*, and so he did. He barreled up the dirt road as fast as he was able. When he looked back in the mirror, he saw that not only was Ronnie back there, so was the town fire truck. Jesus, maybe Roy had a fire.

He gripped the wheel tight and kept his foot on the gas. From this part of the road, the house was a good ways over to the right. He tried to look and see if he could spot any smoke, but there was nothing but the dust kicked up from his tires. The road curved to the right finally and he could see the barn, the house, and the whole setup. No smoke, thankfully. He eased up a bit. Probably just a false alarm. That happened sometimes. Ronnie must have noticed his speed, because he blasted his horn again, this time longer and louder. As they neared the house, Harper found a flat patch of ground level with the road and pulled over on it. Jesus, he'd just let those rescue boys race to the scene.

His daddy had been a member of the rescue squad in Surry

County for twenty years, captain before it was over. Harper knew these boys just loved to show up at any small calamity: kitchen grease fire, fender bender, you name it. Of course, Roy was one of their own. He'd been on the rescue squad until he'd aged out a few years back. Harper stayed put for a few minutes, waited for the dust to settle a bit. He'd let them have their fun. He'd just have to hope they'd cleared what little smoke or whatever it was in a few minutes. Then he and Roy could get on with their business.

Chapter Nine

Harper

The first thing he saw when he drove up to the house was Star, standing by Roy's pickup truck, jumping up and down and clasping her hands together underneath her chin. What was wrong? The truck looked fine, no smoke or anything. The rescue squad boys were scrambling around for their gear, though, and then he saw Travis Diamond and his wife crouched down on the ground beside the truck, tending to a man in khaki pants. Roy.

Star spotted him then, ran toward him at full speed, and threw herself against him. Please, he thought, please. Please don't let it be. She hasn't been driving that long.

"Did he get run over?" he said.

She sobbed into his chest but shook her head. "I don't know what happened. He climbed under the truck, and then he just . . . he just got stuck or something. He was fine one minute, then he just quit talking. Not moving or anything."

Harper looked over his shoulder. Travis was doing CPR. Jesus. Travis's wife—Harper couldn't think of her name—gripped Roy's left leg like she was holding the bone in place. "Is it broken?" Travis asked her in a calm voice. The woman opened her mouth but couldn't manage to speak. Finally, she shook her head.

"Not broken, then. You're just holding on then?" She nodded, crying now. "Okay, good, honey. You just keep him still," said Travis. He called over to the men, "We're going to need the paddles."

"I'll get mine," said one of them.

Harper stood with his arms around Star, trying to think what he could do. Best just to stay out of the way.

"Young lady," said Travis, "did Roy say anything before this happened? Anything at all?"

"He was going to fix up the truck for me, so it's my fault," said Star, gulping tears. "I was getting some flowers and I told him I'd go in the house and get water for the flowers. I went in the house and found some glasses and filled them up and came out here. See?" She pointed to a couple plastic cups lying in the dirt.

Travis nodded and kept up with his compressions. He picked up Roy's arm and put his fingers on his wrist and turned back to Star. "So when you came out, was he like this?" Roy was lying on an old mechanic's creeper.

She started crying again. "When he wouldn't say anything, I pulled him out. He didn't look like he was breathing and I couldn't find a pulse, so I tried to do that." She pointed at Travis. "Like they said in health class." She buried her head against him again, and he could feel her sobbing. "Dad," she whispered into his shirt, "is he dead? God, what did I do? I didn't know what to do."

She looked up at him, and he thought for a minute that he might cry along with her. "No, honey, you did right, just exactly right," he said. He was out of practice with this stuff—maybe he'd never been there in the first place. He patted her shoulder with a steady rhythm, the way he had when she was a baby.

They had the defibrillator in place. Travis gently moved his inert wife out of the way and nodded. They shocked Roy then. The machine made a little buzzing sound and his shoes lifted off the ground. They watched the little monitor they'd attached to him—everyone motionless for a moment.

Please, Harper prayed to the machine.

"We're good," said one of them, and everyone was breathing again. "Let's get going. Let's get him in the rig." Travis pulled out a backboard and joined the three other men around Roy's body.

Star watched all this with a grave, adult look on her face Harper had never seen before. She tore away from him and ran toward the men, as they counted together and, in a practiced motion, pulled Roy onto the backboard. She jumped up and down. "Hurry, hurry, please," she said.

Celeste caught her and held on to her arm so that she wouldn't get in the way. "It's okay," said Celeste.

They loaded him into the ambulance. "We've got you now, Roy," Travis said loud enough for them all to hear. "It's going to be okay," he said, but there was no indication that Roy even knew he was in the world.

Roy

From down in his hole, he heard the big diesel engine of their fire truck. It was idling, just waiting for someone. "Let's get going," one of the guys yelled, and he realized it was him they were waiting for. He needed to get going, he needed to put his boots on and climb into the truck and get to the fire or the wreck or whatever it was, but for the life of him, he couldn't do it. It was these cold mornings, wasn't it? It was so cold sometimes, he had a hard time getting his muscles warmed up, getting himself out from under the covers. He took a deep breath, to see if he could tell about the coffee. Wilma was always out of bed a bit ahead of him, and it was that coffee, the fresh grounds that smelled so good, that got him up finally on these cold mornings. Nothing yet, in fact nothing that smelled like morning. He breathed in again; even that was hard to do and there was terrible pain. He smelled the dirt, oddly, dust and Valvoline and a tinge of manure, like he'd put his work boots under the bed, and then there was that girl's voice again. "Hurry, hurry, please." Who was she again? Her name was right out there somewhere, but he couldn't quite get to it.

Celeste

Celeste did not want to be the one to call Wilma, but it was too late. Travis had been the pillar of strength in a crisis, as opposed to her own self, who had been a blubbering idiot. He had ordered her to do it, the last thing before he climbed in the ambulance beside Roy. She couldn't so much as say no. In fact, she had been unable to get out a full sentence since they'd found Roy beside the truck with Wilma's near-hysterical granddaughter doing chest compressions on him. At this point, she had to admit that at least Star had done something, which was better than she could say for herself. So she was not an ideal candidate for this notification job, and then there was the matter of what to say. As far as she could tell, they still hadn't pieced together what happened. It looked like maybe Roy had had a heart attack or something. He had been working on the truck, maybe, but who did that kind of thing in his good pants? This little Star creature hadn't been able to tell them much, and was at this moment hanging on to her daddy and making baby mewing sounds.

"Why don't we all go up to the house and get water or something," said Josh. He favored his daddy more than Celeste when it came to temperament.

They all trudged up the driveway. Celeste came last, trying to plan whatever she needed to say to Wilma. Best to call right away. There was no telling.

Inside the house, there was an eerily normal silence. There was a little dust settled on the tables and on the floorboards; there were Roy's things, his work boots, his books, his coffee cup from yesterday, all undisturbed. Celeste had not been in the front room in a long time. There was a nearly brand-new TV on a stand in the far corner where there had once been Roy's ancient crank-up Victrola. Beside that was a cabinet where Roy had hidden bottles of liquor. They'd met over here, Roy and her and a few others, for some midnight parties. This was way, way back. She'd been as young as Josh then, maybe younger, and Roy in his late twenties. She wondered if he was dead by now. He had looked completely gray when they put him on the truck. In his twenties, dancing, laughing, telling off-color jokes and then snap, dead.

"The phone's back there," said Harper, pointing to the kitchen. Celeste looked at him. She didn't know him really, except what she'd heard. Why couldn't he call Wilma? They were related. They had been. He was avoiding her gaze, the coward, and seemed intent on getting the girl settled on the couch. Josh was running to get her water.

She found the phone on the wall in the kitchen and then just stared at it for a minute and tried to think about how she would like someone to break this kind of news to her. She would want the person to ease into it a little, not tell her right off the bat. She picked up the receiver, but she didn't have the number. There was a little delay while they came up with it. Star remembered finally.

"Tell her I called the ambulance right away," said Star. She started sobbing again. "Don't tell her he was under the truck." Harper and Josh rushed over to reassure her for the umpteenth time that this was not her fault. Celeste could not help but notice that Josh's attentions included stroking the length of the girl's comely arm.

Wilma answered the phone on the fifth ring.

"Hey, hon, it's Celeste."

"Celeste. How are you?" Somehow hearing Wilma's voice brought the whole thing home to her. She sounded happy to get her call—*How are you? I am dandy!*—so content with her life. And now, a few words more and it would all be gone.

"I'm fine, hon. Listen, I'm out here at Roy's farm."

"You are? What are you doing there?" Celeste didn't like the way Wilma emphasized *you*, like Celeste had done something. She looked around the kitchen, which looked like a woman hadn't been here in about fifty years. The old Victrola was on the far wall now. There were all kinds of magazines and catalogues piled up on it. "Hello? Hello? Celeste?"

"Yes." She couldn't think of what to say next.

"Celeste? Is this one of those calls, then? You know, one of those calls, woman to woman? Do you have something to tell me?"

"Yes, yes, I do." Wilma knew that something was up. Women had a second sense about these things. They could see trouble coming a mile away.

Celeste heard Wilma take a deep breath. "Okay, then."

"Well," said Celeste, "I'm over here at Roy's farm, Wilma."

"So you've said. I suppose you've been there a lot lately."

"No, just today," said Celeste. "Travis and I got a call and we rushed over."

"Wait," said Wilma. "Travis is with you?"

"Actually, he's not. He went with them."

"With who? Went with who? You're not making sense—"

"If you'd just hear me out—"

"Wait, dear, is Roy there? Put Roy on the phone."

"No. I can't, that's why I'm calling. He's not here. He's been taken to Baptist a few minutes ago."

"Baptist Hospital?" Celeste had seen this before at work. She'd have to repeat everything a few times. Shock made it hard to get the facts into a person's head.

"Yes," she said. "Now, deep breath and I'll explain. Where are you right now?"

"On the phone." Wilma sounded like she was in another country now, and slipping further away. "Baptist? What happened? Is he okay?"

Celeste gave herself a moment to collect the relevant information in her head, and then she parceled it all out to Wilma as best she could. Once she thought Wilma had it, at least the basic facts, she took a page from Travis's book and gave her orders. "Okay, you go over to Baptist now, to the emergency room. Careful driving now. Harper's here with your granddaughter, so don't you worry about her."

She said these things several times, and Wilma quickly repeated them, in a hurry now to get to Winston. She hung up, and Celeste stood there in the kitchen for a moment with the receiver in her hand. She hoped she'd done all right. She took a few steps across the yellowed linoleum floor and stopped, wanting a single moment of suspension between today and the time long ago when someone had last cranked up that Victrola. She remembered Hank Williams and other folks that they had all been crazy for back in the day. She remembered Celeste Clay, sneaking out across the fields, running up the driveway with dew all over her shoes, beautiful then, lips like Betty Grable, running with dew on her shoes, carrying with her the kind of hope you can only have when you're very young. She remembered Roy Swan, wavy hair, animated eyes, handsome as the day was long, stretching out his hand to pull her toward him as they danced.

Danced in a time when he was not yet completely out of her reach. She had felt nothing even resembling regret for a very long time, and she did not now, except, of course, for the reminders: the Victrola, the fishing gear hung on the wall rotting, the hum of the old refrigerator that would give up the ghost any day.

Wilma

The doctors were describing the machines to Wilma, giving her chapter and verse on this device and that, telling her what tube was stuck where on Roy. They gently reminded her that he was not conscious, that he could not breathe on his own, that they were all hoping for the best, but she had to be prepared, *prepared for the worst.* They were telling her these things as she stood in the hall outside the hospital room, *his room.* Oddly, she felt like a little child on Christmas morning standing at the top of the stairs, waiting to go down and see what Santa had brought her. She could barely take in a word they said, all for want of nothing, even this vital information, except to see him, to stand by his bed.

This feeling came, she knew, from that hour that she had sat on a dirty plastic chair in the hall in a state of waiting like none she had ever experienced, separated utterly from everything on earth, unable to help Roy in any way that she could think of except maybe to pray, which she did in a silent shameless litany that poured through her mind. She sat on a hard chair, motionless for a whole hour, that hour when doctors and nurses, people in pink shirts and white and blue, people wearing sneakers and nurse shoes, stethoscopes, a young black man rolling a cart bearing a space-age machine, a nurse with a smiley-face button, a short man with wet hair—and who knows who else—had come in and out of that room, working on Roy no doubt, saving his life she hoped but did not know for sure, that hour when almost no one said a word to her, most avoided her gaze as they hurried past and those who bothered to look her way offered nothing more than a half smile that was no reassurance at all.

So, here in this hall where some doctor—she guessed he was a doctor, he was about twenty-five, maybe thirty—was trying his best to explain Roy's circumstances. His heart had stopped for a time but it was going now. A blocked artery in his neck. And now maybe a stroke. The doctor was trying to speak slowly, repeating the important terms: stroke, cardiac arrest, carotid artery, brain damage. She knew that she should be carefully taking all of this in, asking questions perhaps, but those words just floated up in the air like balloons. She could do little more than breathe, as she had not been able to do for over an hour. But she could do that—she could truly breathe in and out now that she knew Roy was alive in there. He was not dead. In a minute, if she would just nod her head to whatever it was they said, she would get to see him.

So of course, when they finally opened the mammoth door to Roy's room, she was utterly unprepared. What she could see of Roy fit no definition that she had of "alive." The room was only half lit, so the details fell away into darkness. There was a fluorescent light shining right down on Roy's face. He was utterly gray; she didn't think it was just the institutional light. She moved toward him, though suddenly she seemed to be wearing a different pair of shoes, as if her low pumps were two sizes too big on this whole new planet of the last three hours. If she didn't pay strict attention, she might walk right out of them. She looked back and saw that the doctors were hovering around the threshold, trying to gauge her reaction, deciding when it was safe to leave her and go on to the next room.

It was surreal, this room with this man in the bed who barely looked like Roy. Sure, there was his nose, his jaw with the little growth of beard that he got by this time of the early evening, just barely scratchy. There by his earlobe was the little brown spot that he would nick if he shaved in too big a hurry. But other than that, other than the plain flesh, the up and down of his chest coinciding with the hiss of the respirator . . .

"Why don't you try to talk to him? Call his name," said the youngest doctor who had been left behind now by his superiors. His overly reverent tone and look of practiced sympathy made Wilma wildly angry. Who was he to see Roy like this, to see her, to tell her to call Roy's name?

"Please!" she said, more harshly than was fitting—though this was probably the guy who had pushed the tube down Roy's throat and had performed who knows what other forms of painful procedures on him while she waited out in the hall. "Just leave us alone for a minute, would you?" She turned back toward Roy. The door whooshed closed.

She could not take it all in. Roy's face had receded somehow, as if everything in him that before had organized the features on his face, set them in motion as if all of this—his intelligence, his wit, everything about him that mattered—was lost, spilled out under that awful truck.

"Roy?" she said, not understanding why she was whispering. "Roy?" Of course, there was no response. He had always been hard to wake up, but she knew that he was not exactly sleeping, not exactly. She did now recall and it was obvious that even if he were awake, he wouldn't be able to speak to her as long as he had that tube. "Honestly, Roy, I really do wish you'd wake up here," she said to him, as if it might be Sunday morning and they were going to be late for church. She surveyed his body for a moment, lifting the covers to find his hand, but it had an IV attached to the top of it and she was afraid she would mess something up if she touched him. She settled finally on his arm, just above the elbow. She grasped it, first with one hand and then the other. It was warm, at least. There was blood pumping through it; she could feel the pulse, could see it recorded on the machine on the far right. That was something. She should be thinking about those things, and not thinking about how this whole situation could not be good, how he could die, or maybe worse, how he could just go on exactly like this. No. Things would get better, and he was alive right this minute. That's what Roy would be saying to her if he were here right now.

She let go of his arm for a moment and located a chair, much like the one in the hall, only this one had a tattered upholstered seat. She pulled it up by the bed so that she could reach under the covers and hold on to that arm. Both hands, she decided. She needed them there, like that would keep him safe, keep him with her while she thought about just what might have gone wrong.

Chapter Ten

Star

Week two in Swan's Knob. Situation: messed up, real messed up. It was hard to know what to do when you were a houseguest and everyone you knew and were almost related to had way bigger problems than yours, like hanging between life and death, okay? One day a little better, maybe, one day a little worse. They'd put a tube in Roy's neck yesterday, for a ventilator. That meant they thought he would be out of it for a while. Nothing anyone could do but wait and see, according to her grandma, who had said this morning, life goes on, get some fresh air with your friend. So.

She and Josh were standing on the edge of the Swan's Knob overlook, just opposite the big pinnacle, where the top of the mountain was so close it looked like you could reach over and touch its granite boulders. It was a beautiful spot, marred only by, well, recent events but also by the presence of a bunch of other people. It was a Saturday, so there were day hikers and some local people who were letting their little kids squeal and laugh and climb all over the rocks.

Josh swept his arm toward the Knob. "It's a monadnock," he said, not like he was proud of himself for knowing the word, but like, *monadnock*, just a fact, a little geographical trivia. He grinned at her then. "Anything else you'd like to know?"

Here's what she wanted to know: did he have any idea how he looked standing there, the sun lighting up his hair, his eyes—a deep green in this light and not ocean blue, God, exactly the green of the pine trees on the top of the Knob—his eyes looking at her like there was not another person on the mountain, not another person on earth? It was freaky, really. She had never done it before, but she just stared straight into his eyes, tried not to blink. He stared right back. It made her heart speed up, and Josh got all spastic for a minute, like he had forgotten how to move his legs and arms in a normal way.

He laughed to cover it up and turned to lean against the rail. "This knob has always looked like a wise old man to me," he said. "A man with green hair and a green turtleneck. Can you see it?"

"No," she said. "It's a mountain."

"Well, yeah, but when you look at something over and over, especially when you're a little kid, it starts to come alive. It's like the mountain was always right over my shoulder, see, when we'd be out in the fields setting out tobacco or something. I'd make up stories. Shit, nothing else to do, you know? Sounds stupid now . . ."

"No," she said. "No, it doesn't. There are lots of places in New Mexico where the rocks look like horses or old Indian chiefs or something. A lot of times, that's where they get their names."

Josh smiled at her, all grateful, like she had saved him from being a total dork. They left the overlook, and headed for the trail. They came to a sign with an arrow reading BIG PINNACLE.

"We'll go down here," Josh said, with a mischievous smile that made one side of his mouth turn up just a little more than the other. "There's something very cool I want to show you."

The trail started with a long staircase of stone that descended into a canopy of hardwoods. As they ducked into the shade, Josh put his hand out for her and she took it. There was not room to walk side by side, but they managed to move along the first easy part of the trail in a slightly sideways fashion, linked together like children playing a game. It was quiet there underneath the trees, and private; Star felt this immediately. They didn't speak down the stretch of the trail that took them across the mountain's saddle.

It was a perfect day. When she looked through the trees, she could see only blue—the blue sky, the blue haze filtering down at some point to the valley, though the land itself was not visible. It gave her the sweet sensation that she and Josh, linked, pulses rushing together, were walking on earth that had been suspended in the air, *terra aeria,* far above everybody and everything, like they were the only people truly, really alive. They approached the first face of the pinnacle. Josh stopped short and Star kept going, smashing into his back. She couldn't tell if she'd done that on purpose, exactly, but it made them giggle. The sound echoed off the stone wall. Maybe it was what Josh had said before, but now that they were up close, the rock face looked like it had been carved in another millennium, by an ancient Picasso or maybe Braque. The rocks were all mismatched noses and stern foreheads, no lips, no rounded chins.

She might've stopped there to take it in, but Josh kept going and she followed. They wound around the mountain, not saying a word, listening to the birds and little animals, squirrels maybe, rustling in the leaves. As they got near the eastern face and turned a little corner, the breeze picked up. Star felt it on every surface of her body, cool and moist like you would never find in New Mexico, air that you could drink into every pore. They were just hiking, okay, no biggie, but somehow she started to think that she and Josh had gotten all wrapped up in this day, in this mountain. That it was all one thing, like breathing in and out, like blood in the veins, like everything. The two of them just kept looking at each other, as if something, something big, was going on.

They came up to a place where a slab of granite had fallen off the face of the Knob and lay flat. "Here it is," said Josh, running up and jumping on top of the rock. "Flintstone's bed. Pretty cool, huh? This was my favorite place when I was a kid. I thought Fred left it here just for me." He sat down and stretched his long legs out in front of him. She followed him and sat as well, but he made no move to take her hand again or even sit close. In a moment, he smiled at Star like he was eight and started singing, *"Flintstones, meet the Flintstones, they're the modern Stone Age family . . ."* The noise made all the birds leave the trees and take off across the valley. This was what he'd wanted to show her. Cartoon furniture. Josh must have seen something on her face because he let the song die with a little croak and then a little red streak grew up his neck. They sat there, quiet again, but it didn't feel the same.

"I always loved that," she said.

"What?"

"You know, *yabba dabba doo* and all that."

"Oh," he said, "yeah."

The heat of the rock was radiating through her jeans now. She lay back and let it heat her whole body. "A hot rock bed," she said. "This is like some kind of spa treatment. I guess this is what Fred and Wilma had going for them."

"Spa?" He looked down at her. Green, green eyes. "Oh, you mean those places with massages." *Maaasages*, he'd said, putting the accent on the first syllable, like he'd never said it aloud before.

"Yeah, massages," she said, pronouncing it the same way.

"Well, maybe that's what you need." It came out halting and barely audible.

"What?" she said, the breathing, the blood all coming back to her, swirling in the air around them.

"Massage," the word barely coming to the surface.

They might have said something else then. He mumbled a few words, she didn't know what she replied. They were talking, she was sure of that, but as they did, he was moving his face toward hers inch by inch. The kiss came like those last words, starting in some faraway corner of their bodies and then surfacing with one breath. Kiss, then kiss. Cheeks, chins, lips and mouth, round and smooth, soft and soft, folded against the heated rock.

She was not sure how long it went on like that. It was like some kind of trance: no thoughts, just the firing of a million fantastic nerve endings. It might have been ten seconds, thirty, two minutes, ten, before they heard the faint rumbling of feet on the trail, followed by a series of high-pitched war whoops. Josh stood and pulled her to her feet just before a swarm of children burst into the clearing and headed for the rock.

They finished their trek around the Knob in no time then, pressing just ahead of the kiddie stampede. They paused only once more at the last overlook before the parking lot, facing south toward Roy's farm and Josh's. He stood real close and had her look down his arm so she could pick them out. He put his other arm around her and laid his hand on the small of her back. For a minute all she could do was feel the imprint of his palm, his fingers. Everything in the valley was just a misty landscape. Finally, she spotted Roy's farmhouse, his barn. She looked for her dad's car—he was staying there to look after things while Roy was in the hospital—and spotted it just beyond the barn.

"Do you know—," she began. Josh curled his hand then, gathering up the fabric of her shirt, flattened it again, and nudged her several degrees east.

"See?" he said, and she could: his place—another barn, another farmhouse, surrounded by tobacco fields.

"You know," he said, "I don't think anybody's home."

Josh

Josh watched her. She stood on the ladder of stairs that led to his room. God. Her head and torso lost in the blackness of the upper floor, her jeans and boots below.

"Wow," she said, standing on her tiptoes. This made her back curve in spectacular form. She took another step up into the dark and called down. "And how did you talk your parents into letting you have your room up here?"

"Their idea. A long time ago." He followed her up the ladder and found her standing in the middle of the room on the braided rug. His mom had given it to him to lay over the floorboards last winter. It was six thirty, near sundown. His parents were at a swap meet in Mount Airy, and her grandmother was at the hospital. There was a soft gray light in the room. He'd never noticed that with the overhead bulb on all the time. The room looked okay, not shabby, not like some kid with smelly socks slept here. It was her, maybe. Like what people said: someone could light up a room.

"So, ZZ Top?" she said. She cocked her head to look at the poster on his ceiling. Her hair (long, dark, like a dangerous cloud) fell over one shoulder.

"Not so much these days," he said.

She wandered over to the poster. On the way, she looked at the things on his dresser: dorky baseball trophy, jar of pennies, half-used tubes of Clearasil (God!), his tape deck. She picked up a stack of his tapes and looked through them. She held up a tape that one of his sisters had given him for Christmas. "You like these guys? Fine Young Cannibals?"

"Oh, yeah," he said. Had he listened to it?

"We played this all the time in Santa Fe. These guys used to be the English Beat, you know."

"Yeah," he said. "Want me to put it on?" But she already had the tape in his deck. The music started. He remembered it then. The guys sounded cool and sort of retro. They had an old-school echo in their mix. He liked it okay, though he should've planned this out, spent less time thinking about kissing Star's breasts. He'd have the perfect music all queued up now. But how could he have ever planned for this? Forget it, this music would do. She was smiling at him the way she had the whole distance around the Knob: lifting up the corners of her mouth and the edge of her eyes at the same time. He hadn't seen her do that to anyone else.

She was still wandering around his room. She came close to the bed. Maybe this would go better than he had any right to hope. Maybe things were more advanced in Santa Fe. Good for one of them to know what she was doing.

He was still standing by the stairs. He'd been planted there ever since they came up. Probably had some dumbass look on his face too. He bent over and tugged on the stairway to fold the steps up. The long spring on the hinge let out an aching creak. The door thumped into place. Josh would hear the same noise a thousand more times in his life, hear it every year of his adulthood when his wife had him retrieve the Christmas ornaments from the attic. The sound would always bring this moment to him: the scent of the wood eaves, his muffled steps across the room, a beautiful young girl in a tattered T-shirt sitting down Indian-style on his rug.

She circled her arms around her knees with one hand clasped around the opposite wrist. He sat down facing her, his muscles as tight as guitar strings. He stretched his legs out to one side. She smiled at him again. She rocked back and forth a little. Her bangle bracelets chimed like they belonged to the music. A silence then, as the first song finished and the second came on. A soulful ballad. He was not sure what happened from there. Hell if he'd ever be able to tell the story, how he'd put the moves on. It wasn't like that. It was like someone had given his body, and hers, a pep talk about what to do. He didn't give out directions or anything. There was no thinking. It was like a horse that knew its way home, or a pigeon, maybe.

He would remember it, though, every second: how he was kissing her face, kissing her lips, how she would lean her head over and there would be her neck, just there, where he wanted it to be and he would kiss it. How his face fell through her hair. How he would put his hands on her shoulders and he would know it was right because they would move just so, and he would press on her shoulders and on her lips and wish that she would fall back to the rug and how she would, like magic, like the force of the ocean. How they crossed over to unknown territory: bare shoulder, fever haze, cloth, buttons melting, scent of skin on skin. They lay down, naked to the waist, twins it felt like, yin and yang. He wanted his ghost to float up from his body and look down on them, but he could not tear any part of himself away. They were sliding their hands over one another.

"Beautiful," she whispered. It was, he wanted it to be, but his dick was straining against his jeans. It was a whole other creature. It was demanding. Star smiled at him sweetly. He had to look away. Demanding. He looked past her face to the poster on the wall. "Outlier," he said to himself. "I am the Outlier." This brought one moment of control; then she tugged on the button of his jeans, and he was lost, in the very best possible way.

Chapter Eleven

Harper

Saturday night was Harper's Sunday morning. It was his church—call it blasphemy—that was the truth. On Saturdays, a couple dozen of the pickers in the county would get together to play music and party on someone or another's porch. Come the real Sunday morning, Harper would be sleeping it off, but Saturday night, it was the whole damn cathedral. Tonight, it was his turn to provide the porch, and since he was staying at Roy's farm taking care of things, he didn't think it'd be any problem for people to gather there. Roy would be okay with it and what Miss Wilma didn't know wouldn't hurt her. All he'd had to do was haul the chairs out on the front porch and put a cooler full of ice on the steps.

About the time he got the whole thing set up, Steve Penley showed up.

"Let's get us a head start," he said, handing Harper a jar of clear liquid with a tiny green peach sitting in the bottom. "Uncle Pete's done real good with this batch." Steve had an engineering degree from NC State and worked for the highway department, but he was a country boy on Saturday night, prided himself on it.

Harper took a short shot by way of honoring Steve and his uncle, then retreated inside to see if he could borrow a bottle or two out of Roy's wine stock right quick. He wanted to be back outside with a glass in his hand by the time people started coming.

Roy had wine in every closet in the house, but most of his own stuff was in the kitchen pantry. As he turned the key that Roy left in the lock, Harper felt a little sad pang. Sure, he was doing what he could for Roy. He'd picked a whole basket of squash this morning and he'd hit the green beans tomorrow. He'd even called that county ag extension guy, Tom Felton, to see what he needed to be doing with all the grapevines. Roy would be happy to know that; he'd be pleased as punch to pull out a couple of bottles for the pickers to drink, more than happy to share that carton of chocolate ice cream that Harper'd had for supper. Still.

Harper grabbed the clipboard that hung from a nail on the second shelf and looked over Roy's scribbled inventory. There was a lot of wine from 1982. He located the bottles in a crate at the far end and took three back out to the porch where Steve was tuning up his banjo.

"Listen to this," he said. "I got it off an old Charlie Lowe recording." Steve was not the best banjo player, not a bit of musical talent, but he knew all the songs, knew the chords, and no one would've thought of leaving him out, though on occasion, as the night wore on, Brother Sully might tell him to tone it down a bit so they could hear the singing better.

In a little while, people started to show up, two or three to a car. Sammy Sparks came first, followed by Clayton Jones, Billy Atkins with his bass, Deanna Lee, and then Brother Sully with a whole gang of boys from over in Round Peak. These last fellows pulled their instruments out of the trunk and tuned up standing out on the gravel. By the time they got into the yard, they had their straps around their necks. They warmed up as they walked, the thin ribbons of music and cigarette smoke swirling around them. They played old-time string-band music, which was all Harper had heard growing up. Now you never knew just who might show on any given Saturday. Tonight, they'd probably play a bit of everything—standard bluegrass, tunes from Surry County and over Asheville way, gospel, folk.

They started up with the songs everyone knew, "Nine Pound Hammer" and "Wildwood Flower." The whole gang was going pretty good by the time his trailer park friend Candace drove up in her old Buick with all the Rondalays. Harper wasn't sure what to expect, but Candace just gave him a quick hug and went to the far side of the porch with her girls. In fact, at the beginning, no one really talked much; they just arranged themselves in the chairs and on the railing in a casual hierarchy that Harper didn't quite understand yet, and joined in playing music like it was an everyday conversation.

The car headlights kept twinkling down Roy's road every few minutes. The newcomers settled in pretty quickly, accepting the wine Harper offered or Steve's brandy, joining in as they saw fit. They played one long tune he'd never heard before, and then it died out, and then someone said, *Well, how about, "Say, Darling, Say" or "Devil in the Strawsack"?* And someone else asked, *In G or A?* And they all laughed and said, *G, you fool,* and started. After a while, some song reminded Billy Atkins of a story about a bear and a spring that had gone dry at the wrong time. Everyone laughed some more, like they had heard the story a thousand times, because they had, but Billy told it anyway, and then that brought to Clayton's mind some other tune, and the music recommenced.

Pretty soon, Candace worked her way to Harper's side of the porch, with one of the Rondalays right behind her. She found a plastic cup and helped herself to the wine and then poured for her friend, a tall girl with long bleached hair and surprisingly perfect teeth.

Candace pointed to Harper's fiddle case: "That's not doing anybody any good in there, you know." Harper shrugged. He'd been a trumpet player, mostly jazz, for his whole adulthood, but there wasn't much call for that in Surry County, so he'd bought a fiddle from a guy at Galax a couple of years back and taken it up. He was nearly tolerable by now, but he hadn't grown up at the knee of Tom Jarrell or any other of those Round Peak greats like some of these boys and girls on the porch, so he wasn't ever going to be real good. He usually waited for the crowd to get warmed up and the booze to go a couple of rounds before he got going himself. Candace gave Harper a creasy smile. "Come on, baby, don't leave that thing in the case all night, now." She poked her elbow into her friend. The friend laughed like the joke was on Harper.

"Girls, girls," he said. "You better watch out, now . . ." He shook his head at them and went back in for more wine. Lord God, this was what happened to him. There was always a woman like Candace, laying it all out for him, just attractive enough to do for the moment. He rummaged around in the wine pantry and ended up pulling out a near-full crate of bottles with a bunch of bells on the label, old Christmas scuppernong wine, no doubt. Harper hoped it wasn't too sweet to drink.

Candace and the Rondalays were singing when he got back outside, which was vaguely disappointing. Harper made up for it by appointing himself the official sommelier, opened some of the wine and tasted it. It was not one bit sweet and nothing near a scuppernong brew, as far as Harper could tell. Maybe this was Roy's first year of cabernet franc—who knew, except that it was fine, mighty, mighty fine. The girls were singing pretty good tonight as well, and started in on another song.

"Belle here wrote this one," Candace said, elbowing her friend again, and then they launched into a sexy girl song, sort of bluesy, *I'm falling off the edge of this cold cruel world,/And into the fire of your heart.* Shit, not bad. Harper thought maybe he really ought to consider putting them in the festival. Hell, he had a lot of time to fill. Wouldn't hurt to have some very local people. Candace was not a guitar player, but the other two girls seemed decent, and that Belle, damn, come to think of it, the girl could sing. She was working it over there across the porch, and maybe he was all ego, but she was working it in his direction. He raised his cup at her and mouthed, fine, mighty fine.

It struck him as he drank his cup dry and poured some more that the whole *mighty fine* business came from Roy. It was what he always said, not just about his wine, but about things in general, those times when the two of them were sitting on this very porch. A couple of guys came over to fill back up. Harper poured the wine and he looked around and counted then. Forty-five. There were forty-five people enjoying the hospitality. Pretty good. Harper raised his glass again, this time up to the stars. A toast. "Roy Swan," he said aloud. A couple of people nearby heard him, a few who knew Roy, a few who didn't, but they all joined him anyway. They said his name all around the porch.

After that, one song sort of flowed into another. That girl Belle, who it turned out was not another Rondalay, but Candace's cousin from Nashville, played some more and then sang like some kind of very cynical angel, and if Harper had not been getting so drunk, he might have made inquiries of both an amorous and a commercial nature. As it was, he didn't feel wholly confident making it across the porch. He had never in his life let a tolerable buzz get in the way of his playing, though, so he did finally take out his fiddle and played along with half a dozen tunes. About two bottles into the Christmas wine, he even took his turn at a little solo break in the middle of "Fire on the Mountain." It didn't suck too badly, though he could have been mistaken. About midnight, he and a couple of the boys headed around the far side of the house to smoke a doobie. They were just about done, when Billy Atkins spotted the bus.

"Lord God," he said. "Man, am I seeing things or is that a big-ass Greyhound bus coming up the road?" Some kind of large vehicle outlined in a host of tiny lights had made the turn onto Roy's farm road.

Sully said, "Maybe they're lost," but Harper didn't understand how something that big could make a wrong turn and end up all the way out here by accident. Whatever it was was barreling down the road toward the house. He wondered briefly if Sheriff Garson conducted raids using these things.

"Do you think it's cops?" he said.

Sully took one last toke on the tiny end of the joint and threw the roach on the ground. "Oh yeah, Harper. It's the man, all right. In a tour bus." He and the other boys laughed.

"Paranoia," someone taunted in the dark, as they all walked back around to the porch. The bus continued to come up the road. Harper felt his pulse speed up, and he tried to take a little inventory of just how ripped he was at this moment. The noise of the engine intruded on the music and some people stopped playing. Harper would have felt better if the bus had showed signs of slowing down as it approached Roy's first streetlight and the row of parked cars underneath, but it blew right on past them. "Mercy me," yelled one of the Round Peak boys as the left fender barely missed his blue pickup. Harper blinked but could see only a blur of trim lights as the thing passed in front of the house. "He isn't going to make it," someone said, in quiet understatement. The spotlight on Roy's barn lit the whole scene: the bus had run out of gravel. It rolled right onto the grass beyond the barn, rolled, rolled, up through the pasture now, no screeching brakes, no noise at all, rolled, rolled, like a ghost bus, no one on the porch breathing, rolled up a little rise, stopped a few feet short of a row of apple trees. Mercy.

For a moment, there was no sound except for the idling of the bus engine. The company on the porch took a breath in unison. The bus, wheel-deep in the grass, seemed to hover over the pasture like an alien spaceship, its headlights illuminating the gnarled apple trees. "Jeeeeesus," said Steve, finally. For about ten seconds, Harper felt sober as a Sunday morning. Everyone was looking at him, as though he should have an explanation for all this, or worse, as if he was in charge of greeting the aliens. He stepped off the porch. One knee buckled slightly, but he steadied himself and started across the yard. After a few seconds, his buddy Steve came stumbling along beside him. He squinted in the dark to see if he could make out the lettering on the bus. He was right up beside the thing before he saw the gilded D plastered down the side. "Delrina!" it said, in ten-foot elaborate script, and in smaller print, "and Little Charlie."

There was a whoosh of hydraulics. The door of the bus opened, throwing out a square of light. Steve and Harper reached it just as a voice called out, "Well, heeeey!" the last word belted out and held a full four counts. It was a sound almost as identifiable as any note in the C scale, Delrina Kay's signature greeting. Harper had no time to react—to be surprised she was there, to be angry that the bus had almost plowed Roy's back field, to wonder what in the world this woman was doing there so far in advance of the festival—none of these things, because in less than a second the owner of the voice, a tiny woman of approximate middle age wearing a turquoise running suit, ventured from the bottom bus step to the surface of the field. The drop was farther than it looked, or Delrina had her own Saturday night already going, because for a minute it looked like she would land face-first in the pasture. She made an awkward lurch forward and then caught herself and stood more or less upright, the whole time with a smile plastered on her face like a veteran performer. "Well, heeey," she said, a little less dramatically, when she finally came to rest.

She looked around for a second, looked at Harper and Steve, and then raised a tiny ring-covered hand to adjust her plastic rain bonnet. Harper's mother had owned several of these at one time, clear accordion hats that folded into a pouch. They used to give them away up at Gregory Chevrolet. Harper wasn't sure where anyone would get one now.

"Well, I hope this is the place, boys, because it's hell to back this rig up," said Delrina.

"What place?" said Harper, still stoned and now unable to leave the rain bonnet behind.

"What place? Well, you know, honey, the place, the place where we're booked to do the festival. Lord, do I need to go back up and get out the paperwork? A farm. Astor's Farm? Shit, that's not it. So and so's farm at sometysomething Knob, where we're doing this . . . Mountain . . . Music in the Shadow of the Mountain or some such. This it?"

"Oh, my God," hollered Steve. "It's Delrina Kay."

"Well, yes, honey, I sure am." She stepped forward, still a bit off balance, to shake Steve's hand. "And you must be Parker, Parker Chilton. We are at the right place. Why didn't you tell me right off?"

Steve took her hand in his two, immediately swallowing it up. "This," he said, "this is a real honor, Miss Kay."

"Sank you, Parker," she said, stumbling over her bottom lip this time.

"It's Harper," said Harper.

"Well, nice to meet you too, Harper. Real nice," she said, with a weirdly executed wink. "Harper and Parker, that's so cute. Cute! You boys twins or something?"

"No, ma'am. I'm Steve. That's Harper," said Steve. He had still not taken his eyes off of her.

"Well, then, where's Parker? I got to find the organizer," she said.

"That'd be me," said Harper. "There's no Parker, it's Harper. I'm the organizer, but you're here a little early." *Two months early,* he wanted to say. *What's with the rain hat?*

"Early? Well, then, what's all that?" she said, pointing an arm toward the crowd on the porch, where a few of the less curious pickers had started up the music again. "Well, heeeey!" she yelled, giving them her onstage wave. She began to charge across the pasture.

"Let's go. I am ready, Freddy."

"Mind the furrows," said Steve. He rushed to catch up with her, but Harper, who had decided that he was quite possibly the most sober of the bunch, got there first. He took Delrina's arm and was about to try to take the whole situation in hand, when she stopped short. They both swayed a bit and then Delrina looked up at the sky like she was about to pray. "Lord God," she said. "When did it stop raining?"

"As far as I know, it hasn't—"

"And you were going to let me go up there to those people in this old thing. Shame on you, honey," said Delrina, whipping the rain bonnet off her head. Underneath was a shock of shoulder-length beaded braids, dozens of them. Harper did not remember this look from Delrina and Little Charlie's last album cover. He was not sure the country community was ready for it.

Delrina saw him staring. "It's wild, isn't it? Little Charlie just hates the new hair, but I tell you what, honey. I hadn't got nothing wild left in my life anymore. I go to bed early, eat right, toe the line. This hair's the only fun I got left. That, and playing some music once in a while. Let's get to it."

"What about Little Charlie?" Harper looked back at the bus, where there was no sign of life.

"Charles. Don't call him Little Charlie, hon. He doesn't like that at all. Not at all."

"Okay. Charles. Should we get him and the rest of your crew? Your driver must be . . . must be a little tired." Or drunk. It occurred to Harper suddenly that it might be his job to feed all these people.

"Oh no, honey. Charles won't be bothering us tonight."

"And the driver?"

"You're looking at her, baby," she said, with another one of those winks. That explained several things. Harper just hoped she had remembered to put the bus in park. Delrina seemed to take a little inventory of herself as they neared the crowd. She tossed her braids around, unzipped her windbreaker six inches or so, and adjusted the ropes of turquoise necklaces underneath. He expected her to climb onto the porch with a star's fanfare, but by the time she got close to the pickers, Delrina seemed nearly shy. "Hey," she said in a normal tone of voice to a few people standing in the yard. "How y'all?" And then she sat down on the porch steps to listen to the music. As he passed her, she pulled Harper's face down level with her own, and with whiskey breath whispered, "What you got to drink? I am real thirsty."

To the credit of all the folks on the porch, no one made any big deal about having a star at their gathering. Of course, by the time she'd walked up from the bus, everyone had to have known that it was Delrina joining them, but apart from a few stolen looks, some whispers in the back, no one said a word beyond hello. Harper loved his buddies for this. In Surry County, it was a big deal to see a star up close, even if she was on Top 40 Country side of things. He knew they would be bragging on this long past Christmas. But for tonight, they wouldn't treat her any different than Candace's Nashville cousin Belle, who already knew Delrina, it turned out. When Harper brought back a cup of wine, the two women were hugging each other's necks, saying how long it had been.

"Girl, I thought you moved to L.A.," said Delrina. "Thought you went Hollywood."

Belle kicked up one of the nicely shaped legs Harper had noticed earlier, and pointed to her white cowboy boots. "Girl, does this look Hollywood to you?"

"Hell, no," said Delrina, accepting the cup of wine and drinking. "How about these?" She tugged at her running pants to reveal her own boots and, Harper saw, a pair of calves that were not half bad. Harper tried to get a little better look at her. She was younger than he'd thought initially, about his age, late thirties, maybe forty, maybe a few years younger. She was an attractive woman, doll-baby eyes set under an overmanicured brow, Cupid's bow lips, nice boobs. The faint light of the porch, mostly a glow from a few candles and the lamps inside the house, was a kind light, he knew. Best then to avoid the sober dawn.

Billy Atkins tapped him on the shoulder, and there was more tok-
ing around the side of the house, more music, and more drinking.
Harper lost track of his duties as host and gradually became too
messed up to be much more than a spectator. He sent Steve in to get
more wine, and at one point, he did stand and give another heartfelt
toast to Roy. There was singing, a lot of singing: Belle and Candace
draping their arms around Delrina, harmonizing on old-time songs,
and then late into the night, hymns. The crowd dwindled slightly
without Harper seeing anybody leave and when he went in to the
bathroom, he saw a few folks crashed on the couch. Sometime later,
Delrina pulled a stool up beside his chair and handed him the wine
bottle she was drinking from.

"So whose place is this again? The winemaker you were toasting
earlier?" Delrina's speech seemed less slurred at this hour, though
possibly Harper just couldn't tell the difference.

"Roy Swan is his name. God bless him. He's had a heart attack
and then that caused some kind of stroke. I'm taking care of the place
for him while he's in the hospital. Cheers, Roy." Harper toasted the
stars again, and wondered if that was bad luck.

Delrina looked around the porch. "You're some caretaker."

"He wouldn't mind."

"I would," she said, "if this was mine." She took the wine bottle
back and took a drink. "Is he bad off?"

"Yes," said Harper. "He's been out more than a week now, so
that's bad. They're not sure—"

"Have you seen him?" She was looking at Harper now like the answer was important.

"No," he said. "I'm not sure what good that would do."

"Maybe," she said, "you need to find out." She fished around in
her pocket and pulled out a cork and stuffed it into the wine bottle.
"Maybe we need to bring this party to him."

It was the kind of idea that could only make sense, if that was even
the word for it, after a night of partying and aliens and something
close to a complete disaster. Just an idea, which was, of course, where
trouble always started.

Roy

Roy heard the whoosh of waves, the tide going in and out with incredible regularity. He saw himself on a beach and then he was a boy standing between his parents. The sun shone on his face, but he could not quite feel the warmth. The waves broke and made foam on the sand at his ankles, whoosh and whoosh. He reached out his arms and his mother grabbed his right hand, his father the left. They lifted him in time with the tide, whoosh and whoosh. And then everything went white, but the sound remained, engulfed him, took over his breathing.

Later, the beach was gone, and the sun, and maybe he was awake now. He could still hear the waves. They broke on his chest. Off in the distance, a melodic laugh began and then was stifled.

Shhh, shhhh, someone called, like the rustle of sheets.

"Well, why, tell me why," said a woman. "Isn't the whole point to wake him up?"

For a time, he was lost in the waves again, and then he heard glass clink against glass.

"Let me help you with that," said a man's voice, one that was familiar, but before Roy could grab on to it, he heard all that glass again. It was a bushel basket collection of those green glass bells, the insulators they used on telephone poles. He and little Celeste were each holding a basket handle and running with everything they had through the apple orchard. The insulators they had swiped from the fallen telephone pole were sliding from one side of the basket to the other, chiming like dozens of champagne toasts.

"What are we going to do now?" Celeste said. Though her voice sounded like a throaty grown woman, she looked up at him with a sweet cherub face.

"Bury them," he says, and she nods, though he hasn't actually said this aloud. They both know, him especially, that they will face the hickory stick if anybody finds out they have run up to the road and raided a downed utility pole ten minutes after a lightning storm, while a live electricity wire was still dancing in the road like a snake.

They head toward his family burying ground. When they get to the hill, they fly up the path like they have wings, like they are angels, and then they dig a hole in white, white sand, though the ground there is red clay. They throw the glass insulators into the big hole, clink and clink, only they are no longer insulators but a mound of sea glass the color of the ocean.

"Bottoms up," says Celeste, over the grave. "Here's to you, Roy Swan. Take a drop and come back to the living."

And then, it is the oddest thing, Roy can taste salt, as if he has dipped his fingers into the ocean, and then he tastes wine, his own fine wine infused with the red clay it was grown in.

Chapter Twelve

Star

Her mother called from Kuala Lumpur just as they were leaving for church. Star was wearing her lacy white skirt, which made her look shiny and new, which was how she felt and how the morning felt, even though she had to go and sit indoors for over an hour. She didn't even care about that because, see, she'd take it all with her. She was walking in some kind of bubble where everything light came in and stayed there. It was like one of those bubbles you made out of dish soap and glycerin, a thin shiny membrane that had surrounded her ever since yesterday afternoon. She tried not to think about it at this moment, there in front of her grandma, because she was afraid that it would show, everything that had happened, including—let's face it—her truly becoming a woman.

When the phone rang, her grandma dropped her keys and rushed to the phone with a jerky walk. It had happened like this a million times yesterday, mostly people asking about Roy. Star wondered if people knew that every call caused Wilma a fit of terror, the kind that made her eyes open up wide and then shudder closed one long moment before she lifted the receiver.

"Hello?" Her grandma's voice did not let on a thing. "Hello. I can't hear you."

Star was lucky that her grandma barely looked at her this morning, hadn't noticed the change, though lucky was not the right way to think about it. Her grandma was worried. Star got that. She did. She was worried too, right on top of the bubble of happiness. It was a sick combination. God, maybe Roy would die, he could really die, at least she thought maybe he could. No one had actually said that, and it was not the kind of thing you ask. She especially wasn't going to ask her grandma. In a way, her grandma looked as if she was walking around inside of some kind of bubble too, only hers was filmy and gray and didn't have a lot of air inside, maybe. Her face was chalky and streaked from putting on her makeup too fast. Star wanted to hug her. She wanted to say a lot of things to her, like, *Sorry, so sorry* and *Do you want me to go back home?* and even, *Can I use the truck to go see Josh this afternoon?* but she didn't say a word because her grandma was too far away. As bad as it looked inside that bubble, it might be worse if Star somehow popped it. That's the way she looked—like if Star said the wrong thing, her grandma might move her face the wrong way, even a little twitch, and she might crumble like chalk into a million pieces.

"Hello? Oh, it's fine now. I can hear fine. Sarah. Sarah, honey, how are you?" Wilma gave Star an anxious look related to the fact that it was time to leave for the service. It was the same time every Sunday. Had Star's mother thought of this? Had she done the math? Sure, there was the international date line and all, but somehow, Star didn't think that was the trouble.

"We're all fine here," Wilma was saying. "What do you think of Malaysia?"

She had been waiting for her mother to call for days, ever since she got to Swan's Knob, ever since Josh, and ever since Roy. Maybe when Wilma told her about Roy's stroke, they would come back.

Star could hear her mother's voice, at least a tinny version of it, coming through the receiver in Wilma's hand. She couldn't make out any words, but she could recognize excitement in the avalanche of sounds her mother was showering on her grandma. Her grandma listened, pacing around the kitchen with a dishcloth in her hand, wiping up invisible dirt.

"She's right here," said Wilma, finally. "She's doing fine. She's a joy, just a joy. She's the toast of East Surry High and has found herself a nice boy to date already . . . No. I'm not kidding . . . Well, yes, sure you can." Wilma looked pointedly at Star now, and said into the phone, "Wait a minute, she was just here. Let me see if I can find her." She put her hand over the receiver, smiled at Star, and said, "Now, there's no need to tell her about Roy at this point. She's halfway around the world, and her knowing and worrying won't do a thing to help any one of us. You hear?" And then to the phone, "Okay, here she is . . . You can ask her all about him . . . We'll talk to you soon, honey. Bye-bye!" This last sounding more cheerful than her grandma had ever sounded in her life.

She handed Star the phone but hovered around still wiping the counters, probably to make sure Star didn't let the cat out of the bag. Star didn't get it. Why didn't she want to tell her? What was going to happen if Roy died? God, her mother would probably be mad at all of them.

She held the phone to her ear and said hello.

Her mother sounded like she was speaking with her lips pressed against a metal screen. "Star? Star? Hi, honey. What's this I hear? A boyfriend already? What's his name? Can this be true or is your grandmother just delusional?"

Beautiful. Star was not sure what she wanted to tell her mom about Josh, wasn't sure what she wanted to "share." That was what Sarah called it, "sharing," said with her wispy, hippy voice, reserved for the most embarrassing topics: tampons, wet dreams, red meat, Republicans.

"Star, can you hear me? Wait until you see the photographs of this place. It's sooo amazing. Last night, after dinner, we walked . . ." Half a world away from Kuala Lumpur and from her mom and her step-dad, from her little half sister, Star stood in the pool of sunlight that shone through the kitchen window. She kept the handset to her ear, but found the OFF button with her thumb. When her grandma turned from her to stow the butter in the refrigerator, she pressed it down quickly and released it. "Star?" her mother said, not so easily de-terred. "Star?" Star pressed the button again, and this time held it down.

Josh

Josh sat on the church steps, feigning boredom, nodding politely to anyone who came into the building. Of course, he was watching for her, any sign of her—her grandmother's LTD, the old Chevy truck, anyone with long hair and a beautiful neck. Since yesterday afternoon, she had invaded his brain. He couldn't think of another thing. He kept replaying every minute of what happened, or else he had to recite a string of prime numbers. This was the only way to prevent a mishap on the steps of the Lord's house. 1, 2, 3, 5, 7, 11, 13 . . . It was like a disease out to obliterate the rest of his life: before and after. He had known her thirteen days. He had been alone with her exactly twice, and the first time didn't count because it was after the ambulance took Roy away.

She appeared now with her grandmother at the far end of the sidewalk. They had parked the car across the street. He stood without thinking about it, but it was too early and he had nothing to do with his hands as they approached. God, she was beautiful. It was like that Shakespeare thing. She was the sun.

Yesterday afternoon, once they had—God, even thinking the word got him into trouble—17, 19 . . . Afterwards, they hadn't talked much. She seemed okay, not hurt or anything, but there'd been some blood. He'd worried.

This morning, she wore all white, smiled at him as they came up the walk. It must be okay, then. He smiled back, tried to speak to Miss Wilma. He managed a mumble that his mother wouldn't have been proud of, but she just charged past both of them.

Star noticed. "Late," she said and shrugged.

He looked at her for a place that he could touch. Mr. and Mrs. Snow were helping Mrs. Reardon out of a Camry in the handicap space just across the lawn. He reached up and clasped the crook of her arm with two fingers. He imagined he felt her pulse under his thumb.

"Ow," she said and laughed, and he moved his hand to her back as they walked into the narthex. She leaned close to him. "Let's sit in the last row," she whispered.

He was not sure what kids did in Santa Fe. He had a feeling now they were more advanced. He wanted to tell Star that church in Swan's Knob was not like going to the movies. It was not dark, for one thing, and Mrs. Snow would be standing right behind them in a minute, ready to note any indiscretion and report back to his mother in the middle of the grocery store line next week.

Star took his hand and led him across the back of the church to the pew in the far left corner. He did not have the guts to tell her that this was Mr. White's normal spot. What was worse was that he was out of place as well. Since he was a kid, he had been assigned the third row on the right, where his parents could keep an eye out for him and his siblings from the choir loft. Thankfully, he didn't see any of them at this moment.

He opened his bulletin and pretended to study it. Star did the same, though she giggled slightly and fanned herself. A small breeze crossed his face, bringing her scent with it. 23, 29, 31 . . . Yesterday, after he'd taken her home, he'd come back to his room and sat there on the rug for a long time. The air still smelled good from her breathing it.

Miss Wilma came in through the side door and climbed up to her organ. She didn't check to see where Star was sitting as far as he could tell, and started right into playing. It sounded okay. According to his dad, you never knew what Miss Wilma might make people listen to these days. Josh didn't know much about it. He'd heard her play a couple of things that sounded like the soundtrack of a scary movie, and once, there'd been a choir anthem where a few people had to shake maracas. That had really set his dad off, but Josh didn't see anything wrong with it.

Star put her bulletin down, crossed her legs, uncrossed them. She watched her grandmother for a moment, and bit her lip, worried. Josh kept his head facing forward, but cut his eyes to the side so that he could observe her, her breasts rising and falling with each breath. He wondered how long he could keep her. *Please God.* 37, 41. This was nothing to pray for, he knew. His parents filed in with the rest of the choir. The first hymn began and he found it in the hymnal and held it open for her, though she didn't sing. He didn't either, but mouthed the words in case someone was looking. When the prayer of preparation began, he couldn't help it. He prayed anyway. *Let me keep her. Please, God. Let me keep doing what we did yesterday, 43, 47, and I will marry her sometime, I will and I will bring her here on Sunday mornings, that's what I'll do, right after we do it and it will all be okay, okay in your sight, and in Mrs. Snow's, for thine is the kingdom and the power.*

Wilma

She has been sleepwalking through the entire service without missing a note: a simple Bach prelude, a hymn or two, just numbers in the hymnal, all under her fingers, not really getting to her brain. She has done fine, and is comforted, in fact, by the familiar ritual. She is fine. That's what she has been saying in the choir room this morning, when they've asked, and they've all asked her, every person in the choir. Celeste has insisted that she and Travis will be over to sit with her in the hospital this afternoon. Cynthia Trolley has once again offered herself as a substitute organist, but Wilma has refused. She needs Cynthia's high clear soprano for the anthem.

So, by the eleven o'clock hour, Wilma has waved everyone off and climbed into her organ loft. She is enduring the service so far. Somnambulant, that is the word that she wants. She says it to herself instead of thinking of her still, unknowing husband lying over in Baptist Hospital with his brand-new tracheotomy, a hole they put in his windpipe on Friday, a hole he doesn't even know about yet. Somnambulant. She says it over and over, somnambulant, somnambulant—anything to keep the word "tracheotomy" out of her head—and now comes time for the anthem. It's another Fauré piece. She pulls the sheet music out and gets set, and then looks up at the choir. They are ready, poised on the edges of their seats to stand at her signal, so she raises her left hand so they can see it, and then scoops the air to bring them up. She is surprised when for once they do it in unison, and then she is unnerved by the attention of their thirty sets of eyes. She looks over at Travis to see if he might want to shake his head one last time in derision, but he is all business, broad shoulders under the cream pleats of his robe, clasping his music folder between two mammoth hands.

The first part of the piece is a cappella, so she gives them the notes softly on the organ with her right hand and then counts out the beat with her left. She hears their collective breath on the last beat and then the perfect unison attack as she directs it. There is music, then, filling the space where a moment before there was only musty chapel air. It is an everyday miracle, more than the sum of the blended voices and their owners. Once captured in this tide, the singers out-do themselves. The anthem is better than when they practiced it, more beautiful, and to Wilma's sad and desperate ears, more holy. As she looks out over the faces of her choir, it occurs to her that they are doing this for her. A gift: their best effort, inspired.

She is unprepared for the effect that this has on her. The sound waves crash into her body and wash over the seawall. The choir is coming to the part where the organ joins in, so she looks down to find her place, and as she does, tears splash on the keys. This is a first in her entire professional career, spanning how many decades? How many years? She madly tries to compute the number as a way to pull herself from this moment, from the flood of everything that is rolling from her eyes and down her face and onto cream pleats. Thirty years? Forty? She can't lift her hands from the keyboard long enough to wipe her face, so she has to let everything go. Fortunately, the choir is able to find its own way through the music, and she does not even need to worry if she is following the choir or they are following her. She bows her head, first to make sure that she continues playing decently, and second, to hide her face. The choir has seen her crying, that can't be helped, but she would like to avoid a display for those in the congregation with a view of the organ loft.

By the time they reach the end of the piece, there is so much water on her chin that it actually drips when she is forced to look up to conduct the ending. She sees then that Cynthia Trolley, Celeste, and several of the older women look ready to cry as well, and she manages a smile to convey the fact that she is fine, really she is. She does not dare glance out at the congregation, though she doubts that anyone has noticed anything unusual. The choir settles in their seats, stows their music folders. Wilma looks across the church and sees that Reverend Berry, usually making his way to the pulpit by now, is still seated and he is looking straight at her with a pastorly expression.

Wilma cannot explain it, but this makes her mad, this look on his face, this mixture of concern, pity, and maybe, a bit of eagerness. She tries to look back at him with a completely composed face, a face that says that he may have mistaken a bad case of sweaty hot flashes for a crying jag, one that says, *Get on up there and preach, for God's sake, and leave me alone,* but the man smiles at her, one of those sugary saintly smiles that she cannot abide, and then he stands and mounts the pulpit and Wilma knows that she is in for it.

Reverend Berry is a man who is sure of himself. If you asked him, though you wouldn't want to in Wilma's opinion, he would say that all his certainty comes from his love of the Lord Jesus Christ. Wilma is not so convinced. It seems to her that this man might love the sound of his own voice more than anything else. "Friends," he calls out ten times each Sunday, hanging on the consonant combination at the end: "Friennndddsss, I'm here to tell you today . . ." Wilma hates this kind of familiarity in the pulpit, and she has a strong notion that she is about to hate whatever he might say now.

"Well, amen and amen on that," he says.

This was another one of his catchphrases. He turned his rotund body and swept his arm with its long preacher sleeve toward the choir assembled behind him. He went on for a few minutes about the anthem, managing to take something truly beautiful and walk all over it. Wilma tried not to listen, but nevertheless she was obliged, with all eyes on her and the choir, to sit up on the bench without moving her face, which was in need of some repair, though that was of little use since the tears continued to run down her cheeks. Her hiccups started at the moment that the man said, "And we are especially thankful to have Miss Wilma with us this morning—"

The first hiccup, a complete surprise, was surely audible in the front pews. It nearly launched her off the organ bench, just at the moment that people in the congregation were craning their necks to look at her and throw a sympathetic smile her way. Several more came in rapid succession as Reverend Berry described, in stark detail, his visit with Roy in the hospital. Most of what he said was lost on her then. She raised her hand to her mouth as she struggled to stifle either sobs or hiccups or whatever other animal sound that might be trying to emerge from somewhere in the pit of her stomach. She was two seconds from throwing herself on the floor and thrashing about when the sympathetic remarks were concluded, apparently, with the reverend turning around to her once more and saying, "And you know, dear sister, that His eyes are on the sparrow . . ."

She could not fathom in a million years what he might mean by that, but it was not important. The man had stopped finally and was bowing his head for his presermon prayer and mercifully, everyone else did the same. The anger returned as the hiccups receded. This was big anger, not the small irritation she might feel with a student who hadn't practiced her lesson or a butcher who didn't trim the beef properly. No. She was mad as a hornet at just about everybody she could think of. This stupid idiot of a preacher, all those people sitting in the pews all sorry for her, the choir—even though they had just sung their hearts out. Every one of them, everything they did was feeling sorry for her, which was something she really, really hated, and what's more, it seemed to her that they were homing in on her tragedy, hers and Roy's.

And they were all thinking now—oh, she just couldn't stand this—they were thinking, *What a pity, what an awful shame. The two of them found each other so late in life. They went to all that trouble to get married, to set up that pretty house, and look what's happened.* And now they were looking at her in that same way they looked at her when Harry killed himself. They were wondering how she would react, if she would crack. She knew she should feel more charitable herself, she knew they meant well, but she could not feel this in her heart. In a small town, sometimes it felt like this kind of tragedy was just grist for the mill, that little extra drama that people needed to make their week a little more interesting. She hated it, this being the grist, being the tragedy.

Reverend Berry went on with his sermon, the sheer flow of unintelligible words reminding her of the time that she and Roy had been on a wine tour in France and she'd spent the day listening to a hail of foreign words that bounced against her until she thought they would make her sore. That was what she felt now, hailed on, weary beyond belief, mad at everybody, mad at God, beyond belief.

And while she was at it, she would admit this to herself. She was just as mad as she could be at Roy Swan himself. Yes. Roy. Her beloved, who had taken her to France, a place she'd never thought she would go, and who had taken her that night when she was so tired from being a stranger, had taken her back to their little room with the lumpy thin mattress and made the whole thing right. He had been more gentle than she could imagine and he had touched her on her arms and legs and all over her body in a way that was more than sweet and she had found it pretty easy then to completely forget about how dog-tired she had been.

She was aware that she ought not to be reviewing these things in church, right here in the middle of the sermon, which turned out to be, as far as she could tell, about the story of Lazarus. Again. So she allowed herself for just five minutes to wallow, to roll herself in that night in Beaune, and then in a million other times just like that, when Roy Swan had made her change her mind or her own bad mood or had surprised her with his love. This was why she was so mad at him now, for leaving her, for leaving her but not quite leaving yet, so that she had some room to hope, some awful hope, and some awful bad feeling that he might not come back and that if he came back, it would be as something not much more knowledgeable than one of his prize tomatoes. It pained her to think of this now: it was a sin to think of the worst. Well, hell, she'd already thought about how she was mad at God, hadn't she? And while she was thinking about that, and the preacher was winding up that sermon and asking them to bow with him, she would say it to God now, as a prayer: *I am mad at you.*

Star

Star could not sit still. She could not find a comfortable position on that hard bench. She was not the twitchy sort, okay? She could sit in a meditation class with her mother for an hour or more. She could sit perfectly still, center her energy, do that low humming, *ooomm*, follow her breath. No problem. But this bench was just two inches too deep for her legs, and Josh, God, Josh was watching every little thing she did out of the corner of his eye. She liked this in a way. It made something swell up in her chest, squeezing her breath out of her. Maybe this was the way it was going to be now: Him, next to her all the time watching. Her, forgetting how to breathe. Maybe this was love, but she didn't think so.

She tried once again to shift from one butt cheek to another and concentrate on the service. It was almost over, as far as she could tell. It had never been this boring when she had come to church before, but that was mostly at Christmas and maybe once at Easter. The minister had finished his talk, but it looked like he was going to pray again. Yep, everybody in the church bowed their heads. She leaned forward and snuck another glance at her grandmother. The two of them were the only ones in the church with their eyes open. Her grandma was paging through the hymnal, getting ready for the last song. She was a scary white: she had been ever since the anthem. Star had wondered at first if her grandma had been disappointed by the choir's countrified pronunciation of French, but it had been the best thing in the service, a beautiful song by Fauré, the bulletin said, "Cantique de Jean Racine." It had been full of interesting minor harmonies that Star was going to try to keep in her head so that she could play with them later. She always needed new stuff for her own songs, and the harmonies made the music sound like it didn't belong on earth, much less in a little country church.

She had been thinking about this, about the chords and things, so she couldn't be sure what had happened exactly, but when the choir had gotten to the most incredible part, the part about God pouring out the fire of His grace, her grandma had started crying. At least that's what it looked like. It was hard to be sure, because she had never even seen her cry before. She felt bad for her grandma. And she felt bad for being her selfish self, sitting there thinking about her guitar and about Josh and what song she would write for him and about what they did and not thinking about Roy and not even praying for Roy. She wasn't sure if it would do any good, but while she was here, she would go ahead and do it, she would pray for him. *God watch over Roy. Make him better.* There.

People were standing up for the last song, and she and Josh did too. By accident, they ended up with their hips leaning against one another. Star felt a charge run up her leg. Like lightning. Neither of them moved, but Star decided she would cover her bases and send Roy some of this good energy as well. So while everyone else sang, she would center herself, she would follow her breath. She would breathe the breath of God and send lightning, all that lightning to Roy.

Chapter Thirteen

Celeste

"I think they made these mashed potatoes with something other than potatoes," said Travis. They were eating their Sunday dinner in the hospital cafeteria. The food was bad, Celeste had reminded him of that beforehand, but he had insisted.

"Probably powdered," she said. "Want some of my Jell-O?" She sat back and eyed the table of her friends over by the window, a little group of nurses and LPNs who usually stopped in for coffee before their shift. They smiled at her over Travis's left shoulder. She felt like a calf separated from the herd.

"No, I paid for this, I might as well eat it," he said. He had dragged the sleeve of his suit jacket through his gravy. Grease. It would never come out, which was just as well. Celeste had seen about enough of that seersucker over the past few decades. She'd be happy to retire it right directly into the trash.

She picked up Travis's cup and hers and headed up to the coffee urn. Most of the time she got her coffee as she went through the line, but she knew to wait to get Travis's at the end of the meal. He wouldn't drink it unless it was burning hot. When she got back to the table, he had discovered the gravy and was making it worse with the ice water from his glass.

"I'll take care of that later," she said.

Travis took the coffee cup from her and brought it straight to his mouth. He always drank it black. Before Celeste could sit back down, he checked her plate and said, "Are you almost done there? I've got to get up to see Roy." He slurped down most of the coffee in one gulp. The sound, loud and just unusual enough to be heard clear over at the window tables, made Celeste want to reexamine every single decision she had ever made in her life.

She folded her napkin and laid it over her plate. "Now, Travis, I've told you. I'm not sure you can go up. Wilma said no visitors when you asked her this morning."

"She didn't mean it. They always say that, especially people like her. They don't want anybody's help, even when they need it."

"I didn't get the idea—"

"Roy's my friend. He'd want me there. Besides, we're talking about possible healing here, salvation even." Celeste didn't know what to say. Roy wasn't Travis's friend. Travis didn't have friends, as far as she could tell. Travis stood up and walked around to pull her chair out. She noticed the gravy had dripped down the front of his pants as well. He bent over and whispered, "Come on, sugar, you just take me up there with you. No one will mind."

She had gone over this with him in the car. She'd told him she could lose her job for such a thing, though this wasn't strictly true. In fact, he was right: no one would notice. She tried to think fast as they walked past her friends and down the corridor toward the elevators. "Why don't you go into the gift shop and pick out a card or a little gift or something?" she said. "I'll go up and check on Roy and come back down and let you know how he's doing."

She didn't want Travis up in Roy's room. There were a million reasons why this was a bad idea. Roy, of course, probably wouldn't know any different one way or the other, which was part of why it bothered her. She wouldn't want someone looking at her if she were lying there, wearing next to nothing, one corner of her mouth sagging down. She would especially not want Travis, who would provide the details in grave tones to every person he saw over the next forty-eight hours. She paused in front of the gift shop and waved at her friend Clara, who always volunteered there on Sundays. "Go on now. That woman in the pink jacket will help you pick out something real nice."

Travis paused with his back to the door and gave her a suspicious look. "What do you mean, me get Roy a card? Men don't get each other cards. Besides, I got everything he needs right here." He fished around in the pocket and brought out a tiny glass vial with a black top. It was filled with a clear liquid. For a moment, she thought he was intending to foist one of his home remedies on Roy. At home, he was all the time trying to get the children to use that nasty Raleigh's Ointment on every blessed thing from jock itch to ringworm.

Travis held the vial delicately in his calloused fingers, held it up to the light. Celeste saw then a small cross etched in the glass and caught the unearthly shine in Travis's eyes, and she knew.

"Where'd you get that?" she said. She did all their shopping and she had no clue where you bought holy oil, if that was what it was.

"Mail-order catalogue," he said. "You'd be surprised what all they got—prayer cloths, baptismal vestments." She had to wonder how Travis thought up these things. Just last month, he'd had an altar call in the middle of his Sunday school class. And several times lately, he'd spoken to her about going down to be rebaptized in the Ararat River. None of this was standard Methodist practice. No matter. He was smiling at her now, and here came the scripture: "He anointeth my head with oil—"

"Yes, yes, your cup overflows," she said, a little more harshly than she'd intended.

"Surely goodness and mercy!" he said, the last word a rebuke. They stood there for a moment and stared at each other. Celeste was afraid to say anything else. There had been many times she'd made Travis angry, which could have ugly consequences, especially in public. But right now she wasn't sure he was mad exactly. He was too quiet. She looked into his eyes, trying to make up her mind, and darned if he didn't look hurt more than anything else. It almost looked like he would cry.

"I'm going to be late for my shift," she said.

"Look," he said, "this is important. Take me up there." He put his hand between her shoulders then, and steered her toward the elevators. It was a familiar sensation, one that she usually found comforting, but today he pressed his palm, his fingers against her with a force just a hair stronger than it should have been.

Wilma

She would ask herself later why in the world she had left Roy's room, why she had wandered down the hall and pressed the elevator button. She could never quite remember—a candy bar from the gift shop? A breath of air not processed in a hospital building? No matter, the doors opened. It had seen better days, this particular car. It had the same scuffed tile as the ward halls, the same wall covering (probably a hygienic thing). She stepped in and joined the other refugees, everyone a walking tragedy, everyone with a ready story of some loved one on the edge of death or maimed for life.

The hospital was such a public place, too public to bear almost, for such very private occurrences—death, birth, and occasionally, healing. She would never get used to seeing perfect strangers rolled down the halls, unconscious, fresh from the violence of some surgical procedure.

She took a step toward the front of the car, avoiding the gaze of her fellow occupants, hoping to avoid even the most cursory of contacts. Yesterday, she'd had a long conversation with a long-haul truck driver with a wife in ICU. The man had told her his whole story—of his wife and her stomach, filled with cancer, of her chest cavity and its drain and its sepsis, all this and the woman only forty-five. Then he'd asked her and she'd found herself telling him all about Roy. Had it helped them at all, her and this trucker, to float the sorry details between their two blue plastic chairs that had been nailed to the floor in facing rows? She hoped so, she really did.

The elevator door opened onto the lobby, full of the same people you saw every year at the Winston fair. Wilma stepped out into the fray, spotting Travis Diamond just a few seconds too late. He fairly ran at her, all red faced in his ill-fitting seersucker suit.

"Wilma!" he shouted. He had been waiting for her. Celeste was right behind him, wearing that horribly dogged expression she got when Travis was about to have the prayer, or else misbehave in some other way.

"Wilma, Wilma." Travis took both of her hands.

Over his shoulder, Celeste flattened her mouth out and lifted her eyebrows in silent warning. *This is going to be ugly,* said that expression, *and there is not a thing I can do about it.* "I've got to go clock in," she said.

"We'll just come on up with you. Roy's right on your floor," said Travis.

Travis meant well; everybody did. But Travis would not be going to Roy's room. Wilma give him a smile to buy time while she thought of a nice way to say no. But it was the oddest thing: instead of coming up with words, her brain gave her a strong craving for a holster, a holster containing some kind of gun, like on that *Gunsmoke* show Roy had liked so much. For the first time in her life, though she couldn't say why exactly, she wanted to draw a pistol on this man and tell him, *Hold it right there, buddy. You are not going near my man.*

It was Celeste who found the words: "No. No, Travis honey, you stay down here and visit with Wilma," she said. Sweet Celeste, sweet and meek Celeste, was Wilma's sidekick and her genuine friend. Celeste knew. She knew it all.

"Well," said Travis.

"Yes, stay. I could use a breather, let me tell you," said Wilma. *Kerpow, kerpow.*

The elevator doors opened again and Celeste popped in. "I'm about to be late for my shift," she said, waving. "I'll see you later."

Travis stood flat-footed beside Wilma, but only for a moment.

"So, how's Roy doing?" he said, making a little melody of the last word, sounding every bit like their pastor.

"Not good," she said, feeling less murderous, but still sick of all this goodwill, sick of smiling.

"I want you to take me up to see him," he said.

"Travis, that's not such a—"

"I know, I know you think he doesn't need visitors. But he needs me, trust in this, Wilma. I feel a little strange telling you, but I've got to. I've been called, called to anoint our brother, to claim his healing. It's as simple as that. It came to me in church this morning long about the end of the sermon."

Celeste

Roy had been on her unit for over a week now, and though she had read every word of his chart every day, she had hardly darkened his door. The other girls on the floor understood—he was a friend. This happened to all of them now and then. Angie Glass's mother had actually died in one of their beds last year. But today was Sunday. They were always shorthanded on Sundays. She signed in and checked with Sally Rothrock, the RN on the unit. The other nurse was busy with a discharge, and Sally had a real problem down in 405, a woman just admitted in the last hour, breathing issues, thready pulse, the doctor on his way in. Sally asked her to check on Roy and three other patients. Celeste couldn't say no.

Celeste looked at Roy's chart first. It hadn't been a good night. Roy's breathing had slowed, and the nurse had turned up the ventilator. That had helped, but overall the signs weren't good: diminished heart rate, minimal urine output, everything grinding down. She thumbed through the other patients' paperwork, all routine, and then gathered the things she needed. She made her way down the corridor. At the far end, something had happened to one of the fluorescent light fixtures. It blinked on and off maddeningly. She ducked in and out of the rooms, recording temps and other vitals. Each time she reentered the hall she looked to see if Wilma had come back upstairs, or worse, Travis. No sign of either of them. Poor Wilma down in the lobby, handling Travis. Celeste felt bad, but she just could not control Travis twenty-four hours a day. Her job was up here. It was time to go take care of Roy.

She took a breath as she reached the threshold, as if the air in the darkened room wouldn't keep her alive. She walked in, telling herself he was just one more patient, but one of his arms was dangling off the side of the bed and when she saw that, it liked to kill her then and there. It was so pitiful, so awful pitiful and happening to a man who hadn't had a minute of pitiful in his life.

She rushed across the room and grabbed his hand, but she didn't put it back by his side. She couldn't help it, she held on to the hand, stroked it a little. She looked at him, looked at his face, his lips. He had damage on the right side, that was easy to see. What didn't show was the brain swelling. It was impossible to tell just how bad it was, just how many of the cells had been destroyed. The longer he went like this, the worse it got, and the less chance of recovery. Soon, his face would swell too, and his hands. They'd have to kick up the ventilator, though that would only prolong it. To distract herself from this, from what might come over the next few days, she tried to picture Roy in another time, a happy time. Tried to think of what his lips had felt like when he had kissed her that once—his lips when they were not thin with age and his mouth not creased and turned down on itself. He had been a tender kisser, like he understood that he was already past thirty and she was still a girl really, nineteen, not even out of the house. There was a sweetness, a softness, but also an urgency in it like they better hurry up right quick and take everything they could from the moment.

Oh, she had not put a candle in the window for him all these years. Lord no. She had not thought about what had gone on between them in decades. She doubted that it was something he would even recall. Well, and certainly not now, or ever again. Roy was a man without a country now, a man without a life really, past even his memories, past everything on earth. This was something that Travis could not understand. And Wilma, she had been in this room for days now, and Celeste could tell, especially after church this morning, Wilma was getting the idea by now that Roy wasn't coming back. Oh, he might wake up, Celeste had seen it happen. It was still possible, but then there was the damage done. He could wake up a baby, a little child, unable to do for himself, crying easily, the old Roy gone away— or worse, trapped like some animal in the cage of his body.

Celeste placed Roy's arm by his side and walked around the bed to check the machines. The respirator hissed and she turned up the volume on the heart monitor, so the sound of whatever life Roy had left rang out in the room. It wasn't much more than a little electricity. She listened for a minute and then muted it. She finished her work, recorded the information, and then she couldn't resist. "Roy," she called out. "Roy, it's Celeste." There was nothing, of course, no sign from him. She decided to cut on the radio. Maybe that would get to Roy's ears somehow—he always loved music—and if not, maybe it would cheer up Wilma when she came back.

Roy Orbison came on the radio: *"One look from you, I drift away . . ."* And for some reason, the idea came into her mind right then: *Take him out of this world.* This came in like the light from that broken fluorescent fixture, all bright for just a second, perfectly bright, and then gone.

No.

The light flashed back on, *yes, yes, take me*, as if Roy, her old friend, was pleading with her. The other Roy sang, *"Anything you want, you got it . . ."* Mr. Orbison himself was sitting somewhere in Nashville at this very moment, wearing his sunglasses and his spangledy coat, totally oblivious, having not the first idea that his hit record was doing the devil's work. She looked around and saw a dozen things that would do it: a drawer of empty syringes, a breathing machine that could be stilled for just two minutes, a pillow behind Roy's head. "Dear God," she said out loud. "Dear God." And then for a moment, she wondered if in fact it was God and not the devil that was calling to her.

"Dear God," she said. *Give me a sign.* She didn't say this last out loud because, well, because, she didn't want a sign. *Remove this cup,* she wanted to say. But then she walked around the bed, and there it was—Roy's arm hanging off the bed again, his palm up, his fingers curled slightly, looking just like that picture she had seen of Adam's hand, lifeless, suspended in air, just before it was touched by God's.

Chapter Fourteen

Wilma

They were still standing in the lobby, right in the middle of a sort of thoroughfare, people streaming all around them. He stepped close to her. She couldn't look him in the face, so she stared right into his jacket. There were crumbs scattered down the front of it and a greasy food stain. Looked like gravy. She could smell his awful aftershave. Just what were men thinking when they slapped that stuff on their faces in the morning? Who or what did they think they would attract?

Travis was starting to quote scripture then, which was nothing new. Wilma was so busy trying to figure out how she was going to keep him out of Roy's room, she didn't follow most of it. Eventually though, he got on to Lazarus. Lazarus, Lazarus: "As Jesus commanded him to rise—"

"Wait right there,' she said because this just burned her up. "Don't you say that. Don't you say that. Lazarus was a dead man. Do you get it? Dead. I won't have it, you hear?"

"Of course not," said Travis. "I meant only . . . Look, Jesus healed the man, that's all I'm saying. That's what we want for Roy, isn't it? The anointment of healing."

She felt that need for a weapon again. She thought about taking off her pump and beating him over the head with it. "Travis, please—"

"Cleansed in the Holy Spirit, raised unto Him, Wilma."

"You're not going up there." She had shouted this, but no one passing seemed to take note. Travis stopped talking and looked at her from under his blond bushy eyebrows. He opened his mouth, thought better of it, closed it with the clench of a martyr.

"All right," he said finally. "You're the boss."

"Thank you, Travis. Thanks for understanding." Wilma did her best to smile, and at the same time to check out the light panel at the bank of elevators. It looked like a car was about to arrive. She experienced a moment of divine, light-headed release and took a step in that direction.

"Hold up a minute." Travis cupped his hand around her lead-off shoulder. "Here's what we'll do." He thrust his other hand into his pants pocket, and pulled out a small, somber-looking vial filled with a clear liquid. The elevator door opened. Wilma felt her spirit leap forward, but the rest of her just stood there like an obedient child.

"You can take the healing to Roy. How about that? Holy oil. Accept the mantle of the Holy Spirit and bear it unto him."

"Yes, okay fine." She looked him in the face finally, and put out her hand. She'd take his oil and that would be the end of it. He took his hand off her shoulder, and she was planning her retreat—looking past him, through the crowd for the next elevator, so she did not fathom his intent until the top was off the vial. He dipped his forefinger into the oil, and before she knew what was happening, he raised his other hand and drew a cross on her forehead with his oily finger and commenced a prayer in a loud Sunday voice: "Lord, bring Thy healing power to this woman . . ."

The lobby was constructed mostly of cement blocks. Travis's voice resonated pretty well off the walls. There was nothing to do except bow her head. That way, she didn't have to see the curious faces of all the people as they floated by. She could hear their shoes sliding along, giving the two of them a wide berth. Beyond that, there was a certain shocked quiet. As he went on, Travis lifted his voice a bit further, and she could hear whispers in the stream of folks around her. She felt tingles in her scalp, like little pins, the ancient flight instinct. She wished that she could be washed away, taken by the swift current with the others, down the halls, down the steps to the basement and beyond.

Travis prayed for a few minutes—it was impossible to judge how long, exactly—asking God to sanctify her and save her beloved Roy. Since Wilma knew He would not, she used this time to look down in detail at the brown and green terrazzo floor, at Travis's scuffed shoes. The shoes were brown brogans, which looked okay with dungarees but silly with seersucker. The laces were black and had been double-knotted. Travis paused for a minute. She lifted her head an inch or two, thinking he might be done. It was a false alarm, though, and since she was trying to keep all movement to a minimum, this left her looking squarely at Travis Diamond's trousers. There was another stain, more gravy, dribbled down the front, right across the puckered zipper.

She closed her eyes, not wanting to see another thing on the earth. Travis let out an Amen. His gravy breath washed over her, eroding the last bit of faith she possessed. Later, she would not remember the moment when he released her. She would not remember how she made her way to the waiting elevator, or what she might have said. She would remember only the doors sliding closed in Travis's shiny oblivious face and the car lifting her up off that floor. This was her very own benediction.

Roy

It was a country station playing. It had been going on a while, and right this minute, he could hear Hank Williams, whom he had loved in his youth even more than Sinatra. *Gonna find me a river, one that's cold as ice* . . . It was an old record, he thought, something he hadn't heard in a long time. He made a note to himself to dig around the farmhouse and see if he could find that old 45. He'd seen it around there someplace. He thought maybe Celeste or one of her friends had brought it over for one of their party nights, right before he left for Korea. Maybe it had been Bill Surratt or Inez Whitaker who left it at the house one night and then, pretty soon, they'd stopped all that, stopped the parties. He ought to return it, to Celeste maybe, but he would listen to it first.

Where had he last seen the record? The front closet maybe, with the rest of his old vinyl, or maybe he'd taken it to his house in town. Had he fixed that old Victrola? Maybe that was his old record playing right now. It sounded scratchy and far away. Or maybe it was coming from one of the old transistor radios, the ones that were a dime a dozen in Seoul? Could be, he was mixed up. Maybe he'd gotten that fever his CO was always warning against. *She's looong gooone*. Roy liked this sound, liked it a lot, though now there was also another voice: a woman calling to him, calling his name. He couldn't be sure, but it seemed that it was his mother, and she was calling out to God, to him and to God. That made no sense. *Roy, Roy*. Still, he'd better answer. He tried, but he couldn't. He tried again. The effort produced nothing more than a low, low groan, and even that seemed to blend in with the song, a kind of humming right there along with the bass line.

Somewhere in there his mother was humming along with him. It was her evening song now, a lullaby. He could feel the bed give slightly as she sat down beside him, the warmth of her body next to his. "You're dead," he said to her. For sure, this was a dream.

"Yes," she said. "Long ago. Let's fix these pillows." She cupped his head in her hand and held him up while she moved the pillows behind him. She gathered his hair in her sweet fingers before she slid her hand away. He drifted down into the bed, surrounded by the bedclothes, warm and tucked in for the night.

Harper

He wasn't sure if it was the sound of breaking glass that woke him up or the mammoth headache. Either way, he was conscious and viciously hungover at this point, which was, according to the clock, 12:45. That would be P.M., if his brain was still serving him, which was a miracle, since it was housed in a skull twice its normal size. Harper turned over and tried to block the light with a pillow. This made him seasick and, of course, full of remorse. Though it was a predictable and wholly familiar outcome, a hangover was always a bit of a surprise. He'd felt so fine when he turned in, hadn't he?

He heard another crash, more glass breaking. He was at Roy's, so who was downstairs? He tried to think. Some of the big drinkers, Brother Sully and Clayton, had left early on. He'd sent Candace home with her cousin right before he'd driven down to the hospital. Ah, Jesus, right, he'd gone to see Roy. Goddamn. He couldn't believe he'd done that, driving and all, though . . . Right, Delrina. Delrina Kay had shown up in her bus, and she'd been the one. She'd talked him into going. She was the one who drove, but not that bus. She'd driven his van, that's what they'd done.

He couldn't believe they'd found their way to Baptist Hospital. It was a further miracle they'd located Roy's room. Delrina had sweet-talked the night guard. Carousing with a minor celebrity, these things happened. Doors opened. You could visit a sickroom in the middle of the night. The whole memory was disorganized like a dream now. He did not think they'd been in Roy's room very long. They'd opened some wine, made a toast or two. He thought Delrina had tried to wake Roy with a song, and that had brought in the night nurse, who kicked them out right quick. After that, he wasn't clear on much.

He threw the covers back. He hoped that Roy had a Coke or something in the house. Of course, if it had been there last night, it was gone, drunk up by locust musicians. He found his pants. As he put them on, he had a final thought about the evening and rechecked the bed. He had fallen into the covers late and scarcely moved them. Mercifully, only his side was disturbed.

When he came downstairs, he found Delrina on the porch with a plastic garbage bag in her hand, looking like a normal everyday person in a T-shirt and jeans, except for her hair, which was still strange. She was chinking wine bottles into the bag, enjoying the sound of their breaking.

"Well, look who crawled in from the swamp," she said, a little louder than necessary.

Harper wondered again what in the world she was doing there, why she had shown up for a gig eight weeks early, but he was not about to ask while she was cleaning up.

"There's coffee in the kitchen," she said. "I hope you don't mind, I helped myself."

"No," said Harper, "it's fine." He sat down on the front stoop. There was very little evidence of the party at this point. The size of the garbage bag worried him. He wondered how much of Roy's wine they had run through.

"I have an espresso maker on the bus," said Delrina, "but I didn't bother to get a hookup last night, so there's no electricity. God, it made the back room really stuffy this morning."

"Is anyone else up?" said Harper.

"Who do you mean? Is there someone upstairs?" She smiled at him.

"No." Lord God, where did this woman get off? "I meant in the bus. Where's Little Charlie, the band?"

"Oh," she said. "Them."

She twisted the top of the bag and tied it like it was something she was used to doing. "Ain't none," she said. "I should've told you. Charles, as he wants to be called, he ran off sometime last week. I don't know where, and we haven't had a band in a long, long time. It's me. It's just me and one very nice damn tour bus."

Wilma

It was the same elevator car as before, the one used for people and freight. There was a girl in there with her, a young girl about Star's age, but a little less worldly maybe, wearing a neat skirt and blouse, hose and heels. She was very pretty and fresh, the way Wilma imagined herself at that age, out with her girlfriends for a day of swimming at White Rock Lake.

They would go right after church, on a day like today, change into their suits when they got there. The water in the lake was an emerald green and made her skin glow underneath the surface. She was a good swimmer. She would always swim far out into the lake, beyond the buoys, beyond everything. There was one boy, Cy Jenkins, who swam after her one time, pretended that he was worried for her safety. A girl swimming so far from the shore. But when he had reached her, he had put his arms around her, and pulled her close. He slid his hands under her suit and across her soft skin, making it shiver and burn, until she got away from him and swam for the shore.

Damn Travis Diamond and his little magic vial. Who did he think he was?

When she got to Roy's hall, she ran into Celeste, who looked just about as bedeviled as Wilma felt. She was pale and she'd been crying. "I left him in the lobby," Wilma said.

"Who?" said Celeste.

"Travis." Surely she'd known what he was after. "Travis and his holy oil. I told him he couldn't come up."

"Oh." Celeste looked like she had forgotten all about him. "Good." She looked hard at Wilma, like she had just now recognized her. "Sorry."

It was strange. Wilma had fairly well been assaulted by this woman's husband. But somehow, looking at her—her sun-freckled face, runny eyes marked with little creases, one ruined hand nervously picking at the other—it was Wilma who felt sorry for Celeste. What would it be like to be married to Travis? Hell on earth, that didn't begin to cover it.

"So how's Roy?" she said. "Any change?"

Celeste went from pale to red now and began scratching her palm with a fingernail again. "I haven't gotten the chance to look in on him yet," she said. "I have to finish taking vitals. You go on. I'll stop by directly."

Later Wilma would try to replay the moment, the very second when she put her hands on him.

At first she did not touch him at all; she didn't even look at him. In those first minutes, she wasn't really thinking about Roy. She wasn't worried about what kind of condition he was in when she walked into the room. She was thinking about her own damn self, about how Travis had embarrassed her, about how he had chased whatever she had left of God right out of her. She was thinking about how she was just a breathing machine away from being a widow again. She was filled with pity, not for Roy—truth be told—but for herself. She felt completely alone, for the first time in a very long time. Alone, without a friend, cold as a slab of stone. She avoided the bed, went straight to the window and sighed a few deeply self-oriented sighs, looked out at the trees and the sunshine. Behind her, the machines whirred along: *hiss inhale click, hiss exhale click.* There wasn't even Roy's breathing to reassure her.

When she turned around, it was the wine bottle that she noticed. It was one of their wedding bottles with the special labels Roy had made, silly wedding bells with their names and their wedding date. What was that bottle doing on the medication tray? Roy had made the wine from his first vines of cabernet franc, used it for the toast at their wedding. It was a big deal to him, her special wedding present, and he had packed away extra cases, a bottle to drink on every anniversary.

"There's enough to last us to 2015, dolly," he'd said when he'd opened one this last June. "It'll be vinegar by then, but if we live that long, we won't know the difference."

She picked up the bottle, nearly knocking over the dirty glasses that were lined up beside it. There'd been a party. The bottle was open, half the wine gone, the cork wedged back in the top. She tried to think how it could've gotten there. Most likely, this was the work of some of Roy's rescue squad buddies. Beyond riding around in fire trucks, these men didn't know what to do with themselves other than to hang out at Squirrely's and drink. Roy had probably given them a few bottles some time back. Maybe they'd come by to visit him, and they'd brought the wine along. She'd ask Celeste if she'd seen them. It was nice, when she thought of it, that they'd come by. It lightened her heart in a way nothing else had in days.

She still had the bottle in her hand when she looked up at Roy. Finally, she looked at him, thinking, *Shame on you, Wilma, for not even saying hello,* thinking, *Surely not, this will not do here for you to think of Roy as nothing more than a whirring machine. He's right there, and he will be better and you two will be drinking this wine again in no time.*

She put down the bottle, walked over to his bed, and put her hands on him, one on each side of his shoulders. He was warm. Later, she would try to remember whether she had felt some kind of charge in that touch, a flow of any kind go out of her hands, anything like that at all, but really, there was only the warm reassurance of his living, everything that she would feel through his blue cotton pajamas. In that exact moment, she was thinking that she would need to change them that afternoon, that she would trade the blue pair for the yellow. Pajamas. That was exactly what she was thinking about, her hands on his sweet shoulders, when Roy without any warning whatsoever opened his eyes, looked straight into hers, and whispered, "Glass breaking."

Chapter Fifteen

Celeste

Most likely the chill in the air had kept people home lighting the first fire of the fall, so there was a small crowd in the Coach House Restaurant. Celeste had gotten off her shift on time for a change and arrived before Travis. This gave her a few minutes in the back booth to peruse the menu and contemplate her eternal damnation.

She had seen a special on TV over the summer where they had talked about people who could read auras, how auras were different colors depending on a body's spiritual makeup. If there was such a person, an aura reader, at one of the front window tables right now—for instance, that woman wearing the nice red pants suit—if she were to look back at Celeste right now, all she'd see was a swirling cloud of black pestilence. Celeste could not see her own aura, but she had felt it hovering all around her from the very minute that she had made her attempt on Roy Swan's life.

Since she had decided that she would have baked chicken with dressing, green beans, and cucumber salad, she took a moment to thank her lucky stars that she was a mostly stupid woman. In Roy's room, she had been so tortured, so intent on thinking exactly what the right action was—to kill or not to kill—that she had not focused on how she could best do it. It occurred to her now that this was how many criminals got caught. She was lucky in that way. She hadn't been caught, she had got off scot-free, and there was no reason to think that anyone would ever know, except, of course, she would know.

What she had done was take a pillow from behind Roy's head and press it tight over his face.

Mary Beth came over to her table now and asked her if she wanted tea while she was waiting for Travis. Celeste asked for it unsweetened. This was the first thing, the first penance she would give herself for what she had done: unsweetened tea. She would take it from there.

She had held the pillow over his face for a good couple of seconds, crying as she did it. Then she had realized that the man was on a respirator. Covering his face with a pillow wasn't going to make him miss one breath. All in all it was just about the stupidest thing anyone could do, much less a licensed practical nurse.

Once this occurred to her, Celeste had pulled the pillow right off. Then before she could think further about whether she ought to pinch the respirator hose or find an empty syringe, or maybe even just go down to the nurses' station and drink a Coke, the miracle occurred: Roy's eyes fluttered for a few seconds, and then he let out a little noise. It wasn't much: no one with a trach could really talk. The vocal chords just didn't work. Still, Roy was trying. He made a low hum in the back of his throat, the kind of noise you might make if there was a waitress standing at your table and you hadn't quite figured out what to order. *Ummm.* That kind of noise, like he wanted to say something but couldn't quite get it from his throat to his lips.

"Roy," she said, what little training she had coming back to her. "Roy." Louder, since the idea was to bring the patient up from the last brink of unconsciousness.

"Ummm," he answered promptly.

"Roy Swan, can you hear me?"

"Ummm." This went on for a few minutes. Celeste kept thinking he would open his eyes or try to say a real word, but he never did. However, it was clear: he had turned around, he was walking away from death. Two minutes after she had tried to throw him over the edge.

Mary Beth brought the tea. It was bitter, bitter, but Celeste refused to put anything in it. She wouldn't even use saccharin, though that in itself was a trial.

Josh

His dad had made him put on the sweater from last Christmas before they got in the car to go eat. It had reindeers on it and shit. Made him look like a dork. Didn't matter, though. He was walking misery, had been all afternoon. He ached. It wasn't sore muscles. Something else had gotten to him, like a weird sunburn or a rash in a place he couldn't scratch. Guilt, maybe, or love. It was hard to tell.

He took a quick look through the window of the Coach House before they walked in. There wasn't anyone he knew inside. Just a few tables of old people and his mom sitting in the back booth in her hospital clothes. This afternoon, he'd put that *Fear of Flying* book back in her drawer. It was a little dog-eared, but she wouldn't notice. He'd done the dishes too. Hard to say why. Penance, maybe, or maybe just something to do with his hands. Other than. Again, hard to tell.

He followed his dad inside. There was a delay while his dad spoke to every person he knew at every table. Like he was running for mayor, or maybe chief evangelist.

"Get your hands out of your pockets, son," his dad mumbled between the first and second tables. Josh did. Shook hands with Undertaker Snow, gross enough. Mrs. Snow too. She held his hand with both of hers and he got a nose full of her perfume. Eau de dead.

The air was clear at the back booth. Good, because he was hungry. His mom smiled at them both, made it plain he was to sit next to her. So, okay. He'd watch his elbows. He looked at the menu, trying to remember which combination would yield the most food. Country fried steak. Potatoes. Pintos with onions. Maybe he could get a shake. Travis started right in on the sick list. Like always. Josh wished they would do this at home. In a minute, his dad would use the blessing to pray for anyone in their town that was up in Baptist Hospital. His mother was Travis's undercover spy for the sick and dying. Josh normally tried to block this out. This litany. Who had twisted intestines, who was eaten up with cancer. Bad for the appetite.

Tonight, though, he listened. For Star, he listened. For any mention of her name. And for Mr. Swan, whom he'd always liked. Roy

Swan was first on the list. His mom seemed all jittery about it. Dumped about half a cup of sugar in her tea.

"Celeste, honey," said his dad. "Mary Beth will bring you some sweet tea if you ask her."

"I know, I know," his mother said. She stopped clanging her tea-spoon in her glass then. Put her palms down on the table and a weird smile on her face. "Good news, I think, about Roy. Wilma was up on the floor with him this afternoon, and he came to for a minute—"

"Praise Jesus!" said his dad, too loud, but no one looked. They were all used to it.

"—said a few garbled words and that was it. But still, that's better than we expected. It's a start." Josh was happy about this, for Mr. Swan, for Star, but he was also afraid of what his dad would do next. One time in church he had yelled "Amen," right in the middle of the sermon. No one else did that at their church. The lady next to him in the choir had jumped a foot off her chair.

"Praise Jesus. By His will, we have healed Brother Roy!" His dad grabbed his mom's hands. Josh ducked his head. Here it came. But his dad was silent. When he looked up, his dad was crying. Really. Like, big tears. Dripping off his eyelashes.

His mom kept talking. "Wilma was with him when it happened. Some of the nurses thought it might all be wishful thinking, but you know Wilma, she wouldn't—"

"Did she do the laying on of hands?" his dad whispered, but he didn't wait for an answer. "She did it!" He was shaking a little bit now. "She took the healing to him. Praaaaise Him. Praise His Holy Name." Tears and spittle flew all over the table. Oh, God.

Mrs. Appleton came to take their order. His dad gave her the news straightaway. A vial of holy oil. His anointing of Miss Wilma. This, just prior to her touching Roy and healing him. And Roy, just prior, on the point of death. Healed. He said that a few times. Healed. He showed Mrs. Appleton the vial.

"Well, isn't that just the best news," said Mrs. Appleton. She didn't look at the oil too close. She held her pad up in front of her. Looked at Josh. He ordered and then pointed at his mom. He'd seen his dad do this. It moved things along.

His dad looked at the two of them, like, *How can life go on?* He
threw his hands up in the air. "A miracle," he said, and then he asked
for the hamburger steak, fries, and a salad. He finished up with a
"Praise God."

"Yes," said Mrs. Appleton.

More people they knew came into the restaurant. They dropped
by his family's table. His mom stayed quiet. His dad told the story. He
added a few things every time—how the lobby of Baptist had got
quiet when he anointed Miss Wilma. How her forehead glowed with
the oil. How Roy might be sitting up having supper by now.

"Well, that's a bit optimistic," his mother volunteered, when his
dad said this last to Mr. and Mrs. Snow, who'd had their food and
were headed home. Josh couldn't believe his country steak was taking so long. He reached for the crackers.

"Nonetheless, it's just wonderful news. An answer to all of our
prayers," said Mrs. Snow, and then, without warning, "I know Josh
here has got to be happy, Roy being his little girlfriend's stepgrandfa-
ther."

"Girlfriend?" His mother and everyone else looked at him.

Mrs. Snow gave him a perfumy smile. Like he had made National
Honor Society or something. She looked over his head to his mother.
"Rachel and her boys were up at the Knob yesterday and saw the
lovebirds on Table Rock. You all, well, Celeste, you remember Table
Rock, right? Kind of a tradition." She said that last word funny. Like
some adult code.

His dad hadn't heard any of this since he was busy showing Mr.
Snow the oil vial. Josh was in trouble, though. His mother smiled
back and gulped her tea. What had Mrs. Snow's daughter seen? He
steeled himself for what came next. The Outlier, he was the Outlier,
but just then their food got to the table. Mrs. Snow said, "Come on,
Ronald, let's let these people eat. They've had a big day."

Celeste

Celeste looked over at her son, who was eating the food on his plate like it was his last meal on earth. What had he been up to with that Star? Part of her wanted to wallop him right there, but then, maybe this was the time to live and learn, to rise above Grace Snow and her Chanel No. 5. Maybe this was no more than talk.

Just like Table Rock. She would never live it down. Not one thing had happened. Nothing at all, thanks to Roy being the kind of person he had been and was now, come to think of it. Still, she wouldn't live it down. As long as there were Grace Snows in this world, there'd be a town full of people thinking she did the deed with Roy Swan on Table Rock the day before Easter, 1953.

Maybe she should give her son the benefit of the doubt, just like someone should have given her long ago.

She put down her fork.

Yes, that was right. Someone should have given her the benefit of the doubt. When she had that thought, something happened. It had been a red-letter day, full of every kind of emotion, and here came another big one. It was like one of those scenes she saw on television when the actress found out something big and had to put her hand up against her chest. Celeste understood this now. She felt her very spirit overcome her black cloud aura. She felt her essence fly up to the ceiling. Of course, her body remained in her seat. And right there in the back booth of the Coach House, right in that moment with her spirit swinging from the antique brass light fixture, it became clear unto her.

If she stepped back and surveyed the course of her life, it was clear as it could be. She had been set on this earth to heal Roy Swan.

Wilma

He hadn't said another word. He had blinked a bit, smiled at her as if he had awakened from a nice long nap, and then closed his eyes again. She had called in the nurses, everyone. They had looked at Roy, taken his pulse, then looked her over good, like she was a patient too. They had given her a few contained smiles. "Maybe," one of them said. "You never know."

Celeste was the only one who set store by what Wilma reported. "Don't worry," she had said right before the end of her shift. "He's coming back. Just you wait and see."

Wilma sat beside Roy with her heart beating up into her throat for the rest of the evening, looking for another sign, wondering if he had actually said "glass breaking," whatever that meant, wondering finally if he had said anything at all. It had been a sort of whisper, after all, not much more than a hiss. *Glass breaking, glass breaking,* or had it been *gas station*?

They made her leave at nine o'clock.

She was in no mood to go back to Swan's Knob. She couldn't shake the feeling that at any minute, Roy would wake up again and ask for pancakes and bacon. She didn't want to go anywhere, but there was nothing to do but climb into her car. Maybe she needed some food herself. When had she last eaten? Nor many places would be open, except maybe Krispy Kreme. She hadn't been in years—doughnuts were the kind of thing she tried to keep away from Roy—but tonight this appealed enough to get her to start the car and head toward Stratford Road.

When she got into the parking lot and looked in the front windows, though, she was reluctant to go in. The whole place was lit up as bright as an operating room, and there was all of that hospital white tile. Still, there was a gnawing in her stomach, and hot coffee, that would be good.

There were two groups of people sitting at the counter inside. At the far left was an unsavory cluster of men who hunched over empty coffee cups, smoking. On the other end of the counter, there was a young family, a skinny wife and a fat husband with two toddlers out past their bedtime. Wilma took the nearest stool, even though she hated to sit on a stool—made her feel as if she wasn't exactly sitting, somehow, precarious, as though she could fall off any minute. That, and her backside always dumped over the sides.

No matter. Here she was out in the world, in the Krispy Kreme, where there was no one who knew her, no one to ask her how Roy was doing, no one to look at her with sympathy and pity, out here where she was just a woman who looked unattractive sitting on a stool. She allowed herself two doughnuts, three sugars in her coffee, and ten minutes of unmitigated hope.

During the first few months, she and Roy had conducted their courtship in secret. Wilma had insisted on this, initially because she just hated to be the subject of gossip, but then simply by choice. In public, at the church or in town, Roy would greet her as he always did with courtly formality: "And how are you today, Miss Wilma?" He would come upon her at church, standing with several other women from the choir, and compliment them all on the anthem, but then as he walked away, he would turn and wink at Wilma behind their backs and mouth the word "tonight." This sneaking around made their little private meetings even more delicious.

Roy would come over to her house at ten o'clock, or later, walking the three blocks from his house to hers. He would call her on the telephone first. This would give her just ten minutes to get her wherewithal together. At first, she would put the kettle on the stove, like she thought maybe they'd have tea. Roy had laughed at this, hugged her good, and said, "Who's the tea for, darling? You expecting company?" He had that easy way about most things. He made it easy for her to say yes to him, to say yes, in fact, just six weeks or so into their courtship. This was entirely new to her. Before Roy, of course, there had been only one man, her Harry. She and Harry had gotten along all right in the bedroom over the years. She couldn't say she didn't enjoy it, but still, there had been a certain routine developed early on. That worked just fine, as far as Wilma knew, though she wondered now why they'd never been free enough to look one another in the eye, not once, not even in the semidarkness of their own bedroom.

But Roy, Roy would look at her like she was the most beautiful thing on earth, like he was a lucky man. He would say that sometimes the minute he came through her back door. He was sweet to her, and tender, that was the word—the physical manifestations of this tenderness almost too much for her to think about in the garish light of the Krispy Kreme: his hand brushing lightly in the small of her naked back, the graduation of his kisses from soft grace to sweet insistence, the moment when he would be aroused against her and transformed into a young man again, needing her guilelessly, at her sweet mercy, and she would have the hands and beating heart of an ingénue. Their lovemaking was never the same from one time to the next. Each time was its own story, written in its own incandescent ink, an arc stretched out over their hills and valleys, body and spirit, sheets and soft evening light.

Together, they had collected the tiny miracles of sensation and of caring, and in this, they had discovered their own secret clearing in a wood. It was an amazing thing, the eighth wonder of the world, but they never discussed it. They never said a word. This was the way she'd wanted it. Maybe it would've been more modern to talk about sex, but it was not their way. If it had been, months ago she would have simply asked, "Honey, what's wrong?" That way, she might have known; she might have figured out that he was getting ill.

But no, she had spent her evenings silent, speculating about his fidelity, imagining him catting around out at the home place with Mamie Brown or Celeste. She was ashamed now that she had lost faith in their love, and doubly ashamed that she had missed all the other signs. She had gone over and over this by now, and of course the signs were there: his ankles had been a little puffy sometimes, which she had attributed to too much country ham. He had put on a little more weight, she'd noticed; he breathed a bit heavier. Often, his face got red. He had told her several times that he'd gotten dizzy, "swimmy headed" he called it. She had prescribed nothing more than a sun hat.

She realized now that she'd eaten both doughnuts without tasting them, which was a shame really, since they contained more calories than she should have in a day. The little family to her right was getting ready to go home finally. One child had given up the ghost and was sleeping on her mama's shoulder, the other was whining.

"Do-over." Wasn't that what children called it? She still had a dozen or so piano students—she only taught the most diligent these days—and when one of them, like that sweet Lauren Burgess, had a bad run at a piece, she would look up with wide child eyes too big for her face and say, "Please, Miss Wilma, can I have a do-over?" These days, in these precious days, these near eight years since she'd had her Roy, since they'd had each other, Wilma always said yes. Yes, honey, go right ahead. Do it all over again. So she had learned something, but not quite enough. She wanted to believe that Roy would come back to her, all the way back, that she would put her hands on him in the morning and get two more words out of him, any two at all, and then the next day, two more, and on and on until she got every bit of him back. She wanted to believe this, she really did.

She finished her coffee, which was sweet and lukewarm.

Chapter Sixteen

Celeste

It was hard to eat when you had just had a major revelation, so Celeste just picked at her food. She ordered a fresh glass of tea, sweetened this time, and when Mary Beth came back around, she got pecan pie with ice cream for dessert. Josh joined her, and they ate it all up as Travis went over the miracle story one more time. He kept asking her for more details. What had Roy said, exactly? Did Wilma say how she touched him? Where? Celeste said as little as possible so as not to rip the curtain in the universe, the one that had just been pulled back, revealing all.

When they got out to the cars, she told Travis he should take Josh home in his truck. He agreed, and Josh seemed eager to go along with that. No way he wanted to talk about Table Rock with his mama. He was hoping to dodge that bullet. He had, in a way. It was a day for dodging bullets all around.

And it was a night full of stars, crisp as a new crop of apples. Celeste aimed her Taurus out into the new world, rolling down the road like she was piloting a spaceship past the known universe.

Celeste had set her cap for Roy back in the days when girls did such things and their mothers told them not to. She had been smitten from that first day he took her out of the apple tree, smitten in that way that little girls are before they know what's what. A few times, he let her come with him as he wandered the creeks around the farms, messing with crawdaddies and box turtles. They'd found abandoned treasures in the woods and other places (car parts, arrowheads, old glass) and buried them on Roy's graveyard hill. They'd played out in the rain, but then he'd grown up long before she did. He left.

She had pined for him during that year or so at the end of the war, when he was out on the West Coast, when she wasn't any older than twelve. He had answered her letters. She had them still in her bedside drawer. When she read them now, she could see that he took pains not to look down on her, to treat her as almost grown-up, even when she sent him a chalk drawing of the apple tree with their initials on the trunk. He had not led her on either. He'd returned from the war before she was wearing her first bra, only to abandon her for Washington and Lee.

When he finished, he was home for a full summer, the best one of her life maybe. She'd been fifteen and smart enough to know that he saw her as a little sister. That was fine. She wore Peter Pan shirts and a ponytail, just like Judy Garland in those movies with Mickey Rooney. Celeste played the part: kid sister was fine with her. She spent the summer tagging along with Roy and his friends to White Rock Lake and church dances, begged them all to teach her how to shag, how to do the sidestroke. She bumped herself against Roy every chance she got. "Oops," she'd say with a giggle and act like she'd forgotten the step. She had a tube of red lipstick and a Playtex C cup. They'd had their effect.

Her mother had seen through it all.

"Missy, you are too young for him," Ramona had said after watching Celeste dance at a church ice-cream social.

Roy had danced with her more than anybody that evening. She'd counted. And he'd almost breathed on her neck. "I don't hear anybody complaining," she'd said.

"He's not going to complain," said her mother. "That's not the way it works." Her opinion didn't matter to Celeste by then. She was bitter as hell about everything. The year before, Celeste's dad had disappeared with all their money right after harvest. Whatever looks Ramona had left had dried up with the stalks in the field. She looked like one of those dehydrated apple dolls, and she wasn't even thirty.

"Just you wait until Erma Swan gets a wind of this, missy. She'll put an end to it right quick. She has big plans for Roy, and they do not include him marrying a Clay girl, red lipstick or no." This stung, but Celeste closed her ears. Roy was no mama's boy.

Roy left again, though, this time for the war in Korea. Celeste tried not to take it personally. He reenlisted, got his commission as an officer. He planned it for a long time, in secret. His parents disapproved. They wanted him to go to law school. But it was already done and he was off to a boat in San Diego inside a week. He had time for only one last party for their little gang out at his farmhouse.

Ramona let her go but sent her out the door with a warning: "Don't get caught doing something that will leave you out in the cold. He's off to war." Her mother didn't understand a thing. Celeste had walked across the fields to the party, scraping her penny loafers on the frozen furrows. She'd heard the music as soon as the white clapboard house came into view. Hank Williams's "Long Gone Lonesome Blues" had been their particular favorite that summer. They played it over and over that last night, and the girls cried their eyes out. Celeste got the idea then, from all the crying and the hugging, that those older girls, the ones who had taught her to smoke and wore neck scarves and stockings, they had set their caps as well. This made her mad and jealous, but it added to her resolve. She would wait. These other girls, they were nearly grown. They didn't have the time.

Celeste was almost right. Those girls, they were mostly married or otherwise eliminated by the time she saw Roy again. When he got home, the war in Korea was over. His parents were dead. And Celeste Clay had waited. Her brothers and sisters had all gone the way of their father and dispatched themselves to the far corners of the state, but Celeste had stayed. She had gotten a job taking care of an old lady in town. She had saved her money and herself. She had been courted by boys well beyond her mother's expectations, but she would have none of them. Ramona saw what she had on her mind. "Erma Swan may be dead," Ramona said in her husky emphysema whisper (she was nearly dead herself by then and six months behind on the mortgage), "but that don't mean she's gone. Roy's going to hold her up against every girl that comes his way. Don't be dreaming. You'll miss your chance in life."

She got just one kiss.

Roy came home a full-grown man, filled in around the shoulders and neck. He smiled less than he had before, spent most of his time with the men at the pool hall and at the rescue squad. And when he looked at her, well, Celeste couldn't tell what he was thinking. She walked his land with him late one afternoon just a few days after he returned. It was springtime. She'd worn something like she'd seen on Doris Day in her last movie, a crisp shirtwaist dress, very ladylike, though once they started walking she felt too dressed up. They crossed over the fields and down to the creek, and then found themselves on the path up to Swan's Knob. The talk had been easy enough, though she'd been careful to use good grammar and keep her hands ladylike instead of waving them all around. She caught Roy up on everyone, the weddings, new babies, college degrees.

He talked about Korea, what the country looked like, the arid mountains with scrub bushes and not a decent tree in sight, how it was mostly all brown there, everything. "The noise, Celeste," he said. "You never get used to all the shelling, day and night. We shelled those hills until we blew off what leaves they had and the topsoil too. There wasn't a thing left but chalky rock underneath. From a distance, it looked like it'd snowed."

"That sure is a foreign country," she said, for lack of anything else.

They ended up at Table Rock. It was right at the end of the footpath, next to the Knob. They had leaned on it first and then pulled themselves up to sit and dangle their feet off it. Celeste didn't care what anybody said later—they had not laid down. They kept on talking about all kinds of things: the new radios Roy had used to call men on the front, the way he had rigged one up one time to pipe Hank Williams out to men ten miles away. After a while, Celeste wished that they could talk about something else, like how her hair glowed in the dying sunlight, how she looked like a beautiful statue of Athena. There were places in the conversation where Roy could have worked that in, and she tried to keep real quiet and look at him just a little dreamy-eyed, hoping he'd find the moment to say how he had thought about her on those lonely nights in Korea. But he did not. He said, finally, "Well, I'm probably boring you with all this war talk." He asked her then about the funeral, the service for his parents that he had missed. She obliged, feeling sick, just sick on her stomach because she was starting to get the idea. Her mother was right. It was no use.

They had stayed in that spot until past dark. Neither of them thought one thing about it. They knew the path back down, every rock and tree, even without the moon that was shining, bright for being half phased. When they got back down to the house, at the edge of the last field by the barn, Celeste got her kiss. She was not even sure why he had done it, or even if he did—maybe she had kissed him. She had been waiting for it all those years, that kiss, but it came and went, soft and sweet and as arid as the hills of Korea.

On her way home that night, she carried very little of the hope she'd saved up along with everything else.

She never found out who it was, but someone had seen them back up at the Knob, someone with an imagination every bit as inventive as her own, for it was claimed far and wide, from one end of Swan's Knob to the other, that Celeste Clay and Roy Swan had been having relations on top of Table Rock. And this detail was added: that Celeste's dress had been bunched up around her waist, with her knees shining in the moonlight.

Before that year was over, three things happened: Ramona Clay died of the emphysema. Celeste inherited their shambledown farm, mortgage and all. And Travis Diamond brought her mortgage up current as a wedding present for his bride.

Celeste, she did look like a statue of Athena at her wedding. Radiant, of course, with the sunlight making her hair glow. But no one said so. That was a thing that did not happen.

Celeste had not thought about any of this in many years. Certainly none of it was a secret, except perhaps for the fact, known only to her and Travis, that she was a virgin on her wedding night. In small towns, there wasn't such a thing as a real secret, only a rickety kind of history—and everybody held on to a piece of it. Didn't matter if it was *true* true, like it happened, only mattered that it was true to you. Like tonight, like Roy. In a few hours, everyone in town would be telling it. Travis, his holy oil, Wilma's laying on of hands. But Celeste would know better. She had touched Roy first, even though it had been to kill him. She, Celeste, whose name meant "sky," had scared the life into him, sent his eyes all fluttery, and brought him back finally from a foreign country.

Roy

Okay, this he knew: he had come back, or maybe it was he'd come up, because when he did, it was not so much a struggle as a surfacing. He'd floated—without weight, without his own propulsion—a divine buoyancy brought him ever closer to the world. At the end, at the very surface, he felt a resistance, a coating like ice—whether it was in his head or not, it shattered as he broke through, shattered and fell away from him and he listened for the sound of it falling, he listened for his own voice calling out, but there was nothing except the infernal metronome of breathing, which went on without even the most minute deviation, on and on.

He'd discovered his body first. He could feel every inch of it, heavy beyond belief, laid out on a bed, pressed by a hideous, unfamiliar gravity. In this altered place, one without the joys of his dreams and the comfort of the long-dead, he could locate his eyelids—his only moving parts. This was not good news. They'd fluttered aimlessly at first, shifting him between dark and half dark. When he'd first managed to hold them open for a few seconds, he could see only shadows, and then close up, some tubing. He was lying under a machine. His eyes closed before he could get a good look, and he lay there, heavy, heavy, and tried to think. A truck? Was that where he had been? The thought washed away.

He'd managed to get his eyes open again. He saw more shadows but in a longer field of vision. A bed. He could see the end of it, the footboard, maybe, and beyond, a chair. He was in a small room. He had been looking out into the darkness, into the far corners, when something moved, and a gray light filtered into the room. A hand held back some kind of curtain. It was suspended in the light of the small window at first, disembodied, maybe his own, unbidden by his brain and stretched out across the space. But no, he could make out a person standing there, a woman. She stepped forward to look out the window. He had no idea what she might be looking at, maybe nothing. She stood perfectly still for several minutes, and he could see her face in profile: her features softened by age and rendered handsome in soft gray light. He looked again. He did not know her, but he was taken by her expression: she looked as if her mind were untethered and wandering in an unknown country.

He wanted to speak then, to call out to her, but his eyes were like tiny peep shows. They closed—his money had run out. He heard then, in this true world, he hoped, and not the other, the sure timpani of footsteps, as the woman walked across the room. This was a sound he loved, he knew this, but no more. She stood beside his bed then, and he'd struggled mightily to give her a sign.

She touched him. Had he been able to speak? Maybe, maybe he had. He had grabbed up whatever wits he could find, but of course everything was awry. There was no time to choose the words, not enough air to carry them out of his throat. Whatever noise came out surprised them both. He opened his eyes then, just in time to see her face light up like someone had set a big birthday cake in front of her.

And that was all. He had gone back under, as far as he knew, gone back into the sleep of the dead until just five minutes ago, when he had awakened, just plain woke up, in a bed in the dark, alone, pressed down, it felt like, an astronaut returned to earth. All that he possessed at the moment was a thin assurance: that woman, the window, his few words, had not been a dream. They belonged to this world, the world right now, where he had a mind that was working and a body that was not. He had awakened, but he knew then, beyond doubt. He had in no way been released.

Harper

Even in the upstairs bathroom, with the door closed, Harper could hear her voice. Delrina had been on the phone all morning. He hadn't been able to quite make out what she was saying—and Lord knows who she'd been talking to. It sure wasn't anybody local. There'd be long-distance charges. Worrisome, except that Roy was rich as hell.

Harper hunched down in the bathtub so that he could immerse his ears. This drowned out Delrina and allowed him to totally zone out for a few minutes. The old tub was deep and just long enough for his body, perfect after his run this morning. He had to admit that he ran best if he did it first thing, though of course yesterday he'd been too hungover to even think about it. Today, though, he was pretty clearheaded, and in just a few minutes, he was going to get busy on his to-do list. Totally.

Having Delrina around had reminded him of everything he had to do yet. She was a little hyper, that one. After she'd cleaned up the party debris yesterday, she'd made them omelets, tossed in zucchini and herbs from the garden (surprisingly good) and then she got to work asking all kinds of questions about the festival. She'd made him walk the land yesterday afternoon, hungover or not, so he could show her where the stage would be. Hadn't acted too impressed either. She'd just looked at him the whole time he was explaining where he'd park the cars, where he'd put the concessions, how the bands would set up on the stage.

"I've got a big banner to stretch across the top of the light grid—FESTIVAL OF THE KNOB," he'd said. The "Knob" letters were in the shape of the Swan's Knob itself. It was going to look really cool. He told her all of this, but she only asked who had come up with that name. He told her he had, and she'd said, "Oh, well, I see," and then adjusted her big Richard Petty glasses.

This pissed him off. Who was she, Miss High and Mighty in her celebrity Greyhound? He didn't ask her why it was she'd shown up in Swan's Knob weeks before her gig. He didn't ask, because he knew the damn answer—and that was, Miss Delrina Kay had nowhere else to go. He knew the look of someone at the end of their luck. He was not sure what had gone on with her son, with her band, but he was willing to bet she didn't have so much as a quarter tank of gas left. Celebrity or not, if it wasn't for him, she'd be parking herself and her bus at the nearest KOA.

She was in the kitchen still on the phone when he got downstairs.

"Yes, honey, that's exactly what I'm talking about. Well now, I just knew you were the very man to call. Those Fenders will do fine. And how about the mikes? We need at least a dozen. Maybe more. You remember what happened that night in Dollywood when the thunderstorm came through." She looked up from her seat at Roy's desk and smiled at Harper. She had pulled all that hair up into a ponytail and was wearing a hot pink *Delrina!* T-shirt. "Yes, you did save the day. I haven't forgotten. Oh, yes, I remember that part too."

As she spoke, Delrina unraveled the phone cord that had gotten tangled with the papers on the counter. She straightened the papers and then poked her fingers in the holes of the dial rotary to release the dust. "And as I recall, you were not so bad your own damn self." She looked at Harper now and shook her head to let him know this was all a put-on.

Without her makeup and a couple of quarts of wine in her, she had a sort of mid-thirties cuteness. She said, "Well, Superman, that is quite an offer. I'll have to think about that. In detail. In the meantime, sugar, you just get your crew and that equipment down here to Sewanee Knob. Then we'll see about all those superpowers. Okay, you too. Bye-bye!"

She hung up. "Hot damn!" she yelled. "We got us a sound system."

"Well," he said. That had been on the top of his list this morning.

"Well, what?" She walked over to him and looked at him with her haughty little smile. He measured, force of habit. In her cowboy boots, she was almost as tall as him, but not quite.

"Well, thank you," he said. "Sounds like there's going to be a little extra special payment due when it gets here."

"Harper, darling, you let me worry about that. You just concentrate on coming up with the twenty-five hundred dollars for the rental." She walked into the front room and he followed her.

"What?"

"Money, honey. But don't worry—Superman Dan, he won't expect a dime until the whole thing is over. I got that arranged."

"Sounds like it," he said, equal parts grateful and outdone. Delrina ignored his sarcasm and retrieved his notebook from the desk. She started making notes on the list he'd started yesterday. He was considering the best way to get it out of her hands when he heard the front screen door squeak. Star opened the front door.

"Oh," she said. "Good morning. I didn't want to knock. I wasn't sure you'd be up yet."

"Oh yeah, I've been up a long time. Took a run and everything," he said, overselling, though there was no reason to feel guilty. No one moved or said anything for a moment. Star had stopped at the threshold. "Come on in," he said.

"Yes," said Delrina. Her voice sounded funny.

Another silence, then finally, Star rescued them. She walked over to Delrina with her hand outstretched. "Hello, I'm Star," she said, so grown-up all of a sudden.

"Oh yeah," said Harper. He always forgot this part. Introductions. "Star, this is Delrina Kay. She's going to be in the festival. She's . . . she's come early."

"Oh, I know who she is," said Star. "Miss Kay, I am a really really big fan."

"Delrina. Call me Delrina. I'm not that much older than you, honey." Delrina didn't use her melodic charm voice on Star. Maybe that was reserved for people who could do something for her. Too bad, since Star was bestowing one of her rare smiles on her.

"Delrina, then," Star said. "I am so amazed you and Little Charlie are going to be in the festival. I used to play 'Standing Tall, Thinking Big' over and over all the way through elementary school."

"Elementary school? Well, just rub it in, darling." Delrina headed toward the kitchen. "I need another cup of coffee."

When she left them, Harper took a moment to give Star a hug.

She still smelled like a little girl. He'd talked to her several times since Roy had gone into the hospital, tried to get her to come out to the house, but this was the first he'd seen of her. "How you doing, baby?" he said. "Any news on Roy?"

"Yeah," she said. "Good news. Really good news, I think. I tried to call you but your phone is always busy."

"No surprise there," he said. "I've been trying to get things lined up for the show. It's coming along too."

Star looked toward the kitchen. "Do the acts always show up this far in advance?"

"Not usually," he said. "But first, Roy. Is he okay?"

"Well, better. That's what Wilma said this morning. She was at the hospital most of the night."

"You want coffee?" Delrina yelled from the kitchen.

"Yeah," said Harper. "Black."

"How about Star?" This said grudgingly.

Star smiled anyway and headed toward the kitchen. "I'll come fix mine."

"Sugar is over there, but I don't think there's milk," Harper heard, and then Delrina charged out of the kitchen, a small but intense thunderstorm accumulating on her face.

"I cannot believe you," she said in a spitting whisper.

"What?" he said, uncertain why he was whispering as well.

"She could not be more than eighteen," she said.

"Seventeen, actually, just turned seventeen."

"This does not bother you?" Star was back before Harper could ask what she was talking about.

"So Wilma came back early this morning. I'm not sure when it happened, but she said Roy woke up." She held her coffee with both hands.

"Woke up?"

"Just for a minute. She said he woke up and said a couple of words and then went back to sleep. But it's good, that's what she said. Hopeful." She smiled. "Good coffee, Miss . . . Delrina."

Harper looked around the living room, at Roy's nice stereo, his books, his duck decoys. He'd live to see them again. Harper was

flooded with a light-headed feeling. Relief, he guessed, followed by a
creeping guilt that maybe he'd given up on the guy. Given up and
started in on his wine.

"Wait," said Delrina. "Is this the guy, Harper?"

"What guy? Roy? Yeah, it's him all right." He shook his head,
hoping she would get the clue.

She didn't. "The one we visited the other night?" Fortunately, that
sounded fairly benign. No mention of all the drinking, the broken
wineglass in the hospital room.

"Yeah," he said. He turned to Star, wanting to get her talking before Delrina spilled the rest. "So this is great news—"

"My God!" Delrina put her hand on her chest in dramatic fashion. "Star, when did this happen?"

"Yesterday sometime. In the afternoon," said Star, still a little
awed at Delrina and wanting to be helpful. "He just opened his eyes
and said, 'Glass breaking,' at least that's what they think he said,
'glass breaking.'"

"That's it, that's it!" Delrina screamed.

Star

She didn't have a lot of experience with celebrities, but she realized
now that what set them apart was the whole larger-than-life thing.
Maybe they felt things more deeply, because they sure did act more
dramatic—like what Delrina Kay was doing—waving her arms big,
looking up at the deer antler chandelier and yelling, "Thank you,
thank you, thanks be!" Best Star could make out, Delrina had met
Roy once. Her dad had taken her up to the hospital. Roy hadn't even
been conscious, so that barely counted. Still, here she was, nearly
having an epileptic fit over the news that he might, just might, recover. "Oh my God," said Delrina. "Harper, don't you get it? It's a
miracle."

Star looked at her dad for a clue about this woman, but he just
smiled, like, *Bear with me here, okay?* Maybe he had a thing going
here. Delrina was about his age, though he usually went for someone

younger. He kept looking at Star to make sure she was all right with this ranting celebrity. She was. Her dad's life was never boring, that was for sure. In the middle of the next round of "Thanks be, thanks be," the phone rang.

Delrina stopped immediately. "I better get it," she said in a controlled, totally different voice. "Could be the guy from *Rolling Stone*."

She went into the kitchen and answered the phone. "Hello?" she said, a little arpeggio. "Well, yes, you've got her. It's Delrina. Heeey!"

Star looked at her dad and made a couple of oh-my-God faces.

"Oh, Benny, of course I'm happy to talk to you. Anything I can do to get the word out about the festival. It's going to be quite a show."

Her dad grinned at Star and said quietly, "That's him."

"*Rolling Stone?*" She couldn't believe it. Her dad.

"Hey, you know what?" He pulled her over to the couch to sit down. "How about we put together a song or two for this thing, you and I?"

"I don't know," she said. "I'm not good enough."

"Sure you are," he said. "It'd be fun."

"I'm not sure about the full lineup," Delrina was saying in a kind of stage voice from the other room. "I know I'll be singing my little heart out throughout the day and night at the Sewanee Knob Fest. Of course, that will be in combination with some of the other top talent—"

"Oh God," said Star's dad. He grabbed a notebook off the coffee table. He found a blank page and wrote "Festival of the Knob, Swan's Knob, NC" in big letters across the top and then he scribbled down some names.

"Yes, you're so right, Benny, these little festivals are the heart and soul of what I call *real* country music, as opposed to that mess they play on the radio out in L.A. That's why I've gone back to my *roots*, to the root of it all. What's that? Well now, that's just a bunch of folks, folks like you and me, setting on the front porch, singing and playing."

Star's dad rushed into the kitchen with the notebook.

"Just the other night, when I got up here to Sewanee, there was a whole party of folks waiting to welcome me. And how did they do that? Well, they all assembled on Roy Swan's front porch with their instruments and such. When I got here, we had us a big time, I'll tell you, honey."

Her dad came back into the front room, but he couldn't sit down. He walked between the couch and the door to the kitchen, back and forth, listening to Delrina, alternatively wincing and nodding as she made her points using a mix of down-home expressions and melodic bad grammar.

Eventually, Delrina began to feed the guy the list of names. Star's dad seemed to relax a little then and sat back down. He asked about Roy again, and Star told him again everything her grandma had said on the phone.

"Wait," he said, finally. "She was gone most of the night. What did you do?"

"Went to sleep." What did he think, she was ten still?

"Ah, baby, why didn't you come out here?"

"It was late. It was no big deal."

"Still, Wilma's going to be at the hospital even more now, and you don't need to be alone all that time—"

"Well, that's done!" Delrina was off the phone, but she hadn't dropped the celebrity-vibe speech yet. "Did you hear? Benny out there in L.A., he just loved it! How about all that stuff I said about picking on the porch? You got to mention the porch, honey, or it's just not country to those people. I'll tell you, not a bad bit of work for a Monday morning!"

"It is Monday, isn't it?" Her dad looked at the clock and back at Star. "And why aren't you over at the high school, come to think of it?"

"High school!" said Delrina. "Goddamn."

Star was never prepared when her dad slipped into father mode. "Dad—," she started.

"Dad?" said Delrina. "Goddamn, Harper. She's your daughter?" She let out a huge laugh and then ran over and pulled Star up out of the chair. "Oh, sweetie," she said and hugged her tight.

Chapter Seventeen

Roy

Come dawn, which he witnessed through a small gap in the curtain, Roy was clear on several things. He was in a hospital all right. He had been out for a while, unconscious or doped up, something. Something was wrong with him. He could move a few things—a couple fingers, couple toes under the covers—but his right side was dead as a doornail. Stroke then, that's probably what it was, damn it. The woman who'd been in his room before (last night, last week, last year?) was not there. A nurse had come in and out several times, but he hadn't quite been able to get her attention. They had him on some kind of breathing machine that was about to drive him crazy, *heave ho heave ho*. He wanted to get the nurse to turn it off, but his eyelids didn't always work when he told them to, and she was gone before he knew it. As far as she was concerned, he was probably some kind of vegetable. This thought pissed him off so bad that out of nowhere, he started crying. Pretty soon, he could feel tears running down his face, but couldn't summon up a hand to wipe them away. Goddamn.

The next time the nurse opened the door, he made sure to hold his eyes open. She was not the kind of looker that a man might hope for first thing out of a coma or whatever, a little hard for his taste, harsh red lipstick, tired eyes. She was nice enough to look his way, though, and when she did, her eyes lit up with surprise.

"Mr. Swan?" she said. "You're awake!"

No kidding, he wanted to say, but it came out as a kind of low hiss. "Kuh, kuh, kuh . . ."

"Cup?" she said, in the kind of voice you use on a two-year-old. "You want a cup? Of water? Oh, I'm afraid not, not with a ventilator." She checked the machines and then asked him to follow her finger as she moved it slowly from right to left. He did it, trying his best to appear more with-it than a vegetable.

She grabbed his left hand and said, "Don't try and talk anymore. Just squeeze my hand. Once for yes, twice for no." She proceeded to ask him a bunch of things—like was he in pain and was his name Roy—things he mostly knew, damn it, but he was busy with the joy of actually being able to feel her hand, her soft, cold fingers. She didn't really give him enough time to get his squeezing going. He just sat there, Roy, the tomato.

"Don't be afraid," she said. "You've had a stroke. You're in Baptist Hospital. I'm going to go get a doctor. You hold tight, okay?"

"Tuuh," he managed, though this was not at all what he intended. There was a whole river full of words dammed up inside him, and after she left, the sheer force of them made him feel like he was going to blow a gasket. What the hell was all this? Where was everyone? "Kuuh. Tuuh." Was that all he had to say? The outrageousness of his situation just flew at him, burned him up, and of course, here came more tears. *Easy, Roy,* he told himself, *don't want to have another stroke.* Goddamn.

Over the next hour, there were a bunch of people in and out of the room, all of them talking fast and not giving him much of a chance to respond. He wasn't a vegetable. He did undertand them. He was more like someone's old dog, lying there, everyone petting him, but too dumb to do much of anything. His only consolation was that there seemed to be some talk about the breathing machine. One of the young men, a doctor maybe, kept fiddling with the dials.

"Better call his wife," said one person, and this seemed to open another compartment, and he was flooded with the feeling he had every day when he walked in his back door. He could picture her clearly, the woman who was his wife, standing in the yellow kitchen with a row of canned tomatoes behind her. Her name didn't come to him. There was a warm spot where that name should've been, but he tried not to panic over it—*goodly wife of Roy Swan,* was all he knew.

Oh, and there was his name, *Roy Swan*. Very good. He would try to hang on to that for the next time one of these people asked him. How about, he would just say it now: "Roy Swan." There. A man didn't forget how to say his name. Still, he hadn't heard much of a sound.

The man over by the machine looked up. "Wait," he said to the others and then leaned down right in front of Roy. "What did you say?"

He moved his mouth the same way again.

"Roy Swan. Yes. Excellent. That's your name, Mr. Swan." He smiled, but used that tone reserved for toddlers. "I know all of this is a little confusing, but it'll get better. It's impossible for you to talk with your trach in. I've turned the ventilator down now, and in an hour or so, I'm going to be able to take it away. Then you'll be able to try speaking again. How's that?"

Great, he wanted to say, but the guy had already looked away. Roy guessed he was the doctor. He was acting like he was the most important person in the room, though he was the youngest for sure. Roy tried to read his nameplate, but he had turned to scowl at the nurse with the red lipstick. "I remain appalled that you didn't call me overnight," he said in a mean voice. He proceeded to tell her what all she'd done wrong. Roy didn't catch most of it, but he couldn't get over the tone of the man's voice, mean, mean, mean. The woman had had a hard life, that was clear, lines all over her face, slumpy boobs. Once again, he felt the tears coming down again, and then, most awful, a rivulet of drool from the left corner of his mouth.

The nurse drew her lips into a frown. "You're scaring him," she said flatly and left the room.

The doctor turned. "Mr. Swan," he said loudly. "Your wife will be here in a few minutes." He left the room then too. Roy was worn out and drifted into sleep. He dreamed, though he didn't go far. He dreamt of the woman by the window. In his dream, she floated from the window to his bed and hovered over him as he slept, dream within a dream. He understood then that she was an angel, that she was not real. He understood this now, the real world and the others.

When he woke up, there were more people around. Foolishly, he looked for her, but there was no one and nothing in the least familiar.

He was in a mad cycle now: each new waking brought him to a different shore, where he could never tell if he was coming or going. This time, he had raised his arm before he knew it and started batting away something that was pulling at his throat. Someone restrained that arm now, which made him mad as fire—he had just gotten it back. "Take it easy," he heard. It was the surly doctor. "We're going to get this thing out of here and you'll feel much better."

And then he did feel better, breathing on his own, though it seemed the wind was whistling through his neck for a minute. He opened his eyes to see the ugly nurse bandaging his throat. His arm was tied to the bed rail.

"Take off," he said, and it sounded almost right, though slurred slightly. They must've used novocaine on one of his molars.

"Take off?" she said. "You wanting to leave us already, Mr. Swan?"

"No," he said as loud as he could and pulled on his tied-up left arm. He couldn't move the right one at all.

"Oh," she said. "I can't take that off, hon." This made him mad again, and he would have done something about it, but just then the door swung open with considerable force. Roy craned his neck to see if there was someone coming to help him, maybe that angel, but this was someone else, a nicely dressed woman who rushed to his bed and dropped her brown pocketbook on the floor. He recognized her as soon as she grabbed his hand. "Goodly wife," he said, clear as a bell, and he had never been prouder of himself.

"Roy," she said, not like he was some two-year-old, but like he was a man come back from the dead, which maybe he was. She had the same crying disease he did, because tears came up in her eyes and started spilling out the little corner creases, and then he started in too, which was a mess.

Josh

Star had not shown up for school. He wasn't sure what this meant. He thought Roy was better, but maybe not. School sucked without her, frankly. There was no one to look for, no shining face to pick out of the crowd between classes, during lunch. Math was his last class. Total drag to sit there and look at her chair.

"Where's the new girl?" someone asked him. He didn't answer.

He headed into town just after the last bell. He made it to Fowler's Market in about five minutes, and from there, it was just another five to the Swans' corner. The house was right across from the library, and almost as big, white with lots of ornate kinds of woodwork. Nice. From the sidewalk, it didn't look like anyone was home. Looked more like they had gone on vacation—the grass all grown up, the big fig tree full of birds helping themselves to the ripe figs. He stood there for a minute, then decided he might as well see if Star was home. He had a right now, didn't he? A little bit.

He climbed the front stairs and stepped over a bunch old newspapers. He rang. The bell echoed through the house, but no one came to the door. Maybe she was at the hospital with her grandma. Maybe he should go down to Hardees and get something to eat, but he hated to leave, so he sat on the steps. A couple of cars went by, and probably they were looking at him. He stood back up and started collecting the papers, put them in a neat stack by the front door. This gave him an idea.

Roy's lawn mower was right where he looked first, in the shed in back, and there was plenty of gas. Josh rolled it into the front yard. It took a few minutes—the spark plug was old—but he got Roy's mower started and from there it was easy. As he mowed, he practiced the look he would have when Star showed up. He'd shake his head in a modest, manly way, like, *Hey, no big deal, this is the kind of thing I do. No problem, little lady.* She would tell him to come inside when he finished up, and she would go and make him lemonade. No, on second thought, she would look out the window and see him sweating, and she would draw him a bath, that's what she'd do. He'd take off his clothes and get down in the water, and that's when she'd bring him the lemonade.

Wilma

He looked just awful. They'd told her he was awake when she'd come onto the floor. She couldn't get into his room fast enough. There was a nurse bent over him, and she raised up as Wilma walked in and sure enough, there he was: still gray, one side of his face tilted like an image in a fun-house mirror, his ventilator gone, and his ample mouth mawing open so that you could see all his dental work. It would take her a long time to erase that particular picture of him, to forget how it felt to be happy and terrified in the same moment. She heard the contents of her purse clatter to the floor. She'd dropped it. Change rang out and her lipstick rolled. She just let it go and went over to him.

"Piddly knife," he said, with a smile like a two-year-old. She didn't know what this meant, but it was clear that he knew her.

She called his name, and then the two of them just sat there and cried. This was a first, as far as she knew. Roy wasn't big on crying, he would hate it when he thought about it later, but for now, it felt good to do anything, anything at all together. She reached for his hand, then saw that they had it tied to the bed rail.

"Can't we get rid of this?" she asked the nurse.

"He was pulling at his trach wound earlier. Best to leave it for now." The woman picked up Roy's chart and got out of the room before Wilma could say another thing.

"Off." Roy tugged at the restraint.

"I know, Roy, it seems silly, but we need to keep it that way right now." She patted his arm. "I'm just so happy you're back. You've been unconscious for over a week now. We didn't know . . ."

Roy's eyes darted around the room. She looked at him and waited. It looked like it was hard for him to come up with the words. "Get off," blew out of his mouth finally in a big rush, clear as a bell.

"I understand, Roy. You want me to take this restraint off your hand. But they told me not to, honey." He looked at her then, and though he didn't say anything more, she could see exactly what he wanted to say, which was, *This is me here, Roy, and this is a stupid ridiculous situation. You know me better than these others. Do what I'm asking* . . .

"Look," she said. "Do you promise not to pull on those bandages?"

"Ummm," he said. "A course."

She looked at the door to make sure no one was coming, though it wasn't as if she was about to commit a criminal act. As she started to work on the ties, she looked up and saw the pure fury in Roy's face, the complete animal anger derived from being subjected to this folly along with everything else. As she worked—the cloth strips were double knotted and not easily released—he grunted and pulled against them, his hand in a tight fist.

"Hold still," she said. "You're making it worse." Just then the thing came undone, surprising them both. Roy's arm flew up in the air, and his fist smacked hard into her chin.

It was a baffling offense: the sting of contact, the displacement of her jaw, every thought in her head rattled to kingdom come. An instinctive anger crested in her chest and then receded instantly, but a yelp of pain had already escaped. Roy yelped too, horribly, like a dog run over by a car, and gripped the bed rail.

From the doorway, where the nurse was standing at that moment, it must have looked much worse than it was, for the woman didn't even enter the room but turned and ran down the hall in search of help before Wilma could set her straight.

Roy

He was alone and utterly exhausted, so they hardly needed to restrain his good arm, and now, his good leg. There had been many people in the room, trying to get the "situation under control," as that surly doctor had put it. No one had said much to him, and he had been unable to tell them, to explain, though that hardly mattered. There was no excusing the fact that he had hit Wilma. Oh, and yes, *her name, of course, Wilma, Wilma and not miss and not wife and not even goodly wife, but Wilma.*

Wilma had understood what happened. He saw an expression of (oh God) pity flash across her face even as the pain registered in her jaw. This only added to his horror. She had bitten her tongue when he hit her and blood had come pouring out of her mouth. There'd been a big fracas: an orderly tied him up in a pretty rough fashion while the doctor attended to Wilma—dabbed her tongue, shone the light in her eyes, just like they did to him a hundred times a day.

"This is silly. I'm fine. It was just an accident. A silly accident," she'd said over and over, the "S" sound thick on her injured tongue.

They gave her ice. They lectured her about letting him loose. They talked of sending her down to the emergency room, which she refused.

Go, he wanted to say, *go,* but they had put some medicine in his IV that made him too sleepy to speak. She didn't say anything to him—what could she say with all those people in the room?—but smiled in way she meant to be reassuring. After a few minutes, a blue bruise was rising underneath her chin, and he noticed she tried to hide it from them (and him) with her ice pack. This made him want to roll over and die right there. They made her leave finally, told her she had to go home.

"Roy," she whispered to him before she left—they wouldn't leave her alone with him—"forget all about this, sweetie. Forget it. Oh, I hope when this is all over you won't remember it. But remember this: I love you. I'm so, so glad you're back."

Roy's parents died in a train wreck on the Silver Star just south of Baltimore. A switch malfunction, two trains collided. His parents had been in the first-class car, just two back from the engine. They had been dead and buried for six months by the time he got home from Korea.

"Terrible accident, but they died on impact, from the look of the bodies." That's what Ron Snow had said when he picked him up at the airport in Greensboro. "Probably never knew what hit them."

And though it wasn't strictly a funeral director's job, that day Ron had taken him by the cemetery at Old Salem, God's Acre, where his folks had been buried with his mother's kin. It was just a few days before Easter, and people were everywhere tending the graves, washing the headstones, staking up pots of fresh lilies and hydrangeas. Roy was still in his dress uniform on that afternoon, full starch, spit shine. He'd come through the war; he'd fairly strutted past all the girls in the airport. Everything in working order.

There came the moment finally when he had to stand on the Easter basket–green grass by his parents' grave, the moment when the theory that he'd held in Korea, that of his parents' passing, moved over into the realm of fact. This was, as Ron Snow surely knew, the purpose of the graveyard, to remind the living as much as to remember the dead.

A breeze blew through God's Acre and ruffled Roy's auburn hair like a mother's hand. He felt for the first time the guilt of his own survival, the hubris of his living, and the burdensome force of his future. In the next few weeks, he would receive all manner of *welcome home*s: farm field kisses, pool cues and corn liquor shoved in his hands, pound cakes and jams. These would continue, these things: his life would go on. He would get a gut and lose his hair. He would travel, romance women, marry late. He knew all these things now, the course of his life less in some ways than the man-boy might have dreamed on that day, and also, far more. But he and the man-boy, they had the same lack of imagination when it came to that grave. For it was unimaginable, completely so, that resting in those few square feet, in those two elaborate boxes, was all that remained of his parents.

At the time, it had seemed a heinous thing, for Erma and Charles Swan to die without knowing, alive one minute, out of this world the next, but now, from his hospital bed, such a death seemed to Roy to be the height of luxury, a Pullman car with velvet seats. They had died together in an instant, without knowing they would.

Chapter Eighteen

Wilma

She hadn't been gone but a few hours, but as she drove through those blocks of Main Street on her way home, it seemed like she had been on a monthlong trip. Little things had changed—a new display of rust-colored sweaters in the window of Traditional Shop, mums in the flower boxes, a tree with just a tinge of yellow in its leaf tips—but it was more than that.

Roy was going to be better, she said to herself over and over, sure of it now. She knew this feeling, the sheer giddiness of a second chance. Her life had been full of them, and here was another. A new lease on life. She loved that expression. That's what she had, and that was what Roy had. He'd see. His broken speech, her aching jaw, his drooping right side, all trivial. Okay, they had some work to do, and they would do it. But right now, she couldn't even think of that. She could only drive in her nice new Ford LTD through her town, slowly, glad for two red lights so that she could stop and take it in, glad to roll by all that was familiar: the drugstore, her little church, that nasty old pool hall, the Coach House, the bank, and behind each building, right out her car window, the familiar slopes of their mountain.

She was most anxious to get home, and she made a note of this as she neared their block. Roy would feel the same way. That would be the first order of business. As she steered the LTD into the driveway—excellent turning radius for such a big car, that's what Roy had said when he bought it for her. No sign of Star. Poor Star, she had barely seen her grandmother these past days. She had been asleep when Wilma got home last night and asleep when she left for the hospital at dawn. Wilma only hoped Star had noticed the box of doughnuts she'd left on the kitchen table for her breakfast, though Lord, Sarah was such a health food nut, she would be appalled to hear what Wilma was feeding her daughter.

She turned off the car and gathered her things, all the while trying to calculate the current time in the Pacific. She had to call Sarah and give her the news about Roy's stroke. She should have done it before, of course. Sarah was going to feel left out, held at arm's length. This was something she had complained about before. Wilma hadn't really said much about her relationship with Roy until shortly before their wedding. Sarah was still mad over it, but in that case, and in this one, come to think of it, Sarah's strong, vocal, and mostly offbeat opinions were not always what Wilma needed. In a pinch, she could pick out her wedding dress by herself. She would rather go it alone if she was going to have to hear how the traditional marriage ceremony was all about the transfer of property and how, in that case, maybe the best color to wear was black.

She was trying to remember where she'd put that last number Sarah had given her when she heard the whine of Roy's lawn mower. Her first impulse was to look around for him, though of course that was silly. Then here came Celeste's youngest boy, Josh, around the side of the house, pushing the thing.

She had to smile when she saw him—she hadn't had a lot to smile about lately and this felt good. He was cute as he could be: sweet eyes for a boy, taller than she remembered, and more handsome. Looked a little like Troy Donohue. And those ears, well, he would grow into them maybe, that or develop a fine sense of humor. When he saw her, he fumbled with the mower to shut it off and walked over to her, buttoning his shirt up.

"Did your mother send you over here? You are just the sweetest thing," she said. Celeste and Travis had a large, immaculately groomed front yard, and now she knew why.

"Uh, no, ma'am. I was walking by, and well, the grass looked tall. It'll go to seed if you let it go too far, so I thought . . . Hope it's okay." He didn't quite look her in the eye until he got to the last part.

"Okay?" she said. "Son, it's the nicest thing you could do. Roy will be so pleased to have this done. And in fact, I'd be more than happy to pay you."

He took a minute to consider this. "No, thanks," he said finally, and then after another pause, "Do you have any idea when Star might be back?"

Now the whole thing made sense. Of course. Anothing thing she'd missed. She looked at her watch. "Well, she should be home from school any moment."

"She wasn't at school," he said, and then his ears turned bright red. "I mean, well, I didn't see her. She could've been there."

Star had skipped school. Great. Wilma felt that guilt rise up again, along with a bit of irritation. Why did teenagers always pick the worst moment to go down the wrong road? Okay, she would not go crazy over this. She would not imagine Star lying dead in a ditch somewhere or smoking cigarettes and swigging moonshine behind the pool hall. No. Second chances. It was a day for second chances, that's what it was, if and only if everybody would just have the courtesy to make it through the entire twenty-four hours without dying.

Wilma smiled again at Josh, who was bathed in sweat over having told on Star. "She'll be back soon, I'm sure. When you finish," she said, "how about coming in for some lemonade?"

She went inside and changed out of her hospital clothes, found her slippers. She got back down to the kitchen and was rooting around in her freezer for the frozen juice when the phone rang. For the first time in two weeks, her heart didn't beat up into her throat at the sound.

"Hello?" She'd hoped it would be Star, but instead she heard the crackle of an overseas connection.

"Hi, Mom, it's Sarah." The connection was pretty good this time.

"Hi, honey. Where are you?"

"Still in Kuala Lumpur. It's really hot, but we're happy to be here. Korea was okay, but everyone seemed so downtrodden there, so un-interested in things. I had enough pickled cabbage for a lifetime." Wilma could hear the fatigue in Sarah's voice. In this state, whining was not unusual for her, but it was rare to hear her dismiss an entire culture, unless of course it was her own.

"Well, you never did like chowchow either," said Wilma.

"Oh God, chowchow, that's what you call it. Of course. Yuck! I was trying to tell our host about it just the other night. It's really not that far from kimchi, but listen, tell me, how are you doing? How's Star?"

"Well," said Wilma. Not the time to say she didn't know where Star might be. "Fine, we're all fine. Roy's had a bit of a setback, but he's better now. We're all fine now."

"What kind of setback?"

"He's had some sort of cerebral event. Scared us all, but he's back now."

"Mother! Roy's had a stroke? Oh my God. When? Why didn't you call me?"

Wilma took a breath. "Honey, what could you do, all the way over there? Nothing but worry, honey. And now you don't have to. When I saw Roy this morning, he was conscious and even spoke a few words. He's going to be fine."

"Wait. Let me get this straight." Here it came. Righteous indignation, a specialty. "Roy is in the hospital. The hospital. With a serious stroke. Oh my God, you've had your hands full, I'm sure. Did you think that I might want to be around—or God forbid, just be available—to comfort my daughter in such a stressful situation?" She had a point there, and she was getting mad. "No, you decided to go it alone, as always. With Star in tow. God, Mother, have you completely lost your mind?"

"Honey, after the week I've had, that is a really poor choice of words." She laughed, hoping to lighten the situation. No dice.

"And this has been going on how long, a week? So you knew when we talked last Sunday?"

"Well," said Wilma, and there was a silence abroad.

"Okay," she said finally. "We're coming home. I don't know what else to do. I don't know how we'll manage, how we'll arrange it, but that's it. Put Star on the phone. We're coming home."

Star

Delrina ground into the next gear and turned her tour bus onto Main Street. Star clung to the cheetah-print captain's chair behind the driver's seat, regretting her decision to accept Delrina's offer.

"Come on, I'll take you back to your grandma's. How many times do you get to travel in a first-class genuine tour bus?" Delrina had said when Star asked her dad for a ride. She wanted to leave Roy's truck at the farm since, technically, Wilma had never said she could drive it. She'd wondered why her dad hadn't been so crazy about Delrina's idea.

Now she knew. First, there had been the ordeal of backing the thing out of the field. Next was the difficulty posed by a 5'2" woman handling a steering wheel the circumference of a hula hoop. There was now a big question in her dad's mind of whether they had enough gas.

"Sit tight," said Delrina. "I'm telling you, once that low fuel light goes on, you've got a minimum of sixty miles before the tank is dry." Star had to laugh. Her dad and mom had had the very same argument a thousand times when she was a little girl, only it was always her dad who would make the "sit tight" speech.

"I'm just saying," said her dad, from the dining booth that converted into a bed, "that we don't need to get stuck in this thing in the middle of downtown."

Delrina just shook her head, which made her beaded braids clack against each other. She'd loaded one of her latest recordings into her compact disc system when they boarded ("See? State-of-the-art!") and her songs had been blaring out of ten speakers ever since. Delrina mouthed the words and smacked all of her silver rings against the steering wheel in time with the music.

"The house is just two blocks down on the right," Star said over the racket. "It's on the corner, just past Murphy Street." She hoped her grandma hadn't made it home yet.

"Is that Murphy?" said Delrina. She pointed, and the bus wobbled. Star was about to say yes, but her dad yelled, "Shit!" They had drifted into the left lane. Delrina jerked the bus to the right, missing the oncoming conversion van but bumping up over the curb on the corner. The sign saying "Murphy Street" loomed briefly in the windshield before it was mowed down. Delrina kept on turning the wheel, pulled into the street proper, and managed to stop the bus basically parallel to the curb. She pulled on the hand brake and then swiveled her seat. "Harper, don't you ever scare me like that again! We could've been killed!"

Star did not wait for her dad's reply. From their parking space, she could see her grandma's LTD in the driveway. She grabbed the lever to open the door and ran down the steps. If she could get inside, maybe her dad could persuade Delrina to get the bus turned around and out of town before anyone noticed.

She made it across the street but didn't see Josh until he was standing right in front of her. He was so tall. He looked at her in that cute cockeyed way he had, his head tilted to the side, hand on his hip. He gave her a crazy wide smile and then looked back at the bus. "Well, hey," he said, "have you joined the tour?"

"I hope not," she said, forgetting for an instant the need to hustle into the house. "What are you doing here?"

He was about to tell her when two horn blasts sounded from the bus. The door whooshed open again and, natch, here came Delrina around the bus. Her dad followed, calling Delrina in his be-reasonable voice.

"Is that her?" said Josh, real low.

"Oh yeah, Delrina Kay." Star was getting used to all this.

As they approached, her dad kept looking back up at the house. And, of course, just then, the back door clicked, and the screen door creaked open. Her dad closed his eyes for a moment. Grandma Wilma came out onto the stoop in her apron with the fall leaves on it. Maybe she had just gotten up from a nap. Her face was all puffy on one side and further messed up by a tight frown. She headed down the stairs, managing to stomp even though she was wearing her bedroom scuffs. She didn't look at Star right away but checked out the bus and then Star's dad. He was the one who was going to get it. Totally unfair.

"Well, heeey!" said Delrina, stretching her hand out. Star's grandma just looked at her like she was a dead animal, and then turned back to her dad.

"I hear Star wasn't in school today. Where has she been?" said her grandma, actually putting her hands on her hips.

Her dad didn't say anything right away, but he got that look that her mother called "the brick wall." He made his face very smooth and still, but hard as a rock.

Lovely, great. Family drama. Josh standing right there. Josh thinking, *No one acts weird like this in my family.* Now he would break up with her for sure.

Harper

Easy, he told himself, *go easy. Remember she's had a rough time lately.*

"Wilma," he said. "This is Miss Delrina Kay. I'm sure you've heard some of her music." Wilma gave Delrina a reluctantly civil smile. Harper made a quick decision. For once, Wilma would get a dose of her own Emily Post. He adopted the mannerly tone he'd heard Roy use with the ladies. "Delrina, Wilma is just about the most famous piano teacher in three counties. She's taught about a zillion students, including one concert pianist. Isn't that right, Miss Wilma? And now she's a choir director too."

Miss Wilma did not seem impressed by the compliments, but now that he'd pulled out the script, centuries of arcane social encoding kicked in. She had to be nice. It was in the genes. And lucky for him, the rules provided no means for a quarrel in front of strangers.

"Miss Kay, nice to meet you. What a lovely bus you have," Wilma said on cue. She did not, however, offer her hand. Perhaps this was not strictly required.

"Hello, Miss Kay," Josh said, sticking out his hand. Delrina shook it and then looked back at Miss Wilma.

Harper held his breath, hoping that somewhere Delrina harbored some scrap of the code, but of course, this was the woman who had grilled him on the way over about the location and quality of the nearest pawnshop.

"Oh, Wilma, honey, I just want to say how sorry I am that your husband has had such a hard time. But I was so glad when little Star here came out to the farm this morning and told us that Roy is doing better."

"So Star's been at the farm all day?" Wilma looked from Star to Harper and back. Then to Delrina: "And you're staying at my husband's farm as well?"

"Well, yeah, getting ready for the festival. It's just a few weeks off, you know. Lots to do."

"I see," Wilma said.

Delrina, finally sensing they were in trouble, looked at Harper for help. He needed to make a quick case. There was a short silence while he gathered his argument, then everyone spoke at once.

"Grandma, there was no way I could deal with school today."

"Harper told me it'd be all right to park the bus at the farm—"

"I'll just go finish up the mowing."

Wilma swept her hand in the air as if to dismiss them all. "Look!" It seemed she might cry for a minute, but then she calmed herself. "You know what, Josh, that is a good idea. It's not long until dark. Go ahead and finish up. And, Star, why don't you help him with the trimming? There are clippers in the back shed where the mower was." The kids scuttled off.

Wilma looked at Delrina. "Miss Kay, it is a delight to meet you. That bus looks very comfortable, so I wonder if you wouldn't mind sitting in it now while I have a quick chat with Harper." She smiled in dismissal and turned to march up the driveway. "Family business," she said over her shoulder. "Won't take but a few minutes."

Harper had no choice but to follow.

"Well, hold on a minute," said Delrina.

Wilma acted like she hadn't heard and kept walking.

"Wait just a *damn* minute!" Delrina shouted this time. Was there a way to signal her? She had no idea whom she was up against. Wilma turned and looked Delrina up and down. Delrina was dressed in studded blue jeans and a chartreuse Western shirt that threatened to burst open at the bust. Thankfully, she'd gone light on the makeup.

"Please," he begged, without moving his mouth.

"Please what?" Delrina used her stage voice. "Please allow this woman to treat me like trash? Please act like it's okay she don't want me in her house?" She charged past Harper and approached Wilma.

"You would not be doing this if you knew," she said. She shook her head so violently that all of her braids got tangled up. "Tell her, Harper, tell her what we did. How we brought Roy back from the brink of death."

Oh, Jesus, not this. Please not this again. Hadn't he taken her aside not an hour ago and asked her to keep her theories about Roy's revival to herself? He looked over to the front yard, where that boy had just put his hand on the small of Star's back. When he turned back, both women were looking at him, and shit, of course, both of them were mad now.

"Well?" said Delrina.

He wasn't going to say a word.

"Okay, fine." Delrina dismissed him. "It started with Roy's wine. We were all out at the picking party on the porch. Me and Harper and a bunch of other folks were drinking Roy's wine."

"When was this?" said Wilma, feigning interest now, forming a noose.

"Saturday night," said Delrina. "Harper was telling me what bad shape Roy was in, how he was dying, and I says, 'Let's go take him some of this stuff,' and so we did, though God, we probably shouldn't have been driving." Delrina detailed their ride over to Winston and their entry into the hospital. Harper tried not to listen. He looked back up toward Star and Josh. That kid's hand was resting lower now, just above her studded belt.

"We were just a-carrying on at first. We made a bunch of toasts, spilt wine all over the place, so on. You know what it's like. You been drinking most of the night, you get silly, you get a little sloppy, but you also get deep thoughts. Drinking can be mystical. I got to looking at Roy after a while. He was so alone in that bed, even though we were right there. I just wanted to do something. And that's when I thought of it. To give him a taste of his wine, the fruit of his own soil, the fruit of his labor. Course, I didn't get the full mystic understanding of this until today."

Star and Josh had disappeared around the house, leaving the lawn mower in the far end of the front yard.

"You gave him wine?" Wilma looked at Harper now. "You gave a man on a ventilator *wine*?"

"Just a little bit," said Delrina. "Harper was worried we'd choke him, but I just dipped my pinkie in a glass and stuck it in his mouth."

"What?" This yelp blew past Miss Wilma's genetic composition and came out her mouth with such force that Delrina needed to take a step back.

"Well, my finger was clean," she said in a wounded voice. "We didn't hurt him. Don't you get it? The wine, the wine woke him up. We saved him."

"Saved him?" Wilma headed up the hill so fast that one of her shoes came off. "Hell's bells!" she yelled, and then at the top of the steps: "Harper, get in here!"

Harper looked over at Delrina. "I have never in my life met a more ungrateful woman—," she began.

"Please," he said, "get on the bus. I'll be back in a few minutes."

He trudged up the driveway. It had been a long time since he got a spanking. He looked around the front yard once again, but Star was not there. She could well be in the potting shed at this moment, becoming the wrong kind of flower.

Wilma

Her jaw ached. She had a ringing in her ears brought on either by her injury or her sudden fury, and she had an odd craving for a glass of wine. She'd take a page from that nutty woman's book—a little wine might cure all three of her ills, and if she could drink fast enough, it might prevent her from killing her former son-in-law. Four miracles. All in one day. She took a bottle from the refrigerator and was rummaging around in the drawer for a corkscrew when Harper knocked lightly on the back door and then let himself in, making a show of wiping his feet. He had always been a performer, that one, musician, husband, family man—talented, charming, handsome in an elfin way, everything peachy until the real work began or the light bill was due.

"Let me explain," he said.

"Good idea." Why had she even agreed to let him take care of the farm? It'd have been better to just let the grapes fall to the ground.

"Everything has been going along fine. Just like I told you, I've been looking after things out there—the last of the vegetables, the grapes. I called the ag agent. He's going to come by in a few days and tell me if the grapes are ready. There are not a lot of them this year—next year will be the first real production—so we'll just go through and take what we have to next week."

"You've got a crew lined up?" she said, knowing the answer.

He licked his lips and narrowed his eyes, like he was calculating his workforce. "Oh, yeah, I'll have plenty by then."

"What'll we need to pay them?" The corkscrew had not gone into the bottle properly, and she was having a hard time getting it out. This was usually Roy's job.

"I haven't got that far yet," he said. "Do you need help with that? I'm not sure I've ever seen you take a glass of wine."

"Never did much," she said, "until Roy and I got acquainted." For Roy, no vacation was complete without a visit to a winery. They'd been all over by now, Napa, Green River, Loire Valley, Umbria. She'd developed a taste for it. She gave a last tug on the cork and it popped out of the bottle.

"Good job," Harper said. He sat down at the kitchen table.

Wilma remained standing. "I'd offer you some, but you've got your friend out there in the bus."

"She can wait," he said, using that smile that showed off those soulful brown eyes, the look that must have gotten her daughter in trouble those years ago, and the one that made it hard for anyone to stay mad at him for long. It hadn't worked on her in the past, and it sure wouldn't work today.

"Look . . ." she said.

"I know, I know, Delrina is a real piece of work. I apologize, Miss

Wilma. She just showed up out there, just showed up, no warning. I mean, she's booked for the festival, but why she got here eight weeks early I don't know. She may be a little down on her luck."

"And the communion miracle?"

He laughed. "Oh God, sorry about that too. You've been around musicians. They can be a crazy bunch. Always making things up, injecting drama into a situation. It's what makes them good performers. And Lord knows, Delrina is that. Just this morning, you should've heard her—"

"You know, this is none of my concern." Wilma got one wineglass out of the cabinet, then another. The alternative was to wait until he left, and they had some business to settle yet.

"Look, she's just camping in her bus out there at the farm, and she's even helping me with the last arrangements for the festival. I don't think Roy would mind at all. No harm done."

"No harm? What did she say about a party? You're supposed to be looking after things and you have a party."

"Practice. It was a practice for the local festival musicians."

"Practice? And you raided Roy's wine while you were at it?" This argument was undermined slightly by the fact that she had just served him a glass of Roy's good white burgundy.

"Well," he said. "You have a point there. I did borrow a few bottles of Roy's wine. But I was careful not to take something real good. I got some of his old Christmas wine."

"Christmas wine? The scuppernong?"

"No, I don't think so. It was something else, had bells on it."

Of course. The bottle in Roy's room. Their wedding wine. "How much?"

"How much what?"

"Of the wine. How many bottles did you take?" Maybe she had gulped the burgundy too quickly. She was queasy.

"Not much at all, just a couple of bottles, two or three," he said, but the color of his face told her to multiply that by ten. "We'll replace it, of course. In fact, I am planning to take this year's grapes—"

"You know," she said. "I am going to need you to clear out of the farm."

"What?" said Harper.

"Clear out."

"What about the grapes? There are still lots of zucchini."

"It can rot. Everything can rot."

"Wilma, come on, you've had a rough time. Let me help you."

"Harper, I can do without your brand of help."

He started on a lengthy argument then, a list of items that needed his immediate attention, issued in low soothing tones. He evoked Roy's name, what Roy would want, what Roy would say, how Roy wouldn't want her to bother. She didn't listen really. She sipped her burgundy, and she thought about those few cases, the wine Roy had put aside, enough bottles to last a lifetime. The sweet fruit of his labor, diminished now, swilled down by who knows who.

After a few minutes, Harper got round to the festival plans, what all he needed to do to get things ready. "Here's the thing," she said. "The festival is canceled."

"Wait," he said, and put down his glass. "You can't."

"I can," she said. "You can't use the land."

"Wait. You need to think about—"

"Sorry," she said, though she wasn't.

"Roy isn't—"

"Roy is ill. We need to concentrate on getting him better. Period." She stood up and gathered their glasses.

"We can't stop it at this point. There's media—"

"We've got to. Figure it out," she said. "Maybe put Delrina on the case. She seems like a resourceful person."

Harper's face was drained of color by now, making his eyes look black and feverish. He might have started in on another round of arguments, but there was the scuffle of feet in the mudroom. Star came in with Josh right behind her. They had been working hard in the yard, both of them with little red cheeks, the boy still sweaty. Poor Josh, how long had he been working out there?

"Oh, I promised you lemonade," Wilma said. She was on overload. One thing after another, first Sarah, then the bus. Sarah. She had to make sure to remember to have Star call her later. Maybe Star could convince her to stay put. Sarah, someone else who wanted to help. Assault from all sides.

Harper was standing finally, put his hands in his pockets. "All right," he said. "I hear what you're saying, Wilma. I think it's a hasty decision here. Disappoint a lot of folks to cancel the show." He looked over at Star. Always playing to the crowd.

"Cancel? Cancel the festival?" Star said. "Why? It's going to be so good. Why cancel it? Grandma?"

This caught Wilma flat-footed. Harper was strategically silent for a moment. He shrugged. "Star, honey, I know it's disappointing. I'm disappointed too. But you know, your grandmother's been under a big strain."

"It's not me, it's Roy," said Wilma. "I'm just worried—"

"I thought about that too," Harper put in quickly. "He's been so excited about this. I hope this news—"

"I only meant that—" Damnation.

"But, Daddy, you can't cancel now, can you?"

"Star, shh . . ." Harper put his hand on Star's shoulder as he passed her, and then nearly ran into Josh as he made for the door. Josh slid quickly aside, but Harper glared at him anyway.

At the threshold to the mudroom, Harper stopped and turned around. "I gotta go, but you know what?" he said, as if he had the perfect solution for this problem and for world peace as well. "I am just going to wait a few days, Wilma. I hear you, I hear what you're saying, but you may not be thinking straight. I'm going to sit tight. I'll get those grapes harvested, you'll get Roy on the road to recovery, and then we'll see. If you still want to cancel, fine."

Wilma tried to formulate her reply—she needed to watch her tone with Star in the room—but before she could open her mouth, there was a loud horn blast, the kind produced when someone with poor breeding presses her hand without pause on her bus horn. The noise insulted Wilma's sore jaw. It sounded without mercy in and around her house and throughout her neighborhood, where it was supper time for decent people.

"Harper. Cancel it," she said, once she caught her breath, but he was gone.

Chapter Nineteen

Roy

*H*e slept a lot, but every time he woke up, things got a little better. He could answer all the dumb questions they asked him now, about what day it was (Thursday, he'd been here over two weeks), where he was, what his name was (Roy Swan, he knew it every time now). He was starting to remember the names of things, though some words wouldn't come when he called them. Often, an orphan brother word would show up instead. This happened especially at the end of a sentence. When Celeste started her shift this morning, she'd come into his room like usual and asked how he was doing. He'd said, "I am funny," when of course, he meant he was fine.

Fortunately it was Celeste asking him. He'd have thought he'd be embarrassed by having someone he knew take care of him, but Celeste was very professional and understood when he might need to have the bed cranked up another way or when he could use a little ginger ale. She did the more personal stuff like it was no big deal, just part of her job. And best of all, she had a sense of humor, unlike that other nurse, June. She never smiled, no matter what he did. However, Roy preferred June, he preferred his old friend Celeste, or even his surly teenaged doctor to everyone who lived in the world outside the hospital. And that included Wilma.

He loved Wilma. There was no damage to his brain that could make him forget that he loved her dearly, more than he had ever loved anyone. But right now, he did not want to see her. He was a big mess. The right side of his body was inoperative, looked as if someone had let some air out of it. His face drooped, his shoulder sagged, the skin bunched up. The real him was on the left, with the right part gone to a different universe. Over there, it was two decades later and he was an old man. Down his middle was a kind of crude international date line. Unfortunately, in this territory, where some very vital parts were located, his body didn't seem to know what the hell was going on. Good God, he didn't want to think about all the tubes and things, but overall, there was a kind of weird numbness. This worried him, but frankly he couldn't see himself asking Celeste or June or one of the other nurses about it.

As for the teenager, Dr. Matthews, he only presented his smarty-pants self in the room with a bunch of other folks, including those nurses, and he said just about the same damn thing every day: "Mr. Swan, your carotid artery was blocked during your heart attack and the left side of your brain lost oxygen for a time. This has caused damage. But you're improving, and you'll keep on improving."

"All the way?" Roy had asked this morning. He still had to keep his sentences short, but he'd hoped the doc would understand his full meaning.

"Hard to say," said Dr. Matthews. "Some people do. Sure. What happens is that you'll get a lot better real quick and then whatever is left, a little paralysis, numbness, speech issues, some of these linger. We'll get you into rehab to work on these. We'll see. Over time . . ."

Wilma had been in the room when the doctor said all this and she'd looked at Roy to see how he'd take it. "We'll just have to have a little patience, Roy," she'd said, and she meant well, he knew that, but damn, it was the tone she took. Careful, as if she couldn't upset him, as if she had to watch which words she used. "Oh, I'll bet you're glad to see that ventilator gone," she said, then caught herself. "You know, the machine to help you breathe?" And she'd made motions at her throat. "Are you glad it's gone?"

"I know," he said. "I know what that is."

"Of course you do," she said.

He tried not to be ill-tempered, he tried not to cry every five minutes, but he didn't have a lick of control over it. That's why it would be best if everyone left him alone. He'd said as much to Wilma several times, but she'd just laughed and said, "You can't get rid of me that easily, Roy Swan."

Celeste

Travis slammed in the back door and walked through the kitchen with little pieces of sawdust flying off his work clothes. "Got any coffee?" he asked. The full pot was four feet in front of him. She handed him a mug, but he stared into it, as if the coffee might magically appear. Since the healing (that was what he called it now), Travis had been so full of himself. You'd think he'd been bathing in that holy oil, that or some potent male hormone.

"Hang on," she said and grabbed the pot. She stepped forward and began to pour into the mug, but she was too far from the rim and the coffee splashed up onto Travis's hand.

"Ouch, woman!" he said and jerked the mug away. Celeste couldn't say why, but this irritated her to the point that her reaction time got fouled up and she didn't get that pot upright until about a half a cup of coffee had landed on Travis's feet.

"Oh," she said, "goodness." He stared at her, like, *God forgive her, she knows not what she does,* and then sat down at the table. Travis had eaten earlier and gone on out to his workshop to get busy on the big kitchen cabinet order that was due this week. This was his coffee break.

She wiped up the floor, poured him another cup of coffee, carefully this time, and then pulled the roast chicken out of the refrigerator. Josh loved her chicken. There was plenty left over from last night's supper, so she would just make him a sandwich for his lunch. If he made it downstairs before she had to leave for work, she could stuff it in his backpack as he left. That way, maybe Travis wouldn't notice and tell her that she ought not to baby Josh, that he was nearly a grown man and didn't need his mother sending him to school with a bag lunch. She finished up the sandwich, wrapped it in wax paper, and then hunted in the refrigerator for an apple.

What Travis didn't know, of course, was that Josh was on his way to being a little more of a man than his daddy thought. That cute Star had picked Josh up for school every day this week. She seemed a nice enough girl overall, but too much freedom was no good. Celeste had seen her driving all over town in Roy's old pickup. She'd said something about it to Wilma at the hospital. Wilma had reminded her she didn't have much choice given Roy's situation. She was right, of course. It was clear now that he would make it, but he had a long haul in front of him. Most of this was going to fall on Wilma, so she didn't have a lot of time to be driving Star around. But Wilma would die, just die, if she had seen what Celeste had seen on Friday when Star had dropped Josh off after the football game.

Celeste had happened to be in the front room when the headlights shone through the window. She'd stood behind the curtains. This was her right as a mother. After a few minutes, Josh had gotten out of the truck, but instead of driving off, Star had hopped out of the cab. And right there in front of the house, that girl had closed her door and then leaned back against it in a way that reminded Celeste of Vivien Leigh in *A Streetcar Named Desire*. And of course, what did Josh do? It was too dark to see exactly, but as far as Celeste could tell, he did what any boy his age would do, and that involved not only kissing but putting his hands in places they ought not to be. After a few minutes, Celeste didn't want to see anymore. She went upstairs and took a bath.

Under normal circumstances, she would've mentioned this to his father, and Travis would've had a man-to-man talk with him in no time flat, but she hadn't said a word. Honestly, she did not want to risk it. There was no telling what His Holy Oily-ness might say. Plus, she couldn't help but worry that maybe that book of hers had given Josh an idea or two. If Travis started in on him, Josh just might spill the beans.

Travis peered up over the sports section. "What time does your shift end today? I was thinking about going up to see Roy."

"He's not having visitors yet, honey." She'd explained this how many times?

"He's not or Wilma's not?" said Travis. "Because I'm betting he'd love to see me, love to have a visit from some of us rescue squad boys."

Celeste poured him more coffee and got herself some too finally. "It's not Wilma who doesn't want people, Travis. It's Roy."

"That's hard for me to believe."

"Trust me, he doesn't want anybody. He can barely tolerate having Wilma. She's up there every day, but she no sooner gets in the room than he sends her back out to get him things from downstairs, from home, everywhere. She'll get back and he'll keep his eyes closed, doesn't want to talk, nothing."

"Well, she's his wife, I can see that," said Travis. "But his buddies . . ."

Celeste decided to ignore this comment. Josh wandered into the kitchen now. "Morning, honey. You want a little cereal?" she said.

Josh shook his head, but his hair stayed put. He'd used some kind of gel in it. "I'll just take some toast with me. My ride'll be here in a second."

"Ride?" said Travis. "Since when did you stop taking the bus?"

Celeste couldn't decide if Travis's weak powers of observation were a blessing or a curse. "I take the bus," said Josh smoothly. "Only this morning, I've got to get to school early to work on a math project."

"Math project?" Travis said this like it might be contagious.

"Yeah," said Josh.

"*Yeah*, you say?"

"Yes, *sir*," said Josh.

"And who's giving you the ride?"

"Star, you know, Miss Wilma's granddaughter. She and I are working on the math project together." Josh smiled when he said the name. Celeste would bet the only math those two were working on was one plus one.

Josh looked out the window. "Gotta go," he said.

"Son," said Travis, "you need to comb that hair a little more. You've got it standing up straight."

Josh

She noticed as soon as he got into the pickup. "Your hair looks cool," she said. Then she gave him that sly grin. "Did you raid Travis's stash of holy oil?"

He laughed and brushed his palm over the top of it. "Yes, ma'am. I did. Can't you see how it's levitating? *Praise Him!*"

She wound the engine out on the gravel driveway, popped it into second. "Praise Him and pass the pork chops," she said.

He'd told her the whole story about his dad anointing Miss Wilma. She had laughed—not like his family was pitiful, no, like he was funny, clever. He'd done a great imitation of Travis in the Coach House, holding his hands in the air, saying, "Praaaaise Him. Praise His Holy Name," while Mrs. Appleton was trying to take his order. Star had cracked up, and now that was their joke.

"Yes, Lord," he said, "and how are brother Harper and sister Delrina this morning?" After his Travis imitation, Star had filled him in on Delrina's story about the wine. Here was the freaky thing—his dad was not the only fool claiming Roy's recovery.

"Who knows," she said. "When I left them last night, they were singing and partaking of the holy grape."

"You know what we have here, Star," he said. "Between our two families—total freak show."

"Total," she said. "Tell me about it."

Star didn't like to drive fast, which was fine. He could ride around with her forever. They rode in silence for a few minutes. Not twitchy silence. Just silence, which was cool. The sky was that great clear blue that you got on these fall mornings, and about halfway to school, the dew evaporated from the passenger side rearview. Josh leaned forward to check it out. The Vaseline was working out okay. His hair hadn't lain down a bit.

"God," she said. "I almost forgot. I finally got my mom on the phone last night. In Singapore. She was all ready to pack up and come back."

"To Santa Fe? You're not going back home?" This idea made his stomach hurt.

"Oh, no. My mom was thinking of coming to Swan's Knob. She's halfway through her bodywork course back home. She said that she could help Roy get better."

"Bodywork?"

"You know, all that massage stuff—Rolfing, craniosacral, deep tissue. I think she's even started acupuncture."

"The needles?"

"Oh, yeah. It's big in Santa Fe."

They were getting into town now. Too bad. "So is she coming?"

"No," she said. "I talked her out of it." She stopped at the light on Church Street and waved at a few random kids crossing the street. Josh waved too as they passed them. "It would be great to have her here. Sounds dorky, but I miss her. And she really can make someone feel better. When I was a little kid, she could take a stomachache away just by putting her hand on my belly. But I don't think my grandma wants her here right now. I convinced her she could do just as much good sending positive energy from Singapore."

She looked sad for a minute. Josh scooted over in the cab and put his arm around her. She looked up into his face until the person in the car behind them tooted his horn.

She said, "Do you think it helps?"

Josh turned to see who was behind them. "What?"

"The energy," she said. "All these people, freak show and everything. People trying to make Roy well. I think it does."

It was Wiley Grissom, junior class president, behind them, all studly in his Jeep Cherokee. Josh would let him wait. Let him watch through the back window. Josh bent down and kissed Star. She kissed him back and then shoved him aside as she pulled onto Main Street. "Anyway, she's not coming. Too bad. I told her all about you."

"You did?" This made him blush. Wiley gunned his engine and drove right behind them with his grille only a few inches off their bumper.

"Oh, yeah. She said you sounded very cool."

"Really?"

"Of course, then I had to hear a big lecture about birth control. God, what is this retard doing behind us?"

"Wait," he said. "You told her? You told her about . . ." As they turned into the school parking lot, Wiley zoomed around them. He put his left arm out of the car and flipped them off.

"Wow," said Star. "Get a life." She found a parking place and then looked over at him. "You okay? Wait. God, Josh, don't worry. It's taken care of. I thought I told you."

"You told her?"

"Well, yeah, I told her too. I'm on the pill. Did that a while back, just in case."

"No," he said. "I mean, good, that's good. But wait. Wait. You told your mom that we did it?"

"Yes. I just said. Can you hand me that green notebook? It's on the floor under your feet somewhere."

"Didn't she freak?"

"Oh, no. She's totally cool with it." He couldn't believe she could sit there organizing her backpack and say this to him.

"And your dad, you didn't tell your dad, did you?"

"Not yet." Still calm, not getting it at all.

"Okay, don't."

"Why not?" She bent down to retrieve something else from the floorboard, and God, the slope of her left breast peeked out of her top.

He felt that rush of blood again—it was happening now with ridiculous frequency—and this time, it rocketed beyond his crotch and up through his brain, causing fireworks of images that included Harper's fist barreling toward his face, his parents standing in solemn judgment, slamming the front door. He saw Star waving good-bye forever. "Don't," he said. "Just don't tell your dad. Promise."

"God," she said. "Okay. No biggie."

Harper

The door to Roy's room was open six inches or more, so he walked right in and called out hello. He didn't say it too loudly in case Roy was sleeping, but he wasn't. He was propped up in bed. Wilma, who was sitting next to him, gave Harper her standard who-invited-you expression.

"Harper," she started, "Roy doesn't—"

"Ask him," Roy said out of one side of his mouth. Harper tried not to stare. Roy had looked better unconscious. Now that he was awake and moving a little, you could see how many things didn't work at all.

"Ask him what, honey?" said Wilma.

"I. Asked. Him. Here." Harper couldn't tell if Roy was angry or if it just took bluster to get the words out.

"Oh." Wilma looked surprised. "How?"

"Phone," said Roy and rolled his eyes.

Wilma eyed the phone on the nightstand to Roy's right. Harper could tell she wanted to ask Roy how he'd managed that. She let it pass.

Harper walked to the end of the bed. "Good to see you. Glad you called and asked me to stop by." A sour-sounding nurse had actually made the call for Roy, but Harper'd be damned if he'd say so.

"Thanks for coming backwards," said Roy.

"Happy to do it, buddy," said Harper, hoping he'd understood right. "Good to see you getting along so well. How are you feeling?"

"Shit," said Roy. Wilma opened her mouth in surprise, then shut it again.

"Like shit," said Harper, relishing the occasion to say the word in front of Wilma. "I hear that. Shit. Well, I guess that's to be expected." There was a little silence. Best to keep talking maybe. "Well, I guess Wilma told you, I've been out at your home place, looking after things." Roy nodded. She'd told him.

"Everything is going along fine. We'll start harvesting what grapes there are soon, real soon. Tom Felton showed me what to do. He's lined me up with some boys to help pick them." Roy nodded.

"Tom had me call up to Asheville, those Biltmore people. They said they'd take the grapes, so nothing's going to waste.

"They can send you a check or they can deliver some cases to you. Your choice. Of course, if it were me, I'd take the wine." Harper waited. Roy looked like he wanted to say something else.

After a bit, Wilma said, "Well, thank you, Harper. We appreciate it. Like I said the other day." Roy nodded again and then turned his head slowly and looked at Wilma.

"How about . . . how . . . about," he said. "Dewar's?"

"Scotch?" said Harper. "Little early, isn't it?"

Wilma crinkled up her forehead. "No. God. That's not it. He means Dewey's. Right, honey? You want me to go to Dewey's Bakery? Again?"

Roy smiled, but it was a sorry sight. The left side of his mouth hitched up, showing his gums; the right side was immobile. "Coffee cup," he said.

"Yes, yes, the coffee cake." Wilma sounded tired. "This is the third time this week he's sent me for it."

"Go ahead," said Harper. "Roy and I will hold down the fort here. Take your time."

"I don't know," said Wilma. "You're his first visitor. I don't want to get him tired out. We can't have any setbacks if we're going to move him over to Stewart's in a few days."

"Stewart's?" said Harper. That was a nursing home. Nice one, but still . . .

Wilma saw his look. "They have a rehab facility," she said. "Totally separate from the nursing home. Right, Roy?"

"Shit," said Roy.

"Roy," said Wilma and she stood up. "I don't care what kind of stroke you've had, no reason to start that kind of talk."

Roy looked over at Harper. "Sit," he said.

Harper moved around the bed and sat in Wilma's chair. Wilma remained standing, reluctant to leave them. There was a silence while Roy stared her down. Finally, she had no choice. She picked up her pocketbook and smoothed her skirt. "Okay," she said. "You two behave yourselves." She gave Harper a pointed look. "Remember. He doesn't need any excitement, none at all. Nothing upsetting or otherwise."

"Okay, Wilma, I get it. You win. I'll cancel the dancing girls and the three-martini lunch." Harper got it. Wilma didn't want him talking to Roy about the festival. She probably hadn't even told him that she was trying to cancel it.

A nurse came in as Wilma was leaving. "June, you better keep an eye on those two," Wilma said.

The nurse gave Wilma an officious look and said she would, and then went about the business of checking Roy out. She took his vital signs and adjusted his IV. Roy asked her to help him sit up more in the bed. When she bent over to adjust the control, Harper caught Roy looking down her shirt. He laughed. Roy looked up and gave him a wink that filled Harper with relief. The nurse puttered around for a few more minutes and then left them alone. Roy looked at Harper, looked him in the eye, then pawed the bed with his good hand. He seemed to be working hard to string the right words together. Before he found them, tears came running down his face.

"Listen," he said. "Please. You got to hell me out."

Chapter Twenty

Roy

It took the longest time to get Harper to understand what he needed him to do. It was like the time he and Wilma were in France and trying to find their way to a tiny winery in the Loire Valley. They started out with a very sketchy map and a combined vocabulary of about twenty words of French. They'd had to stop in three or four small villages along the way to ask directions—each time attempting to talk to some interesting characters, gesturing wildly, picking up a few more words or cheeses or pastries, getting sent on detours across the countryside. Ultimately, they'd made it to their destination by noon only to find the winery closed for lunch. This was his path for conversing with Harper, a sorry linguistic venture, only this time he was not diverted through the lovely French landscape but sent back again and again to the hard ceiling of his limitations.

Finally, he made Harper understand—he did not want to go to Stewart's. He refused to go. He did not care what the doctors thought. He wasn't going. He wanted Harper to get him out of the hospital. (Harper: "Come spring?" Him: "No! Spring me, spring me.") He wanted Harper to take him out to his farm, where he could get better without anyone hovering over him. (Harper: "Far piece?" Him: "Farm. Get better in peace.") When he finally understood, Harper looked at him real good and said, "Miss Wilma doesn't know a thing about this, does she?"

This was the hard part: she couldn't know in advance, or she wouldn't let him do it. She was hell-bent on following every order that doctor prescribed. She was probably out pricing walkers this very minute.

"She'll kill us all," Harper said.

"Yep," Roy said. "Please." He was fuzzy on a number of things. He couldn't quite remember having the heart attack under the truck, he couldn't remember parts of the last week, he was still looking for the angel that had visited his room, but this he knew: he had picked the right guy to help him out. Harper had always lived on the far side of reckless, and if Roy remembered correctly, he was the one guy in town who might still need something from him.

"Roy, buddy, I want to help you out, but you can't walk, can you?"

"Not yet."

Harper put a hand on his hip and looked over at the side of Roy that didn't work. "Then how are we going to do this?"

Roy had a plan, and after a few minutes, he conveyed it. They'd buy everything they needed—wheelchair, hospital bed, that goddamn walker. They'd hire nurses and physical therapists. Let them come to him. He'd do his rehab, only he'd do it at the farm.

Harper listened to him, Roy had to give him that, but he didn't show much enthusiasm. "And you want to do this when?"

"Soon. Saturday?" Roy said, hoping that he was right about today being Thursday.

"Why so soon?"

"Stewart's . . ." he started and then thought of something that would work better. "Festival," he said. "Got to get ready."

This got Harper's attention. He looked at Roy as if he was still considering the entire plan. "Well," he said. "There is the festival. We could manage that ourselves now, but it'd be great to have you there. And as for this plan for avoiding Stewart's, I can't argue with that."

Roy nodded his head and tried not to smile. Good to know he hadn't lost his last bit of wits.

"Here's what I don't understand, though," said Harper. "Why can't you do this at home, with Wilma? She'd go along with all of this."

"No," he said. Harper was right, she might go along. But he couldn't have it. Just this morning, he'd wanted to turn over in the bed. She'd tried to help him, and even though he'd been cross with her, she'd been patient and kind. She'd kept a calm look on her face as he'd flailed about, she'd given his shoulder and backside a little shove at exactly the right moment, and he'd rolled into place. In the process, his covers had bunched up along with his hospital gown, and for just a moment, his midsection had been exposed—his belly fat and sagging, other things lying there past recognition. She'd covered the whole awful mess without a word, without any reaction whatsoever, which was, of course, what killed him.

He could not bear for her to see him like this, could not bear for her to see him struggle. He would not make her the chief witness to the sweat and shit and painstaking exertion of his recovery. Better to sneak away, to let her breathe free while he got himself in order. Then she would see only the end result. She would have him back whole and they could go on just like before. Oh, she wouldn't like it, not a bit. She would not allow it if she had any choice whatsoever, so he would not give her one.

Of course, there was no way to explain all of this to Harper, so he just said, "No way. No Wilma, okay?"

Harper stood up and walked to the window. He put his hands in the back pockets of his jeans. He was calculating, Roy knew, as he had many times over the course of his shiftless life, trying to decide which brand of trouble he was willing to smoke. Harper owed Roy, no question. On the other hand, a man needed courage and foolishness combined to invite the wrath of Wilma Mabry Swan. Lord, they both knew this from grim experience. Harper took his time looking out that window.

When he turned back around, Roy could see he had a deal. There would be terms, but at this point, he was ready to discuss most any crazy thing Harper had in mind. It was at that moment that Travis Diamond walked into the room, with Celeste trailing right behind.

"Well, hey there, buddy boy. What's shaking?" said Travis, in the voice he used over in the rescue squad hut on stew night.

Celeste looked pained. "Roy, I told Travis you weren't quite up for visitors—"

Travis stared at her in a way that made her shut her mouth mid-sentence and then turned toward him and Harper. "I told her it'd be all right. Thought you might've had enough of all these women telling you what to do. I know I have." He looked at Celeste again, lowering his bushy eyebrows down over his lids. Wilma had Roy trim his.

Celeste smiled at Roy, embarrassed. He smiled back best he could; then she left the room. Roy himself had never thought much of handling women this way, but this morning, he felt a slight bit of admiration for Travis.

Travis hustled over to Roy's bed and took the chair. "Praise the Lord that you are healed," he said.

"Well," said Roy and cut his eyes toward his right hand. It lay on the outside of the covers, palm up, with his fingers curled up in a way that told the world he was a cripple.

"Oh, that's just a matter of time," said Travis, waving his own hand with the confidence of a man sitting beside the bed instead of in it. "Besides, let me tell you what, I've just come from the funeral of Tom Green. You remember old Tom Green, don't you, Roy?"

Roy didn't, but nodded anyway.

"What about you, Harper? Did you know Tom?"

"I don't think—"

Travis didn't bother to wait for his reply. "Well, thing of it is, this was Tom's Green's *second* funeral. How about that? Harper, now I know you're wondering how this is possible, but it is. Let me tell you, me and Roy, we were at Tom's *first* funeral—remember, Roy?—and that was quite a show." Travis was sitting with his hands clasped between his legs and a look of suppressed glee on his face.

Harper hadn't spent his life hanging out at the rescue squad, so he was slow on the uptake. "Travis," he said, "I don't know if this is the day to be talking about funerals."

"Oh, but it is, son. It truly is, because Tom Green was such a wonderful man, and his first funeral was a grand affair. Hundreds of people turned out. There was a sad service with three preachers a-preaching for two hours going. There were ladies weeping, and most of all, the widow Green. Remember, Roy? It was an awful rainy day. It just rained and rained as if God himself was crying, and when the time came, there were six pallbearers called to carry the coffin from the church out to the grave. There was a little rise in that grave-yard and old Tom Green's grave had been dug just at the top of it. And those poor pallbearers, they had to heave and ho and I don't know what all to get that coffin up the hill."

Travis was in full swing now. This joke was Travis's trademark. Roy had heard it on many occasions, but he didn't mind hearing it again. Travis could tell a story. Even Harper had caught on now and walked around to the end of the bed to catch the full act.

"Anyhow, here's the thing. About halfway up that hill, one of the pallbearers—I believe it might have been Sonny Fulp—well, Sonny falters. He slips in that good old red clay of ours, and he lets go of his end of the coffin. This causes the others to lose their footing and down comes Tom Green's coffin. It hits the ground, bam! And wouldn't you know, the lid flies open and out pops Tom Green. Only, here's the thing, he isn't dead! All the commotion has woke him up. Well, there is a big celebration. The widow Green has everybody over to the house and everyone rejoices. And Tom Green lived another two years until just last Monday.

"That brings us to today, boys. Today we went to bury Tom again, and wouldn't you know it? It was another awful stormy day, mud everywhere. Them pallbearers had to go up that very same hill, and oh Lord, Sonny Fulp, he gets halfway up that hill again and he begins to falter. Only this time, the widow Green, she steps right up, she puts her hand on Sonny Fulp's back. And she says, 'Steady, boys!' "

Roy laughed with abandon, the same way he had been crying the past few days, way over-the-top. In ten seconds, the tears came with the laughing, though that was all right with him. Of course, since Travis had told the whole thing to cheer him up, he laughed along with him.

"Steady, boys, steady." He repeated this several times.

Even Harper laughed and said, "Travis, you had me going there. I didn't know what in heck you were doing."

It took them a few minutes to settle down, Roy especially. He had never thought much of Travis. He was mostly a big pain in the ass, al-ways holding up Sunday school with his prayer list, agitating about some fool thing he'd heard on the PTL network, and most days Roy

wasn't too crazy about the way he treated his wife. But today, he was
the tonic that Roy needed. He settled in now for a visit, leaned back
in the chair, and Harper started looking at the door.

"I suppose that Wilma told you all about last Sunday—," said
Travis.

"I'll let you two talk," said Harper. "I need to get back to the
farm, Roy. Got stuff to do."

Roy caught his eye. "You do what we said?"

"On Saturday, you mean?" said Harper. "Yeah, of course. I'll
come back. No problem. Might bring a friend to make things easier."

"Great," said Roy, hoping they understood each other, and mostly
hoping Harper wouldn't alert Wilma.

Harper made for the door, and Travis was about to launch into a
conversation, but Harper stopped and said, like he'd just thought of
it, "Now, just so we're clear here, Roy. You want us to go forward
with the festival, right?"

Roy nodded.

"So you don't want to cancel?" Odd question.

"No."

Harper smiled. "See you Saturday."

"Steady, boys!" Travis said one more time, and Harper closed the
door, laughing.

Wilma

Instead of toddling on down to the car and driving to Thruway Shopping Center to Dewey's, Wilma went to the visitors' lounge. She'd
find the newspaper and see what might be going on in the world after
all these weeks. Roy might bellow later, but she was not going on a
fool's errand. He no more wanted Moravian coffee cake than the man
in the moon. He wanted her out of his way, which would've burned
her up under other circumstances. But today, she couldn't complain.
He was getting better, that was plain. After nearly a week of half
sleep, half sentences, and a fair amount of self-pity, he was feeling
good enough to arrange for Harper to come by all on his own, with

no help from her at all. She didn't like it, being shooed out of his room, but this amounted to the man getting a little of his spunk back, which was what he had been missing and what he was going to need for the next few months.

The waiting room was disheveled, as usual. There were all manner of trashy celebrity magazines, mostly outdated. She'd read all of them by now and was no better for it. She began straightening them up, throwing away the plastic cups and candy wrappers people had left, but then caught herself. Enough. Not her job. She should be calling Stewart's again to see if they'd finished all the arrangements. She was not putting Roy over there until they showed her where he would be—she'd asked for one of their nicest rooms, one facing their gardens, away from the nursing home patients. She wanted Roy assigned to their best physical therapists, and she wanted to make sure he'd have nice food, a private nurse, the works. You had to stay after people or they just wouldn't get things right. She needed to call them, but she couldn't bring herself to do it yet. She tried to sit and watch TV, but it was one of those morning shows where people shouted at each other. After a few minutes, she couldn't bear the noise. She headed down to the nurses' station to see if someone had today's *Journal Sentinel*.

Celeste and Travis were just walking into Roy's room when she passed it. "What's shaking?" she heard in Travis's booming voice. Roy must have summoned all of Swan's Knob overnight. She walked on by and tried to shake herself, to get rid of that feeling of being left out. Hadn't she been worried for days that Roy would be totally dependent on her? Now that he was getting better, she should be thankful. She'd work on that right after she got things lined up at Stewart's.

There was no one at the nurses' station and no sign of a newspaper. Wilma decided to wait. She wanted someone to look at Roy's chart for her anyway. She didn't have to stand there long because Celeste left Roy's room not two minutes after entering it, dismissed as quickly as Wilma. Celeste shook her head when she saw her. "I'm sorry," she said.

"Why?" said Wilma.

"I know y'all haven't wanted Roy to have any visitors, but I just couldn't convince Travis."

"Well," said Wilma, "from the looks of things, it's all okay. It's a sign."

"A sign of what?" Celeste looked wary, and then Wilma remembered she lived with a man who dropped to his knees several times a day.

"I just mean, it's a good thing he wants to see people. Maybe it means he's getting better. Isn't that what the doctor thinks?"

Celeste didn't rush to agree with her. "Well, anything's an improvement over last week, that's for sure," she said finally.

"What about the chart? What does that say?" Celeste, being only a practical nurse, wasn't the best person for her to be asking maybe.

Celeste went behind the desk and began hunting through paperwork. "I'm not supposed to be showing you the chart," she said. "I don't think there's much to see anyway." She located Roy's, thick with reports and printouts, and thumbed through it idly for a few minutes. Finally she looked up at Wilma. "Look," she said, "I'm not the doctor here, but I've been around these kinds of patients for a long time. I want to warn you a little. Roy is doing good, he's doing real good. He could've died, after all. But it's going to take a long time for him to get better." She looked down at the chart again as if it could maybe tell her how long.

"Oh, I know," said Wilma. "The doctors said. We're going to have to take our time getting Roy back up on his feet, getting him to speak fluently, getting his energy back. He's going to need exercise for his heart problems, a new diet. It's going to take work. I understand." The thing was, Wilma realized suddenly, it was the thought of this work, the idea that there was something she could do for Roy, to get him better, that was holding her together right now.

"Good, that's good," said Celeste, and she nodded her head. "But, sweetie . . ."

She stopped and Wilma smiled at her. No one in town ever called her "sweetie." Celeste said, "Prepare yourself. He will only go so far and no more. And probably not far, sweetie. He won't be the same."

Celeste said all of this most gently, lovingly even, but Wilma was not prepared, not in the least. It was worse than the accidental punch Roy had thrown at her. She knew right there—Celeste had told her the gospel truth. Roy, the man who had courted her ardently, the man who knelt in her flower bed with his green clogs, the man who always knew what to say to make her laugh, to make the world right for her, that man was not coming back. Tears came up and she wanted to punch back for a moment. Then she looked into Celeste's kind face.

Another person, like that intelligent young doctor or the preacher Berry or even Travis, might have told her this truth. They would have conveyed it, however kindly, as a display of wisdom or as a means to witness the terrible toll of sorrow. But Celeste looked at Wilma with the simple expression a woman uses on a child who's just seen that first awful example of the world's cruelty. This kindness broke something loose in Wilma and she sobbed out loud. Celeste hung her head for a moment. Then she walked around the nurses' station, silent in her white nurses' shoes, and threw her arms around Wilma with abandon.

Wilma was able to hug this woman, with her gardenia perfume, her thin arms, and her massively padded bra, a woman whom she had known for years, whom she had wholly underestimated as a person and as a friend—she was able to hug her without reservation. They cried there, both of them, until one of the nurses, June, Wilma thought it was, the one who used all the starch on her uniform, came back to the station. Celeste stepped back then and pulled some Kleenex out of her pocket and began to clean the mascara that was smudged all under her eyes.

Harper

"Finally," Delrina said to him the moment he came in the door around dinnertime. She had pretty well quit using the bus as her living quarters, except during those few hours a night when she slept. He wasn't sure how she maintained her constant level of energy, but she showed no signs of winding down at this early stage of the evening. That would take hours and a considerable quantity of alcohol. "I can't wait to show you this," she said and led him into the kitchen.

On the table was a large and detailed drawing of Roy's farm. Delrina had pieced together several brown grocery bags and drawn on them, first with pencil and then with a black Magic Marker. The result was far more professional looking than Harper would have imagined. She had laid out the entire site, locating all the things needed for the festival.

"I didn't have anything but a ruler," she said, "so it's not completely to scale, but it should give you some idea."

"Wow," he said. He was beginning to see now how the Delrina and Little Charlie act had gotten itself on the charts.

They had talked several times about how things would be arranged, but it was great to see it all laid out in detail. Delrina had come up with the brilliant idea of making the barn part of the backdrop of the main stage. That way, performers could use it as the backstage area. There was a wide, flat area in front where people could set out their blankets and lawn chairs. She'd decided that Roy's front porch was a fine place to gather all the amateur musicians, and they'd have the food vendors set up their booths along the fence bordering the back vegetable gardens. She walked him through the plan, parking, traffic, and all.

"You are a logistical genius," he said.

"Why, thank you, sir," she said. "Now, have you talked some sense into Wilma? We've only got six weeks, you know, and pretty soon, it'll be too late to do anything."

Harper wondered when exactly the festival had become a matter of "we," but there was no stopping the Delrina train. "Good news," he said. "Problem solved. Just like I told you. The Festival of the Knob is on."

Delrina jumped up from the table and hugged his neck. "That is great, so great!" Harper was getting used to her hollering. "Let's have a toast! How in the world did you convince her?"

"Well, sometimes you have to go around the mountain," he said. "I'll tell you the whole story a little later, but let's have a few drinks and some dinner." He sat down and folded up the site plan. "I am going to need to borrow your bus, though."

"Borrow away," she said. "You're the one paid for the tank of gas. And one more thing. We're changing the name." She said this from the wine closet.

"Name of what? And stay away from those bottles with the bells on them," he said.

She emerged with a bottle of wine from a commercial winery. It was a red wine, French, less than five years old, from someplace he'd never heard of. Acceptable. Delrina put out the glasses and a plate of saltines.

"That ag guy came by again today. He said the grapes are ready, showed me where you need to start down on the south field," she said. Tom Felton was a somber fellow, earnest, used to dealing with tobacco farmers and worm infestations. Harper pictured him walking down through the front pasture with Delrina, wearing pink leather pants today and a tight T-shirt with "Country Music Awards" across the front. No doubt this had been a big day for Tom.

"Did he say anything about a crew of guys to help harvest?"

"Well, he said he didn't have anybody right yet. He said, with no more fruit than is on the vines this year, we might consider just going ahead ourselves." She held up the highball tumbler that she favored over wineglasses. "Cheers," she said, "and please tell me that man is not saying what I think he's saying."

"Well," said Harper. Obligations were piling up.

"Now, honey, Harper honey. I have been willing, more than willing, to help you out here—talking to the magazines, using my two semesters of drafting class, being the chauffeur to your daughter—but honey. Honey. Delrina is no field hand. No, right there is where I draw the line."

Chapter Twenty-one

Celeste

There was a tour bus parked in the employee lot when she came in to work on Saturday morning. She recognized the name on the side, a big country act from a few years back, and figured they were putting on a show for some of the kids. It was right in the front by the entrance, and when she walked by, she saw that two of the bus's wheels were up on the sidewalk. So maybe it had been an emergency, one of the band members OD'd or something, and they'd overshot the emergency room entrance.

She went on up to the floor. Someone there would be sure to know. There was always a little buzz in the hospital when a celebrity was around. The news could travel the four floors from the ER up to the ICU in the time it took to draw blood.

When the elevator doors opened onto the ward, she could see immediately something big was up. Cerebral hemorrhage brought on by cocaine use, maybe? She'd seen it before. As she walked down the hall toward the nurses' station, though, there was no mistaking. The activity was concentrated on Roy's room. Nurses and technicians going in and out, several guys from the Surry County rescue squad standing by the door, looking nervous. This made her heart take a dive to the bottom of her stomach. Surely not, surely not. He'd been doing so well.

Beatrice Stubbs, a weekend part-timer, was behind the desk. "What's going on?" Celeste tried to ask as if Roy was just another patient, but it was no use. "Has he coded?"

"I don't think so," Beatrice said. She started to say more, but at that moment, the door of Roy's room burst open and Dr. Matthews emerged. He was red-faced and had pinched his eyes and forehead down into a small knot. Celeste was instantly relieved. This was the face he used on careless interns and tardy nurses, not the look of quiet defeat he got when he was about to lose a patient.

"Get me a discharge form," he said to Beatrice.

"You're discharging Roy Swan?" Celeste said, ignoring protocol. This was not a question for a nurse's aide.

"No, I'm not, Celeste," he said, equally out of line in using her first name. "Apparently, he is discharging himself." He looked impatiently at Beatrice, who was fumbling through the file drawer. "Good thing I'm not asking you for a syringe of adrenaline, Nurse Stubbs. We'd have a dead patient before you could locate it."

"He's checking out?" This made no sense.

"As far as I can tell. His speech is not the best, as you know, but we've got a whole delegation in there speaking for him."

"So his wife is taking him over to Stewart's?" She and Wilma had talked at length about this, but she'd understood the plan was to move him in a week or so.

"Let's have it, Nurse Stubbs," he said. Beatrice was frantic by now, starting to tear files out and throw them onto the floor, but she had the wrong drawer. Celeste went over to the large lateral cabinet and pulled out the right form.

"Thank you," said Dr. Matthews, changing his tone. "His wife isn't in there. It's some other people."

"Who?" said Celeste. "Does Wilma know?"

"It's Delrina Kay," said Beatrice, with reverence. "You know, the singer." This explained the tour bus out front but little else.

"How does Roy know her?" said Celeste.

Beatrice pointed to the two men Celeste had seen in the hall. "She came in with three or four men, including those guys over there." Celeste looked at them again and tried to think of their names. She'd seen both of them over the years at some of the rescue squad fundraisers.

"I haven't seen Little Charlie, though. Delrina Kay and Little

Charlie have had several number one country hits," said Beatrice, trying to be helpful after the problem with the discharge form. "I think
'Just Loving You' is their best."

"Maybe that's what I need to put on the form," said Dr. Matthews.
"Reason for early discharge: *number one country hits*." His pen
scratched across the paper. *Released against physician's advice,* he
wrote.

"What does Wilma say about this?" said Celeste.

"That's right, you know Mrs. Swan, don't you?" said Dr.
Matthews. "I suggested that we call her earlier, but Mr. Swan refused." He looked at Celeste. "So, as his physician, I can't call."

"But a friend could call, right?" He nodded and Celeste headed
to the desk phone and dialed as Dr. Matthews read the number from
the chart. Waiting for the connection, she panicked briefly about
what she would say. "Who all is in the room?" she asked. "Is it just
Delrina?"

"No," said Dr. Matthews, consulting the chart. "The person actually signing him out is Harper Chilton. There's some familial—"

"Oh God." Wilma was not going to be happy at all.

"Who is he?"

"Ex-son-in-law," she said a bit too harshly. She gulped down a few
breaths as the phone began to ring.

"Should we call the police?" Dr. Matthews looked alarmed.

"No, he's not that bad." At Wilma's house, no one was picking up.
Eventually, the answering machine clicked on, but Celeste had no
idea how to leave this kind of news after the beep. She hung up. "No
answer," she said.

Dr. Matthews, who normally looked right past anyone not wearing a white coat, motioned for Celeste to come around the desk. He
pushed back his own coat and put his hand on his hip, the way he did
when he and some specialist were conferring on a difficult case.
"Look, this guy is just a few days off a ventilator," he said. "He's still
got his IV. I removed the catheter this morning, but you know how
that can go."

She did know. She was the one who had to clean up that kind of
mess. "I don't understand," she said. "Where are they taking him?"

Dr. Matthews shook his head. "Some farm, I think. Mr. Swan has a farm?"

"Yes," she said. "It's right next to ours in Swan's Knob."

"Oh," he said. "Okay. How about this: can you talk to them? I've tried, but Mr. Swan has given his instructions to these people, and they just won't listen."

"Well," she said.

"Thanks," he said, putting his hand on her shoulder and gently steering her toward the door to Roy's room. "Let me know what they say."

Celeste couldn't move for a minute. She needed to find Wilma, that would be the best thing, though, God, if Roy was as hardheaded as Travis, there would be no talking to him.

"Do you know Delrina?" said Beatrice. "Do you think she'd sign an autograph?"

Celeste ignored her and went toward Roy's room. The two men flanking the door obviously recognized her. "Well, hey, Mrs. Diamond," said the one on the right. He was really young and had a head of curly red hair. He was one of the Snow boys. Celeste remembered now that she'd seen the hair.

"How are you today? And how is your mother doing?" she asked. The young man opened his mouth, but she plowed through the door before he had the chance to answer.

The room was nearly full. There was Nurse Baker securing Roy's IV, someone else, a PT maybe, trying to check the reflexes in his extremities, Harper packing up clothes and get-well cards, and then that singer Delrina standing at the end of the bed, wearing one of the cutest outfits Celeste had ever seen—dark jeans with lace sewed all over them, lizard-skin cowboy boots, and a boxy cheetah-print jacket. She looked like she was all ready to be in one of those videos on the Country Music Channel. Roy was totally engrossed in whatever she was saying to him, but when he saw Celeste, he made a little braying noise that had become his greeting over the past week. "Eeey!" He couldn't manage the "h" sound. Everyone turned to look at her.

"Well," she said. "I'm not sure there's room for one more person in this room, but I did have to come in and see what you are up to, Roy Swan."

"He's getting hisself out of here, that's what's up," said Delrina.

Celeste, by nature, gravitated toward celebrity. This was one of the traits of her personality. She had so many questions for this woman, but right now, she had no choice—she had to ignore Delrina if she was to complete her mission.

"Of course, Roy, I know you're getting out of here and soon," she said, and as she did, she tried to watch her posture. Posture was a big thing in people with Delrina's training. "Why, Wilma and I were talking yesterday about how she was going to get you out of here and into rehab ASAP."

"No!" Roy said and hit the bed with his hand.

Delrina turned toward her and gave her a raised eyebrow. "You heard him, honey. He isn't going to the nursing home. He's going to his farm." Celeste hated to get off on the wrong foot with this woman. For one thing, she would like to know how long it took to put your hair into all those little braids.

"Of course you are, Roy. Wilma wants you home more than anything, but rehab is the first step. And you need to think twice before you go out to the farm. It's not going to work." This got Harper's attention, though Delrina and Roy seemed unfazed.

"We've been through all this with the doctor," Harper said. "We're going to get a nurse for Roy, physical therapists, whatever he needs."

"How are you going to get him home, that tour bus out there?" Celeste laughed.

"Well," said Harper. "Yeah."

"And what nurse have you got to look after him?" Celeste hated to talk about this with Roy sitting right there, but he was in no shape to answer.

"We're working on that," said Harper. "I called an agency this morning."

"And who are they sending?"

"They haven't called me back, but the woman said she thought they could send someone by the afternoon." All the hospital crew had left the room now. Celeste eyed the two who were left. What was Roy's chance of surviving them? Maybe Delrina had some sense; it was hard to tell on short notice. Harper was worse than useless. And Roy, Roy really needed care right now.

"This is crazy," she said. "Let's assume that you can get Roy up in that bus, which is doubtful. Who's going to look after him for the ride home? What if something happens to his IV? What if he's got to go, for God's sake? Roy, you have to stay. Just for a few days, even. Let me help you get the right people lined up. Then you do what you want."

"No. Now," said Roy. He hit the bed again and frowned at her like she was the enemy. Celeste had heard about strokes changing a person's personality, and she had to wonder about Roy. Had he been so stubborn before?

"You heard him, Celeste. You are making way too much of this." Harper spoke as though he had the situation all under control, but she could see him eyeing the IV line and the wheelchair someone had pulled up beside the bed. "You saw Hollis and Ronny out there. They're the best rescue squad guys in the county. Ronny is even certified in handling IVs, and Hollis can do CPR. They've lifted a lot heavier men than Roy. So we're set. We're going to be fine. Right, Roy? You ready to go?"

"Fine!" Roy smiled at Harper, who had not the first clue about step one, which was to get Roy into that chair.

Celeste considered her options. Delrina had been quiet for a few minutes, which made Celeste wonder if maybe she was getting a little worried as well. She decided to appeal woman to woman. "You know, Miss Kay," she said. "I'm not sure how a famous person such as yourself has gotten involved in this, but I have to let you know. This here is going to kill Roy's wife. She is just going to *die* when she finds out you've taken him out of here."

"Well, she should've thought of that before she booked him in the nearest nursing home," Delrina said and walked around to hold the back of the wheelchair. "Hop on in, Roy, honey. Delrina's going to take you for a ride."

Roy actually threw back his covers with his good hand and began to move his left leg off the bed. This was the problem with a partially paralyzed patient—there was no sense of what the deadweight could do. The moment Roy put that foot on the floor, the rest of his body would follow. Delrina only watched and smiled inanely. "Wait!" Celeste screamed. "Stop!" But of course, he didn't listen to her. She rushed across the room and got to the side of the bed just as his entire torso began to topple off. Roy was heavy. Celeste had to use everything she had to keep him from falling. Everyone else just froze until she said calmly, "Some help, please." Harper came over and helped her push Roy upright in the bed. When it was done, they were all sweating.

"See? You see?" Celeste didn't think it could be more clear.

"Sorry. You okay?" Roy said. He looked at her the way a dog does when it's peed on the rug. He looked so old, his eyelids falling down over his eyes, slack jaws, sickly pale skin. She tried to picture what he had looked like back in those days when she had loved him, but it wouldn't come.

"Oh, yeah," Celeste said. "I'm fine."

Roy straightened his hospital gown, pulled at his covers, trying to recover his dignity. He took a deep breath and held his head as straight as it would go considering he was missing some neck muscles at the moment. "Okay, bring in the boys," he said slowly but clearly. "Let's go."

"Roy, are you—," Harper began, but Roy just held up his hand like a stop sign.

"Let's go." Roy looked at Celeste then. "I'll be funny," he said, then realized he'd got it wrong. "I'll be . . . you know. You know."

"Roy." She was pleading now.

He held up his hand again. "No," he said. "Going."

Afterwards, she did not remember making the decision. "If you're going," she said, "I'm going with you."

Star

Her grandma was so busy chirping about Roy, about how much better he had gotten, about how thrilled he would be to see Star now, she didn't even notice Delrina's big tour bus pull away from Baptist Hospital at the same moment that Star turned into the visitors' parking lot. Star didn't say anything. Her grandma didn't like Delrina. Star didn't want to hear about it again.

"Park here, honey. It's closer to the door." Her grandma had let her drive her land barge this morning, but she had given her lots of advice. On the highway, she had read off the numbers on the speedometer: "Sixty-six miles per hour, sixty-seven, sixty-seven . . . Oh, Star, the speed limit's sixty-five here."

Her grandma had been totally hyper about everything since Roy woke up. Star heard her clomping around late at night and then again really early in the morning. She had cooked food they didn't need. Plus, she would not shut up, okay? As they went into the hospital, she kept on: "When Roy first gets home, the stairs might be too much, so here's what I'm thinking—I'll redo the den. I'll paint it navy maybe, get those antique bedside tables from the guest room, maybe the rocking chair. Make it masculine but homey."

The hospital was creepy. Her grandma had gotten used to it and kept on talking. Going through the lobby, you never knew what you would see: bandages covering nasty wounds, people slumped in wheelchairs, women with no hair. Maybe it was best to keep talking and walking. Here, it hit you, it was a fact—old people got sick. The chairs were full of them, poor people too, people who looked like they'd come from somewhere way in the country. They camped out on the sofas with little kids and sack lunches. Seeing all this made Star feel sick and also sorry, like she was some ungrateful princess who didn't have a clue and didn't want to.

They got into the elevator that smelled like cooked cabbage. The hall where Roy's room was smelled better. It had green walls and a shiny green floor, gave her the sensation she was walking through an aquarium. She tried to look straight ahead and close her ears in case there was moaning or something. Star was nervous about seeing Roy. She had visited him a couple of times. She hoped he was looking better. But here was the problem, okay? What would she say to him? Where would she put her eyes?

It was quiet all of a sudden, and Star realized her grandma had stopped talking. She stood in the hall about ten feet behind Star.

"Oh, sorry, is that Roy's room?" Star said. She was being a total space princess. She backtracked and joined her grandma. She looked into the room. There was no one in the bed. This panicked Star for a minute, but then she saw there were sheets on the bed, blankets, all messed up, like Roy had gotten up, gone to the bathroom or something.

"Is this it?" she said.

Her grandma nodded and then seemed to come unfrozen. "I'll bet they've taken him down to physical therapy," she said. "They were supposed to tell me first. Go on in. I'll be right back." She marched down toward the nurses' station. Star went into the room, but she could hear her grandma's footsteps loud and clear, and she could hear her voice as well: "Excuse me, excuse me. Nurse! My husband is not in his room!"

Star sat down on the chair next to the window and looked around. All of Roy's stuff was gone, his cards, the flowers, his clothes. There was nothing in the room but messed-up sheets, a water pitcher, and some wadded-up gauze. Star had seen things like this happen on TV, but now that this was real life, and really happening, it seemed some kind of weird dream, a dreamworld where the floors were a shiny emerald green, and the fluorescent lights were humming like insects and her grandma's monstrous footsteps tapped down the hall toward her.

Her grandma came into the room with a nurse right behind. Star jumped up and ran to her. Her grandma seemed unprepared to receive her, but after a few seconds she hugged her anyway.

"Will you tell me what's going on?" her grandma said. Star couldn't answer, didn't want to say, but it turned out she was talking to the nurse.

The nurse said, "Now, Mrs. Swan, let me assure you again, nothing has happened to Mr. Swan." Problem was, the nurse didn't sound that assured.

"Where is he then?"

"I've called Dr. Matthews. He'll explain."

"What in the world is there to explain?" Star could feel her grandma shaking, so she held on tight.

Josh

He put a fried bologna sandwich in front of his dad, along with a glass of tea.

"You'll make someone a lovely wife someday," his dad said as he bit into the sandwich.

He laughed at his dad's stupid joke. Okay. Now he'd try one more time. "I've been giving some prayerful thought to what we talked about earlier," he said, hoping that didn't sound too kiss-ass. "Here's the thing: those grapes over there are not wine. They're not even grape juice at this point. We don't even know if they'll be made into wine."

His dad had a response, but his mouth was filled with bologna. Josh charged on, "I think that the main point is that we have a neighbor who needs our help. Mr. Swan's grapes need to be harvested in the next few days or they'll be useless. We can't let that happen."

"Son, that is real nice. I hear you, but wine making is something we can't be part of. I wouldn't say this in front of Roy, but it's the devil's work. Understand? Would you go over there and help Roy out if he was running a brothel?" said his dad.

Several responses tempted Josh. He kept them to himself, though a smile escaped.

"Okay," his dad laughed. "Bad example, maybe."

Josh liked his dad once in a while. He could be okay when no one else was around. Maybe Josh should be going to him with things now instead of his mom. "Dad, my problem is my friend Star. I can't let her—"

"Oh Lord, so this is what this is about. I should've known. Puppy love."

Okay, now he felt like killing his dad. He hid this behind his sandwich.

"I was wondering why you were so keen on picking grapes all of a sudden." His dad gave him a tight little certain laugh—true and actual chuckling, which was something a person should never do. "This is Wilma's granddaughter, right?"

"Yes," Josh said, thinking of all the sharp heavy tools in his dad's shed. "Look. Give me a break, okay? If I don't go over there to help, she'll have to do it practically alone. There's no one else. Her dad asked us. He said there'd be pay and everything."

His dad took a long sip of tea. He folded his arms over his chest and then sat back and looked at Josh with one eye closed. Josh had seen this before—Travis lording it over someone who needed something from him.

"Well," he said finally. "I guess you could say in one way that our Lord Jesus Christ was a winemaker. That was his first miracle, turning water into wine. Remember?"

"Sure," said Josh, thinking, thank you, Jesus. "The wedding at Cana, right?"

"Of course, during biblical times, it wasn't the same thing. They didn't have strong wine. It was more like grape juice."

"Same as Roy's. Like I said, who knows how they'll use it," said Josh. "Could be grape juice. Roy's not going to be able to make it into wine this year."

"Not likely," said his dad. "I saw him yesterday. He is doing better, praise God."

"Yes," said Josh. "Then I can go?"

His dad handed him his plate and glass and got up from the table. "I'm going to let you," he said, "in the name of being a good neighbor."

"Thanks, Dad." He headed toward the back door and grabbed the old sweatshirt he kept for outdoor chores.

"Hang on," said his dad, taking his keys out of his pocket. "I'll take you over there. I want to see this Star that's got my son aching to be a farmhand."

Star

Her grandma didn't say another word after they left Roy's room. Had she been a little girl still, Star might have tried to fill in the silence, but she was old enough to know now—something awful had happened. Roy had not died; he had not gotten worse. In a way, these were the things she might've expected. These were things that maybe her grandma had been preparing for, but this was something else.

Her grandma got into the passenger side of the LTD and planted her feet firmly, one slightly in front of the other, as if seated at a piano. Star had to remind her to put on her seat belt. Star headed out to North 52 without even asking. She tried to drive textbook perfect: hands on the wheel at ten and two, not one mile per hour over the speed limit, a turn signal for every lane change.

They traveled up the highway, past Rural Hall, Tobaccoville, into Surry County, where the surface of the road changed. She had not noticed this before. There were seams in this section that rumbled, *ba-bump ba-bump,* made her grandma's chin jerk up and down. There was nothing Star could do about it.

Pretty soon, the highway turned slightly and Swan's Knob loomed ahead of them. Here at the end of September, the leaves on the mountain hadn't begun to turn. The mountain was all green, the pines on the very top the deepest blue green against today's pale sky. It was beautiful, a view you could never get tired of, one you would always notice, even though something terrible had happened to you. She hoped it helped her grandma, even just a little bit, but she couldn't tell.

When they got to the next exit, her grandma said, "Take this," and Star didn't say anything; she just did it. "Left," her grandma said at the bottom of the ramp, and pretty soon Star was driving the car up to the top of Swan's Knob, winding around in the trees. When they got to the top, her grandma pointed to a parking spot at the far end of the lot, and Star headed for it. She pulled in carefully; it was on the edge of a big slope. A good place to stop and gather your thoughts.

This was what her grandma wanted maybe, a stopping place between before and next.

Star was only seventeen. People always said it that way: *only* seventeen, like, what could she know? But she did know some things and she knew about this. Sometimes you needed to stop the world from spinning around, even for a few minutes. You could do this every once in a while, if you tried real hard, but you could also get lucky, and it would happen all on its own.

One time, when she was little, she and her mom and her dad were driving home to Santa Fe from her grandma's. There had been a big fight between her parents during their visit in Swan's Knob. She had been too little to understand much about it, though, and once the trip started, everything had seemed to settle down. It was a long trip and they drove straight through, late into the night. She had fallen asleep. She woke up under the lights of a Jack in the Box. Her parents were sitting in the front seat, sipping coffee, eating hamburgers, and talking in quiet tones. She listened for a few minutes to the hum of their voices, watched the steam rise off their cups, and drifted back to sleep in the calm assurance of their presence, of her safety, in the perfect knowledge that everything was right with the world.

This was her favorite memory and the saddest too. When someone said the word "family," this was what she would see—the three of them in that old car cruising home. It was like a time capsule, an old one, rusted in her memory. Of course, as her mom was always saying, families come in all shapes and sizes. Okay. But for her, "family," this word was completely contained, forever, in that car. It had all been broken, natch, the minute they arrived back in Santa Fe. Her mom dropped her dad off at the La Quinta. Star and her mom had moved in with Jonah a few months later; Verity was born in the spring. The three of them—her mom, her dad, and her—they had not shared the same space for more than five minutes since.

Her grandma leaned forward in her seat, looking down into the valley. At first Star thought she was looking at the big thunderstorm that was coming across the distant farmland, but she wasn't, exactly. Her grandma got out of the car. She walked out to the little overlook, with her gray hair blowing all around and her neck scarf stretching out behind her like a miniature cape. She put her hands on the guardrail and leaned farther, not exactly contemplating her fate, as Star had thought, but checking something out. Star got out and joined her. The wind was fierce and chilly. She could see the goose bumps on her grandma's skin, but she was afraid to put her arms around her. She followed her gaze instead. Roy's farm. Of course, the doctor had said they took him there. You could see the whole thing from the overlook. Delrina's bus was parked up close to the porch, the rescue squad van behind it. It was too far away for Star to be able to see if they were bringing Roy out of the bus. Maybe he was already inside. Her grandma squinted, trying to see herself.

"Get back in the car," she said finally, "and let's go down there."

Chapter Twenty-two

Harper

The phone started ringing the moment they brought Roy into the house. Harper prayed it was the home health agency saying they were sending a nurse. Celeste had been helpful, but they needed someone with more skills and fewer opinions. Of course, when he answered, it wasn't the agency, but someone from the *Winston-Salem Journal Sentinel*, a reporter on a deadline for the Sunday feature section. Harper talked to him briefly and then motioned to Delrina.

She came into the kitchen. "Jesus," she whispered, before she took the receiver from him. "What are we going to do with this guy? He's a sack of potatoes."

This was not kindly put, but it was accurate. He said, "It's Roy's house, Delrina. Don't forget." He pointed to the phone. "Doug, *Journal Sentinel*."

Delrina took a breath. "Hello, is this Doug? Well, hey!" She winked at Harper. "Oh, honey, just wait until you see our festival grounds," she said. "We have a brand-new open-air amphitheater. Doc Watson was over here the other day just raving about it. Yes, he's on the bill, of course, and we'll have a few surprises as well."

Harper started to go back into the front room, but they were busy transferring Roy to the bed, and he couldn't bear to watch. He turned back to the kitchen to hunt up the coffee and found Delrina stretching the phone cord to its limit to get to the far counter. She retrieved an open bottle of wine she had somehow failed to consume earlier and emptied it into the biggest coffee cup in the kitchen.

Roy

He was home, the thing he'd wanted so badly. It'd taken more doing than he would have ever imagined. Turned out it was a long, long way from the hospital bed in Winston to his little frame farmhouse. And where was he after all the fuss? In a hospital bed, just like the other one, except that now he was lying smack in the middle of his front room. He was flat-out worn out too, could hardly keep his eyes open, even though there was more bustling and arranging and hollering and phone ringing than he could ever remember in all his times in this place, worse even than a house full of his wild Indian cousins. His dead side—that was how he thought of it, *dead*—had been as heavy as a load of firewood, heavier even. What's more, the side that worked wasn't too much help. He was weak as he could be. His rescue squad buddies had been forced to lift every ounce of him, all umpty-ump pounds. It had been ugly. Ugly. Turned out plain old brawn was not enough. Ronny and Hollis would have dumped him on the floor six or seven times if Celeste had not been around to supervise.

Good God, that was the other thing that was making him tired, all this supervision. Harper had supervised Delrina the whole way home, telling her where to turn, where to slow down, how she'd better "fucking stop running up over curbs." Celeste had supervised Harper's use of bad language and his method for anchoring Roy's wheelchair to the banquette table leg, and she had advised him on the correct temperature on the bus so that the "patient" (she called Roy that, her lifelong friend) wouldn't get pneumonia and die. She had supervised his litter bearers, yelling, "Careful not to bang his head on the door frame! You'll knock the last bit of sense out of him," as they'd come in his own front door.

Did he have any sense? He was not certain.

Celeste

At the hospital, at least they had the illusion of control—sterile conditions, patient charts, a plan of care. Here, the old wood floors creaked under their feet, there was too much furniture, too many people, and Roy looked like a lost soul. The trip had tired him out, she could see. His skin looked nearly transparent and his eyes wandered around the room without lighting on anything in particular. Pretty soon, his bladder would be full, whether he knew it or not.

As a defense against the sight of the man in the bed, she tried again to picture Roy as he had been those years ago in this house—curly hair combed just so, swept back with Brylcreem, his smile wide with the pleasure of the evening. He was a tolerable dancer, not as good as most. He would stay back and watch most of the time, crossing his arms across his plaid shirt. She could see his spot over by the fireplace, marked now by an IV pole wrapped in plastic, where he would preside over the Victrola and nod his head in time with the music.

Roy's rescue guys had located themselves just beyond the bed, by the bookcases, shuffling their feet and feigning mighty interest in a shelf of old duck decoys. They'd gotten Roy into the house and into the bed. That had been some job and they were not all that practiced at it. Celeste was sorry she had been short with them, though bless them, they had taken her yelling and Roy's situation in stride, pretended it was all routine. The Snow boy had even joked with Roy about what a lousy pool player he was. Now there wasn't anything for them to do, really, but they were hanging out just in case.

"Hey, guys, thanks for all you did," she said. "Can I raid your rig out there? I might need a few things."

"Sure," said the Snow boy. As he left, he walked by Roy's bed and spoke to him like they'd just had a beer together. "All right now, Roy. Once you're better, I get the first game you play at Squirrely's, you hear? I'm going to hold you to your bet. You knock the cue ball on the floor, and it's drinks for every man on the squad."

"You got it," said Roy, with more gusto than any of them felt.

Celeste followed them to their van, hoping to God they had something resembling a bedpan.

Roy

He was almost asleep when it occurred to him that he had to pee real bad. He opened his eyes. For the moment, there wasn't a soul in the room. He didn't want to call out. That might summon all of them, and he didn't think it would take the whole crew to empty his bladder. The misery of his situation combined with the sudden urgency overwhelmed him, and Jesus God, he began to tune up and cry again. This was the kind of self-pity that he could not bear in others. He tried for a moment to concentrate on his surroundings instead. Back when he was staring at the four walls of that hospital room, he had longed for the familiar, and here it was. Yes, he might prefer his and Wilma's nice bedroom—their antique four-poster bed with the nice covers she'd had custom-made right after she moved in, but he couldn't think about that, about her, about their bed, the only one he'd ever shared.

He heard Harper and that singer woman banging around in the kitchen. Harper stuck his head in the door, and asked if Roy wanted coffee. He nodded yes, and Harper disappeared again before Roy could describe his predicament. He looked around for a solution—a cup, a bowl, hell, he did not care.

There was nothing within reach. On the bookcase nearby, a collection of his dead relatives looked down on him from their various frames with focused reserve. Only Granny Swan provided a modicum of sympathy. In the picture, she was just like he remembered her. She was wearing a black dress and black button boots and standing in front of a huge hydrangea that still thrived in the south corner of the garden. She had a large watering can in her hand and looked out of the photo at him as if she'd certainly lend the thing to him if she could.

Harper came back in. "How do you take it?" he said.

There was no choice. "Look," he said. "Gotta piss."

"Oh," said Harper. "Hang on." Roy wasn't sure that he could. Harper ran back into the kitchen and began to open and close the cabinets frantically.

"What are you looking for?" said the singer woman.

"A pot to piss in," he heard Harper say. Roy was afraid to laugh.

Granny Swan had died in her bedroom upstairs without any fuss at all. No one mentioned a cause that he remembered. Old age, is how they would've put it. She had been laid out on a dining table right about where he was lying now. The Swan relatives had gathered, carrying on their business in the same room, all around her coffin. His mother had objected mightily. She had insisted that even if they did plan to bury Granny Swan on their hill in the morning, she should be taken to the funeral home overnight. When this did not happen, his mother took a few of the littlest cousins back to the house in town and left the rest of them to sit up with the body all night.

Josh

"Well, I don't like the looks of this," his dad said when they came up Roy's driveway and he saw the rescue squad van parked behind the bus. His dad pulled his own truck up into the grass by the porch so he wouldn't block anyone in. When they got out, they could see that the doors of the van had been flung open. The guys from the squad were inside, going through drawers and bins and handing items out to a waiting nurse. The nurse turned around. It was Josh's mother.

"Where is your car?" was the first thing his dad said to her.

It took her a minute to think. "Left it at work," she said, real short. She turned back around. "Boys, how about a box or something for this stuff? My arms are full."

"What are you doing here?" his dad said, but his mom didn't hear. She stepped up into the van.

"What's happened?" his dad asked. This is what Josh would've asked first.

"Nothing," said his mom. She shoved a box into Josh's arms and went back for more.

Ronny Snow came out of the van now. "We've just brought Roy from Baptist," he said quietly.

"What?" said his dad. "Who let him do that? Are y'all crazy?" His mother didn't answer right away. His dad put his hand on her shoulder and gripped it, but his voice was calm. He said, "Celeste, why are you not at work?"

"Roy," she said. "He insisted on leaving Baptist and I couldn't let him go alone."

"Looks like he had plenty of help."

"He needed me," his mom said. She turned toward Josh then and pointed to the box. "Honey, take that inside."

Josh went up the walk and the front steps, looking around for Star. There was no sign of her. At the door, he thought about knocking but decided he could just go on in. The door opened straight into the living room. There was a bed right there. Roy Swan was in it. "God, sorry!" he said. Yikes, not what he expected.

He turned the other way, but then he nearly ran into Star's dad, who was carrying a cook pot. Whatever was in it sloshed up a bit but didn't go over the side. "Watch out!" Star's dad screamed anyway. He gave Josh a look like he was ready to kill him.

"Sorry!" Josh said again.

Roy

Celeste's boy, the one Star liked, stood at the end of Roy's bed with a box in his arms, not sure what to do next. What was he? Sixteen? Seventeen? Roy could smell the outdoors on him, the sweat from his old work shirt, and Lord knows what else. He wondered if there was some way to put that into his IV.

Celeste and Travis came in with more medical supplies and a damn oxygen tank. Travis looked as jolted as the boy to see him. Damn near dropped the tank, which would have been bad. The singer woman came in from the kitchen with a tray of coffee cups. At the back of the house, there was the sound of the plumbing and then Harper reappeared. Five people. No one sat down. It got quiet suddenly, after all that ruckus, and everyone looked at everyone else.

This was a brand of awkward he could usually handle, but he was not able to play the part of host this afternoon. The silence stretched on, making the moment as uncomfortable as the worst date he had ever been on, which had to be—no question about it—a Saturday night in the late fifties in the back booth at Green's Supper Club. His date was a pretty black-headed girl he barely knew. They'd started with a simple conversation, but nothing he said seemed to amuse or interest her in the least. Before they'd finished their first drink, he'd said something to offend her in some way. She virtually stopped speaking by the second drink and refused to order another one, which might have helped. Before long, he was rendered completely speechless himself, couldn't even recall how a normal date should go. He could only sit in the leatherette booth and look across at this lovely girl with the sour expression and know the whole evening was ahead—oysters, steaks, the works.

This was more than a disastrous evening, this folly of coming home. He'd had the silly notion that he could go on living almost as before. And he had brought these good people with him. He had to make this right, if he could. To pretend, as he had that night, that things could only improve. Well, he would try, but he would not make them suffer long. He started by smiling at Harper, who had just done way more than any friend should have to do. Then he looked at Delrina. "Coffee," he said.

Celeste

Celeste wanted to go over and check on Roy—he was looking flushed—but she didn't dare for fear that her dear husband would pitch a fit right there in front of everyone. Did he not understand and appreciate simple human kindness? Apparently not. He was not about to give any out. He stared at Roy like he was a corpse at a viewing.

"He doesn't look so good," he said. The comment was for her, but everyone could hear.

This wasn't the time for her to tell Travis that she had not been for this, that she had left work at her own peril for fear Roy would be hurt, that she had personally prevented several disasters already. Now she had to defend the whole thing. She said, "He's just a little tired is all. The ride took it out of him."

"Well, at least take the poor man upstairs. Give him a little dignity," Travis said.

"It was hard enough getting him this far," said Delrina, but she was kind enough to add, "No offense, Roy." Celeste noticed that Delrina was making her way around the sofa and old chairs that they had pushed aside earlier, carrying the tray like she had done it all her life. Now there was kindness. This woman was a celebrity, and yet she had pitched in and made coffee, in that nice outfit too. She was about to put a mug into Roy's hands.

"Wait a minute," Harper said. "Don't give him that."

"He's got to be thirsty. It's all right, isn't it, Celeste?"

"I don't see why not." Actually, coffee was probably not the best thing, but Celeste couldn't help it—she didn't want to go against Delrina now that the singer knew her name and thought to call upon her for advice. "Be careful, though. You might want to hold it for him. We don't want him dropping hot coffee in his lap."

Roy

When he and Wilma had visited Versailles a few years ago, he had been fascinated by King Louis' bedchamber. Folks had been tiny back then. Louis' bed was only five feet long, but it had rested on a tall platform in the middle of an opulent room—gilt trimming, paintings by great masters on the ceilings, tapestries and draperies everywhere. A king's bedchamber was not a private place. His courtiers clamored for the privilege of attending him—only the most favored could draw near to wake him, to wash him, to empty his chamber pot. Roy tried to think of himself thusly, as a king, attended now by this woman whose relation to the situation escaped him. He tried not to mind that she climbed up on his bed beside him and held a sturdy mug up to his lips. He took a little sip. Maybe his taste buds were off, but the liquid was not hot and it was not coffee.

Harper

He wondered if he should open a window or something, get a little air into the room with all these people. There were just too many for the space, but he looked around—whom could he ask to leave? At any minute, he might need the services of any one of them. He looked at the kid, Josh, who'd put his box on the floor and was standing with his hands in his jeans pockets. Maybe he could go. He didn't look like he wanted to be here anyway. Take his daddy with him too. Harper started to say so but remembered that Josh was one person whom he'd actually asked to come. The grapes. Right, there was that.

"Josh," he said. "Sorry. You're here to help out with the grapes, right? Star said you'd be coming. Let me take you down and get you started."

Roy, who seemed to be wholly comfortable now with Delrina and her big cup lounging on his bed, perked up at the mention of the grapes. "Yes?" he said. "Grapes ready?"

"Tom Felton came on Thursday and said get them off the vines," Harper said. "He didn't come through with a crew for us, so Star and this young man here have volunteered."

"Nice," Roy said. "Thanks."

"You're welcome, sir. Happy to help out," said Josh politely. For the moment, Harper tried not to think about what else Josh might be happy to help himself to.

Celeste sent Harper on another errand then for more linens and some pillows. He climbed the stairs and took his time looking through the closets. In the bedroom he'd been using, he looked out the window. Dark afternoon storm clouds coming up from the west. A storm might not be so good for the grapes, but it was going to delay their harvest. He wasn't sending the kids out in a thunderstorm.

When he came back down the stairs, it was completely quiet. There they were—Star and Wilma.

Wilma was focused like a hawk on the bed, where Roy was still being attended by his courtesan Delrina. Everyone else looked up at Harper, but it was Star he noticed. She looked at him with the wild, wide eyes he'd seen when she was a little girl stuck at the top of a big jungle gym, unable to make her way down.

Roy

If he had thought it through, he could've predicted she would come, and come the minute she heard. But that particular part of his brain—the thinking-through part—was not really functioning.

"Hey, Wilma," he said, like it was normal for him to check himself out of the hospital, to move himself into this farmhouse, perfectly okay for him to be lying in a bed with a shapely singer, sipping out of her cup.

"Well, heeey!" said the singer. This would make things worse.

Suddenly all of these people who'd wanted nothing more than to help him five minutes before were busy looking at their shoes. Harper was the first one to speak.

"Star," he said. "Glad you're here. Let me take you and Josh out to the barn and get you started. Maybe you can get in a little work before it rains."

The others made departure noises as well—Celeste pointed her husband toward the kitchen, and Delrina gave Roy one more quick drink. Wilma did not budge from her place. Roy swallowed the wine, if that's what it was, and took a deep breath. He'd make her understand. But of course, this was not going to be his day for dignity. The last sip went down the wrong way. He began coughing and sputtering, and then gasping in the most pathetic way possible, causing everyone in departure mode to rush the bed. This gave all those present in the king's chamber a perfect view when he sprayed red wine all over his covers.

Wilma

Riding down from the mountain, Wilma had decided that Roy was going to kill himself with this foolishness. That he would die from his own stubbornness. But she was not thinking literally *die*, like he was now, hemorrhaging in the front room of the dusty farmhouse.

Delrina jumped down. "Uh-oh," she said, though that hardly covered it.

There was not a doctor in sight, and God, not even a nurse. They had told her he'd hired a nurse. Roy's very life was in the hands of Celeste, an LPN with nothing to offer other than trade-school training and the box of gauze pads that she carried toward the bed now.

"Do something," Wilma yelled at her, at which point she dropped the box onto the world's filthiest floor.

Celeste crouched down to retrieve her supplies. "He's hemorrhaging," said Travis, yanking her to her feet. Roy continued to cough and waved one hand in front of the mess.

Wilma, by his side now and uncertain how she had gotten there, grabbed his hand and held it tight. It was important at least that she not get hysterical for his last minutes on earth. "It's okay," she said. "We're going to take care of you." She searched out Harper. "Call an ambulance," she said.

"Really?" said Harper, who had always been a stupid man.

Roy shook his head and opened his mouth. Wilma steeled herself, but it was only a short dry cough this time. He shook his head. No. No. His face was crimson. Maybe it was okay with him to die of stubbornness, but she would just not have it.

"Roy Swan, you are not allowed to die," she said. She meant this. She would not have it.

"Oh, for Pete's sake," said Delrina.

"Wait," said Celeste, who was standing beside her now. "Hang on." She looked down at the covers and then back up at Roy. He had stopped coughing. "This isn't blood."

"Then what is it?" Wilma said. The color in Roy's face was returning to normal.

"It's wine, red wine," said Delrina. "I been trying to tell you."

Roy

He was not sure what was worse, the abject fear that had turned Wilma's green eyes to midnight a moment ago, or the fury that he could see building now in the veins of her neck. As she looked over at Delrina and then at the rest of them, she began shaking, the enormous tide of her fear and anger engulfing her entire body. She clung to his arm still as if the danger had not passed, as if she were afraid of being swept away from him, afraid that if she let go for a second, something else foolish and random would take him away. He closed his eyes. This was the reason he could not bear to have her near him now. Everything, every cough, every miscued word, every bare-assed indignity—all this suffering doubled in her presence. Quadrupled. He felt it twice, for them both, and she did too.

Celeste

She allowed herself two seconds of relief that Roy was not actually hemorrhaging and going to die right there in front of everybody. Then she reminded herself that for once she was the one in the crowd with the qualifications. She needed to get hold of things. This was not going to be easy. At least one person in the room, and that would be her husband, was screaming, "Wine! Wine?"

Delrina, completely unrepentant, lifted her tray in the air, like her coffee cups would defend her. She did have wonderful posture. It added dignity to her situation. "Yes," she said, like she was on a stage. "Wine. It worked before. You people need to know. Roy, we brought some of your wine to you in the hospital the other night and that's why you are here today. Isn't that right, Harper?"

"Jesus," said Harper.

"No, it isn't," Travis put in. "Far from it."

In the middle of this mess, Roy looked tired and a little confused. He looked at Celeste for help. "Who is that woman?" he said slowly. She got the idea that he was asking about Delrina, but Wilma, who looked like she might have her own stroke, didn't understand and began to shake his arm.

"Don't you know me, Roy? It's Wilma. Wilma." Roy didn't say anything, kept his eyes on Celeste.

"Look," said Celeste. "He's tired. It's been a long day for him."

Wilma let go of Roy's arm like she'd been scolded, stepped away, and sank down into the old couch. Everyone seemed to take a breath then. Josh, who had been trapped all this time on the far side of the room, slid past her and went over to Star. Celeste retrieved the extra linens from Harper and set about changing Roy's sheets. She was careful of his modesty since she had an audience. He didn't pay much attention to what she was doing, just looked around the room from face to face. When he got to Star and Josh, he gave them a special smile and lifted his hand in a little wave.

Delrina wandered through the room trying to foist coffee, or maybe it was wine, on people.

"No, thank you, ma'am," said Travis when she got to him, like she was Jezebel or Eve or something.

"It's coffee in these mugs," she said. "That's all. What's your problem?"

"My problem," said Travis, "is a person who claims healing with an alcoholic beverage."

"Roy," said Wilma from the couch, "are you feeling better?"

Delrina slammed her tray onto the nearest lamp table. "Have you ever heard of a little thing called the Lord's Supper?"

Roy looked over at Travis, who sputtered, "That is not the same thing, not in the least."

Delrina had her hands on her hips and was about to reply when Harper looked up from his conversation with Star and Josh. "Delrina, how about you come outside with us and help with these holy grapes? Roy would sure appreciate it."

Roy

He tried to look at anyone but Wilma. This was not easy, because she had called his name several times and had the idea now that he did not know her. Maybe this was best.

Celeste was fussing over him, Harper was in the corner trying to explain how to cut grapes, and now Travis and the other woman were having some kind of religious debate. He was still not sure what this woman's name was and why she was there, though he remembered tasting his wine, and not just now, but somewhere in his dreams in the hospital. Maybe she had been there. He didn't know.

"Roy. Roy." It only got worse. He closed his eyes, but Wilma didn't stop calling him.

"Wilma," he heard Celeste say quietly, "he's tired."

"I don't think that's it," Wilma said. She touched his arm again. "Is it, Roy?"

He didn't know what else to do. He opened his eyes. "Go," he said, though it could have sounded kinder. "Go home now."

Celeste pulled a blanket up on him. "I can't go yet, Roy," she said. "I'll wait until a nurse gets here."

"No," he said, hating it. "Her. Tell Wilma to go."

Celeste

Travis had always had the knack of making a bad situation worse.

"Now, Roy, wait a minute here," he said. "You need to listen to me. That is Wilma. That is your wife. Keep thee only unto her, buddy."

"Travis, it's all right," Wilma began, but he pushed past them and leaned up into Roy's face.

"Talk about healing, Roy. This is the one who done it. Wilma. She has claimed the healing I brought to her with holy oil and prayer. She's the one that done it, laid her hands on you and made you whole."

"Whole?" Roy frowned at Travis, even tried leaning up toward him, but Travis stood his ground.

Wilma got up from the couch. "Roy doesn't need to hear all this now," she said. "Star, let's be—"

"Yes, he does," said Travis. "About our prayers, about the oil I ordered from the Holy Land. He needs to know so that he can claim the rest of it."

"Well, it could have been the wine," said Delrina. "We were there first."

"Star," Wilma said, "get the car."

Celeste thought that they might all leave then, that she might get a chance to get Roy settled and to find out what had happened to that home nurse, but this time, it was Roy who would not leave it alone.

Roy

"Angel," he said. "Angel." That got their attention.

If he was going to be the victim of a faith healing, he might as well put in his two cents. If someone or something had awakened him, maybe it was the woman he saw by the window in his room. She had touched him, hadn't she? He hadn't seen her since. And maybe, she had not been there to heal him at all. It took him a minute to think of the words, but finally he did: "angel of death."

Josh

He'd been wondering if he and Star would ever get to the field. He wanted to go a million times, but he couldn't find an opening. Now it was pouring rain, and her grandmother wanted to take her back to town.

Okay, he'd pick grapes solo. He'd do it in the rain, risk getting struck by lightning. Happy to. Give him the clippers. This was messed up. Mr. Swan was lying in his living room in his pajamas. It wasn't right for everyone to be standing around, watching the guy puke and arguing about who saved him. Poor Star. She looked freaked. So did his mother. She was trying to keep Mr. Swan calm. His dad, on the other hand, was being a nightmare.

His mom put her hands on Mr. Swan's shoulders. "No, no," she said. "There's no angel of death."

This didn't help.

"Yes," Mr. Swan said. "Like that. Just like that." He looked at Celeste and his eyes got real big. "You?" he said suddenly.

"Celeste," said his dad then, "you're getting him all worked up."

"I think he's feverish," she said, but the guy went off then.

"Was it you? You?" He said this over and over.

"Celeste, have you been touching Roy?" said his dad, like it was a dirty thing.

"I am not the angel of death," said his mother. "It didn't work. It didn't work, Roy."

"What didn't work?" said his dad. Now his mom was freaking out big-time.

"The pillow," she said. She didn't look at his dad. "You were bad off, Roy. I was trying to help you. But it didn't work. Maybe that's what did it. Maybe it was the pillow that woke you up."

"You telling us you tried a mercy killing?" said Delrina. "Lord God."

Star

She wanted to help her grandma somehow, but it seemed to her these people had already been over-helping. It was complicated, all right? Maybe she missed something between the coffee cup and the oil from the Holy Land. Roy was alive. But he wasn't so good. She didn't get why everybody had a claim on this.

It had been raining hard for a while now. You could hear the plunking sound it made on the tin roof. The thunder rumbled through the old house and rattled the old knickknacks on the walls, but no one said anything about it, since they were all playing their little parts. There was no way she was going to be able to pick grapes with Josh, which was a shame since he had come over here to do that and not to see some freak show.

One time her mom had gone to a party at a hotel in Santa Fe where they played murder mystery. They gave everyone costumes, like boas and mustaches and stuff. Someone got fake killed and they had to guess who had done it, with what, and why. Her mom, who hated all kinds of parlor games, had said it was the longest night of her life. She wished she'd gotten to be the murder victim because that woman got to spend the entire night in the bar, drinking free margaritas.

The lightning cracked now, and it sounded close. The lights blinked off and on and then off again.

"Ooooh, spooky," she said, but no one paid any attention.

Even though the storm was loud, Roy kept closing his eyes. It looked like he just wanted to go to sleep. *I think it was Colonel Mustard in the observatory with the candlestick,* she wanted to say, but she didn't think anyone would think it was funny.

Roy

He was startled by what Celeste said. Moved too. Of everyone, maybe she was the only one who had it right. Maybe she had known what was ahead and wanted to spare him. After a few hours away from the hospital, he was starting to get the picture. He was less than certain he wanted to live like this. Everyone thought he owed them now. Owed them at least his best effort. Did he? Did he owe Wilma, and all these crazy people who had prayed on him and poured holy oil and wine and tears all over his pajamas?

Lord, they had gone to some effort. They all looked at him so earnestly now. With such concern. Only Harper, his buddy Harper, smirking over there in the corner, seemed to understand the real stupidity of the situation.

Harper spoke up. "Roy, bottom line, I think, is that everyone here cares about you, wants to see you come back. You'll just have to forgive us if we went a little overboard."

"Yes," said Wilma. "The main thing is that you're alive."

Alive? This made him furious suddenly.

"Who said? Who said I wanted to live?" He said this with as much volume and meanness as he could muster. Then he made Celeste chase everyone out of the house.

Chapter Twenty-three

Wilma

"I'm going to send you money for all these phone calls. I can wire it over," Wilma said. Sarah had called her almost daily since Roy had left the hospital and moved out to the farm. It had been more than six weeks. International long distance was expensive.

"I've told you: we'll charge it to the magazine," Sarah said. Her voice had a determined edge. "And stop changing the subject. I keep calling and all you want to talk about is the weather or the leaves or the long-distance charges. Meanwhile, Star says you're running around in the middle of the night scrubbing bathrooms and polishing the silverware. What's going on?"

"I'm staying busy, that's all. What else should I be doing? By the way, I found your grandmother's asparagus tongs the other day. They've been missing forever."

"Oh God, Mother. Why can't you just go out there and see Roy? What's he got, an invisible force field around the farm?"

Yes, Wilma wanted to say, that must be it. Maybe that's why I've driven my car out Dobson's Mill Road about twenty times and never gotten farther than the Ararat River. A force field. "Roy told me to leave. He said for me to stay away. You can't go where you're not wanted." She sounded testy but that was better than blubbering herself into a puddle of sadness. She tried to save most of her crying for the shower.

"How do you know that?" said Sarah.

"Know what?"

"That Roy doesn't want you around?"

"He said. Simple as that." She had been over this many times now, with Sarah, with Star, with herself.

"That was when he first got out of the hospital. He's better now, right?"

News was scarce. Roy hadn't let anyone into the house except the medical people. She was lucky that included Celeste or she wouldn't know a thing. "Yes, he's better. That's what I hear."

"Much better, is what Harper told me. Roy's able to walk a little now. His speech is really improved."

"Harper's seen him, then?" This she hadn't known.

"Just in the last week. Roy invited him over to talk about this concert thing Harper's doing. They're using the farmhouse as their headquarters. It's Grand Central over there by now. You knew this, right?"

"About the festival? Oh sure." Another battle she had lost. Wilma held the phone between her ear and her shoulder and began fumbling through her kitchen cabinets for a tea bag, any tea bag. She appeared to be out.

"See? Then there's your chance, Mother. Roy's better, the barriers are down. Perfect time."

So now Sarah was in cahoots with Harper—her ex-husband, no less—and no telling who else. They were all on the line together, talking about festivals and treatment plans, talking about poor old Wilma, back in town, polishing the silverware in oblivion. She was happy that Roy had survived, glad that he was healing, but she also wanted to lie down and die over this latest news. He was letting people back into his life. Most people, but not her. So it was what she'd feared. That force field, it was not around Roy—it was around her. "You don't get it," she said in a tone she rarely used on her daughter. "He doesn't want me."

Sarah sighed all the way over there in the Pacific—Bangkok, it was this week. Sarah put on her therapist's voice. "I hear your anger, Mother. I hear you. I, for one, am angry as well. Roy is being very withholding. I don't understand how he can even begin to heal with all that bad energy inside him. We've just gotten back from Rayong, where I talked with this wonderful healer, Jitra Wongyai."

Sarah was off then, launching into an account of her visit with the amazing Mrs. Wongyai. Wilma put her kettle on the stove. Surely she had a tea bag somewhere. Sarah continued, but Wilma didn't feel obliged to pay attention. Sarah had provided similar stories in the past weeks, complete with prescriptions for all manner of ills. Nice of her, of course, kind. But. There was nothing that was going to cure Wilma's particular ailment, which was nothing more than plain awful sadness, the kind that buckled her knees, sent her to the tile floor of her shower. Sadness. That's what she felt. That, and a creepy sensation akin to losing a limb, a longing for something vital that no longer existed. Only it was not her right arm missing, but worse, her true love.

Nothing would fix this, nothing. But how like her daughter, all the way over there in Thailand, to try. Yesterday, Wilma had received a package from her containing the ugliest root she had ever seen in her life. It looked like a miniature naked old man, dried-up, fat in the middle, spindly limbs, thin wiry hair. Maybe she could make comfort tea with that.

As Sarah continued to chatter, about the healer woman's dirt floor, her beautiful hands, her salve made from cabbage and beeswax, Wilma tried to let herself be soothed by her daughter's weird brand of optimism.

"By the way, thank you for the root," she said.

"Oh, the ginseng, you got it. Great!" said Sarah. "It's for Roy, really. Ginseng is highly prized out here. Asian men like it because it does wonders for their get-up-and-go, if you take my meaning. I know that can be a problem with stroke victims. I was wondering if maybe that was part of Roy's—"

"I am just so sorry that Star isn't home from school yet. She's been working on some new songs for the festival," said Wilma.

"Okay," said Sarah. "I got it. End of subject." The therapist voice again.

"Thank you," said Wilma. Roy's get-up-and-go was the least of her worries. She'd be happy to see the man walk across the room. Happy to have him call her name. In fact, she'd take less than that. This was exactly the thing that Roy Swan did not understand.

"Look," said Sarah. "I'm just trying to help."

"I know, sugar, I know, and I appreciate it, really I do." And she did, to a point. "I need to go now. This is costing you a fortune, and I want to get my shower before Star gets home."

She heard the hiss of distance on the line then and thought she'd lost the connection, but after a moment, Sarah's voice, clear and soft, came over her receiver. She said, "It's like I tell my students: you can't be too proud, Mother. Ask for help, I tell them. Ask for what you want. Go for it. Be shameless."

There was the hiss again, and it may as well have been the sound separating Wilma's own time from the next—where shamelessness was a good thing and pride was not.

"Look, forget the ginseng. Bad idea," Sarah said finally.

"No, honey, thanks, I know—," she began.

"Just go talk to Roy. Don't hang on to your pride, Mother," said her daughter, her sweet girl who could still put faith in an ugly root. "Pride won't get you anywhere."

"Maybe you're right," Wilma said then, mostly to get Sarah off the phone. But what she didn't say was this: that her pride, her own precious allotment of it, was the only scaffolding she had left, the only thing to keep her from washing right on down the drain.

Harper

Harper let himself in through the back door. He found Roy alone, pulled up to the kitchen table in his wheelchair, finishing his breakfast. He threw the magazine and the contraband box of doughnuts onto the table and sat down beside him.

"Here we are, buddy, wait till you see. *Rolling Stone* magazine. All written up, a week in advance of the festival, so time enough to help with ticket sales."

Roy smiled at him, the right side of his face almost even with the left. "That is fine, mighty fine." His speech had gotten so much better, and the rest of him was coming along as well. Maybe that was why he had let Harper and Delrina back in the house. Roy thumbed through the magazine with his good hand, looking for the article. "What's Delrina think?"

"I haven't shown her yet. She's all wrapped around the axle with some singing group this morning." Harper had spent the last month camped out in Delrina's tour bus. This had its pluses and its minuses. They'd run a phone line out there, hooked up electricity, gotten to know each other a little better. They'd been able to keep getting ready for the festival without a hitch, but still, it'd been hard to watch the parade of medical professionals come in and out of the farmhouse, knowing that except for them, Roy was pretty much on his own.

Harper flipped through the pages and located the article for Roy. Roy stared at it for a few minutes. Was reading a problem? Harper didn't know. "Mind if I read it out loud?" he said. "I'd love to hear the sound of it. It's pretty short."

Bluegrass Heritage Fest Set for Blue Ridge Foothills

Swan's Knob, NC—Headliners Delrina Kay and Little Charlie, Doc Watson, the Del McCoury Band, and a host of other bluegrass, old-time stringband, and country acts will gather in the foothills of the Blue Ridge Mountains next weekend for the first annual Heritage of the Foothills Music Festival.

Organizers expect more than five thousand to make their way to the festival site overlooking Swan's Knob in Surry County, NC, for two days of old-time bluegrass, folk, and new country music. Modeled on the old-time fiddlers' conventions, attendees will also have a chance to make their own music at one of several pickers' tents to be set up throughout the venue.

"Around here, we pass many a Saturday night sitting on the front porch picking. Our idea was to take this tradition and make a big old party out of it," said Delrina Kay, who is helping to organize the music lineup. Delrina, returning to the music scene after a two-year hiatus, will be joined by her son Charles Kay, formerly known as Little Charlie, and accompanied by a local gospel choir.

"Really?" said Roy. "Her son coming?"

"Beats me," said Harper. "Last I heard, he was hanging out in Key West somewhere."

"And you got a gospel choir?"

"Well, she's still working on that. We'll see." Harper didn't want to tell him.

"I am real excited about the music I've developed over the time I took off," said Delrina, whose last album, Tell It All, *was nominated for a Country Music Award. "I've really gone through a spiritual thing lately, based on some very personal happenings. It's just all flooded out into the music."*

"Oh Lord," said Roy. "She's not going to talk about the wine again, is she?"

Harper laughed. "Roy, you know I have no control over that woman. Listen to this last part."

"We hope lots of folks will come on out and enjoy the music and the fellowship," said festival organizer Harper Chilton, a local fiddler and Delrina Kay's new manager. "We couldn't ask for a better location. We've got wide-open spaces—room for RV and tent campers, a new amphitheater, lots of good food, the works. It's a beautiful spot. No better view of Swan's Knob in the county."

Roy Swan, whose historical farm and vineyard are the location for the festival, has provided inspiration to all those organizing the festival, said Chilton. Swan is a lifelong Swan's Knob resident, the festival's benefactor, and a paraplegic, whose recent health struggles have spurred on the efforts of all of those involved, noted Chilton.

"Paraplegic?" said Roy. "Where'd you get that?"

"Delrina's idea," said Harper. "She said it sounded more heroic than recovering from a stroke, more like a skiing accident or something. The rest of the article just talks about the lineup of musicians, which I think you know by now."

"Does it say anywhere in there what you're going to do in case of snow?" Roy cut his eyes over to Harper then. And there he was again, the old Roy, the sly dog who hung out at Squirrely's and played incompetent pool, who loved to tease a guy. He'd come up with at least one nightmare scenario for Harper every day this week. Yesterday's had been a sudden infiltration of cicadas.

"Well, no, Roy, I hadn't thought of snow since it's only mid-November. We've set up some campfire rings in case folks get cold, but you're right, maybe we ought to order snowshoes."

"Just a thought," Roy laughed.

Harper got them both more coffee then and took a few minutes to hang out at the table, watch Roy eat doughnuts, and shoot the breeze about nothing important—the high school football team, the price of tobacco, the new fire truck the rescue squad was taking delivery of in a few days. Of course, Roy didn't mention that he'd donated the thing, hoses, siren, and all, and Harper didn't let on that he knew about it, that the whole town knew, that there were folks saying this was evidence that Roy had truly lost his marbles—donating a whole fire truck.

Harper didn't think it was one bit crazy. For one thing, it had made the mayor, Chief Henry, and the rest real cooperative about all the permits they'd needed. They'd even volunteered for traffic control. Anything for Roy. Everyone knew—he was a generous man. This was the part of him that had survived everything, survived his black moods over the past months, survived despite his need to cut everyone out of the picture, to suffer through rehab all on his own. Harper did not understand how a man could be so generous, how he could write checks to build a new stage by his barn, outfit the whole thing, but still refuse to let anyone—family, friends, even his own wife—close enough to return the favor. This was the hard fact of the last six weeks.

But now, as long as they were sitting at that table, Roy smiling and sneaking one more doughnut, the night nurse camped out in the next room, it was easy to pretend nothing much had happened to Roy. Maybe that was how he wanted it. Roy wanted everyone to just skip over the past couple of months and move on. Harper thought he could do that, but he wasn't sure about everyone else.

Celeste

She put on her uniform, the shoes, stockings, her LPN pin, everything, before going over to Roy's. It was the standard issue from Baptist Hospital even though she was on leave at the moment. A uniform was not strictly required for her work at Roy's, but she always wore it anyway. She tried to tell people, and she'd told Travis about a million times now, that it was her medical training that had made her useful to Roy in his recovery. This had not been an easy sell.

She walked through the kitchen on her way out. There was no one around and nothing but an empty cereal bowl and a bunch of crumbs on the table. As usual these days, Travis was already out back. Ever since it had come out that she had tried to mercy kill Roy, that she had gone home with him from the hospital, and that Roy had put her in charge of his care, Travis had rarely left his workshop. He was pretty much living there, even sleeping most nights on the old camp bed he had. He had never scolded her for what she had done, not even that first day over at Roy's. In fact, he had not said much of anything.

She had tried to explain. About the pillow, about Roy's awakening, about how Roy might have died or at least broken something if she'd let him leave the hospital with the rescue squad. Travis's sole response was to say, "Woman, I have vowed to keep me only unto you as long as we both shall live. I will do that no matter what you have done." He said these exact same words every time she tried to speak with him. At first, she had felt horribly repentant, but by now, she was ready to take a pillow unto Travis's sleeping face.

She grabbed an apple and some Nabs to take with her to Roy's. Of course, her pillow days were behind her. Sure, it was a nice fantasy, to picture your husband's limp body lying on the camp bed. But that was all it was, a daydream you used on mornings you thought you would die if you had to wash his cereal bowl one more time. If she had learned nothing else in the last few weeks, it was that her talents lay elsewhere.

This was what she would call a hard-won lesson, the result of hours and hours of sitting at Roy's bedside, confused, lost, and even bored. Once he was home, Roy had lived in a dark, dark place for many days. He was so low that he would not speak and would not participate in any way with his care or share even the tiniest optimism about his recovery. After a few days of watching this, she'd stopped waiting for his instructions and started to use her head. She'd called up physical therapists, speech experts, nutritionists, more nurses, Dr. Matthews even. Together they had put him on a plan and she made him follow it. She tried to be cheery, tried to urge him on. His dark mood did not lift, but he had done what the PTs had asked, he had eaten what was put in front of him. She made sure. It had not been fun, but then, what was? Even his considerable progress had not brought him visible pleasure. Until this week. The change had been so sudden, Celeste had called Dr. Matthews and described Roy's new-found liveliness.

"These things happen, Celeste," he said. Dr. Matthews called her by her first name all the time now. "I think your hard work has paid off. Maybe Roy's brain has healed. Even we scientific types can't always explain what will bring a patient around. I just thank God and move on. I suggest you do the same."

This made Celeste feel good. Dr. Matthews actually thought she deserved some of the credit for Roy's improvement, and he'd called her a scientist. That was a first. Of course, he had cautioned her that Roy's recovery was not complete, that he could feel good and all optimistic one week and come crashing down the next. So her work was not done, but at least now she understood her calling.

She was called to heal. She decided to cling to this idea even though she did not know where it might lead her. She tried to ponder it in her heart. This did help her endure her punishment.

It was an informal thing, of course: no one told you exactly that you were now dirt in the eyes of most everyone you knew, so it had taken her a little while to catch on. Apparently, Grace Snow, who thought she knew everything, had distributed her own version of events. And she had pretty much spoken for the entire town on the one night Celeste had gotten up the courage to show up at choir practice. "Oh, Celeste, honey, there's a lot of women who finished that little six-week LPN course over at Surry Community. It's not your practical nursing skills Roy's after over there in that farmhouse."

Celeste had not even known how to respond to that comment. It was one of those times she'd wished that Travis had been at her elbow to set people straight. But she was pretty much on her own. Now that she was, though, it occurred to her that it wasn't so bad. Between her mama and daddy and her sisters and brothers, then Travis, then their six kids, she'd never had one minute in her life alone.

As she walked out of the house to the car, she tried to remember a single weekend, or even a single day, she'd had to herself. There wasn't one. She started up the Taurus, but it needed a few minutes to warm up. She sat there—it was a perfect fall morning—watching her breath fill the air and then disappear. She looked around at the freshly turned fields, the orchard beyond. She leaned back against the seat. The moisture cleared off her front windshield and there, rising up in front of her, where it had always been, was Swan's Knob, majestic as God Almighty. It sat alone in a plain of farmland, sixty miles short of its sibling mountains in the Blue Ridge. And here she was, Celeste Clay Diamond, breathing her own breath, all peaceful and noble, like maybe Joan of Arc had been at one time.

Roy

Celeste had helped him out onto the porch and made a big deal about his being able to sit in a normal chair. It was a nice day, he tried to appreciate that. They had been lucky. It had been an unusually warm fall, not too much rain, so now it was the same for the grapes and the leaves on the trees—a late, short season. Under the clear morning sky, the sourwoods and maples on the mountain were blazing red, just succeeding the fading yellow hickories. One more week and all this glory would be gone.

There were people in every corner of the place, getting things ready for Harper's festival. The stage was looking great. He tried to appreciate that too, to locate a little gratitude inside his mess of a body. He was trying these days to be more appreciative all the way round. It would make it easier for folks later. Down on the stage, they were testing out the sound system. Harper was out front and spotted Roy from the distance. "Testing, testing, Roy, can you hear me?" Roy picked up his left arm and waved big.

"Yeah, boy," Harper said.

Now that Roy had made his decision, it was not so bad. In his mind, it was not unlike his leaving for Korea. He had done that against all reason, against the wishes of those who loved him, but it had been his second war. He'd known what he was getting into. This was no different, really. He had been dead, or nearly so; it was not so bad. Better than what he had now.

His death, which he would bring on himself in just three days, would disappoint people. They would think he was ungrateful. They would think he had been too hasty. They would think he was depressed, not in his right mind. He knew better. He had taken the time to think it through. Yes, he could almost walk across a room now, but he would never do it again without having to quarterback every step. He would improve his vocabulary, speak in public even, but only with a third grader's labored cadence. Every day would be in some way the kind of trial he had endured these few months.

He did not want it. This was his choice.

And whether Wilma understood this or not, she didn't want him either. Not like he was now. It would be hard on her, doubly hard since her Harry had done the same thing. She'd survive, though, just as she had before, and he'd provided for her well, so she wouldn't want for anything this time. He was right to stay away from her, and he was right to finish things now. Otherwise, he might feel just a little better one day and end up seeking her out. No. Best for them to stay apart. This way—by perpetual separation—their love could remain untouched. It would belong to another time, those seven short years when they had stood together as man and wife, and not to this era of deadwood.

Harper had finished his sound check and was striding across the mowed field toward him now, Delrina by his side. Roy felt a stab of envy. Harper looked several inches taller at this moment, and it wasn't just those new cowboy boots. He was a man getting some loving, a fact hard to miss for Roy, whose loving days were over, whose own equipment was erectile non grata, and whose libido had been lost in the desert for forty days and forty nights.

Star

It was getting to her, okay? Her grandma was zoned out big-time over the situation with Roy. She was totally wrecked. Star could tell. She still did the things she was supposed to do—she taught all her piano lessons, went to choir practice, she took care of the house—but she did it like a kind of robot. She fixed fancy meals and made them eat in the dining room, she pressed Star's jeans and T-shirts and her sheets, but she also went upstairs sometimes and left the water running in the kitchen sink.

Star was trying. Like right now, sitting across the booth from her grandma in Surry Drug, she smiled and said, "I'm having a cheeseburger, what about you?" trying to put a little excitement in her voice like this trip downtown was the best thing she'd done lately.

Her grandma shrugged. She hadn't put on any lipstick before they left the house, which for her was just about as bad as leaving the water running.

"Limeade?" Star said, all Miss Perky again.

"Sure," said her grandma, remembering to try a little herself. "Did you see Josh today?" This was her code, her way of asking if Star had gotten any more information about Roy from Josh since the last time she'd asked. Josh's mom Celeste was the only one who knew anything.

They ordered then and sat there without much to say. People came in and out of the drugstore. A couple of them, Grace Snow and some other choir lady, stopped by their booth. They were nice, but they didn't stand there long, because they didn't have much to say either.

"So I talked to your mom today," said her grandma. "They're in Thailand somewhere."

This was a good topic. "Right," said Star. "She said she was working with some healer woman."

"She talked to Harper this week. He's been over to see Roy. She said they're all working on the festival."

"Oh. The festival." Star had heard this from Josh, but she hadn't passed it down the grapevine.

Her grandma smiled, but it looked lame without the lipstick. "He must be better, then. That's really good."

"Yeah," said Star. "Real good."

The guy behind the fountain put their food down then, so they didn't have to talk for a while. They were almost finished when Celeste came in, wearing her white uniform. Star was facing the door, so she saw Celeste spot the two of them in the booth and start walking real slow, like she didn't quite know what to do and was hoping she could sneak by. That wasn't going to happen. The whole drugstore was about thirty feet wide.

Celeste gave up about the time she got to the greeting card rack. "Well, hey there, you two," she said. "Hey Star. Hey Wilma." She made a little lame wave and was about to walk on, but for once, Star's grandma came out of her zombie state.

"Celeste, oh Celeste!" she said and gave her a big smile.

Star could tell Celeste still didn't know what to do. Her grandma filled the gap. "Won't you join us for a limeade or a hot fudge sundae or something?"

"I'm on duty," said Celeste. "I've got to get these prescriptions filled for—before the druggist leaves for the day."

"Of course," said her grandma. "Of course. You go on."

Celeste stood there looking at them when just a second before she had been in a real big hurry. "Well . . ." she said, and rubbed the back of her ankle with her white nurses' shoe.

Her grandma smiled a little tight smile. "Oh, don't let us keep you."

Celeste started to walk toward the back of the store to the pharmacy window, but then stopped and pointed at them. "Wait, I'll be right back. I'll just put these prescriptions in, and then I'll come get me a cherry Coke." She made her way past the bandages and foot remedies, nodding to herself like she had decided something, and yes, yes, she had decided it right.

Her grandma folded the paper around what was left of her hamburger and began cleaning up the table like she was getting ready for a guest. "Finished?" she said.

"Almost," said Star, chewing. She had been the go-between for these two for weeks, and now she wanted to duck out. It was bad enough to watch your grandma try to get over the real sickness of grief. She didn't want to be there when she was forced to ask somebody else what was going on with Roy. At least it was Josh's mother. Star had been around her a bit lately and she seemed nice, really nice.

When Celeste got back to the table, Star jumped up. "Here, Celeste, I'm taking off anyway," she said.

"You mean, Mrs. Diamond," said her grandma.

"Oh, it's okay, Wilma. Star's practically family by now, anyway," said Celeste, grinning at Star like she knew a secret.

Star hated it when people said weird stuff like this. She didn't know what to say back, so she just tried not to turn red and left as fast as she could. Of course, when she got outside, she peeked back in through the window. Celeste leaned over the table and reached for her grandma's hands. Here's the thing that surprised her: her grandma did the same. The last thing she saw was the two of them, their heads inches apart, talking at the same time, like a dam had broken in a rush of words she could not hear.

She made her way straight home, past the little stores of the town, the yards planted with mums and pansies. She had the feeling her mom must have had the first day she left Star in kindergarten. As in, she hoped her grandma would be all right back there. There was not much she could do but hold her breath and trust that Celeste would not tell her grandma what she'd told Star a few days ago: that Roy had not even said the word "Wilma" since the day he came home, he hadn't mentioned her once, and that when Celeste finally asked him last week—after he started inviting other people into the house—if he wanted to call Wilma, he had turned his head away and asked Celeste not to mention her again.

Wilma

In the end her salvation came, as it had over and over in her life, from an unexpected source. It began with a ride on the church bus, taking her and her choir out to Roy's farm for the Heritage Festival on a pretty November day. Of course, it did not feel like the trip to salvation. It felt more like the beginning of a ride on a rickety roller coaster, the part where the cars creaked and strained up the first long incline, giving you time to think about the possibility of a high-speed derailing.

The atmosphere on the bus was festive, the women chatting, the men practicing their harmonies for "I'll Fly Away." Wilma sat near the front and held on to the back of the seat ahead of her. At her age, she should have been wiser. Her first instinct, when Delrina Kay had shown up at choir practice a few weeks back, was to expect trouble. She should have gone with that—she should have resisted Delrina, who, it turned out, could be very charming. Instead, Wilma had stood right in line with the rest of the choir and bought her ticket to this crazy carnival ride. She and her choir were going to sing onstage with Delrina this afternoon. They were the backup group for Delrina's second set, the one she called her "Gospel Quest."

They were almost up to Roy's farm road now, which made Wilma slightly queasy. The bus had to stop in a long line of traffic. They inched up to the turn, where Chief Henry himself was out in the road in a brand-new fluorescent vest, managing the turn lanes. There were people everywhere, walking along the road, loaded into vans and buses. It was a huge crowd, much larger than Wilma had imagined. Cynthia Trolley, sitting two rows in front of her with Mimi Salter, turned around and looked at her for a moment. "Amazing, isn't it? I came out here yesterday to check on our choir robes, and I couldn't believe what they'd done."

"Amazing," she said. Unrecognizable. All these people, signs everywhere, food vendors, T-shirts, festive banners. She had spent these last weeks banished in a locked box with little more than the exacting torture of her own imagination. All the while, she'd pictured Roy full of pride, lonely, stubborn, struggling to recover from his stroke without her, whispering her name in his sleep. She had entertained the notion that one day, in a moment of revelation, he would call her back to his side. What she had not imagined was him hosting a hootenanny.

"You all right?" Cynthia mouthed.

"Fine," Wilma said, but she must not have been convincing, because Cynthia got up and slid into the seat next to her.

"You are going to be pleased with our new choir robes," she said. "Delrina and I decided on purple, a deep purple, not a lavender, mind you, real regal looking. You'll see for yourself. They are not one bit tacky." She said this mostly in a single breath, with a guarded eye on Wilma. Cynthia was trying to distract her, which was most kind but not a bit effective.

In fact, everyone had been most kind—Celeste sitting down with her at Surry Drug and giving her all the little details about Roy's condition: how she had brought him a brand-new pair of sneakers when he built up to walking across the room, how she had him reading poetry out loud to improve his speech. Wilma had wanted so badly to hear that Roy had mentioned her, but Celeste didn't say a word about it, and finally Wilma asked. "Oh, honey," Celeste had said. "I think it's just a matter of time."

Wilma had taken that thin explanation and run with it. In a way, that was why she was on this bus. She had been clinging to those words, *a matter of time*. She had decided that Delrina's invitation was her salvation, her chance to put herself in Roy's path. But as the bus pulled into the parking area, she could see that Celeste had been too kind to give Wilma the full story. All this careful preparation, this festooned stage and the prettied-up farmhouse, all of this was an elaborate announcement of Roy Swan's recovery. He had done it without her. Without her. She would not be called to his side, at any time now or in the future.

So what was she doing here? She had to ask herself this question now. And then, of course, it came to her, the story of her life: she was the accompaniment, nothing more. That was what she had always been: the piano teacher in town, the organist at the Methodist Church, the choir director, the one who provided music for the high points of other people's lives. Yep, just part of the choir for a country singer's second set.

Chapter Twenty-four

Star

She wondered what her mom would say if she were standing beside her now in the middle of the sea of lawn chairs that filled the Heritage Amphitheater. Onstage, her dad was introducing the next act. He'd been doing that all day. She made sure she was around to see it every time. He sounded cool and important and got people all excited the way he said, "And now, the Dixie Ramblers!" The crowd got up and cheered, waved their souvenir Heritage Festival gimme caps as the band walked out onto the stage.

Star had a backstage pass, but for now, she just wanted to walk around and look at this thing that her dad had put together, all from an idea in his head. It was amazing, and she thought her mom would think the same. Even the details, which her dad was not so good at, were all worked out. She walked by Port-o-lets and souvenir vendors, Baptists selling ham biscuits, and band members fixing hot dogs and drinks. Everybody happy, having fun.

In the crowd, she spotted a bunch of kids from school, people she'd seen downtown with her grandma. Everybody said, "Hey, Star, how are you today?" and "Hey, isn't this great," or just "Hey!" She said it right back. She was getting used to this. And even though it had been a strange couple of months with Roy sick and then weirdly stubborn, the whole rural high school thing had turned out fine. She was glad she'd come, and considering her grandma's deal, the way Star had been able to be here with her through all this and be her trusty spy, she was sort of thankful.

She stopped on the path up to the farmhouse and turned around to look back. Someone should take a picture, she was thinking, and then she felt familiar hands around her waist. It was Josh. "Hey, doll baby," he said. She always felt a little thrill when she saw him, which was totally part of the fun, totally. Now that she would be going home in a few weeks, she felt like Dorothy in *The Wizard of Oz*. She should say to Josh, "Oh, Scarecrow, I think I'll miss you most of all." The coolest of all cool things was that if she did, if she said that, he would get it. But he would not go all ape, like, *Let's be together forever.* He understood. He wasn't like that.

"Idea," he said, which meant he had thought of another place where they could do it. "How about we go up that little hill over there in a few? We can look over the whole place. I'll bet we'll still be able to hear the music too."

"You are so bad," she said. "It's still broad daylight, and my grandma's choir goes on with Delrina next."

"Noted," he said. "What about after that? Sunset. What do you think?"

"Deal," she said. "Only I've got to get back later to do the pickers' tent with my dad. We can't forget."

"Deal," he said. He was so cute. Star had checked it out, and it was like her grandma said, he did look like Troy Donohue. When she got back to Santa Fe, that's what she'd tell them, that she had dated a country Troy Donohue.

Harper

Backstage it was a totally crazy scene, more folks than he could've ever imagined. They were a loud-talking bunch, these music folks, but it was hard to tell the performers from the crew just by looking. The days of spangles and long fringed cowboy shirts were over, except of course for Delrina, who liked to dress in what she called traditional country, which meant the whole nine yards—sequins, satin, cleavage, bright colors, big hair. She was sitting over in the far corner now, holding court with Sam Bush and some boys in Ralph Stanley's band. She had forsaken her beaded braids at the last minute, requiring Harper to make an emergency call to Maizey's Beauty Shop in town. Maizey herself had come running. The results weren't awful, but Harper didn't know how a woman would sleep on such a head of hair.

His stage manager, Ronny Snow, came by with a clipboard and a checklist for the next three acts. This young man's years of watching his daddy put on funerals had made him the master of operating a tight ship. The show was actually still on schedule, a small miracle.

"And what'd you decide about Roy?" Sammy asked. "Did you talk him into it?"

"No," said Harper. "He said no way, he doesn't want to go out on the stage. Doesn't even want me to introduce him."

"How about a spotlight?" said Sammy. "You could say something and then I get one of the guys to throw the spot. He'll never know what hit him."

Harper laughed. This was going to piss Roy off, but that was okay. Maybe a little getting pissed would be good for him. Better than folks walking on eggshells all the time. "Okay," he said. "Do it at your own risk, buddy."

He was about to go out front and hunt up Star, but he glanced back at Delrina for a minute and caught a look he didn't like. Ralph Stanley's boys were nowhere in sight now and Delrina looked like she might be talking to herself. He had made a career out of reading her moods the past few weeks. She had been a little pissy this morning but wouldn't say why. He'd just steered clear for the rest of the day. It paid to get out of the way when she was about to blow. In this setting, however, maybe he'd better attend to her before it was too late.

"Well, hey there, you manny man. Here we are," said a voice, and he turned to find his friend Candace.

"Well, hey, Candace. How are you, girl?" he said and gave her a big hug. He loved everybody tonight. And Delrina had steered him right about Candace. She was not the greatest, but Delrina knew all about that cousin of hers who'd come to his picking night. Delrina had seen that Belle Taylor sing at the Blue Bird on several occasions, and she thought Belle was going to be a big star. She'd played him one of her albums and told him if he had any sense, he'd beg the woman to do the show and let her cousin and the Rondalays sing backup. He had.

When he got to Delrina, she was smoking, which he'd never seen her do before. She was also drinking from a big stadium cup. "You okay?" said Harper. Shit. If there was anything he had learned over the course of his life, it was that "are you okay?" was one of the worst things to ask a woman. The answer had never been to his benefit. But here he was, asking it anyway, risking life and limb in the name of star management and maybe even love.

For once, there was no explosion, no list of what all he'd done. "Yes, I'm okay," said Delrina, but her bottom lip trembled. This puzzled him. She was not a crier.

He sat down beside her and took her hand. What else could he do? "Okay," he said. "What's up?"

"Charlie," she said. "He's not here."

This had not crossed his mind. "Oh, honey," he said, "you didn't think he was coming, did you? Didn't you say he was down in Florida, hanging out with the Jimmy Buffett crowd?"

"Yes," she said, "but I thought he'd see all the press. I thought he'd get himself up here somehow. I never thought he'd quit for good. We're a team."

"You are great together," he said. "Great, but here's the thing. I have heard your rehearsals, and you have assembled a really good team here too. The musicians, the choir, all good, but at the center of it all, it's you, baby. They'll be another time for Charlie, but tonight, tonight, it's all Delrina."

He said her name last thing, the way he knew she liked to hear it, hanging on the "l" and then ripping through those last two syllables like he was starting an engine. He'd introduce her just that same way. He said her name again, only real real soft, and looked her straight in the eyes. Then a miracle occurred: she absolutely believed him.

Roy

They rolled him out to what they called a place of honor in the front row. Here was reason number forty-one why he wanted to end it all: crippled person on display. He had told them, had he not, he did not want to be onstage. He had told them to just let the whole thing be. But had they listened? No. Harper took the stage, the one that Roy had paid for, and Roy heard his name, *Roy Swan, Roy Swan*, like he was a saint on earth, and then someone took a spotlight, which he had also paid for probably, and trained it right on him. Oh, it wasn't close to dark yet, but even so the light turned him and his chrome chair a sickly blue. People gave him a standing ovation, for being crippled was the only thing he could think of. It made him sick. Reason forty-one, right there.

Wilma

She'd started looking for Roy the minute she got off the bus. She walked through the festive crowd and among the musicians backstage, fuming, half expecting to see him in the middle of it all, more recovered than she could imagine, wearing a *Delrina!* T-shirt, dancing maybe.

She was standing backstage when they introduced him. They announced his name over the sound system, and it rang in her ears and echoed out into the amphitheater. She looked out at the crowd just as the spotlight found him.

He was totally changed. She had seen him in the hospital, and yes, he had looked awful then, deathly pale and slack jawed. He did not look that way today. The musculature of expression had returned to his face, but his features were sewn together now with different thread and a cruder stitch. He looked sorry, so sorry, to be sitting there in his wheelchair, furious at the bright blue light that shone on him—on his scrawny limbs, on his shoulders that turned inward, his hands gripping the shiny arms of the chair. They moved the spotlight then but she kept her eyes on him, searching for something familiar, but—she couldn't help it—to her, he looked for all the world like that awful ginseng root. She tried to banish this thought, to gather a little reassurance from the diminished but familiar curve of his belly, to take comfort in his frayed button-down, in his wiry gray hair that had grown way too long. It was no use. The longer she looked, the more she saw the resemblance, and the more she came undone. And then Delrina was on the stage, and her choir was marching out, and her with them. After that, she could not see him beyond the spotlights.

Roy

Delrina came on again, and with her what Harper called a full gospel choir. The purple robes threw him off for a minute, but when the choir's director walked out, she only had to take three crisp steps before Roy recognized her.

Swan's Knob United Methodist Church choir had been waiting in the wings, of course. They were standing on the stage right in front of him now in two rows, ordered by height. He could only pray that Wilma had been too busy lining everyone up to catch the whole cripple spotlight announcement. Her perfect posture, the arc of her arms in the air as she counted out the beat, these gave him no clue. Though she surely could not see beyond the edge of the stage light, she turned toward him as the music began, and he could look up finally at her sweet face. When he did, there they were, shining in the light, two rivers of tears running down her cheeks. This produced the thing he had most feared, the worst kind of cardiac event. Over the slow sweet introduction of "Bye and Bye," his heart beat out a crude animal cry of agony and fiercest love.

The two rivers that marked her face were reasons number forty-two and forty-three. Two more, and maybe the final, reasons why he and his sweet Wilma would not be seeing one another again.

Wilma

Later, she would not remember a moment of the performance, not a single thing about it. When it was over, she ran back into the wings and looked out at those first rows, but he had gone.

Her heart started beating like a bird's. Cynthia and Mimi were waiting to walk with her to the barn, but she waved them off. She looked out at the crowd, trying to trace a path from the empty space in the front row down the aisle. She couldn't spot him. *Wilma, you can find him later, if that's what you want,* she told herself, but then her bird heart talked back: *No, you can't.*

She turned away from the crowd and went to the backstage area that used to be Roy's barn. She found the choir having soft drinks and mingling with all the musicians. Delrina was showing Cynthia the finer points of her costume. Wilma accepted a cup that someone gave her, and tried to get ahold of herself.

This was not an emergency. She would talk to Roy when all this was over. She'd think of what to say, come back out here on a quiet day. They'd work it out.

Her stomach was not listening to reason, of course. It lurched like she was on a carnival ride, and her heart would not calm down. This was the legacy of her years married to Harry, of course, of him taking his life, of her missing all the signs. Ever since, she'd spent an awful lot of time looking for signs of impending tragedy. But here was the problem: there was always tragedy coming. She had to stop looking for it or she'd miss everything else. She could breathe easy: Roy was not Harry, nothing like him. He was a stronger man. She would bet her life on it.

Maybe that was what she would tell him, the first chance she got. But—though her bird heart still insisted—there was no reason to run after him in all this crowd.

Josh

He loved her more than life itself. Was that a song or something? He couldn't place it, but that was what he was thinking as he and Star climbed the footpath up to the hill in Roy's north pasture: that he loved her more than life. When they got up to the top, he took her hand and led her over to a little flat rock that he had found earlier when he had scouted this place. She smiled at him, her private smile with the little crooked part in the left corner of her mouth. *I love you more than life.* He wanted to say it but hesitated.

"You're not thinking here, are you?" she said, staring at the rock.

"Well," he said.

She wrinkled her nose. "Kind of exposed."

"Well," he said. Now that he couldn't use that good line, he didn't have anything else ready.

She looked around and into the trees. "How about back there?"

He hated to tell her. She might get freaked and that would be it. "Well, it's a little cemetery," he said. "An old one."

"Yeah?" she said. "Wow." She sat down and looked out over the farm.

The hill wasn't very high, but it was still a cool view of the stage and all the people. "Cool," he said.

"Yeah," she said. "Let's just sit here and watch for a little while. The sun's setting. We'll go find a little vacant spot back there before it gets too dark."

"Really?" he said. For him, there was a slight debate here between superstition and his penis.

"If you're not too freaked, that is."

No contest. "Not at all," he said. "I mean, they're dead, right?"

She leaned back against him, and maybe that would have been the moment, the moment to say *I love you more than life itself*, the moment to tell her everything he had been thinking. He wanted her to stay in Swan's Knob. He thought that might be what she wanted too. She could stay, then, they could pick the same college, get married sophomore or junior year. They would be together forever.

Even in the later years of his life, with his own kids in college, his second wife next to him in bed, he would think about this exact moment, the very wind that blew across his face, and he would wonder if she'd have said yes if he had only asked. But in that particular twilight, with the lights of campfire circles glowing in the distance and Belle Taylor singing "Fiery Hearts," it did not seem to be the moment, so he pressed his face into her hair and said nothing. For most of the rest of his life, he would carry the CD of that song of Belle's around in his car. He would play it when he was alone.

Roy

There was a trick to his plan and it was this: no one would believe in a million years that he could make it to the top of the hill. But he could.

He had one of his keepers from the rescue squad roll him back to the house in his chair. When they got to the front porch, there were a bunch of local boys, Harper's buddies, playing some fine music. They were going at it real good. He pretended to be captured by it all and told the guy to leave him right there.

He had one more important thing to do. When there was a break in the music, he called that boy Steve over. He was a good friend of Harper's. Roy hadn't left a note inside, but he did want to leave a message.

"Steve," he said. "Harper and Star are going to be here playing together in a few minutes. Can I trust you to deliver a message to them?"

"Sure thing," said Steve, but he was busy tuning his guitar.

"You won't forget, now?" For the first time, Roy felt slightly panicked.

"No," said Steve. "I won't. I promise."

Roy hadn't thought a whole lot about what to say, but he did want to get it just right. Suddenly, he got another one of those lumps in his throat. He didn't trust himself. He didn't want to cry. If he did, if he started acting funny in the least, someone would call a nurse or worse. He cleared his throat. "I was hoping to catch the two of them playing, but I am plumb worn-out. I'm going to have to go on. You tell them for me, Roy says, he is really sorry that he missed their playing. He's sorry for everything he's missing. Tell them, Harper and Star and her grandma too, tell them I love them more than life itself. Got that?"

"Got it! More than life itself," Steve said and smiled. Maybe he'd forget it in five minutes. Roy's consolation was that he wouldn't be around to find out.

When the pickers started playing again, he rolled his chair around and retrieved his walker. It was right on the front porch from this morning. He looked a little strange carrying the bulky thing across his lap, but folks didn't ask people in wheelchairs many questions.

Everything else went according to plan pretty much. He got his chair through the crowds easily enough, and out on the path through the pasture. There hadn't been much rain in the last week or so. That could've been a problem, but as it was, he arrived at the bottom of the hill, right at the footpath, without having spent much of the precious energy he was going to need to get up the hill.

There was still plenty of light left. He figured he'd get to the top long before dark. He was right about the climb. He got himself at least three-quarters up the hill using his walker. His kin had been hauling coffins up the path for over a century now. It wasn't that steep, and it was fairly wide. This took time, though. Eventually he got to the place where the walker just wasn't going to do him any more good. He threw it in the bushes. Good riddance.

He stood upright, hanging on to a tree limb. He was really sweating now, and tired out. The little pistol that had fit so neatly in his pocket this afternoon was making his pants slide down on one side. He had to wonder for just a minute why he'd decided to get himself all the way up to his graveyard. Sure, he'd shoot himself. Then what? They'd take him down to Snow's Funeral Home before they brought him back up to put him in his grave. He sure wasn't saving anyone a trip. It did seem more gentlemanly, though, if he had to do it during the festival, to get himself well away from everybody.

He took a few steps and made some progress. This was better. He was determined if nothing else, and hell, he'd crawl to the top if he needed to. He took a few more steps and did a little more tree hugging. His legs were trembling like a little girl's, but all in all, this was not a bad deal. Doing it his way. It beat sitting in his front room, looking at his gun for twenty minutes, trying to get up the courage. "We found him lying across the grave of his uncle Sherman," is what people would say. That sounded okay.

When he got to the top of the path, to tell the truth, it was a little anticlimactic. He had actually made it in better shape than he would've thought. Hats off to Phyllis in physical therapy. He sat down now. He'd go over to the graveyard in a minute. Resolved, that's how he felt. Completely, totally resolved. He sat there for a few more minutes, looking out over his land. It was pretty, no question, and made prettier by the lights from the stage, the campfires, the tail lights of cars in the distance. And closer to this hill, row after row of vines, that was what pleased him most—the geometry of the unburdened vines after the harvest, the certainty that next August, they would be hanging with precious fruit.

He turned around so that he could see his mountain one more time, a dark outline. It was the single thing that would carry on his name. The town too, of course, the town had his name. It would be there after he was gone, but no one living, no little Swan boys and girls, to walk this land, harvest those grapes. The only Swans left would be buried on this hill, except Wilma of course, and that was by marriage. She could do as she wished with the farm and the vineyard, everything. She could let the grapes rot, though that wouldn't be like her. But it wasn't going to be his problem. All he had to do was get himself hauled up these last few steps and cross into the trees.

He ducked into the grove. The wind was up, rustling the leaves of the trees and muffling the music below. He felt peaceful then, and soothed to be completely alone after these months of supervision. He looked over the gravestones, which blended into the landscape in the twilight. He couldn't see the lettering on the stones, but no matter.

He was thinking about pulling out his pistol when he heard the first sound. It was a sound out of place, not a leafy sound or a scratchy squirrel run or a bird twitter. It was more of a low animal moan, faint at first and then a little more urgent. His first thought was that there was a deer, or a bear even, trapped somewhere nearby. He stepped quietly toward the noise, which was a tough trick. He heard more noises, and this time he caught on. A pair of lovers had found their way up here to his hill. They were just on the other side of the stones, in the clearing beyond the first trees.

It was none of his business. Except this was his graveyard and he was up here for his own important business. Also, and this was not to his credit, his illness and the resulting infirmities, these things had not killed the curiosity he had been born with. He was surprised now at his ability to shuffle quietly beside his family headstones. He reached the far trees, grabbed on to one of them, and peered around. He could not see a thing. All for the best, probably just make things worse. The faint, sweet moaning continued, though, like a song he adored but had not heard in a really long time. He listened, and though he had promised himself he would not, he could not help it— he thought of Wilma, of their short time together. He held on to his tree and listened—the rattle of the leaves, the music from the lovers and the stage below, the timpani of his own tired heart.

It was a bird chirp at first, down on the path. He imagined it calling his name. "Roy? Roy?" The call got louder, though, and human. And then he recognized her voice. His bird, no one else. He barely had time to let go of the trunk and get himself upright before Wilma appeared in the frame of the trees. She spotted him, breathed in a single breath, then held it. She stood completely still, not a statue but a wide-eyed woman in a choir robe.

"Roy," she said, a single beautiful note from her quaking throat.

And of course, that did it. For a moment, he thought his pistol had been displaced by the climb and was pressing against him. In a second, though, he knew this was not the case. There was the familiar but not recent sensation of fullness around his crotch, and pretty soon it was completely unmistakable.

Roy Swan had come in from the desert. He gasped with surprise. He was able to call out her name before the sensation began to flit away, the fate of all flesh. Then it was gone.

"What are you doing up here, Roy Swan? What are you doing by all these graves?" Her voice trembled, and her eyes darted all around him, knowing the answer mostly. "Tell me," she said, but he couldn't. He was looking into her eyes, the eyes of a woman who was afraid of losing everything. And now he was afraid for her.

"Stay where you are, dolly," he yelled and got his legs in gear. "I'll be right there." The headstones of his kin stretched out between them like a flight of uneven stairs. He took one step and then another. By the third, his balance was off, and on the fourth, something gave way under his foot. He fell then, straight down through the floor of the forest. For an instant, there was nothing but ancient air and Wilma screaming. Then there were the several bumps of his landing. Glass broke, he hit his knee and his nose, got dirt in his mouth. Everything became perfectly quiet then and he waited for the blackness.

But none came. And no angel either. A mouth full of grit was about the worst of it. He could taste minerals and decaying loam and the dust of quartzite rock—all of the these, the things that made his precious wine sing, only in smaller quantities.

Wilma

She called out for help, like she should have done the minute she found his empty wheelchair at the bottom of the path. She had missed all the signs. Again. She yelled for help once more, but of course, no one was going to hear her. She called to Roy, but he didn't say anything. He'd fallen face-forward in some kind of hole, a grave maybe, though it seemed too shallow. She could hear him moving now, and without thinking she jumped down into the hole herself. "Help us! Help!" she yelled again and was surprised to hear an answer.

"Here, here, we're coming." Star appeared on the far side of the woods, with Josh right behind her.

"Thank God you're here," Wilma said. She wouldn't ask herself why until later.

"What happened?" yelled Star. "Is he okay? Is he breathing? Check his breathing."

"Yes," said Wilma. Roy tilted his head toward her. His eyes were fluttering but he didn't speak. "Stay still," she said to him, and then to Josh, "Go get help." He ran off down the path.

"Tell them we need flashlights," Star yelled after him. She was right, Wilma saw, there wasn't much light left up in these trees. She checked Roy over as best she could. She put her hand on his back. Oh, it was good to touch him. He seemed to be breathing just fine. She put her finger on his neck to try to check his pulse.

Star peered down at them and shook her head. "No, not there, closer to his ear," she said. "Let me do it. I'm coming down." She put her feet over the side. She was barefoot.

"Wait." Wilma ventured a quick look around the hole for the first time. It wasn't a grave, thank God. It was only three or four feet deep. Some kind of old wooden crate someone had used to bury their garbage, maybe. The whole top had given way to Roy's step. The box was scattered with metal tools and ceramic-faced jugs and those old jar things from telephone poles, a few of them broken. There was a rusted rooster weathervane lying up by Roy's head and an old metal sign for a carnival. It looked like Roy had fallen squarely on some moldy stacks of papers and comics, though maybe he'd hit his head. His nose was bleeding and he was spitting dirt.

"Stay there, Star. There's broken glass," said Wilma. Roy was stirring now. He opened his eyes. She bent down close to him, and he looked at her, confused for a moment. Then his eyes lit up with recognition and a kind of silly wonderment. "It was you in that window, wasn't it?" he said, and then he put his hand up on her face.

Okay, he was still a little mixed-up. He might not know her. Far better than his death. She'd take it. "Roy, are you all right?"

He didn't answer for a few more seconds. Finally he said, "Think so, dolly. Sprained my ankle maybe. Bumped my head."

She was the one who couldn't speak then. She had a million questions for this sweet old fool. If they ever got down from here, she was going to ask them. He was going to tell her his answers, and she was going to tell him. They were going to sit down together, in the kitchen, on the porch, with a couple of glasses in their hands maybe. They were going to do this every chance they had. Then maybe the two of them could get back to it—with whatever body parts and wherewithal they had left. They were going to go until they emptied every bottle of wine in the closet.

For the moment, however, Wilma did not seem to be of much use to anyone, except to laugh and cry all over Roy. Star took charge for the three minutes before help began to arrive in the form of every person in the county with medical training and several without it— the rescue squad again, Chief Henry, Celeste and Travis, Josh, several members of the choir, and the preacher. Suddenly everyone was shining their flashlights everywhere, attending to Roy and Wilma too. Two men lifted her out of the hole, and Roy's old buddies began to check Roy out.

"What the heck is all this?" said Hollis from the rescue squad.

"Not a grave, is it?" said another guy.

"Just an old refrigerator box," Wilma heard a woman say. It was Celeste, who stood on the edge of the hole and handed a stethoscope down to the men. "We buried stuff in it when we were kids."

"I'm fine, guys. Really, I'm mighty fine," Roy was insisting now, as he batted away Hollis's attentions.

"Lord God, Roy, I'm just trying to get your pressure," said Hollis.

Celeste laughed at this. "Good luck with that one," she said, but nodded when Hollis gave her the numbers. "It's good," she told Wilma and put her arm around her.

The men laid out the stretcher then and began to discuss how to lift Roy up onto it. "It won't be easy," said Travis. "He's gotten smaller, but there's still plenty of him left."

"Just let me get up out of here," Roy said, and eventually, they did. Travis and Josh helped him up onto his one good foot and then the rest half-pushed and half-pulled him out of the hole.

"Whoa, now, that's as far as you go, buddy," said Travis, steadying Roy from behind. "Onto that stretcher."

Roy made noises of protest but complied. Wilma stepped back then. Celeste and Star stayed with her, while every man present vied for a spot next to the stretcher.

"Easy, easy," Travis said when the final six grabbed the handles and began to lift Roy off the ground. For a moment, it looked like the men on the right side would lose their grip and spill Roy right back into the hole, but finally everyone got their acts together. Wilma held her breath as they began to haul him across the little cemetery, past the graves of Roy's ancestors, and past the spot that would be his one day, and hers. She watched for a moment and then caught up to the group. As they reached the beginning of the footpath, she could not resist a caution. Roy might not survive another spill. She put her hand on the stretcher.

"Steady, boys," she said. She did not understand why they laughed as they started down the hill, every one of them. Roy Swan too.

Acknowledgments

Many thanks to everyone who helped me with this book. My amazing writing group members Virginia Boyd and Pamela Duncan, as well as Jim Anderson, Darnell Arnoult, Alyssa Dallas, Quinn Dalton, Jane Danielewicz, Faulkner Fox, Mary Ellis Gibson, Todd Pankoff, Andrea Selch, and Ann York read and commented on various portions of drafts. Russell Beam and Jimmy Chester told me about truck repair.

Suzanne Gluck and Erin Malone at William Morris, Brett Kelly and Trena Keating at Plume, and Marion Donaldson at Headline all offered brilliant and practical advice and shepherded this book from my desk into the world.

Dr. Larry Goldstein, Director of the Duke Stroke Center, and Chair, Stroke Council of the American Stroke Association, was generous with his time and expertise as he answered my questions on the medical details for the book. Any errors are mine.

Others—my children and the rest of my family, Greg Cranford, Kathy Dorran, Megan Matchinske, Beth Stone, and most especially Alan Hirsch—provided everything else I might've needed along the way.

I borrowed all manner of things for this book: song titles, snores, mountains, street names, landmarks. I took the liberty of changing things in any way that suited my story, so I thank the lenders for their indulgence. In particular, Franklin Freeman was kind enough to donate one of his best jokes. Franklin, born and raised in Dobson, North Carolina, is now the senior assistant to the governor of North Carolina for governmental affairs. He tells me he first heard the joke told by Herbert Hyde, Asheville lawyer and former North Carolina state senator. I am proud to have the chance to pass it along.

© Miriam Berkley

About the Author

LYNN YORK's first novel was *The Piano Teacher*. Educated at Duke University and the University of Texas at Austin, she lives in Chapel Hill, North Carolina, with her two children, Anna Lee and Will. Her website is www.lynnyork.com.

LYNN YORK

The Piano Teacher

A Novel of Swan's Knob

Miss Wilma, the resident piano teacher in the small Southern village of Swan's Knob, is blessed with an unexpected visit from her daughter Sarah and her granddaughter Starling. Everything is going well until Sarah's absentee husband Harper shows up on Miss Wilma's front porch moments after a murder shakes the small community–and just two steps ahead of Jonah Branch, the stranger from Sante Fe who's become the number one suspect in the case. Suddenly, Miss Wilma's blessing begins to look more like a house full of trouble . . .

978-0-452-28477-7 / 0-452-28477-5
$13.00 / $19.50 CAN.

Available wherever books are sold.

Plume
A member of Penguin Group (USA) Inc.
www.penguin.com